西北民族大学重点学术著作资助项目

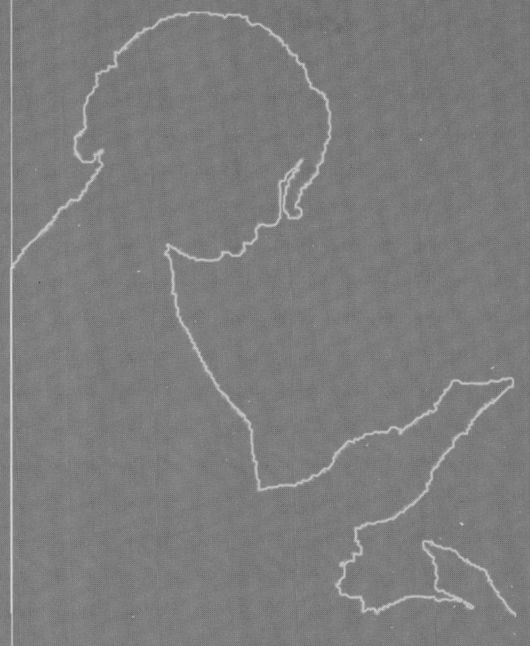

A Study of Alice Walker's Novels

艾丽斯·沃克小说研究

水彩琴 著

中国社会科学出版社

图书在版编目(CIP)数据

艾丽斯·沃克小说研究:英文/水彩琴著. —北京:中国社会科学出版社,2017.4

ISBN 978-7-5203-0192-3

Ⅰ.①艾… Ⅱ.①水… Ⅲ.①艾丽斯·沃克—小说研究—英文 Ⅳ.①I712.074

中国版本图书馆CIP数据核字(2017)第067875号

出 版 人 赵剑英
责任编辑 陈肖静
责任校对 牛 玺
责任印制 戴 宽

出 版 中国社会科学出版社
社 址 北京鼓楼西大街甲158号
邮 编 100720
网 址 http://www.csspw.cn
发 行 部 010-84083685
门 市 部 010-84029450
经 销 新华书店及其他书店

印刷装订 北京君升印刷有限公司
版 次 2017年4月第1版
印 次 2017年4月第1次印刷

开 本 710×1000 1/16
印 张 23.5
插 页 2
字 数 339千字
定 价 99.00元

Contents

Preface

Alice Walker is one of the most remarkable Afro-American women writers in the contemporary American literature. She is not only remembered as the first Afro-American woman Pulitzer Prize winner for fiction but also well known for her promotion of the womanist philosophy and her pursuit of the womanist ideal in both literary writing and social activism. It is a constant theme of her writing and life to strive for a warm, harmonious world, where all humans—male and female, and white and colored—enjoy liberty, equality, independence, and brotherhood, where humankind and every creature in nature coexist equally and peacefully. The culmination of her literary career is marked by *The Color Purple*, her third novel, which is acknowledged as one of the classics in the literary world.

As an Afro-American woman intellectual, Walker first and foremost works as a spokesperson for black women, who are oppressed by whites—male and female—and by black men as well. She has been participating in varied social activities to protest against racism and sexism, and striving for liberty and equality of black women and black people as a whole. In her literary works, she exposes the injustice and sufferings inflicted upon black women in both familial and public lives so as to arouse their consciousness of rebellion and independence on the one hand. On the other hand, she presents the distortion and dehumanization of black men resulting from the white supremacism and the consequent black androcentrism so as to correct their understanding of manhood and awaken their sense of responsibility for justice and equality in the black community. Accordingly, Walker theorized womanism, whose main idea consists of anti-sexism and antiracism, whose emphasis is put on the unity and solidarity of men and women within black communities, and whose ultimate goal is the spiritual survival of black people, male and female.

Walker is a responsible writer with passion and compassion, and an advocate for all underprivileged people. She is dedicated to preserving the rights of children, women, ethnic minorities, and peoples of the third world, and is involved in such nonviolent social protests as anti-war demonstrations and antinuclear movements, which are necessary for the survival of the planet and everyone on it. Her works (especially the later ones) are concerned with the global issues like animal rights, lesbianism, colonialism, nuclear issues, and environmental destruction. As a matter of course, Walker becomes a womanist cosmopolitanist in her later career, be it in social activism or literary writing. Her womanist scope is extended to encompass not just the whole human world but also the natural world. She is shifting to the improvement of humans' relationships with animals, plants and intangible spirits, and to the further involvement with global issues, and striving for a womanist utopia, where people of all races and colors live harmoniously like flowers of different kinds growing and blooming in "our mothers' gardens," where humankind and nature coexist in a peaceful and mutually beneficial way.

Walker is an Afro-American writer with a strong sense of cultural identity. She takes it as her duty to inherit and claim the black culture, the black folklore in particular. She treasures the black cultural heritage and respects the literary predecessors like Zora Neale Hurston in the Afro-American literature, whose works show great admiration for blackness and the black folklore. She not only discovered Hurston's unmarked grave and bought a modest headstone for the gravesite, but also restores Hurston's works to the reading public from oblivion. With Hurston's inspiration and influence, Walker has her fiction deeply rooted in a matrilineal inheritance, and thus becomes Hurston's devoted follower. As a womanist, she pursues equality and harmony between different races but never advocates obliterating ethnic cultures. For Walker, only when people of different races and colors keep their own unique cultures can the human world become thriving and prosperous like a garden of flowers.

To make a long story short, womanism is the quintessence of Walker's philosophy and lifetime pursuit. Its highest end is the equality and harmony of the entire human race, and the peaceful coexistence of humankind and nature. Walker has been striving for the end not simply through social activism but also through literary creation. Her works have incarnated the whole process of her pursuit of the womanist ideal, which has in turn become the soul of her literary writing.

Walker is a versatile and voluminous writer. Among her thirty-nine books, written in the literary forms like fiction, non-fiction, poetry, and essays, the seven novels are the most representative in betraying the author's trace of thought. However, the existing data show that the academic world either choose one (mostly *The Color Purple*) or two or sometimes three of them (one of which is surely *The Color Purple*) to explore its/their themes, characterizations, narrative devices, and linguistic features, or make a comparison between Walker's novel-writing (with *The Color Purple* as the only selected text) and that of such Afro-American writers as Toni Morrison and Zora Neale Hurston to excavate the commonality in any given aspect. Scholars have largely focused on the Pulitzer prize-winning book. The other novels (especially *The Third Life of Grange Copeland*, *Meridian*, *The Temple of My Familiar*, and *Possessing the Secret of Joy*) have not received the deserving attention from the critical world. Therefore the present book, *A Study of Alice Walker's Novels*, attempts to make a thematic study of all the seven novels, reveal the leading theme throughout these works, and trace the development of the author's philosophy.

The book consists of seven chapters, referring to the biographical sketch, the literature review, the theoretical presentation, and the text analysis. Except that the text analysis takes up four chapters, each of the other three forms one separate chapter. The book begins with the biographical sketch, or, to be specific, a profile of Alice Walker. Following a short sketch of her life, from family background through school education to social activism, is a brief introduction to her professional career, including the early academic accumulation and the lifetime literary creation. Ending up with a summary of her contribution to the American literature, the first chapter gives a rough but comprehensive account of Alice Walker's personal life, literary achievements, and social struggle.

Chapter II makes a literature review and presents a survey of the critical responses to Walker's novels. As one of the hot topics in the American literature, Walker's works have gained wide attention from both Western (American in particular) and Chinese scholars. The chapter therefore falls into two sections, handling the Western responses and the Chinese respectively. The former occupy much more space only because the native studies are more systematic and authoritative. The literature research reveals that the present criticism and reviews are mostly concentrated on Walker's early novels—*The Third Life of Grange Copeland*, *Meridian*, and *The Color Purple*, particularly the third one—and that, among the later ones (*The Temple of My Familiar*, *Possessing the Secret of Joy*, *By the Light of My Father's Smile*, and *Now Is the Time to Open Your Heart*), the scholars appear to be most interested in *By the Light of My Father's Smile*, which is praised as Walker's second greatest novel, only next to *The Color Purple*. The visible unevenness in the existing research makes it a necessary and worthwhile undertaking to study all the seven novels as a whole from a given perspective.

Chapter III is an overview of womanism as a theory. To start with, it offers a conceptual distinction of womanism from feminism and black feminism, identifying its connections with and differences from them. Then it moves on to verify the emergence of womanism. Based on the sufficient information about the social-intellectual contexts, Walker's contribution (i. e., the putting-forward of womanism) is introduced and underscored. The focus of this chapter is put on the development of womanism, which is traced from the rudiments to the improvement and the final formation of the principles, whose heart is the ultimate goal of the "survival and wholeness of entire people" and the concern with sexism and racism. (A. Walker, 1983: xi)

The text analysis is the main part of the book, encompassing the succeeding chapters. Chapter IV centers on the elucidation of Walker's womanist ideology implied in the male images in her first three novels. This chapter is subdivided into two sections. Through an analysis of the impact of Eurocentrism and androcentrism (i. e. , the effect of racism and sexism) on the shaping of black male stereotypes, the first section concentratedly explores the limitations of the black male stereotypes and their detrimental effect on the life of black females and the black race as a whole, and thus naturally emphasizes the urgency and hardship for black men to undergo a self-healing change to reach the womanist goal of the spiritual survival. In the second section, the focus directly falls on the long and hard struggle of the stereotypical black men for self-redemption and self-improvement. This section examines how these black male characters strive to shake off the confines of supremacist patriarchy, redefine their notion of manhood, regain their masculinity and humanity, and realize their regeneration in their equal and friendly relationship with other blacks (particularly black women) and even whites. Thus it sums up that the black male characters in Walker's first three novels either achieve their spiritual survival or possess the potential for such survival. They well express the author's womanist ideology.

The topic of the fifth chapter is shifted to black women's struggle to attain their liberty and spiritual survival. The discussion centers around the major female characters in all Walker's novels except the first, to reveal the special power of the black women's alliance in their endeavor to destroy the racial and patriarchal hegemony. The selected texts come down to two kinds of women's alliance, one based on sisterhood and the other lesbianism. Accordingly, this chapter contains two sections. The first section chiefly interprets *The Color Purple* and *By the Light of My Father's Smile*, and analyzes how lesbianism, as a female subversive force, overturns the male dominance in sexual relations. The black lesbianism is of political significance in Walker's womanist texts. It spans the whole spectrum of women's friendship and sisterly solidarity and thus subverts the established cultural narratives (i. e. , masculine cultural narratives) of femininity and desire. The second section explains how sisterhood serves as an effective way to unite black women and support them in their struggle for independence and liberation. The supportive texts include *Meridian*, *The Color Purple*, *Possessing the Secret of Joy*, *By the Light of My Father's Smile* and *Now Is the Time to Open Your Heart*. By dissecting the unique manifestation of the black women's alliance, the chapter tends to lay bare the common underlying aim of Walker's writing to awaken black women's self consciousness and stimulate their fighting spirit.

Chapter Ⅵ discusses about humanity and harmony in Walker's later works, including *The Temple of My Familiar*, *By the Light of My Father's Smile* and *Now Is the Time to Open Your Heart*. It falls into three sections, each dealing with one novel. While the first and third sections place more emphasis on harmony inherent in the novels, the second section puts more concentration on the theme of humanity in *By the Light of My Father's Smile*, though both themes are shared by the three novels. Through analyzing the relationships between men and women, between whites and the colored, and between humankind and nature in these selected works, the chapter tends to demonstrate that the author attempts to incorporate her different 'isms in literary writing so as to highlight her ideal of cosmopolitanism. Walker has been committed to extending and perfecting her womanism, whose goal is now not simply to transcend binary oppositions of male and female, and of white and colored (esp. black), but to attain universal equality and harmony as well. Her writing is dedicated to blurring the boundaries between genders, among races, and even across all species so that her womanism develops into cosmopolitanism.

Instead of a close reading of the selected novels separately, Chapter Ⅶ branches out into a comparative study of Walker's and Hurston's works, which is instrumental in understanding Walker better. As a faithful follower of Zora Neale Hurston, Walker plays an important role in transmitting the ethnic culture. Her works, like Hurston's, are deeply rooted in the black folk culture. The abundant raw materials of the black folklore in their works eloquently prove the common bond between the two great Afro-American women writers. This chapter is split up into four sections, according to the different categories—the literary, the linguistic, the religious, and the artistic—of the folkloric materials in the authors' works, each section focusing on one category. Through comparing Walker's fiction with Hurston's in the four aspects, it concludes that Walker not simply echoes but also revises Hurston in both language and text, and, consequently, has developed a strong bond with Hurston in literary writing. She is thus the deserved inheritor of Hurston's theme and literary craftsmanship, and of the Afro-American women's literature in general.

A Study of Alice Walker's Novels, taking womanism as the key, attempts to do a systematic and comprehensive research on the novels from the thematic perspective. It struggles to achieve logic and coherence within chapters and from cover to cover, notwithstanding its obvious digression and discontinuity. Regardless of the flaws and errors, the book is intended to contribute to Alice Walker studies and spice up the criticism on the author's novels. In this sense, it is worth reading, correcting, and criticizing. Any correction, criticism or comment is appreciated and of great value, and will be welcomed.

Shui Caiqin

Chapter I "In Search of Our Mothers' Gardens": Alice Walker's Activism and Writing

> In my development as a human being and as a writer, I have been, it seems to me, extremely blessed, even while complaining. Wherever I have knocked, a door has opened. Wherever I have wondered, a path has appeared. I have been helped, supported, encouraged, and nurtured by people of all races, colors, and dreams; and I have, to the best of my ability, returned help, support, encouragement, and nurture. This receiving, returning, or passing on has been one of the most amazing, joyous, and continuous experiences of my life. (A. Walker, 1983: xviii)

Admittedly, Alice Walker went through quite a few unfortunate experiences like the shooting that blinded her right eye, the pregnancy that almost led to her suicidal, the divorce, her daughter's estrangement, and the like. She managed to walk away each time largely because of those kind-hearted people in her life, to whom her heart has been swelling with gratitude, as is depicted in the emotional statement above. Life has taught Walker that receiving and returning bring light, warmth, and happiness to each individual, male or female, white or colored. Only when people of different colors and races care for each other and help each other can the world develop equal and harmonious relationships between individuals, communities, or ethnic groups. Hence, as a writer and activist, Walker not simply shows great concern for the sexual and racial issues in her literary writing and social activism but also has put forward and elaborated her womanist philosophy, which stresses the commitment to "survival and wholeness of entire people, male *and* female." (A. Walker, 1983: xi, italics original) Meanwhile she ceaselessly extends her womanist scope to such global issues as animal rights, homosexuality, and environmental destruction, and has been persistently striving for her womanist utopia, where not only people of all races and colors live harmoniously just like flowers of different kinds growing and blooming in "our mothers' gardens" but also humankind and nature coexist in a peaceful and mutually beneficial way. What Walker has done and is doing is attributed to the grateful heart and her belief in a bright future. In other words, out of gratitude Walker is "in search of our mothers' gardens" in her life through literary writing and social activism.

1.1 Striving for the Womanist Ideal

It is not exaggerated to say that Walker's life is one of struggle, a struggle for her own survival and for the "survival and wholeness" of all the underclass. On the one hand, as a girl from a poor sharecroppers' family, Walker got her chance to go to school through her mother's struggle with the landlord; and as a daughter in the family, she not just witnessed the violence and oppression inflicted upon her mother and sisters by her father, and at times, by her brothers (except one), who were all male chauvinists, but also was a victim herself. On the other hand, studying away from home and coming into contact with whites, Walker experienced and witnessed various injustice and inequality in the American society, both inside and outside colleges. She began understanding her own suffering in the social context and came to realize her duty as a contemporary intellectual. She eventually found her role as a social activist or spokeswoman for the underclass, blacks and black women in particular. Walker has been participating in various protests against social injustice and struggles for sexual, racial, and political equality. She is devoted to building "our mothers' gardens," viz., striving for her womanist ideal.

1.1.1 Walker's Parentage and Early years

Alice Malsenior Walker, the eighth and last child of Willie Lee Walker and

Millie Tallulah (Grant) Walker, was born in Eatonton, Georgia on February 9, 1944. Her parents were both sharecroppers and earned only $300 a year from sharecropping and dairy farming. Before the age of four, little Alice went with her parents to the fields and played while they planted, weeded and picked their crops, nobody looking after her on weekdays. Her brothers also worked in the fields and helped milk cows every morning and afternoon. Her father never enjoyed a vacation in his life. Her mother had to work as a maid, while free from farm work, to supplement the family income. Living under Jim Crow Laws, Mrs. Walker had struggles with her landlord who expected the children to work in the fields rather than go to school. She managed to send all her children to school. Alice Walker began her schooling at four, a year ahead of schedule, and enjoyed the school life very much partly because of her first teacher, Mrs. Reynolds. She studied hard with her, though she was just a little girl, and became one of the brightest students in the school. The school life nurtured Alice to grow like one of the flowers in her mother's garden.

Good times never last long. In 1952, the Walkers moved to a farm in a neighboring county, and little Alice, along with her sisters and brothers, was enrolled in a local school. But just before the new term began, her right eye was accidentally wounded in a game by one of her brothers with a bb gun. Unable to afford a car to get her to a doctor's office, her father tried a home remedy and thus missed the best treatment time. When Alice was brought to a physician a week later, a disfiguring layer of scar tissue had already formed over her eye, which was not removed until six years later. In the new school the wounded Alice was teased by the other students and her grades suffered. Therefore her parents were forced to send her back to the old school in Eatonton and let her live with her grandparents there. Every weekend when she came back to her parents, they, to solace the poor girl with the injured eye, would sit around the fireplace telling wondrous stories about her father's great-great-great grandmother Mary Poole and her mother's grandmother Tallulah, and some other stories that had been passed down in the family for generations. When Alice grew up, she learned that these tales could be traced all the way back to Africa and to Native American tribes.

Self-conscious and painfully shy, Alice felt like an outcast and turned for solace to reading and to writing poetry. At the age of fourteen she went to Boston to visit her favorite brother, who persuaded her to go to a hospital for an eye operation. Consequently, the scar tissue was removed although she remained blind in the right eye. Back to Eatonton, Alice became self-confident. She began wondering what she would be in future and got the answer quite by accident: on Wednesday, October 19, 1960, when she learned about Martin Luther King, Jr. and his cause on the television, "as in a fairy tale, my (Alice's) soul was stirred by the meaning for me of his (King's) mission—at the time he was being rather ignominiously dumped into a police van for having led a protest march in Alabama—and I fell in love with the sober and determined face of the (Civil Rights) Movement," became interested in the Movement, and was suddenly awakened to her responsibility and mission as a contemporary black. (124)

Walker graduated from high school in the spring of 1961, honored as valedictorian and voted as the most popular girl in the school. Due to the eye injury, she could apply for a scholarship for handicapped students, which enabled her to go to Spelman College, an institution for black girls in Atlanta. She packed to leave for Spelman College in August 1961, with her mother's special gifts—a suitcase, a sewing machine and a typewriter. As Minnie Walker explained it, each of the gifts bore one of the mother's expectations of the daughter: the suitcase was for independence, the sewing machine for self-sufficiency and the typewriter for creativity. Evidently, as a daughter, Alice fulfilled her mother's wish.

1.1.2 Walker's College Life and Social Activism

On the bus to Atlanta, Alice Walker took a front seat which was reserved for whites only and was ordered to move. She did move but it was in those seconds of moving that she became determined to bring an end to the racial segregation and discrimination. She arrived in Atlanta just at the moment of demonstrations led by the Student Nonviolent Coordinating Committee and some other civil rights activities. This first experience and impression prepared the way for her participation in the activism later. Walker worked hard at Spelman College and was soon rewarded with the opportunity to go to Europe. The trip widened her horizon. Back from Europe, she found Spelman students taking active part in the civil rights activities and joined the student protesters in their sit-ins. But soon Walker realized that Spelman's emphasis on producing "ladies" was an extreme contrast to the changes happening during the Civil Rights Movement. At the end of her sophomore year, she went to Boston first and then near the end of August of 1963, she returned to the Deep South by way of Washington, D. C., where she attended the famous 1963 March on Washington. She received a scholarship from the prestigious Sarah Lawrence College just as the new term began and went to continue her college study in New York in 1963, where she took a B. A. degree two years later. It was during this period that Walker began awakening to intellectual and social issues and participating in the Civil Rights Movement. She met Martin Luther King Jr., whom she credited with her decision to return to the South as an activist for the Civil Rights Movement. Alice Walker, as a young adult, volunteered her time registering voters in Georgia and Mississippi. Just as is depicted in *In Search of My Mothers' Gardens*, "because of the movement, because of an awakened faith in the newness and imagination of the human spirit, because of 'black and white together'... because of the beatings, the arrests, the hell of battle during the past years, I have fought harder for my life and for a chance to be myself, to be something more than as a shadow or a number, than I have ever done before in my life." (125) This personal experience was incorporated into her portrayal of Meridian Hill and the students of Saxon College in her second novel *Meridian*.

During the summer of her last college-year, Alice Walker made a tour to Africa, "and returned to school healthy and brown and loaded down with sculptures and orange fabric" but "pregnant." (qtd. in O'Brien, 1993: 326) At that time, abortion was a sin in the American society. Shocked and depressed, young Alice had no way out but suicidal. "For three days I (Alice Walker) lay on bed with a razorblade under my pillow," saying "good-bye to the world," which she realized she loved so much. (328) Fortunately, one of her friends found an abortionist for her and she had the operation. "When I woke up, my friend was standing over me holding a red rose. She was a blonde, gray-eyed girl, who loved horses and tennis, and she said nothing as she handed me back my life. That moment is engraved in my mind—her smile, sad and pained and frightfully young—as she tried so hard to stand by me and be my friend." (329) This episode affected Alice so much that she "wrote without stopping (except to eat and to go to the toilet)" the week she returned to the school. As a result, she completed almost all of the poems (except one or two of them) in her first collection of poetry *Once*.

After graduating from Sarah Lawrence College Walker continued her struggle for the civil rights. In 1966 her first publication "The Civil Rights Movement: How Good Was It?" won *The American Scholar* essay contest. The following year (1967), Walker married Mel Leventhal, a white civil rights attorney, whom she first met in 1965, and moved to Jackson, Mississippi where she worked for voter registration drives and black studies programs. As the first interracial married couple in the former slavery state, they led a life of constant taunts and even of murderous threats from the Ku Klux Klan. The couple had a daughter, Rebecca in 1969, but divorced amicably in 1976. Rebecca once published a memoir entitled *Black, White and Jewish*, chronicling the effects of her parents' relationship on her childhood. She is estranged from her mother, feeling that she was "a political symbol rather than a cherished daughter," as Margarette Driscoll (2008) described in "The day feminist icon Alice Walker resigned as my mother." In spite of her daughter's misunderstanding, Walker never gives up her struggle.

In the spring of 1988, Alice Walker, along with her companion Robert Allen, joined a demonstration against nuclear weapons at Concord Naval Weapons Station in California. Consequently, they were put in prison for a short time. When asked by a reporter why she continued to demonstrate after a lifetime of marching and speaking out against injustice, she replied that it was what she felt worth doing and that, if she stopped being active in politics, she would feel uncomfortable and wrong. In truth, being an activist is part and parcel of Walker's life.

Walker keeps working as an activist in the new century. On March 8, 2003, International Women's Day, on the eve of the Iraq War, Alice Walker, Maxine Hong Kingston, author of *The Woman Warrior*, and Terry Tempest Williams, author of *An Unspoken Hunger*, were arrested along with twenty-four others for crossing a police line during an anti-war protest rally outside the White House. Walker and 5,000 other activists associated with the organizations like Code Pink and Women for Peace, marched from Malcolm X Park in Washington D. C. to the White House. The activists encircled the White House, holding hands and singing. Interviewed by *Democracy Now*, Walker said of the incident, "I was with other women who believe that the women and children of Iraq are just as dear as the women and children in our families, and that, in fact, we are one family. And so it would have felt to me that we were going over to actually bomb ourselves." Walker wrote about the experience in her essay "We Are the Ones We Have Been Waiting For" (2006).

In November 2008, Alice Walker wrote "An Open Letter to Barack Obama" that was published on Theroot. com. She addressed the newly elected President as "Brother Obama" and wrote "[s]eeing you take your rightful place, based solely on your wisdom, stamina, and character, is a balm for the weary warriors of hope, previously only sung about." In March 2009, Alice Walker traveled to Gaza along with a group of sixty other female activists from the anti-war group Code Pink, in response to the devastation in the wake of the controversial Israeli offensive from December 2008 to January 2009. The purpose of the trip was to deliver aid, to meet with NGOs and residents, and to persuade Israel and Egypt to open their borders into Gaza. In a word, nowadays Walker continues her public struggles to help the entire people of the world attain wholeness and constantly attends to issues that allow human beings to be themselves, whole, free and healthy—issues essential to survival. She is at once active in womanist causes and concerned with issues of environment and economic justice.

1.2 "Living by the Word"

As a writer, Walker has established her reputation in the contemporary American literature by virtue of her great amount of fiction, poetry and nonfiction. She lives for writing and by writing. Hence "living by the word" (the title of her collection of essays) well summarizes Walker's literary career. Since her first publication of *Once* in 1968, she has published altogether seven novels, ten books of poetry, three collections of essays, four collections of short stories, five children's books—*Langston Hughes, American Poet* (1974), *The Life of Thomas Hodge* (1974), *To Hell with Dying* (1987), and *Finding the Green Stone* (1991)—and many other works. The publication of her first novel *The Third Life of Grange Copeland* (1970), together with that of Toni Morrison's *The Bluest Eyes*, marked the beginning of the nascent renaissance of Afro-American women's writing. Her third novel *The Color Purple* (1982) garnered her both the National Book Award for Fiction and the Pulitzer Prize for Fiction in 1983. Most critics applaud her lyrical prose, her sensitive characterizations, and her narrative strategies like folk epistolary style, crazy quilting and mythical history.

Walker's literary career can be divided into two stages by her second volume of essays *Living by the Word* (1988) according to her shift in themes. In the early stage of her literary career, Walker took great interest in social issues and social injustice, especially those concerning black people. So the recurring theme in her works in this period is the exposure of racism and sexism. In her later stage, in addition to her early concerns, Walker turns to subjects like animal rights, vegetarianism, homosexuality, and others. This shift proves her expansion of scope, her involvement in global issues.

1.2.1 Walker's Early Academic Accumulation

Growing up with stories from her parents, Walker began writing, though very privately, when she was only eight years old. One of the positive influences exerted by the eye injury in Walker's early years was that it led the later writer into a self-imposed isolation that was open only to her thirst for reading and her love for poetry. Interviewed by John O'Brien (1993: 327), Walker thus described the early misfortune: "it was from this period—from my solitary, lonely position, the position of an outcast—that I began to really see people and things, to really notice relationships and to learn to be patient enough to care about how they turned out. I no longer felt like the little girl I was. I felt old, and because I was unpleasant to look at, filled with shame, I retreated into solitude, and read stories and began to write poems." Immersed in the literary classics, Walker read earnestly from William Shakespeare through Jane Austen and the Brontë sisters to William Faulkner, and tried her hand at writing poems simultaneously. Thanks to her early years' solitude, Walker developed her later sensibility and shrewdness in examining people and their relationships closely in her works.

Later while studying at Spelman College, she fell in love with the Russian writers of the 19th century like Fyodor Dostoevsky, Nikolay Gogol, Maksim Gorky, Ivan Turgenev, and Lev Tolstoy. She learned a lot from those writers' rooting their souls in the soil of their native land in their literary works, whose example she later lived up to in her own writing. Walker took constant interest in literature while studying at Sarah Lawrence. She added to her reading list the Japanese haiku maters Bashō and Shiki, the Chinese poet Li Po, and the American poets E. E. Cummings, Emily Dickinson, and William Carlos Williams.

Walker's multiple publications in different literary fields benefit from her broad knowledge of other writers. She sees herself as part of an international community of writers from whom she learns and to whom she continually responds. Among those who most impress her are the Russian writers like Tolstoy, Dostoevsky, Turgenev, Gorky and Gogol. These writers render the tone of their entire society through penetrating the essential spirit of individual persons. The result is an interrelation in Walker's fiction between the lives of the black women Walker portrays, the values of the entire society, and the essential spiritual questions that are asked in every human society. The quality of mystery in Walker's poetry, and her preference for economical yet sensual language in her fiction and poetry come from the Japanese haiku poets; the Anglo-American poets like E. E. Cummings, Emily Dickinson, and William Carlos Williams; the ancient Roman writer Ovid; the African poet Okotp'tek; and the Afro-American writers like Gwendolyn Brooks, Arna Bontemps, and Jean Toomer. Walker's courage of illustrating and recording aspects of experiences unknown to or interpreted differently by men and/ or whites, of writing against great social barriers, the ones internalized as psychological conflicts in particular, is attributed to the influence of black writers, especially black women writers like Zora Neale Hurston, and women writers of other cultures like Virginia Woolf, the Brontë sisters, Doris Lessing and Kate Chopin. Among the numerous writers having nurtured Walker, Hurston is the literary precursor, foremother, and spirit-guide who inspired Walker's audacious womanist autonomy in her writing. Walker not only claims Hurston as nurturer of her creativity but restores Hurston's works to the reading public from oblivion as well.

1.2.2 Walker's Professional Career and Literary Achievements

After marriage, Walker first worked as a teacher, or exactly, as a black history consultant to preschool teachers, at the Friends of the Children of Mississippi, which provided underprivileged children with preschool education and meals and health as well. Working closely with those black women teachers, Walker managed to arouse their interest in the black history by encouraging them to write their own autobiographies. The women greatly touched Walker with their vivid and true stories, which were copied and stapled and then handed back to the students as a sort of patchwork quilt in words. In so doing, Walker not only helped her students to understand the importance of history, but also enriched her own writing material. The gestures of wizened women found their way into her short stories.

The assassination of Martin Luther King put Walker in such desperation that even the thought of suicide came back to haunt her. She moved to teach black studies at Jackson State University and attempted to combat her depression with hard work. Around this time, her first book of poetry *Once*, which had been written while she was still a senior at Sarah Lawrence, was published. In 1969 Walker won a National Endowment for the Arts. Meanwhile, she engaged herself in novel writing. In effect, it was her grappling with the characters of her first novel which eventually saved her from the slough of despond. *The Third Life of Grange Copeland* cost its author two years of hard work and came out in 1970, one year after she gave birth to her daughter. However, as Walker once complained, "they (critics) prefer, rather, to talk about the lives of black women writers, not about what they write." (qtd. in O'Brien, 1993: 338) This personal encounter with injustice in the male-dominated critical circle, along with the "mute and absent" state of the past black women writers, awakened her to racism and sexism existing in the academic world, and spurred her on to the commitment to the protest against such discriminations.

In 1972, Walker was offered a teaching position at Wellesley College in Boston, a progressive institution giving her permission to introduce a course in women's studies that concentrated on the literature of female writers whose works had become neglected. The women writers introduced by Walker touched her students a lot and Walker's students came to realize the fact that the opinions and artistic expressions of women were as significant as those of men and that great black artists, like great white artists, spoke movingly to all people. Judging for themselves was what they learned from Walker's teaching. Among all these writers, Walker took a special interest in Zora Neale Hurston, the greatest black woman novelist of the Harlem Renaissance. She began to devote herself to the resurrection of Hurston in particular and of the black women writers in the American literature in general. In 1973, Walker and a fellow Hurston scholar Charlotte D. Hunt discovered Hurston's unmarked grave in Ft. Pierce, Florida. Both women paid for a modest headstone for the gravesite. The 1975 publication of the article "Looking for Zola" in *Ms.* magazine was largely responsible for the renewal of interest in the work of Zora Neale Hurston, who was actually a large source of inspiration for Walker's writing and subject matter. Walker's next contribution to the resurrection of Hurston was her compilation of an anthology of Hurston's best works, *I Love Myself When I Am Laughing... and Then Again When I Am Looking Mean and Impressive: A Zora Neale Hurston Reader* (1979). With the two publications, Hurston's literary reputation became assured.

If Walker's stay in the North during the college days broadened her mind, then her return to the South provided her works with abundant raw materials. During and after her stay in the South, Walker wrote a lot about the lives of the southern rural blacks. Before leaving the South for New York in 1974, Walker had published her first collection of short stories, *In Love and Trouble: Stories of Black Women* (1973), which gained the 1974 Richard and Hinda Rosenthal Foundation Award from the American Academy and Institute of Arts and Letters, and her second book of poetry, *Revolutionary Petunias and Other Poems* in 1973, which won the Lillian Smith Award for Poetry of the Southern Regional Council and garnered a nomination for the National Book Award. The former is "about thirteen women—mad, raging, loving, resentful, hateful, strong, ugly, weak, pitiful, and magnificent, [who] try to live with the loyalty to black men that characterizes all of their lives," about black women who "are the most fascinating creations in the world." (331) The latter contains many of the poems Walker wrote during her years in Mississippi. The title of the book came after her mother who taught Walker about the restorative power of flowers and always planted a profusely blooming petunia bush wherever they lived. For Walker, flowers symbolize hope and determination in the face of hardship.

After her essay "In Search of Our Mothers' Gardens" was published in *Ms.* in 1974, Walker became an editor of the magazine and a leading spokeswoman for black women, focusing on neglect of and injustice to black women throughout history. Her second novel *Meridian* (1976) dealt with activist workers in the South during the Civil Rights Movement, and closely paralleled some of Walker's own experiences. Walker wrote extensively about the Civil Rights Movement both in prose and poetry, but *Meridian* was probably her most considered account of the day-to-day struggle. In 1977, Walker was given a Guggenheim Fellowship (1977 – 1978), which made it possible for her to quit the job at *Ms*.

Since her marriage fell apart in 1976, Walker had written many poems about the pain of divorce. These poems, together with those about her experience since her college years, were collected in her third book of poetry, *Good Night, Willie Lee, I'll See You in the Morning* (1979). Walker chose the death of her father as the centerpiece for the book. In 1973 Walker returned to Eatonton for his father's funeral and watched her mother touch her father's hand for the last time. "Good Night, Willie Lee, I'll See You in the Morning" was what her mother said to her father at his coffin. By using the unusual title, Walker tended to stress the healing power of forgiveness expressed in the last words of one parent to the other. Her second collection of short stories, *You Can't Keep a Good Woman Down*, came out in 1982. It is a collection of fourteen tales written primarily during her difficult years in New York, abounding in anger and confusion of those times.

The inspiration for her third novel and best-known work *The Color Purple* came from a lovers' triangle, which she and her sister Ruth talked about during a walk in New York. Although from then on the characters were trying to contact Walker and speak through her, it was only when she settled down in the hills of northern California that the characters came freely: to set her characters in the right place, Walker left New York for the rural area of northern California just before getting down to the manuscript of *The Color Purple* at the beginning of the 1980s and lived there since then. The book came out in 1982, within just a year after she set about writing it. Under the title of "the color purple" flew a tale of reunion and redemption. *The Color Purple* tells a story of a young black woman fighting her way through not only racist white culture but patriarchal black culture. It proved to be a resounding commercial success and saved its author from the thin time. As a bestseller the book was subsequently adapted into a critically acclaimed 1985 movie as well as a 2005 Broadway musical play. The year 1983 witnessed the establishment of Walker's worldwide reputation with the two most important awards for fiction in the USA given to *The Color Purple* and with the publication of her first and most influential book of essays *In Search of Our Mothers' Gardens*. Covering the topics like the author's favorite neglected writers, her childhood, her struggle with hardship and depression throughout her life, and the Civil Rights Movement, the collection fleshes out Walker's manifesto of "womanism" and may be accepted as an autobiography.

In 1984 Walker at once started her own publishing house Wild Trees Press (closed in 1988) and published her fourth book of poetry, *Horses Make a Landscape Look More Beautiful*. Although the subjects here range from the very personal to the political, the collection mainly focuses on how a person developed an artistic sensibility as a means of making sense of the world. Since her dark days in college, poetry had always helped save Walker from despair, and *Horses Make a Landscape Look More Beautiful* can be read as a sincere gratitude to the spiritual support that helped the poet survive the difficult circumstances. Walker's second volume of essays, *Living by the Word* (1988), not only includes most of her articles about human rights but also the journal entries from her years in northern California. These pieces express the author's willingness to share intimate details about her relationships with animals, plants and intangible spirits and thus marked the author's shift from the early concern with the specific black issues to the later involvement in global issues.

Walker keeps connecting old traditions to the present by novel-writing and each of her novels might be read as an attempt to merge the good and bad parts of American history into a tale that leads people of different colors (esp. black people), male and female, to understanding and compassion. Her fourth novel *The Temple of My Familiar* (1989), ranging across the whole of world history, is an epic about a woman's innumerable lives and experience from the prehistoric world to slavery in the United States. To tell a story about personal relationships spanning countless centuries, the narrator shuttles between the past and the present by employing elements of Zora Neale Hurston's storytelling style and those of other South American "magical realists." In 1991, adding sixteen new poems to the previous four collections, Walker published all her poems in one volume named

Her Blue Body Everything We Know: Earthling Poems 1965 – 1990 Complete. In the same year, *Finding the Green Stone* (another children's book) also came out. Then just a year later, she published her fifth novel *Possessing the Secret of Joy*, which features several characters and descendants of characters from *The Color Purple*. In this novel she chronicled a woman's spiritual trauma after a forced genital mutilation.

Walker continued her steady pace of publication at the turn of the century. Her third volume of essays, *Anything We Love Can Be Saved: A Writer's Activism* (1997), further reveals her wide-ranging interests: oppression, female genital mutilation, the Million Man March, and others, and her emphasis on every person's efforts to make the world a better place. Her sixth novel *By the Light of My Father's Smile* came off the press in 1998. The book examines the connection between sexuality and spirituality, and the relationship of father and daughters is the focus of Walker's concern. In the new century Walker keeps active in the Afro-American literary world and has produced a considerable number of works as a reward for her readers. Her seventh novel *Now Is the Time to Open Your Heart* (2004), ranking among her finest achievements, is at once a deeply moving personal story and a powerful spiritual journey, a story of a woman wonderer Kate's explorations of the natural world and the human soul, or exactly, of her spiritual adventure that becomes a passage through time, a quest for self, and a collision with love. Her first new collection of poetry in this century *Absolute Trust in the Goodness of the Earth: New Poems* (2003) reaffirmed her reputation as one of the best American writers today. Covering a wide range of emotions, the poems explore the fundamental beauty of existence and thus help readers, as at once an individual and part of a greater spiritual community, get across not just the forces of nature but the strength of the human spirit as well. As a persistent advocate of womanism, Alice Walker rewarded her fans and anyone who longs for peace with wise insights and mature compassion in her latest non-fictional work *We Are the Ones We Have Been Waiting For* (2006). In the book she draws on her deep spiritual grounding, her political conviction and experience, and her literary gifts to offer a series of meditations filled with wisdom, hope, encouragement, and, at times, serenity to a world in need of all these things. Walker's other works produced in the 21st century include the collections of poetry like *A Poem Traveled Down My Arm: Poems and Drawings* (2003), *Collected Poems* (2005), *Hard Times Require Furious Dancing: New Poems*, and *The World Will Follow Joy Turning Madness into Flowers (New Poems)* (2013), the third collection of short stories *The Way Forward Is with a Broken Heart* (2000), and the non-fcition books like *Sent By Earth: A Message from the Grandmother Spirit After the Bombing of the World Trade Center and Pentagon* (2001), *Devil's My Enemy* (2008), *Overcoming Speechlessness* (2010), *Chicken Chronicles, A Memoir* (2011), and *The Cushion in the Road: Meditation and Wandering as the Whole World Awakens to Be in Harm's Way* (2013).

In 2007, Walker gave 122 boxes of manuscripts and archive material to Emory University's Manuscript, Archives, and Rare Book Library. In addition to drafts of writings such as *The Color Purple*, unpublished poems and writings, and correspondence with editors, the collection includes extensive correspondence with family members, friends and colleagues, an early treatment of the film script for *The Color Purple* that was never used, syllabi from courses she taught, and fan mail. The collection also contains some hidden treasures including a scrapbook of poetry compiled when Walker was just fifteen years old entitled *Poems of a Childhood Poetess*.

1.3 Striving through the Word

Walker's consistent concern is "the spiritual survival, the survival whole" of her people, of the people of colors, and eventually of the planet. (qtd. in O'Brien, 1993: 331) Interviewed by David Bradley in 1984, Walker said, "I think writing really helps you heal yourself. I think if you write long enough, you'll be a healthy person. That is, if you write what you need to write, as opposed to what will make money, or what will make fame." (qtd. in Bradley, 1984: 36) Accepting writing as a means of achieving health and survival whole, she embodies her idea of wholeness in her characters, both male and female. Throughout her writing Walker repeatedly relates art to what she considers the all-important process of self-improvement. Donna Haisty Winchell (1992: x) points out, while Walker's female characters "achieve their psychological wholeness when they are able to fight oppression" from either racism or sexism or even their own self-righteous anger, her male characters gain their spiritual survival when they shake off the stereotypical patriarchal restraints, redress the definition of maleness and take the responsibility for what they have done to their women and children.

Walker is a respected figure in the liberal political community for her support of unconventional and unpopular views as a matter of principle. Her works typically focus on blacks; particularly black women, and their struggle against a racist, sexist, and violent society. She is well known for her portrayals of the Afro-American women's life. She portrays as part of that life the strengths of family, community, self-worth, and spirituality. Her writings also focus on the role of women of color in culture and history. Many of her novels depict women in other periods of history than our own. Just as with non-fiction women's history writing, such portrayals give a sense of the differences and similarities of women's condition today and in that other time. However, with *Living by the Word* as a turning point, she expands the scope of her concern. In her later works she is shifting to the improvement of humans' relationships with animals, plants and intangible spirits, to the further involvement in global issues. As a writer, Alice Walker keeps striving for her womanist ideal through her persistent writing.

In her quest of the spiritual survival Walker achieves her special contribution to the American literature: the exploration of the Afro-American women writing, her idea of womanism, aside from the sensitive characterizations of blacks in her works. Walker incorporates her intellectual theme into the life experience of the poor, black, plain people. In her works she not only stresses her own history, i. e., the Afro-American women's writing history, but simultaneously the cultural history of southern blacks and American blacks as a whole. Her heritage and history helps her have a radical vision of society and see the world in the way that enables people to realize the necessity of change. As a womanist, she concerns herself with "survival and wholeness of entire people." (A. Walker, 1983: xi) She has become involved in a variety of social issues such as the Civil Rights, the animal rights, and antinuclear movements, which are necessary for the survival of the planet and everyone on it. Her relenting portraits of human weaknesses convey such a message that the breaches and violations must be mended for health and continuity, for survival whole.

Obviously, Walker's political awareness, her southern heritage, and her sense of the culture and history of her people lay a solid foundation of the themes in her works. She is one of the first contemporary black women writers to insist that sexism exists in the black community and is not just an issue for white women. Her uniqueness lies in the fact that she did this at a time when most black leaders focused only on racism and considered her position to be practically heresy. Besides, Walker also dramatizes in her works the nature of racism and the relationship between sexism and racism as modes of oppression that restrict the lives of all women and men in the American society. Walker's writings evoke both criticism and praise while provoking controversy as well as change. As she continues to write from her unique intellectual and spiritual perspective, her contribution to literature and social change grows even more solid and abiding.

In short, Walker's prestige as a writer lies in her skill as a novelist, an essayist, and a poet as well as her role as a promoter and reclaimer of an Afro-American women's cultural heritage and tradition. Her novels help to make the Afro-American literary culture one of the American academic concerns and thus have changed the shape of the contemporary American literature. She has enriched the American literature through rescuing the works of nearly forgotten writers and articulating a black female criticism that has had a major impact on the increase in critical writings by Afro-American women scholars.

Since her first publication in 1968, Walker has become one of the best-known American writers and has won numerous honors and awards, which, in the first period of her literary career, contain Merill Writkins Fellowship in 1966 – 1967, MacDowell Colony Fellowships in 1967 and 1974, the O. Henry Award in 1986 for the story "Kindred Spirits" and the Langston Hughes Award in 1988, in addition to the two great American awards for *The Color Purple* in 1983. During the second period of her literary writing, she received an Honorary Degree from the California Institute of the Arts (1995). In 1997 she was honored by the American Humanist Association as "Humanist of the Year." She has also received a number of other awards for her body of work, including the Lillian Smith Award from the National Endowment for the Arts, the Rosenthal Award from the National Institute of Arts & Letters, the Radcliffe Institute Fellowship, a Guggenheim Fellowship and the Front Page Award for Best Magazine Criticism from the Newswoman's Club of New York. On December 6, 2006, California Governor Arnold Schwarzenegger and First Lady Maria Shriver inducted Alice Walker into the California Hall of Fame located at The California Museum for History, Women, and the Arts.

Chapter II Beyond Measure: Critical Responses to Alice Walker's Novels

> Women writers are supposed to be intimidated by male disapprobation. What they write is not important enough to be read. How they live, however, their 'image', they owe to the race. … I no longer read articles or reviews unless they are totally about the work. I trust that someday a generation of men and women will arise who … will read my work because it is a true account of my feelings, my perception, and my imagination, and because it will reveal something to them of their own selves. They will also be free to toss it—and me—out of the window. They can do what they like. (qtd. in O'Brien, 1993: 338, 339)

Just as Ms. Walker expected in the interview, her works have received condemnations and praises as well. But with the establishment of her reputation in the Afro-American women's writing, particularly after the publication of *The Color Purple*, more and more reviewers and scholars are inclined to explore the positive elements in her works. As Walker's reputation is mainly based on novels, we choose to make a survey of the critical responses to her seven novels to see how her position has been consolidated by the critics.

2.1 Researches in the Western World

A comprehensive survey of Walker studies in the Western world shows that her early novels have been given special attention to, although the later ones, with the in-depth exploration, are arousing more and more interest of the 21st-century native critics. In compliance with the division of Walker's literary career, we tend to classify the critical responses to her novels in the Western world into two categories: those to the early novels and those to the later ones.

2.1.1 Criticism on the Early Novels

Concerning *The Third Life of Grange Copeland*, Jay L. Halio (1973: 465) praises its author for her "firm, tight control" and her eloquent language, adding "it is no surprise to learn that the author is also a poet." Henry Louis Gates, Jr. (1993b: x), in his preface to *Alice Walker: Critical Perspectives Past and Present*, acclaims Walker as "one of the two central figures in the nascent renaissance of Black women's writing," pointing out that, together with Morrison's *The Bluest Eye*, *The Third Life of Grange Copeland* marked the birth of this movement.

Immediately after its publication *Meridian* was listed among the best novels emerging from the Civil Rights Movement and garnered its author a prestigious Guggenheim Fellowship. Tony Gentry (1993: 72) thus sums up the critical responses:

> Among the best novels to emerge from the civil rights movement, *Meridian* was praised by most critics, who were quick to group Walker with Earnest J. Gaines, Toni Morrison, Ishmael Reed, and the other young black writers who had emerged from the civil rights era with a new and encompassing perspective on the black experience. The reaction of a reviewer in *Black Scholar* was typical, calling Walker's book "an extraordinary fine novel... written in a clear, almost incandescent prose that sings and sears." That same journal later named *Meridian* one of the 10 best novels written in the 1970s.

Despite the fame of the first two novels, the birth of *The Color Purple* created a great stir in the literary circle. Shortly after winning the two most important national awards for fiction in 1983, the novel gained "increased fame—and notoriety—in 1985 with the release of the film adaptation, directed by Steven Spielberg." (Winchell, 1992: 85) Also from the brief summary given by Tony Gentry (1993: 81) in *Alice Walker* we can get how the novel is received in the academic world: "*The Color Purple* caused an immediate sensation. *Newsweek* called the book 'an American novel of permanent importance.' *Essence* said it was 'one of the great books of our time.' And *San Francisco Chronicle* claimed that the novel would 'stand beside literature of any time and place.'" Among those critics who have celebrated the publication of *The Color Purple* are Mel Watkins (1993:18) who considers the book "striking and consummately well-written" and undoubtedly Walker's "most impressive" novel, Dinitia Smith (1993: 21) who believes that the novel "marks a major advance for Walker's art" and that "[a]t least half the book is superb [so that] it places her in the company of Faulkner," Elizabeth Bartelme (1983: 94) who hails the novel as an "arresting and touching novel" and its author as "a remarkable novelist … with a strong individual voice and vision of her own, and delicious humor that pervades the book and tempers the harshness of the lives of its people," and others.

Apart from the above general comments on the novels, there are many others focusing specifically on the themes, the narrative strategies, and/or the sensitive characterizations.

2.1.1.1 Critical Concern with the Themes

A typical theme of Ms. Walker's works is her concern with "change," as the author herself proclaimed at an interview that she believed "in change: change personal, and change in society." (qtd. in O'Brien, 1993: 332) At this point, many reviewers echo Walker. Barbara Christian (1993: 50) points out that "the question of responsibility for personal action and societal change is one recurrent motif" in Walker's novels, and that, through continually stitching "a fabric of the everyday violence," her novels are characterized by the "exploration of the process of personal and societal growth out of horror and waste" and of black people's desire for regeneration. She then goes on analyzing how the theme of transformation and regeneration is presented in Walker's first two novels. Christian (1993: 72) argues that in spite of the difference in the focuses of the two novels—*The Third Life of Grange Copeland* on "the Copeland family" and *Meridian* on "the history of black people in the South up to a peak period in the 1960s"—both unify "the bits and pieces of Southern life" through "the potent process of personal change." Different from other echoers, Christian refers to degeneration as well as regeneration in this personal change. She articulates that the process is complicated by the intersection of the two coexisting in the characters. For John O'Brien (1993: 327), *The Third Life of Grange Copeland* is "a novel of education, in which Walker demonstrates a remarkable ability to show the change and transformation of a character without violating either her characters or human nature." Donna Haisty Winchell (1992: 55), after expounding on the burden of responsibility and the flaw of unforgiveness resting with the characters, concludes that *The Third Life of Grange Copeland* is "as much about spiritual change as about social change." Debra Walker King (2001: 414) asserts that *Meridian* "focuses on the Civil Rights Movement and its fight for social change." In "*The Color Purple*: What Feminism Can Learn from a Southern Tradition," Gina Michelle Collins (1990: 78) expresses her understanding of Walker's theme of "change" in the novels, holding that "the refusal to adopt the values and attitudes of a racist patriarchy, to believe in its stereotype, along with a recognition of destructive, limiting effects of adherence to such values, is the key to the power of a Meridian, … or a Celie over those who would silence and enslave them." Philip M. Royster (1986: 348) considers the theme of "change" in *The Color Purple* presented in the action of black women's "overcoming black male sexist exploitation." Melissa Walker's (1991: 69 – 70) opinion about the theme is that, while the characters' transformation in *Meridian* takes place "in the context of a public commitment," *The Third Life of Grange Copeland* and *The Color Purple* embrace the transformations of the characters "in the personal domain." What is characteristic of these critics in exploring the "change" theme in the novels is their nearly identical concern with the female characters. The transformation or the potential for change of the male characters is largely neglected.

As Mel Watkins (1993: 17) reveals it, another "most prominent" theme in Walker's three early novels is "estrangement and violence that mark the relationships between black men and women." Watkins further points out that the focus of *The Color Purple* apparently lies on "the role of male domination in the frustration of black women's struggle for independence" and that, in *Meridian*, this theme is fully explored in the story of one man (Truman) and two women (Meridian and Lynne) in spite of the fact that "the friction between black men and black women is merely one of several themes." In "Violence in *The Third Life of Grange Copeland*" Trudier Harris (1988: 4108) analyzes the theme of "estrangement and violence" in the title novel, arguing that the difference between Walker and most other black writers before her is Walker's shift from their concern with the violence committed by blacks against whites to the focus on the violence committed by blacks "against each other and themselves." Barbara Christian (1993: 53) also expresses her concern with this theme in Walker's first novel, stating that "the story is marked throughout by the motif of physical and spiritual murder, by suicide and infanticide, by wife beating and killing." A similar response is found in Wendy Wall (1993: 261) who insists that, in *The Color Purple*, Walker describes "rape, wife-beating, genital mutilation, and facial scarification" to explain that "a patriarchy maintains power by rewriting the female body into powerlessness, thus denying the woman's ability to authorize herself." Bernard Bell (1987: 263) asserts that the "unrelenting, severe attacks on male hegemony, especially the violent abuse of black women by black men" in *The Color Purple* are "offered as a revolutionary leap forward into a new social order based on sexual egalitarianism." Although Bell goes further by affirming Walker's revolutionary element in her depiction of violence by black men in Afro-American community, he is about level with the other critics in failing to explore the male characters' underlying impulse towards the spiritual survival.

As womanist texts, Walker's three early novels inevitably reflect her great concern with the spiritual survival of her characters, of black people, male and female. At an interview, Walker told John O'Brien: "I am preoccupied with the spiritual survival, the survival whole of my people." (qtd. in O'Brien, 1993: 331) Consistent with this thematic concern, O'Brien figures out that *The Third Life of Grange Copeland* is pervaded by an "optimism … an indomitable belief in the future, and in man's capacity for survival." Thadious M. Davis (1980: 354) holds that, in the title character of *The Third Life of Grange Copeland*, Walker articulates her vision of survival—"at whatever costs, human beings have the capacity to live in spiritual health and beauty; they may be poor, black, and uneducated, but their inner selves can blossom." Christine Gomez (1991: 254) interprets *Meridian* as a feminist *Bildungsroman* dealing with the theme of "self-discovery, self-definition and self-affirmation" of a black woman with positive self-image and social commitment, that is, the theme of womanist wholeness—spiritual survival—of black women. Concerning *The Color Purple*, Robert James Butler (1988: 76) believes that the novel expresses "Walker's desire to achieve personal wholeness." What JoAnne Cornwell (1993: 105) says in "Searching for Zora in Alice's Garden" best expresses her understanding of this theme in these novels: "Ruth [in *The Third Life of Grange Copeland*] … is the embodiment of both male and female transcendence. Already in this first novel, Alice Walker underscores the importance of the androgynous experience in liberating the spirit. This motif comes through even more strongly in her two later novels *Meridian* and *The Color Purple*." These reviewers do manifest their concern with spiritual survival of the characters in the novels. Their focus, however, still lies on the female images with only O'Brien, who is also concerned about the male characters' survival in Walker's first novel, as an exception. In other words, the spiritual survival of Walker's black males in the three novels as a whole remains intact.

Just as *Contemporary Literary Criticism* (Vol. 27) summarizes—"Walker's work consistently reflects her concern with racial, sexual, and political issues"—another recurrent theme of Walker's three early novels is the theme of racism and sexism. (Stine, 1984: 448) The book continues commenting: "like her first novel…*The Color Purple* portrays the devastating effects of racial and sexual oppression." (448) To echo this statement of theme, an excerpt from Carol Rumens follows in the same book, where Rumens asserts that "in *Meridian*, considerations of sexual and racial politics are resonant with universal moral overtones." (qtd. in Stine, 1984: 449) Barbara Christian (1993: 85) also insists that, through the relationship between Meridian, Truman and Lynne, Walker's second novel explores how "sexism and racism have affected the people of America."

For some critics, Walker's attraction also lies in her exposition of the taboo subject. Barbara Christian (1998: 387 – 88), for instance, states that in all the three novels the author explores at least one or two forbidden motifs in the black community, such as lesbianism and incest in *The Color Purple*, family violence in *The Third Life of Grange Copeland*, and "the myth of black motherhood and the idea that revolutionary violence should at least be questioned in *Meridian*." Thus "by critiquing her community," Christian holds that, Walker "affirms our rights to take responsibility for ourselves" and, "by speaking to her community as her audience, she demonstrates how central black people are to her vision."

Besides, the themes like sex, love, animism, motherhood, sisterhood between women, and the creativity of black women are also critics' focuses in studying Alice Walker's first three novels. However, compared with the ones mentioned above, these themes are either less concentrated on or only exposed in one or two of the novels. So they are not to be reviewed in detail here.

2.1.1.2 Critical Concern with the Narrative Strategies

Concerning the narrative strategies adopted in the three novels, Claudia Tate (1991: 511) once points out that Walker's "characters, dramatic situations, and generic forms" employ realism—"social realism" and "gothic realism." He further illustrates that, "rendered in an indelible social realism as vivid as the red Georgia clay, *The Third Life of Grange Copeland* dramatizes the tragic consequences of a distinct form of racial oppression—sharecropping." (512) As for *Meridian*, Tate (514) argues that Walker, detached from the chronological realism in the first novel, adopts the gothic realism to present "a series of small, nonlinear, often grotesque anecdotes about Meridian's experience." To dramatize the "gothic" effect, she also depicts the mythical history in the novel. Tate is echoed by critics such as Jay L. Halio (1973: 465) who asserts that *The Third Life of Grange Copeland* is a "magnificent" novel whose "honest treatment of both past and present, the worst aspects of which Miss Walker does not flinch at, helps make *The Third Life* a convincing and stirring novel"; Melissa Walker

(1991: 110) who holds that "the linear form of *Grange* presumes positive historical progress"; Elliott Butler-Evans (1993: 116) who points out that *Meridian*, with the employment of the gothic realism, "signals a radical departure from the earlier work in its representation of history and its narrative strategies," so, unlike in *The Third Life of Grange Copeland*, the episodes in *Meridian* "are generally not structured by any strict chronology"; bell hooks (1993: 291), who, admiring the "illusory magic" created by Walker in *The Color Purple*, attributes it to the author's remarkable literary technique, that is, "the skilful combining of social realism and fantasy, the fairy tale and the fictionalized autobiographical narrative," and others, to name just a few.

Another important narrative strategy employed by Walker in the novels is the technique of quilting. After an analytic study of Walker's novels like *The Third Life of Grange Copeland* and *Meridian* along with her poetry and short stories, Barbara Christian (1993: 50) asserts that "Alice Walker's works are quilts—bits and pieces of used material rescued from oblivion for everyday use" and that "[t]he bits and pieces are not random fabric… [but] the seemingly insignificant and hidden pieces of the loves of the Southerners, particularly black families," which Walker elaborately sorts out and stitches into a tapestry of society. By naming Walker's works "quilts," Christian centers on the collection of raw materials, while critics like Bell and Wall more stress the structure of her works. For Bernard W. Bell (1987: 260), Walker's first novel "is structured like a crazy quilt in that it is disproportionately divided into eleven parts with forty-eight minichapters that outline the three lives of the patriarch of the Copeland clan." As for *The Color Purple*, Wendy Wall (1993: 268) thinks it difficult to talk about the novel "without invoking the metaphor of the quilt," and that "the appropriateness of this folk craft in describing the epistolary style is obvious in that both are wholes that show the process of their construction." In "Rewriting the Heroine's Story in *The Color Purple*," Linda Abbandonato (1993: 300) echoes that "by adopting the crazy quilt … as the structuring principle of her fiction, Alice Walker places herself within a tradition of black female creativity." Thanks to the craft, "the novel moves freely through time and space, juxtaposing the African motifs with the African American, thus supplying a dialectical commentary on the two cultures." (300)

About symbolism applied in the three novels, Theodore O. Mason, Jr. (1993: 126 – 27) analyzes the "metaphorical values of enclosure" in both *The Color Purple* and *The Third Life of Grange Copeland*, stating that in the former "Celie finds herself enclosed within a series of related imprisoning structures—her illiteracy, the sexist role … and the entire racist political, economic, and social structure of the South, among others," and in the latter "Walker uses the sharecropper's cabin as a charged metaphorical structure indicating the fundamental and irresistible entrapment of its occupants." The metaphorical meaning of colors in *The Color Purple* is also the focus of the reviewers like Linda Abbandonato (1993: 306) who rivets her attention on interpretation of the color purple which is understood "as a sign of indomitable female spirit." She points out that, "[a]ssociated with Easter and resurrection, and thus with, spiritual regeneration," purple may also symbolize the black females' positive sense of sex. As to the second novel *Meridian*, Deborah E. McDowell (1993: 176 – 77) interprets the metaphoric meanings of images such as the changed picture in the church, the branch from the Sojourner tree, Meridian's sleeping bag and others in the ending part of the novel. And Elliott Butler-Evans (1993: 117 – 19) exemplifies "the symbolic representations of disempowerment" through the images like Marilene O'shay, Wild Child and Sojourner tree, while Barbara Christian (1993: 81) argues that "as the image of music connects the motifs of wholeness that Walker uses throughout the novel, so the concept of guilt encompasses the motifs of fragmentation."

Elliott Butler-Evans (1993: 105 – 7) also reveals "the semiotic representation of history in fictional discourse" in Walker's first two novels, which "are structured by their inscription of two historical narratives," i. e., "the racial historical discourse" and "the feminine counterdiscourse." Butter-Evans points out that, to examine Walker's narratives, one not only has to "explore the manner in which the two discourses are inscribed in the text, marking their points of intersection and divergence," but also "needs to examine the manner in which the racial historical discourse becomes increasingly marginalized and is often displaced by alternative narratives of feminist desire." (107) At the end of the same essay, Butler-Evans concludes that, if Walker's two early novels mark a point of intersection and a struggle between two discourses, the full articulation of a distinct feminist position unfolds in her third novel *The Color Purple*.

In addition to these already mentioned narrative strategies shared by the three novels, there exist some other strategies that distinguish one or two of the novels from the other(s). As far as *The Third Life of Grange Copeland* is concerned, Elliott Butler-Evans (108) emphasizes "the constant intervention of an external narrator who comments and interprets for the reader," and affirms the positive function of the narrative which shifts "the centers of consciousness throughout the novel." John O'Brien (1993: 326) expresses his understanding of the novel, saying that "most impressive about her fiction is Walker's power as a storyteller. She does not indulge in awkward asides in which characters have revelations, or in extended dialogues where they work out the themes of the novel. Walker depends on her capacity to render themes in terms of action." As for *Meridian*, Marge Piercy (1993: 9) praises it as "a fine, taut novel that accomplishes a remarkable amount" with "the method of compression through selection of telling moments and her freedom from chronology," while Alan Nadel (1993: 155–56) presents her unique perspective by arguing that "Walker treats narrative as archeology and thus provides instructions for reading Meridian's life as though it were inscribed on the archeological site of her body." In this way Nadel (1993: 158) concludes that the simultaneous breaking down and reconstructing reflected in the body of Meridian is the "uniquely feminist quality" of the novel.

Compared to the first two novels, *The Color Purple* attracts more attention of the critics. Dinitia Smith (1993: 21) focuses on Walker's similarities to Faulkner, i. e., "the use of a shifting first-person narrator, the presentation of a complex story from a naïve point of view, and the Southern fictional tradition." In

"Color Me Zora," Henry Louis Gates, Jr. (1993a: 244) explores the bonding relationship between Hurston and Walker, stating that "*The Color Purple* is replete with free indirect discourse, the double-voiced discourse of *Their Eyes Were Watching God.*" Accepting *The Color Purple* as a feminist text, Linda Abbandonato (1993: 298 – 99) expounds that, to meet the challenge that feminists are faced with, i. e., "to rewrite cultural narratives and define the terms of another perspective—a view from 'elsewhere,'" the novel chooses the ways of lesbianism and of displacing "standard English with the Southern black vernacular." Both Smith and Abbandonato are echoed by Trudier Harris (1993: 40) who insists that, "no matter our approval or disapproval of the incidents conveyed" in the way of folk speech, "they are conveyed in the authentic voice of the folk. … Her first-person narration may be viewed as keeping within the storytelling vein of African-American oral delivery. Walker captures the rhythms as well as the nuances of African-American speech, including signifying and subtle humor." The employment of "the narrative structure of the epistolary novel" is another concern of the critics like Tate (1991: 516) who points out that in *The Color Purple* Walker abandons "the European androcentric literary convention of the epistolary novel" and ushers in the Afro-American women's epistolary novel by giving Celie "the task of telling her own story through her letters," and Henry Louis Gates, Jr. (1993a: 244) who concludes that, before *The Color Purple*, there have appeared no epistolary novels in the black tradition.

2.1.1.3 Critical Concern with the Characterizations

As far as Walker's characterizations in these three novels are concerned, many critical responses focus on her female characters. Philip M. Royster (1986: 360) insists that the major female characters in the three novels, i. e., Ruth in *The Third Life of Grange Copeland*, the title character in *Meridian* and Celie in *The Color Purple* "are masks for Walker's perceptions of herself. None of them has an adequate relationship with a male character. The adult women do not enjoy sex with males." Dinitia Smith (1993: 19) praises Walker's vivid characterization of black women in the three novels, saying that "to read an Alice

Walker novel is to enter the country of surprise … the world of rural black women." The depiction of these women is so vivid and authentic that the readers "are immediately gripped by them." In Deborah E. McDowell's (1993: 168) opinion, what Walker's female characterization presents is "black womanhood and its myriad shadings." McDowell believes that *The Third Life of Grange Copeland* explores "the dynamics of being a black woman," but in *Meridian* Walker "transcends the boundaries of the female gender to embrace more universal concerns about individual autonomy, self-reliance, and self-realization." Through her female image in *The Color Purple*, Gina Michelle Collins (1990: 75) interprets, Walker not only acknowledges "the identification of black women as 'mules of the world' in black folklore" but also emphasizes the "outstanding feature" of such "an ugly, comical creature"—the ability to survive, the talent for survival. At this point, both Mary Ann Wilson and Thadious M. Davis echo Collins. While Davis figures out Walker's preoccupation with the spiritual survival, the survival whole of black people in her characterization in the three novels, Wilson (1993: 57) believes that Walker, by creating black female images, calls for "the force of woman's creative impulse, which must express itself or degenerate into spiritual paralysis, impotent rage, or even suicide if it is denied."

In short, as Walker herself declares, she is committed to "exploring the oppressions, the insanities, the loyalties, and the triumphs of black women," (qtd. in O'Brien, 1993: 331) and her main concern in her writing is about the souls of black women, which Mary Helen Washington (1993: 39) praises as "evolutionary treatment of black women," whose experiences Washington sees "as a series of movements from women totally victimized by society and by the men in their lives to the growing developing women whose consciousness allows them to have control over their lives," that is, from the "suspended women" through "assimilated women" to the "emergent women."

Because of Walker's presentation of black males' weaknesses demonstrated in their relationships with black people, with black females in particular, there exists a controversy about her portraits of black men. The male images have brought the author more censure than understanding from the critical circle. Many reviewers, especially black male ones, condemn her portrayals of black men as unnecessarily negative, pointing to the vile characters in these novels and to her own comments about black males as evidence of enmity on her part. Philip M. Royster (1986: 363) insists that such negative portrayals result from Walker's alienation from black men, "the aftermath of the childhood accident in which she was blinded in one eye after her brother shot her with a bb gun." Bernard W. Bell (1987: 266) also acknowledges that "the implied author and protagonist's hostility toward black men" in the novels is "problematic," and that "the black men are depicted as dogs or frogs … with no hope of becoming princes." In Bell's (1987: 265) opinion, Walker's male portraiture manifests "her sexual, moral, and political closeness to the outrageously audacious black women in the narrative." Although J. Charles Washington (1998: 396, 398) explicitly opposes the conviction that Walker presents "a grossly negative image of Black men, who were portrayed as mean, cruel, or violent, entirely without redeeming qualities" and insists that the positive male image is found in Walker's short stories collected in *In Love and Trouble*, he similarly admits that, in both *The Third Life of Copeland* and *The Color Purple*, the black male characters are "purely negative." Against these negative comments, however, there are still some positive responses. Donna Haisty Winchell (1992: ix), for instance, discovers that "what has too long been neglected in Walker scholarship … is the fact that her male characters also grow and change." Gina Michelle Collins (1990: 86) argues that, though "Walker's male characters portrayed as brutal in their treatment of women and each other, they are not beyond redemption." To illustrate this, Collins takes for example Mr. ——'s rebirth in *The Color Purple*. Yet in contrast to the condemnation against her portraiture of black males, the positive comments are weak and ambiguous.

Despite the nearly unanimous praise, there are also some other negative responses to the three novels in addition to the "anti-male" opinion. Marge Piercy (1993: 10 – 11) finds the ending of *Meridian* unsuccessful, holding that "we are *told* that Meridian has brought off a successful change from victim to fully responsible protagonist. … But *telling* is not enough. Some act is needed to make real the change and it isn't there." (italics added) Commenting upon *The Color Purple*, Dinitia Smith (1993: 20) believes that Walker's male images have "a note of tendentiousness," and their change is too complete to be realistic. Theodore O. Mason, Jr. (1993: 137) criticizes Walker for "the neatness (as well as completeness) of Celie's deliverance at the conclusion of the novel," saying that "it seems to contradict the difficulty and the complexity of the rest of the novel." Regarding the change at the end of *The Color Purple* as a "fantasy," bell hooks (1993: 295) insists that such a "self-recovery without a dialectical process, without collective political effort, without radical change in society" was "dangerous for both oppressed and oppressor."

Obviously, the critical responses to Walker's first three novels nearly cover every aspect from content to form, from themes to writing techniques. The widest divergence lies in her characterization of black men. To make a just and objective assessment of this representative Afro-American woman writer, a further study of her portraiture of black males is absolutely necessary.

2.1.2 Criticism on the Later Novels

The critical world throws less light on Walker's later four novels. The criticism mainly covers the topics like womanist ideal, eco-feminism, sexual overturn, love and violence and female circumcision (genital mutilation), and narrative techniques like conversation deviation, spiritual biography, and shift of point of view. Comparatively, scholars appear to take greater interest in *The Temple of My Familiar* and *By the Light of My Father's Smile*.

2.1.2.1 Critical Responses to *The Temple of My Familiar*

The Temple of My Familiar is an ambitious novel representing 500,000 years of human history, examining the cultural transmission of black and white Americans through the medium of the oral tradition of storytelling. For Ursula K. Le Guin, "[t]he richness of Alice Walker's new novel (*The Temple of My Familiar*

iar) is amazing, overwhelming. A hundred themes and subjects spin through it, dozens of characters, a whirl of times and places. None is touched superficially." (qtd. in Matuz, 1990: 415) However, in the eyes of Debra Walker King, the book is "anything but a novel" and actually "a collection of loosely related stories, a political platform, a sermon, and a stream of dreams and memories" which are strung together to define/explain the present state of human affairs. (qtd. in Andrews, 2001: 387) King holds that, through the stories told by the central character Miss Lissie, who keeps shuttling in the past and present, the author succeeds in presenting a world in which everything is possible through "change, respect and self-awareness." Obviously King's focus lies more on the subjects than on the narrative techniques. King argues that the book was "the ultimate expression of womanism" by covering subjects like "homosexuality, AIDS, drug abuse, racism, religion, parenting, marriage, and death." (387) In the introduction to Alice Walker in the same book compiled by William L. Andrews, King reasserts that Walker's concentration on "spiritual wholeness and cultural connectedness," the core of Walker's womanist ideal, is well expressed in the fourth novel. (414) Mary Margaret Richards (2001: 752) also emphasizes the womanist concern in the novel. She analyzes that Alice Walker "continues the expansion of scope in her novels to include all people" who are descendants of whites, blacks, Native Americans or Asians, and that the book expresses its author's great concern with the wholeness of the world and all its people, among whom black women are consistently Walker's first focus. Richards asserts that the entire book is virtually a myth, a rewriting of history centered on black women in Africa. This is echoed by Paul Gray (1989: 69) who believes that the voluminous story told by Miss Lissie is an extended myth of the primeval Edenic life of human beings and the breaking of the peace by the men's "residence at the women's encampments" and by J. M. Coetzee (1990) who writes in "The Beginnings of (Wo)man in Africa" that *The Temple of My Familiar* is "a myth that inverts the places assigned to man and woman, Europe and Africa, in the male-invented myth called history" and that in the novel Africa became "the cradle of true religion and civilization, and man a funny, misbegotten creature with no breasts and an elongated clitoris." Coetzee summarizes that the book is thus "a mixture of mythic fantasy, revisionary history, exemplary biography and sermon" and needs to be read as an exploration of the inner world of the contemporary Afro-Americans. In the same essay, Coetzee also analyzes racism represented mainly by the female character Fanny. Another topic critics concentrate on in the novel is that Walker seems to make into goddesses black women who are "capable of breaking the bonds of oppression and defining themselves as whole persons." The goddesses, according to Donna Haisty Winchell's (1992: 115) analysis, make up "part of womankind's distant past" and help the contemporary characters in the novel to "redefine relationships between sexes" and eventually to redefine themselves and attain the "balance between the flesh and the spirit." The comment on www.bookrags.com is that Ms. Walker "tries something almost destined to fail." It explains that, on the one hand, the book works as a challenge to the Eurocenticism—the male-dominated white culture which has controlled the Western world for thousands of years—and that in *The Temple of My Familiar* "[f]ormerly marginalized people (principally African American females) take center stage—a much broader one than just Europe and North America—and play the heroic roles." On the other hand, the book, full of stories stressing "connection and equality," is a revision of "the Western representation of reality." Regardless of the negative tone here, readers could find that the ultimate conclusion of the author is that a "central theme in the novel is the challenge marginalized people face everywhere in creating an identity."

Some scholars continue exploring the positive elements in *The Temple of My Familiar*, whereas others clamorously condemn Walker for the ideological weight of the novel or call into question Walker's artistic craftsmanship. For instance, James Wolcott, writing for *The New Republic*, belittles the book into "so much flaky, faddish, New Age starshine"; and in the *Washington Post* David Nicholson describes the novel as a "catalogue of goofy California enthusiasms." (qtd. in White, 2004: 447) J. O. Tate (1989) nearly negates the book in the review for *National Review* by focusing on the flaws in it, the first one among which is "its author's ineptitude" or "the laminated menu device," as Tate names it. For Tate, Walker "has a lot of trouble with basics; or, as a severe judgment would put it, she can't write" at all. Here not only Walker's way of employing several adjectives before a noun is bitterly ridiculed but the "Voices," the "interrelated narratives that are supposed to transcend time and place" are depicted as "float, untethered by coherence yet related by one overriding continuity: they all speak with the voice of Alice Walker" and "don't represent 'characters'—they are instead megaphones for Alice Walker's political fantasies, nutritional obsessions, racial theories, ethnic presumptions, feminist heresies, and intimations of personal divinity." Therefore they "are not connected or supported by the requisite authorial force." With no little irony and sarcasm, Tate states that "Miss Walker has transcended more conventions than those of time and place she has hurdled the conventional demands for technical competence and architectonic ability as well." Christopher Lehann-Haupt remarks that "*The Temple* has the same feeling of over-ambition about it that one sees in a batter so determined to hit a home run that she swings before the ball is pitched", adding that in the novel there is "something to irritate everyone." (qtd. in White, 2004: 447)

As far as the writing technique in *The Temple of My Familiar* is concerned, scholars like Luci Tapahonso, David Nicholson and Mary Margaret Richards focus on the narrative device. Luci Tapahonso points out that "the mode of the storytelling" in the book has "nothing to do with linear time, detailed maps or chronological order" and that Ms. Walker has a series of stories told in the way of kitchen-chatting or over iced tea on the back porch. (Matuz, 1990: 413) David Nicholson argues that it is hard to summarize *The Temple of My Familiar* since it has no traditional structure or plot. For Nicholson, what Ms. Walker gives readers in the book is a "fragmented hodge-podge." Mary Margaret Richards (2001: 752) remarks that "[t]he novel moves back and forth between narrative lines," i. e., in a nonlinear narration, telling stories, many of which are told from the perspective of Miss Lissie and few of which happen in the present of the novel.

Meanwhile, some scholars are concerned with the function of characters, especially of the major one Miss Lissie while others focus on the talk—the monologues and the dialogues—which almost covers all the pages of the book. For instance, J. M. Coetzee holds that Miss Lissie is a "narrative device" rather than a character. Coetzee asserts that, due to the special narrative device, "an ancient goddess who has been incarnated…usually as a woman, sometimes as a man, once even as a lion," the stories could cover both the past and the present, ranging about 500,000 years from the beginnings of (wo)man, and detail the three "ages in human evolution that Lissie lives through." Obviously, for Coetzee, the character works more as a link that strings a series of stories together in one book. In "A Myth to Be Taken on Faith" Paul Gray (1989: 69) is of the opinion that "[t]he skeletal plot" of *The Temple of My Familiar* is just "an excuse to get the conversations going." True, all the characters here either tell or listen to stories. The whole book is made up of voluminous stories in a non-chronological order.

2.1.2.2 Critical Responses to *By the Light of My Father's Smile*

> *By the Light of My Father's Smile* is …a stunning, original, and important book by one of the best American writers of today. (Readinggroupduides. com, 2009)
>
> *By the Light of My Father's Smile* is fresh evidence of Walker's growth as an artist committed to the disciplined exploration of questions which continue to shape and define her fiction. Further, this new novel is an expression of her commitment to use all the forms of literature to express a vision of human experience that, notwithstanding certain bitter actualities, is humane and affirmative. (Findarticles. com, 2009)

Since it first came out, Walker's 1998 novel *By the Light of My Father's Smile* has received almost unanimous praise. Readinggroupguides. com gives a summary of some of the influential comments on the novel, which include "a jubilant novel," "an evocative tale of love, passion, and forgiveness" from *San Francisco Chronicle*, "a powerful story about love, forgiveness, passion and being true to yourself" from *Detroit Free Press*, a "hugely original" novel exploring "what happens—to an entire family—when a daughter cannot forgive her father for a single, hypocritical, soul-crushing act" and "the dangerous bonds of fidelity between sisters, lovers, memories" from *The Baltimore Sun*, and a book fulfilling "a reader's need for wisdom... written in at least two dimensions and across decades" from *Los Angeles Times Book Review*. Obviously, just as Mary Margaret Richards (2001: 755) puts it, although the book "continues many of the themes and narrative techniques" of Walker's earlier work, the author here seems to mainly emphasize "the importance of love and the psychological damage inflicted when a person is punished for loving," which could only get healed through reconciliation of the father and his daughters. Therefore, reconciliation becomes one of the most important themes, second only to love, explored by the scholars. Closely linked with the theme of reconciliation is sexuality, another important theme in the novel the reviewers have been focusing on. Rudolph P. Byrd (1999) expounds that "[t]hese two themes (sexuality and reconciliation) are joined together … throughout the novel in the manner in which fathers are joined to their daughters, in the manner in which lovers are joined to each other," whereas Karen Schechner (1998) in the essay "Sexual Healing: Alice Walker's *By the Light of My Father's Smile*" argues that Walker more "celebrates and revels in the happy subject of sex" than the racism and sexism in her sixth novel. The essay affirms that Walker's depiction of the sex scenes brings the novel a sense of inclusivity, the inclusivity that highlights the notion that "any love is good love," and conveys a message that "not only is sex great, it's good for the soul." The book review from readinggroupguides. com (2009) declares its approval of Alice Walker's own statement that *By the Light of My Father's Smile* is "a celebration of sexuality, its absolute usefulness in the accessing of one's mature spirituality," i. e., an exploration of experience of sexuality as a festivity of life and spirit. As to the confluence of the above observations, Byrd's declaration is direct to the point that "spirituality is a dominant theme." The eventual reconciliation between father and daughters as it is takes place in the spirit sphere.

As is the case with Walker's fourth novel, *By the Light of My Father's Smile* is "artistically daring." The enumeration of comments supplied on amazon. com gives eloquent proof. For instance, Joyce Thompson assumes that the book is intended perhaps as a parable, instead of a story, in which the past and the present interweave to express the author's "cosmology for the new millennium." *Publishers Weekly* asserts that it is the narrative shift "back and forth between living and dead characters, between the past and the present" that makes the novel hard going even in the eyes of Walker's fans. *Kirkus Reviews* holds that, narrated by numerous characters, both living and dead, the book reads less like a novel than "like a series of mournful lectures about the ravages inflicted on the planet, and on women, by the white patriarchy." And it further argues that most of the characters in the book, with too little action and too many lectures, appear "unbelievably serene and rather one-dimensional." This viewpoint is also shared by Rudolph P. Byrd (1999) who reveals that Ms. Walker tends to throw out all taboos and orthodoxies connected with Christianity by calling for "a father's acknowledgement and affirmation of his daughters' sexuality."

Like Walker's previous novels, *By the Light of My Father's Smile* is drawing more and more attention of its readers and there is a good chance that it will become one of the author's most popular novels. However, the current comments are not various enough in form and content, especially compared with the first three novels.

2.1.2.3 Critical Responses to *Possessing the Secret of Joy*

Although among the six novels produced in the 20th century *Possessing the Secret of Joy* has aroused least concern in the critical world, Walker's 1992 novel is expectedly praised. *Newsweek* acclaims it as "a remarkable novel." Its author is honored as "a writer of staggering talent" by *New York Newsday*. A survey of the related studies shows that scholars concentrate more on the themes of the novel. Debra Walker King (2001: 333) thus writes:

> Dedicated "With Tenderness and Respect to the Blameless Vulva," Alice Walker's *Possessing the Secret of Joy* (1992) has raised the consciousness of the Western world concerning ritual clitoridectomy or female genital mutilation (also called circumcision or in-

> fibulation). The novel indites the centuries-old African tradition for its role in the torture, enslavement, and destruction of women. It announces with a vengeance that the secret of joy (that is, the secret of survival) is resistance.

For King, through describing the female genital mutilation and its psychological influence on the heroine, Ms. Walker tends to awaken black women's sense of resistance. Thus female circumcision and resistance become the first great concern of the reviewers who are interested in *Possessing the Secret of Joy*. Gay Wilentz believes that Walker, recounting the psychological suffering and lifetime struggle of Tashi whose life becomes completely destroyed due to the mutilating operation, attempts to expose her readers to "the horrors of female circumcision and thereby invigorate the movement to ban it worldwide." (qtd. in Robinson, 1996: 545) This is echoed by Professor Olakunle George (2001) who points out that Walker's fifth novel "launches an uncompromising attack on both the practice and tendency" of female genital mutilation and that it strongly expresses the author's idea that the practice is "a violation of each woman's right to the integrity of her body" and therefore may be accepted as a violation of human rights in general. Also centered on female genital circumcision in the novel, Dr. Pierre-Damien Mvuyekure(2009), however, explores Walker's "colonial mind" presented in the characters' attitudes toward Africa and African tradition and the European subjugation of Africa through self-conceited, so-called civilization. Mvuyekure applies to his analysis Chinua Achebe's colonialist criticism, which consists of three major parts (i. e., the inglorious past of Africa, the blessing of civilization brought by Europe, and the ingratitude returned by Africa), arguing that "[i]n *Possessing the Secret of Joy* female circumcision is characterized as part of the 'Africa's inglorious past'" and that "the novel contains moments in which European and African-American missionaries bring 'the blessing of civilization' by banning the Olinka practice of female circumcision." According to Mvuyekure, the whole book is permeated by a colonialist discourse throughout its narrative and it is "as colonialist as Joseph Conrad's novella *Heart of Darkness*."

Another topic scholars concentrate on is Walker's emphasis on the internal psychological development of the individual, a shift from reflecting the external conditions of society in her previous works. Donald R. Wehrs (2001: 12) points out that, due to the skilful use of psychoanalysis, Ms. Walker presents readers "a murder mystery," in which she focuses on Tashi's mental suffering, the consequence of circumcision, explores the heroine's psychological changes and successfully helps the victim find the victimizer—African traditional culture—and get cured by turning violence against it. Mr. Wehrs (13 – 14) expounds that, "[b]y drawing upon Jung, Walker emphasizes the transcultural, ahistorical nature of the identity repressed by diverse societies." This statement is apparently based on Jung's "collective unconsciousness" and echoed in Geneva Cobb Moore's "Archetypal Symbolism in Alice Walker's *Possessing the Secret of Joy*." In this essay, Dr. Moore closely examines the three major archetypal patterns of Jung's theory of collective unconsciousness, i. e., the persona or mask, the shadow and the anima/animus, represented in the individuation process of the heroine Tashi. "While Tashi experiences the individuation journey to wholeness, Walker gives specific voice to the inner power of the individual to change and to mature spiritually, a Jungian psychoanalytical discourse that enables Walker to acknowledge yet downplay the power of society over the individual." (Moore, 2000: 113)

Studies on *Possessing the Secret of Joy* cover the field of narrative technique as well. For instance, Gay Wilentz notes that the story "unfolds in fragments of memory in a first-person serial narrative" and the most moving sections of the book "are made up of the dialogue, broken up and dispersed" in the diverse voices. (qtd. in Robinson, 1996: 545) Similarly, Mary Margaret Richards (2001: 753) emphasizes the "multiple narrators" and the nonlinear storytelling format in Walker's dealing with her heroine's "psychological difficulties."

2.1.2.4 Critical Responses to *Now Is the Time to Open Your Heart*

Walker's latest novel *Now Is the Time to Open Your Heart* mainly draws the critical attention to its protagonist's journey of spiritual discovery. Some of the editorial reviews extracted on amazon. com which hails the book as "Walker's most surprising achievement" are as follows: *Publishers Weekly* averts that the protagonist is "a lifelong seeker after enlightenment in the carnal, political and religious realms," who takes a dry river seen in a dream as a "spiritual clue" and makes her "spiritual quests" down two rivers; Vanessa Bush writes for *Booklist* that, having both Kate (the protagonist) and Yolo shaking off the internal and external pressure and dispelling prejudices between men and women, whites and blacks, and young and old, "Walker's dreamlike novel incorporates the political and spiritual consciousness and emotional style." Similarly, in the "Product Description" on the website the book is introduced as "a beautiful new novel that is at once a deeply moving personal story and a powerful spiritual journey," or exactly "a passage through time, a quest for self, and a collision with love." For Nicole Moses (2009), the predominant theme of the book is the theme of "being healed by nature." She holds that the book focuses on "the human spirit and what can happen then it is neglected" and thus sends out an urgent appeal for the acknowledgement of "the existence of Mother Earth and Her healing power."

2.2 Researches in China

To some extent, the Chinese scholars' interest in Alice Walker was roused by Mr. Wang Fengzhen, who introduced Alice Walker in his "An Interview with Alice Walker" published in the Chinese journal *Dushu* in 1983, just a year after *The Color Purple* came out. However, an academic concern with her novels did not emerge in China until 1986. It was Dong Dingshan's analysis of the theme in Walker's works and Tao Jie's translation of *The Color Purple* that ushered in an age of intensive researches on the Afro-American woman writer. With a steady increase of Walker's literary products, more and more Chinese scholars concentrate their attention on her writing, especially her novel-writing.

If the scholarly study in the last decade of the 20th century is apparently limited, the new century witnesses an extensive study of Walker's novels. Essays and comments cover every possible aspect of the novels, ranging from characterization to theme, from language to narration, from realistic representation to psychological analysis. Among them the most representative research ought to belong to Professor Wang Xiaoying and her postgraduates from Nanjing Normal University. Ms. Wang has supervised at least nine theses for Master's degree and finished her own doctoral dissertation concentrating on Alice Walker's works since 2002. Wang's greatest achievement of course is her monograph *Toward the Wholeness of Survival: Alice Walker's Literary Production* (2008), in which she makes a deep study of several of Walker's works including novels like *The Color Purple*, *Meridian* and *By the Light of My Father's Smile*, and short stories such as "1955" and "Everyday Use." Wang at once explores the themes represented in the selected works and the narrative techniques typically employed in Walker's narration. Another diligent researcher in this field should be Ms. Wang Chengyu who mainly examines Walker's novels like *The Temple of My Familiar*, *The Color Purple* and *By the Light of My Father's Smile* from the perspective of language.

Statistics show that, among about four hundred and seventy articles on Walker's novels published on cnki. net, two hundred and ninety or so focus on *The Color Purple* and that, among two hundred-odd theses for Master's or Doctor's degree, more than one hundred choose *The Color Purple* as a text, while fifty-four theses/dissertations make a comparatively complete and convincing study of Walker based on the interpretation of more than one novel by the author. According to the survey, researches on Walker are somewhat limited and fragmented, many scholars focusing on *The Color Purple* only. Her other novels, particularly *Meridian, Possessing the Secret of Joy*, and *Now Is the Time to Open Your Heart*, are nearly ignored. This academic phenomenon does not match with Walker's remarkable reputation in the literary world. Therefore a wider and deeper and systematic study is urgent in this field in China. Since Alice Walker establishes her reputation as a writer mainly on her novels, the book tends to examine all her seven novels to make a comprehensive study of the great Afro-American woman writer's novel-writing.

Chapter III From Lavender to Purple: The Formation of the Womanist Theory

Womanism, as a literary critical movement among Afro-American female intellectuals, grows out of and overlaps with black feminism. It emerges in the early 1980s, when more and more black writing women are devoted to correcting the racial bias of women's studies and communities and the gender bias of black studies and communities both within and outside the academic world, and when there appears an increasingly obvious tendency among black women to be identified with the Third World women and all women of color. To differentiate such contending activists and mark their resistance against "separatism" implied by black feminism, Alice Walker first advocates using the term "womanist." The womanist perspective, with Chikweney Okonjo Ogunyemi, Sherley Anne Williams, and Michael Awkward as its representatives, is deeply rooted in the African culture and tradition. Womanism calls for a commitment "to survival and wholeness of entire people, male *and* female" in literature, and "to a valorization of women's works [and also of men's] in all their varieties and multitudes" in literary criticism. (A. Walker, 1983: xi, italics original; Williams, 2000: 219) Its ideal is thus to furnish a vision that the women and men of different colors coexist like flowers in a garden and yet maintain their cultural distinctiveness and integrity, through exploring how racism and sexism have influenced the development of love, power, autonomy, creativity, manhood, and womanhood in the black family and community.

3.1 Womanism, and Feminism and Black Feminism

"The word 'feminist' or 'feminism' is a political label indicating support for the aims of the new women's movement," which emerged first in the USA in the early 1960s. (Moi, 1997: 104) Feminism is the belief that women are full human beings capable of participation and leadership in the full range of human activities—intellectual, political, social, sexual, spiritual and economic. The pioneering texts—Simone de Beauvoir's *The Second Sex* (first published in 1949) and Kate Millet's *Sexual Politics* (1970)—appropriate literature for feminism. "'Feminist criticism,' then, is a specific kind of political discourse: a critical and theoretical practice in literature committed to the struggle against patriarchy and sexism." (104) It, together with feminist writing, becomes a political means of women's struggle for equality and independence. For feminist writers and critics, the literary mainstream is dominated by the male discourse. They are determined to change the status quo. Thus they develop feminist literary criticism into a dynamic alternative to traditional critical approaches, a method analyzing texts contextually and/or textually.

Geographically, feminism can be divided up into two schools—the French school and the Anglo-American school—or three schools—the French school, the British school and the American school. The leading French feminist critics—Helen Cixous, Luce Irigaray and Julia Kristeva—are concerned with women's relation to language, and examine the construction of the "feminine" in language, philosophy, psychoanalysis, and other systems of discourse. As socialist/Marxist feminism, the British school makes it its primary task to open up the complex relations between gender and economy, stressing the political aspects of feminism, with Mary Jacobus, Cora Kaplan, Michele Barrett, Juliet Mitchell and Rosalind Coward as its representatives.

The American feminist critics usually investigate women's experience and history. The critics like Kate Millet, Elaine Showalter, Ellen Moers, Patricia Meyer Spacks and others take the sex of the author into consideration, regularly scrutinize images of women and gender stereotypes, and seek the "truth" in or behind literary works. Nevertheless, feminism in the white world, as bell hooks (2000a: 131) propounds, "has never emerged from the women who are most victimized by sexist oppression; women who are daily beaten down, mentally, physically, and spiritually." "Past feminist refusal to draw to and attack racial hierarchies suppressed the link between race and class." (hooks, 2000a: 133) Feminists fix their eyes on "the plight of a select group of college-educated, middle-and up-class…housewives bored with leisure," housework and children-bearing. (131) They ignore the nonwhite women, black women especially.

Influenced by the Civil Rights Movement and the women's liberation movement, black feminists began to organize in the early 1970s and directly challenge the racism within the feminist discourse dominated by white women. Inserting the adjective "black" challenges the assumed whiteness of feminism and the term "black feminism" thus disrupts the racism inherent in presenting feminism as a for-whites-only ideology and political movement. Since "any literature, at core, is concerned with the definition and discovery of self in relation to the society in which one lives," black feminist literary critics started to appear in print in the mid-and late 1970s to show their concern with the special identity of black women in the white society. (Christian, 1985: 159) They analyze the works of black female writers from a feminist or political perspective, and attempt to explore issues resulting from not only race and gender but also class, history, and culture. Yet, Sherley Anne Williams (2000: 219) notes that "one of the most disturbing aspects of current black feminist criticism [is] its separatism—its tendency to see not only a distinct black female culture but to see that culture as a separate culture form."

To dissolve the possible "separatism" and, more importantly, to mark its difference from (white) feminism, womanism came into existence. It appears to find ways of fostering interracial cooperation among women and provide an avenue of fostering stronger relationships between black women and men. Although Barbara Omolade (1994: xx) points out that "black feminism is sometimes referred to as womanism because both are concerned with struggles against sexism and racism by black women who are themselves part of the black community's efforts to achieve equity and liberty," African American women who define themselves as "womanist" seem inclined to stress the distinction, i. e., to express their negative attitude toward "separatism." Therefore we may conclude that womanism embraces black feminism and yet implies more. It is black feminism looking beyond the Afro-American society and has harmonious coexistence of all people as its ultimate goal. The following sections are to give a somewhat detailed introduction to the emergence, the improvement, and the principles of the womanist theory.

3.2 The Emergence of Womanism

With the intensifying struggle for black liberation in America from the mid-1950s to the early-1970s, a rebirth—a "New Renaissance" (as opposed to the Harlem Renaissance)—occurred in black arts, including poetry, drama, fiction, and literary criticism. Take the black literary criticism for example only. The editor Hoyt Fuller published his "Towards a Black Aesthetic" in 1968 and explicitly links the project to found a Black Aesthetic with the black power movement, stressing that the black revolt in letters is as palpable and effective as in the streets. In the same year, the poet and editor Larry Neal's "The Black Arts Movement" came off the press only to link the emerging black arts movement with the black power movement. In this widely-read essay of the period, Neal affirms the new black artists' attempts to break away from the dominant (white) artistic modes and to pioneer African-based modes of creativity. Thus the black male literature takes on a new urgency and vigor, especially during the black power movement. Meanwhile, the new women's movement ushers in a new age of white female letters, a feminist age. The publication of Kate Millet's *Sexual Politics* marks the birth of the American white feminist literary criticism. Under such circumstances, black female intellectuals, naturally, couldn't turn a blind eye to the intense change in the cultural circle. After finding that they are either excluded or ignored by both the black male critics and the white feminists, they eventually recognize that sexist practices are as fundamental a problem as racial prejudice and class oppression. A number of black female intellectuals begin to "undertake the total reassessment of Black literature and literary history centering on the cultural importance of Black women writers." (Humm, 1986: 108) Among those who came to the fore in their critical works during the 1970s and the early 1980s are Mary Helen Washington, Barbara Smith, Deborah E. McDowell, Barbara Christian as well as Alice Walker. Just as Deborah E. McDowell (1980: 151) points out in "New Directions for Black Feminist Criticism" (1980), "the recognition among black female critics and writers that white women, white men, and black men consider their experiences as deviant has given rise to black feminist criticism."

Although black feminists, like white feminists, could trace the roots of their movement to the nineteenth century, when several important black women's organizations were built on earlier antebellum programs for abolition of slavery and for women's rights, and when a few important black literary women like Frances E. W. Harper and Pauline Hopkins wrote poetry, prose and novels to present struggle for social change, black feminists in the 1970s still felt themselves isolated and marginalized in American society. It was not until the year 1977 when Barbara Smith published "Toward a Black Feminist Criticism" that black intellectuals took into serious consideration the creation of autonomous black feminist movement and the creation of new theories of black feminist criticism. In this path-breaking essay, Smith sketches the rudiments of a program for cultural criticism. She argues that "a Black feminist approach to literature that embodies the realization that the politics of sex as well as the politics of race and class are crucially interlocking factors in the works of Black women writers is an absolute necessity." (B. Smith, 2000: 134) Black feminist criticism, in Smith's terms, is both dependent on and contributing to a black feminist political movement. A black feminist approach should have a primary commitment to the exploration of the interrelation of sexual and racial politics. Smith (2000: 137) further points out that "she (a Black feminist critic) would also work from the assumption that Black women writers constitute an identifiable literary tradition." Therefore to strengthen the tradition the critic should "look first for precedents and insights in interpretation within the works of other Black women," which is also one of the accessible principles of the later womanist theory. Established on such principles, the black feminist criticism, Smith predicts, would develop into a highly innovative one, "embodying the daring spirit of the works themselves." Smith's essay, as a critical manifesto, represents a radical departure from the earlier work of Mary Helen Washington, by whom the first contemporary anthology of black women's fiction—*Black-Eyed Susans: Classic Stories by and about Black Women* (1975) is edited. Washington, unlike Smith, only concentrates on recovering and situating the neglected fiction of black women writers and establishing the major themes and images for use in a teaching situation, and doesn't explore or define a black feminist critical perspective. In this sense, Smith's "Toward a Black Feminist Criticism" plays the role of a landmark in the history of black female literary criticism.

In the 1980s the black female literary criticism makes a great leap. Deborah McDowell's "New Directions for Black Feminist Criticism" (1980), another landmark essay in this field, embodies an alternative approach to black feminist politics. McDowell (1980: 154) points out that "[b]lack feminist scholarship has been decidedly more practical than theoretical, and the theories developed thus far have often lacked sophistication and have been marred by slogans, rhetoric, and idealism. The articles that attempt to apply these theoretical tenets often lack precision and detail." She calls for an end to the negative project of feminist critique and urges more positive work, i. e., work with precision, detail and sophistication, in gynocriticism and critical theory.

What McDowell adds to Smith is a black feminist criticism rigorous in textual analysis. In other words, on the one hand, McDowell, like Smith, advocates a contextual awareness of the conditions under which black women's literature is produced, published, and reviewed. On the other hand, she holds that a precise textual criticism is essential for formulating the details of a specifically black women's aesthetic. McDowell (156) thus writes: "While insisting on the validity, usefulness, and necessity of contextual approaches to Black women's literature, the Black feminist critic must not ignore the importance of rigorous textual analysis." Besides, McDowell (157) asserts that "an equally challenging and necessary task ahead of the Black feminist critic is a thoroughgoing examination of the works of Black male writers." She argues that, though, like Washington, she acknowledges "the immediate concern of Black feminist critics must be to develop a fuller understanding of Black women writers," she does not support a "separatist position" as a long-term strategy and suggests an exploration of parallels between the texts of black women and those of black men. This lays a foundation of the later womanism, the essence of which is resisting separatism and realizing survival whole of all people.

In the late 1970s and the early 1980s, a flurry of writing by black women sought to correct the racial bias of women's studies and communities and the gender bias of black studies and communities within and outside the academic circle. An increasingly obvious tendency among these black female intellectuals and of their works is their being identified with the Third World women, their aligning themselves with all "women of color" including Afro-American, Asian-American, and Native-American women as well as indigenous peoples of underdeveloped countries around the globe. In her foreword to *This Bridge Called My Back: Writings by Radical Women of Color* (1981), Toni Cade Bambara (1981: xii – xiii) holds that coalitions of the Third World women are an effective means to confront masculinist "divide and conquer" tactics. "The Coalitions of women determined to be a danger to our enemies." Such coalitions would awaken black women to "new tasks" and help them to "create new powers in arenas where they never before existed." Bambara (xiii) argues that "to make the contracts to mutually care and cure each other into wholesomeness" is "to make revolution irresistible" for "the creative combatants." In her essay "Revolution: It's Not Neat or Pretty or Quick" (1980), Pat Parker (1981: 241) neatly expresses her anger at ethnocentrism, saying that "for too long I have watched the white middle class be represented as my leaders in women's movement," and that, as a feminist but neither white nor middle class, "I, for one, am no longer willing to watch a group of self-serving reformist idiots continue to abort the demands of revolutionary thinking women." To hold leadership and direction of the women's movement, she calls for the Third World women to unite and fight. To differentiate such contending activists and avoid the separatism or the possible ethnocentrism arising out of black feminism, Alice Walker advocates using the term "womanist" instead of "feminist."

Alice Walker (1983: 81) originally introduces the term "womanist" in her essay "Gifts of Power: The Writings of Rebecca Jackson" (1981), when she talks about "lesbians" and doesn't think it "suitable (or comfortable) for black women" in any case. For Walker, "black women who love women (sexually or not)" only imagine themselves as "whole" women, "or as 'round' women—women who love other women…but…also have concern, in a culture that oppresses all black people, … for their fathers, brothers, and sons, no matter how they feel about them as males." The more proper term to refer to such a woman should not be "lesbian" but be "womanist," "a word that said more than that they choose women over men," "more than that they choose to live separate from men." Based on this, she further states that, "to be consistent with black cultural values…it would have to be a word that affirmed connectedness to the entire community and the world, rather than separation, *regardless* of who worked and slept with whom." (81, italics original)

Influenced by the 1980s black women's studies programs and encouraged by the numbered male academics and writers promoting works by and about women writers and feminists, Walker improves and redefines the term "wamanist" in her *In Search of Our Mothers' Gardens: A Womanist Prose* (1983). Thus far "womanism" or "womanist theory" forms its rudiments and soon pervades the black female academic world.

3.3 Womanist Theory

Womanism, as a social theory initially concerned with the racial and gender-based oppression of black women and other colored women, emerges to redress the separatism inherent in black feminism. It not only advocates uniting women of all marginalized groups but also seeks for cooperation with black men. It hones in on the everyday issues and experiences of both colored women (black women in particular) and black men. Since its emergence in 1981, the term has been the focus of the black intellectuals, including Alice Walker, who are keen on its definition. They make efforts to provide a concise and all encompassing definition and thus contribute to the improvement of the theory.

3.3.1 The Rudiments of Womanism

In the black culture, "womanism" is a characterization of women as audacious as well as capable, representing an expectation and experience of female knowledge, competence, and responsibilities, which contrasts sharply with the images of females under patriarchy as submissive and inferior in the Western culture. *The Dictionary of Feminist Theory* thus defines: "the term now implies Black feminist" who thinks and acts audaciously but not separately. A black feminist "who believes in womanism is a womanist." (Humm, 1995: 304)

Alice Walker's definition of the term "womanist" in *In Search of Our Mothers' Gardens* covers four laws. Firstly, a womanist is "[a] black feminist or feminist of color." (A. Walker, 1983: xi) The term derives from "womanish," which usually refers to "outrageous, audacious, courageous or *willful* behavior" and represents an attitude or orientation toward life of strong-willed, opinionated self-confidence. Therefore, a womanist is "responsible," "in charge" and "*serious.*" (xi, italics original) Secondly, a womanist is

> a woman who loves other women, sexually and/or nonsexually. Appreciates and prefers women's culture, women's emotional flexibility… and women's strength. Sometimes loves

> individual men, sexually and/or nonsexually. Committed to survival and wholeness of entire people, male *and* female. Not a separatist…Traditionally universalist, …Traditionally capable… (xi, italics original)

Thirdly, a womanist "loves music, loves dance, loves struggle, loves the Folk, and loves herself. *Regardless*." (xii, italics original) That is to say, a womanist is an optimist who loves life and friendship, a liberty-advocator who struggles for equality at any cost, as well as an artist whose creativity relies on all facets of art and life. Finally, a "womanist is to [a] feminist as purple to lavender." (xii) A womanist is not only against sexism like a feminist but against racism as well.

Thus Alice Walker observes that a womanist is a black feminist but not a female separatist. Womanism encompasses black feminism and has also been applied generally to feminists of color. The concerns of the womanist perspective are survival, affirmation, and empowerment of all persons, male and female. A womanist resists systems of domination, and insists on the liberty and self-determination of all people. For Walker, a womanist is spirited and spiritual, determined and decisive, committed to struggle and convinced of victory.

C. Lynn Munro (1984: 161) formulates Walker's womanist theory into three principles. She points out, "at the heart of her (Walker's) perspective is a belief in the importance of continuity—the need to reclaim and celebrate the unsung achievements of one's ancestors, especially those anonymous women." To achieve the "survival and wholeness" of black women and at last, of entire people, reclaiming and celebrating black female tradition is absolutely necessary. Another important principle of Walker's womanist theory Munro stresses is the insistence on "the right of each individual to express his or her particular points of view. Only in this way…can the historic reality in all of its diversity be appreciated." Only in this way can the oppressed reach the goal of liberty and equality. Only in this way can black women "gain a new and larger perspective and benefit from 'a fearlessness of growth, of search, of looking that enlarges the private public world.'" Finally, Walker's commitment to exploring "the inherent interrelationships among all facets of art and life and the need to encourage creative expression" is a drumbeat principle of her womanism. Munro argues that, for Walker, "there are no neat divisions between the literary, social, and personal realms." Whatever one works at, one could make a change and take up "his or her responsibility to contribute to a saner future of the world." Apparently, the heart's heart of Walker's womanism is the ideal goal of spiritual survival of "entire people," i. e., the freedom and emancipation of colored people, male and female.

3.3.2 The Improvement of the Theory and Its Principles

After the publication of Alice Walker's *In Search of Our Mothers' Gardens* in 1983, there appears a heated debate on womanism in the black female literary circle. Some acclaim the birth of the womanist theory and take their stand behind the founder. Others demonstrate resistance against its lack of militancy. Whatever stand they take, they appear to acknowledge the positive function arising from the use of the term that it stimulates black women's great concerns for their reality, that is, how to eliminate the existing oppression of sexism and racism. More and more black intellectuals commit to the improvement of the theory. Among them are the most outstanding critics like Chikweney Okonjo Ogunyemi, Sherley Anne Williams and Michael Awkward.

The 1985 publication of Ogunyemi's "Womanism: The Dynamics of the Contemporary Black Female Novel in English" indicates a new era of the womanist theory. In this essay Ogunyemi (1997: 232) clearly expresses her viewpoint, saying "where a white woman writer may be a feminist, a black woman writer is likely to be a 'womanist' (who), along with her consciousness of sexual issues, must incorporate racial, cultural, national, economic, and political considerations into her philosophy." She holds that, because of similar aesthetic (or, in the words of Walker, similar "tradition") inherent in African and Afro-American women writers, womanism is widespread and binds black female novelists together. Since black women as victims of a white and patriarchal culture are not only victimized by black men and white men but also victimized on racial and class grounds by white men and white women together, the black women writers, Ogunyemi (236) argues, besides writing protest against sexism like their white counterparts, must battle "also with the dehumanization resulting from racism and poverty." To tackle issues aroused by both racism and sexism, black female writers must hold the womanist vision of underscoring the positive aspects of black life. Thus she concludes:

> The intelligent black woman writer, conscious of black impotence in the context of white patriarchal culture, empowers black man. She believes in him; hence her books end in integrative images of the male and female worlds. Given this commitment, she can hardly become a strong ally of the white feminist until (perhaps) the political and economic fortunes of the black race improve. (236 – 237)

For Ogunyemi , the aim of the black women was much higher than only sexual equality. Also, they tend to "knit the world's black family together to achieve black, not just female, transcendence." (237) Ogunyemi (238) agrees with Walker that "sexism is a microcosmic replication of Euro-American racism." Therefore she answers Walker's call in holding that racism and sexism must be eradicated together to arrive at the womanist "survival and wholeness of entire people." Ogunyemi's definition of womanism is:

> Black womanism is a philosophy that celebrates black roots, the ideals of black life, while giving a balanced presentation of black womandom. It concerns itself as much with the black sexual power tussle as with the world power structure that subjugates blacks. Its ideal is for black unity where every black person has a modicum of power and so can be a 'brother' or a 'sister' or a 'father' or a 'mother' to the other. This philosophy has a mandalic core: its aim is the dynamism of wholeness and self-healing that one sees in the positive, integrative endings of womanist novels. (240)

By this definition, Ogunyemi stresses four aspects in her womanist theory—the exploration of black tradition, the eradication of sexism and racism, the dependence on black unity and community, and the realization of self-recovery and wholeness of the black race, male and female. For Ogunyemi, sticking to these principles, the womanist writer will eventually emerge as a spokeswoman for black women through overcoming black chauvinism and the iconoclastic tendencies of white feminism. Thus, despite the slight difference between Walker's and Ogunyemi's emphases in their statements of womanism—the former appears to be a little more concerned about the alliance of all women of color while the latter seemingly more stresses the solidification of the two sexes within the black community—Ogunyemi apparently holds fast to Walker's appeal for protest against both racism and sexism and commitment to "survival and wholeness of entire people."

Exploring the representative works by both African and Afro-American women novelists, Ogunyemi summarizes the common writing techniques in the womanist texts. She notes that "the Afro-American female novelist... employs the mood and structure of the blues in her novels," and argues that, because of the "connection between the blues and the capacity to experience hope," most Afro-American womanist novels "bound in hope." (240 – 241) Another writing technique of womanist novelists, Ogunyemi (242) asserts, is their portrayal of the image of "madwoman." But "[u]nlike negatively presented white madwomen, the black madwoman in novels written by black women knows in her subconscious that she must survive." Hence the black "[m]adness becomes a temporary aberration preceding spiritual growth, healing, and integration." She also discovers that black women novelists, due to their concern with politics and black tradition, "prefer to tell of life as it is, sometimes of life as it is thought to be, and rarely of life as it ought to be." (245) One way of manifesting that the storyteller is "authentic" and "not lying" is some black women writers' "return to the early epistolary form" which is simple, relatively intimate, and candid, and enables the novels to appear "more open and more sincere." The last feature Ogunyemi (246) makes out in the womanist novels is the employment of "songs, verse, and reiterated phrases" which are able to "relieve the tedium of a long speech or a long stretch of narration." Ogunyemi thus develops womanism into a more specific and complete literary theory.

The following year 1986 witnessed the publication of Sherley Anne Williams' essay "Some Implications of Womanist Theory." In it Williams (2000: 220) explicitly states that "womanist inquiry…assumes that it can talk both effectively and productively about men." This assumption is needed because black female images and black female writers are only part of the Afro-American writing. In order to get a full understanding of the Afro-American literature and culture, and their life, the male part should not be ignored. She argues that "a thoroughgoing examination of male images in the works of black male writers" is "a necessary step in ending the separatist tendency in Afro-American criticism and in achieving in Afro-American literature feminist's theory's avowed aim of 'challenging the fundamental theoretical assumptions of traditional literary history and criticism.'" (222) For Williams, through this new approach, womanists will promote theories or ways of reading and enlarge black female literary community and dialogue. Inspired by this point of view, the following two chapters tend to examine the womanist champion Walker's novels from the womanist perspective to explore the ideology expressed in her characterization.

Michael Awkward (2000: 550), a male supporter of womanism, echoes Williams in his "A Black Man's Place in Black Feminist Criticism," acknowledging that "what Williams terms 'womanist theory' is especially suggestive for Afro-American men because, while it calls for feminist discussions of black women's texts and for critiques of black androcentricism [*sic*], womanism foregrounds a general black psychic health as a primary objective" and "aims at 'ending the separatist tendency in Afro-American criticism.'" He further discusses the potential value in developing a male feminist. For him, such "potential value lies in the possibility that," taking black feminists' stand, "black man can expand the range and utilization of feminist inquiry and explore other fruitful applications for feminist perspectives." (548) What black womanism needs is that both black females and males should recognize the gendered inequities that existed and still exist in Afro-American society and determine to commit to work for change. In other words, what is important for the black males to do is "take up a recognizable anti-patriarchal position" and make every effort to dismantle the phallocentric rule in Afro-American society, and acknowledge and celebrate "the incontrovertible fact 'the Father's law' is no longer the only law of the land." (550, 553)

So far, womanism, as a (literary critical) theory, is arriving at its perfection through both Sherley Anne Williams and Michael Awkward's enlargement, and has formed a set of accessible principles, which can be summarized as follows: a) womanism is a philosophy with the spiritual survival of particularly black people as its ultimate goal; b) to achieve liberty and equality, it, as a theoretical whole, concerns itself as much with sexism as with racism; c) it calls for black males' recognition of the gendered inequalities in the black community and their commitment to work for change, and thus stresses unity and solidarity of black males and females; d) it has its unique writing techniques such as the image of "madwoman" in characterization, "the mood and structure of the blues" in theme and structure, and others; e) as a critical approach, it examines male images aside from female ones in both women and men's works.

As a womanist writer, Walker persistently presents black people's hard self-healing process toward the spiritual survival in her fiction through exploring sexism and racism in the American society. Her major characters, especially those in her early novels, male and female, fully illustrate her womanist ideology.

Chapter IV In Pursuit of Manhood and Humanity: The Transformation of the Male Images

> Though Walker does not neglect to deal with the external *realities* of poverty, exploitation, and discrimination, her stories, novels, and poems most often focus on the intimate reaches of the inner lives of her characters; the landscape of her stories is the spiritual realm where the soul yearns for what it does not have. (M. Washington, 1993: 38, italics original)

In Walker's first three novels one can sense the strong influence of the Eurocentric patriarchal ideology upon the shaping of the black androcentrism and their interconnected impact on the Afro-American life, a phenomenon prevailing in the southern area of the United States, where most of Walker's novels are primarily grounded. The white patriarchal ideology not merely preaches the central role of the male/father/husband as the decision-maker of the family and male-female relationships, and as the sole or main authority in both familial and public lives, but also stresses the absolute power of all whites, male and female, over blacks, while the black androcentric ideology just demands the black women's subordination to the black men and their withdrawal from the public male world, and thus seems "simplistically and unself-consciously concerned with justifying domestic violence and other forms of black male brutality." (Awkward, 1995: 53) In her novels, the first three in particular, Walker presents the hazardous and detrimental impacts of such ideologies on black males as well as black females, i. e., the white patriarchal denial and/or erasure of the self-identity of black people, especially of black men, and the black androcentric consequence of dehumanization of Afro-American males, their domestic violence and other forms of brutality, and their twisted understanding of manhood. It is on account of the great harm of the ingrained racial and sexual prejudice that the self-healing struggle of black males appears not only hard but urgent as well. In this sense, the male characters are not set as targets of purposeful condemnation and assault against black men as a whole. Rather, they are portrayed to tell the truth "from a particular perspective that is conscious of their weaknesses—weaknesses they distort into violence against other blacks, especially women and children" and thus to awaken the black males to the hardship and urgency of their struggle for reclaiming their manhood and humanity during the course of redeeming the black race. (Davis, 1984: 45) From this particular perspective of telling the truth Walker enables them to become "conscious, too, of their potential for regeneration." (45) In other words, in the portraiture of the black males Walker virtually more concentrates on how these flawed characters, through a self-improving transformation, eventually reach the goal of the spiritual survival. This just fits in well with the core of womanism—the concern with sexism and racism, and the commitment to "survival and wholeness of entire people."

Evidently, a womanist study can help avoid misreading these male images portrayed in Walker's novels. Confronted with situations challenging and redefining their notion of manhood, Walker's men launch a struggle for redressing their manhood, for "redeeming by learning to love and assume responsibility for their actions." (45) In such a struggle, while some characters fail, others succeed. The redeemed black males and their reclaimed manhood do not grow out of the patriarchal violence against or domination over their women and children. Instead, their redemption and the return of their manhood are the result of their realizing and acknowledging the inflictions by themselves on their loved ones in the past, and the result of their learning from their mistakes, their past and history. For, to heal the black community and fulfill the survival whole of black people, the first necessary step for the black race, for black men in particular, to take, is to acknowledge the fact that black men have participated, whether voluntarily or not, in the oppression of black women. On the basis of such realization, black males can learn to be respectful, responsible, and expressive individuals to understand their own lives and their women and children. Thus, in her writing, Walker fosters a conversation between the black males and females, an interconnectedness needed to offer improvement in the troubled black male and female relationships, which also fits in well with the womanist concern. Therefore, the hard self-healing process of her males toward the spiritual survival is the key to understanding Walker's men and her intention of creating these images. "In presenting these men, Walker first depicts what has come to be the stereotypes of blacks, essentially those set destructive patterns of emotional and psychological responses of black men to black life, their women, children, friends, whites, and themselves. Then she loosens the confines of the stereotype and attempts to penetrate the nexus of feelings that make these lives valuable in themselves and for others." (45) In view of this, the study in this chapter is subdivided into two sections. The first section deals with the limitations of the stereotypes of black males and examines how the black male characters are restricted and distorted in the male-dominated socio-historical settings, i. e., in a racial and sexual society. The concern here is with racism and sexism in the American society during the around sixty years since the beginning of the twentieth century. The second section probes into the process of these black males' self-improvement. To be exact, this section centers on how the male characters face the challenge of claiming black manhood and ensure the spiritual survival of themselves, of black people. The fulfillment of the womanist ideal in the male images is the focus of the second section.

4.1 The Limitations of the Stereotypes of Black Males

In a white supremacist patriarchal society black males not only suffer from material poverty, like black females, but also from emotional destitution. The longstanding Eurocentric patriarchy has structured the stereotypes of black males, the paradox in their notion of black masculinity. On one side, they succumb to the white supremacy and hardly imagine claiming manhood in the white society. On the other, they are inevitably affected by the deep-rooted androcentric ideology of the whites. They are eager to seek a kind of balance as males, as the stronger group in the Afro-American community. In this sense, the worst results of racism and sexism are subverting the most basic human relationships between black men and their women and children and destroying their individual psyches. Black males, suffering the racial oppression and/or defined by the black androcentric ideology, seek their masculinist contentment either by molesting black females, or by inflicting violence on their wives and children, or by abandoning their responsibility as husband/father. Their manhood is distorted. Their humanity is degenerated. To this category belong Brownfield, and Grange in his first life in *The Third Life of Grange Copeland*; Eddie, Mr. Raymonds, Tommy, and Truman in his early life in *Meridian*; and Alphonso, and Harpo and Mr. ——in their youth in *The Color Purple*.

4.1.1 The Degeneration of Copeland Males

In *The Third Life of Grange Copeland*, Walker examines how the racist fabric of the American South affects the black family, presenting the familial conflict and domestic violence inherent in the sharecropping life of the Southern blacks. Since the Copeland men are frustrated by the society in their drive for control of their lives and cannot satisfy their needs for masculinity, they vent their frustrations on their wives. Thus they develop self-hatred and/or racial hatred in their character, which twist(s) and hinder(s) the development of their manhood and humanity.

4.1.1.1 Grange's First Life: The Loss of Manhood

Walker begins *The Third Life of Grange Copeland* with Grange's first life in a run-down shack in rural Georgia, owned by the white man Shipley, in whose cotton field he works year after year. He and his wife Margaret Copeland form the first generation. As a young man, Grange, like millions of other black men in his community, works hard as a sharecropper in hope of providing a home and the necessary subsistence for his wife and his only son Brownfield. Each year, at the end of harvest, he finds that his bill is higher than the pay for his crops. The efficient system of exploitation by manipulation of debt and wage-cutting puts him perpetually and hopelessly in debt and under the control of Shipley. He has no choices in determining his family's future. The reality he must face is "we ought to be thankful we got a roof over our heads and three meals a day," but "it was actually more like one meal a day." (A. Walker, 1970: 5) As the oppression intensifies, he has to send his six-year-old son to work instead of school. He is powerless against his oppressor and has to succumb to endless rounds of hard work. His life

> followed a kind of cycle that depended almost totally on Grange's moods. On Monday, suffering from a hangover and the aftereffects of a violent quarrel with his wife the night before, Grange was morose, sullen, reserved, … Margaret was … exceedingly nervous. Brownfield moved about the house like a mouse. On Tuesday, Grange was merely quiet. His wife and son began to relax. … (11 – 12)

On Saturday afternoon, after a week's exhausting labor, Grange heads for a nearby juke joint only to return "lurching drunk, threatening to kill his wife and Brownfield, stumbling and shooting off his shotgun. … [On Sunday evening] back home again after church, Grange and Margaret would begin a supper quarrel which launched them into another week just about like the one before." (12-13) Thus he turns to exert power in the one place he is presumably dominant, i. e., in his home, and seeks escape from the total drain of physical energy and from an overwhelming sense of helplessness in the arms of the prostitute Josie. He totally ignores his wife's feelings and eventually drives Margaret into protest against his maltreatment—she allows herself to lead a life of dissipation, not even disdaining the white boss Shipley. Under the burden of his psychological humiliation and economic defeat, Grange, despite his basically unchanged love for his wife, eventually chooses to abandon his wife and son to seek relief, and simply takes himself out of a situation he is impotent to change—he goes North to seek for a better life. Till then, Grange's first life ends. Three weeks later his desertion makes Margaret poison herself and her younger son fathered by a white man, only to leave Brownfield fending for himself.

During his first life, Grange obviously lacks masculinity, and his manhood is completely denied both physically and psychologically. Physically, Grange lives a mechanical life, repeating his work in Shipley's cotton field. He is turned to an object, a stone. The stripping of his manhood is presented explicitly through the innocent eyes of Brownfield:

> When the truck came his father's face froze into an unnaturally bland mask, curious and unsettling to see. It was as if his father became a stone or a robot. A grim stillness settled over his eyes and he became an object, a cipher … At first Brownfield thought his father was turned to stone by the truck itself. … But after watching the loading of the truck for several weeks he realized it was the man who drove the truck who caused his father to don a mask that was more impenetrable than his usual silence. Brownfield looked closely at the man and made a startling discovering; the man was a man, but entirely different from his father. (8)

Through Brownfield's eyes, the cause of Grange's inaction and his wearing the mask is thoroughly exposed: Grange needs to wear a mask to help himself hidden from the hostile world which he is impotent to change. He becomes an object, a stone not because of hard work but because of the hopeless debt, the merciless exploitation by the white man Shipley, "who could, by his presence alone, turn his (Brownfield's) father into something that might as well have been a pebble or a post or a piece of dirt." (9) Thus Walker demonstrates to us the truth that it is racism that causes Grange's absence of manhood.

Being physically mechanical naturally leads to psychological numbness. Grange is turned to a numbed person whose attitude toward his life and family is nothing but that of vacancy and bewilderment. "His face and eyes had a dispassionate vacancy and sadness, as if a great fire had been extinguished within him and was just recently missed. He seemed devoid of any emotion … except that of bewilderment." (13) Deprived of his power to support his family and dominate his own life, Grange even does not know "what he was." As a patriarch, he can neither afford to buy a dress for his wife nor to send his only son to school. What he can do is only shrug. After each shrug he becomes more numbed and bewildered than before. Impotence defines his quality at this stage of his life; there are no options open to him for any responsible act.

Turned into a stone and devoid of any emotion, Grange is unable to understand the pain both his wife and his son are suffering. He has no compassion for his family. As a consequence, he is trapped in a state of unconsciousness and inaction and abandons any responsibility for changing this situation. Just as Grange himself explains, "[t]he trouble with numbness … is that it spreads to all your organs, mainly the heart." (211) It deprives one of the ability to love and to be loved. For lack of such ability, Grange's relationship with his family, i. e., the husband-wife relationship and the father-son relationship, is a problematic one. It not only results in his wife's seeking lovers, both black and white, and her eventual suicide, but also sows the seeds of grudge and hatred in his son Brownfield. To some extent, it is Grange who ruins Margaret and Brownfield and therefore is responsible for his wife's death and his son's dehumanization. By creating such an image, Walker tends to awaken the self-redemptive consciousness of the black race, black males in particular.

4.1.1.2 Brownfield's Dehumanization: The Irredeemable Degradation

The second generation of the Copelands is primarily represented by Brownfield, Grange's son. After his mother's suicide, Brownfield chooses to go to the mythical North, following at his father's heels. But having "never heard of the North Star" and unable to find the next railroad, Brownfield wanders for weeks and ends up at the Dew Drop Inn owned by the infamous "Fat Josie," who used to be his father's mistress. (31) The following over two years, he plays the role of resident stud in the life of Josie and her daughter Lorene. His animal-like state of saturation becomes tiresome only when he meets Josie's adopted daughter

Mem, a lovely schoolteacher. Eager to get and marry Mem, Brownfield blindly walks into the trap of sharecropping through contracting work with a nearby farmer. Consequently, within only three years he, like his father, runs hopelessly into debt. Poverty and overwork also drive him to drink and abuse his wife.

The routine quarrel between his parents and their failure to send him to school as a consequence of abject poverty provide Brownfield with a moral environment marked by ignorance and lack of parental love, which naturally determines his eagerness to seek warmth and comfort in Josie's arms and his blindness in running into the snare of sharecropping. Thus since his childhood Brownfield's basic quality of irresponsibility and immorality has already been set. In this sense, his unfortunate childhood, which is the direct result of racism, actually plays a vital role in his later dehumanization. In other words, racism is the key to understanding Brownfield's moral degeneration. In a white supremacist society, the violence and evil doings in his later life seem unavoidable.

The already-set weaknesses in Brownfield's character decide his shortsightedness in treating life. He almost considers nothing but the pleasure of the moment and never takes any responsibility for his wife and family. Married to Mem, Brownfield seeks comfort in Mem and turns to her eagerly every day after his toil in the field. "… She was so good to him, so much what he needed, that … [he] grew big and grew firm with love, and grew strong." (49) And, when facing the heaped debt, he can find no way out but to take it out on Mem:

> It was his rage at himself, and his life and his world that made him beat her for an imaginary attraction she aroused in other men, crackers, although she was no party to any of it. His rage and his anger and his frustration ruled. His rage could and did blame everything, *everything* on her. … Brownfield beat his once lovely wife now, regularly, because it made him feel, briefly, good. Every Saturday night he beat her, trying to pin the blame for his failure on her by imprinting it on her face; … (55, italics original)

Here, we can clearly see that, along with the economic reality, the white supremacist patriarchal system in the Afro-American community works to deprive black men of their humanity. For one thing, Brownfield cannot help his family out of debt or "save his children from slavery" in the white world (54). Nor dare he dream of the dignity as a man before his white boss. "He jumped when the crackers said jump, and left his welfare up to them. He no longer had, as his father had maintained, even the desire to run away from them." (59) He completely yields to the racial prejudice. His pride is crushed and his ego battered. For another, the overwhelming black androcentrism in Afro-American society reminds him about his sense of superiority in sex, which urges his absolute domination over his wife and children. His ill-treating and oppressing them, his wife in particular, is, in effect, a hysterical way of seeking a sort of psychological balance.

Poisoned by the androcentric ideology, Brownfield virtually becomes an obstacle to improving his family's lot. He does not allow Mem to do anything that might outshine him, even though her purpose is to offer a better life for the family. At first, he drags "Mem away from schoolteaching, and sends her into white homes as a domestic" to meet "his need to bring her down to his level." (55) For this already distorted patriarch, his pride before and control over his woman are far more important than a better existence of his family. Then, he steals the money Mem has saved to buy a house, the first time to buy a diseased pig and the next time to buy a car. Even when Mem succeeds in renting a house and getting a job "in town" and offers a better and comfortable life in the new house, Brownfield does nothing to help her but simply waits to take vengeance, to destroy what Mem has created, and to make the whole family return to the past life. In so doing, Brownfield seems to maintain *his* notion of pride and power, his special position as a man in the family. But he loses the basic quality of humanity and responsibility of a man. Thus in the character of Brownfield, Walker presents how destructive a racist patriarchal society can make a black man and emphasizes such a fact that sexism is as detrimental and hazardous to the survival whole of the black race as racism is.

Brownfield's dehumanization is manifested not just in his irresponsibility for the family and maltreatment of Mem in body but in his trying every means to destroy his wife in mind as well. At first, he "accused Mem of being unfaithful to him, of being used by white men, his oppressors" and "determined … to treat her like a nigger and a whore, which he knew she was not." (54) Then "he was determined to change her. … The first thing he started on was her speech." (56) In Brownfield's opinion, Mem's Standard English is a threat to his dominating position in the family. Therefore

> [i]n company he embarrassed her. When she opened her mouth to speak he turned with a bow to his friends, who thankfully spoke a language a man could understand, and said, "Hark, Mah *lady* speaks, lets us dumb niggers listen!" Mem would turn ashen with shame, and tried to keep her mouth closed thereafter. But silence was not what Brownfield was after, either. He wanted her to talk, but to talk like what she was, a hopeless nigger woman … a woman who deserved him. He could not stand having his men friends imply she was too good for him. (56)

By changing Mem's words, Brownfield virtually deprives her of her self-confidence and of her right to express herself. Her intelligence and education, which were once her pride and charm, now become a proof of shame. Her speech seems to her "flat and ugly" so that Mem almost has no courage to open her mouth.

Brownfield's dehumanization reaches its culmination in his cruel murder of his wife Mem on Christmas Eve. Fired by his new boss Mr. J. L. and out of work for several weeks or months, Brownfield desperately finds himself even unable to earn his own living. Now that he dare take no step to oppose the white injustice though he curses it and his white boss many times to himself, he vents his frustrations on Mem. For Mem, it seems to him, always manages to get a job and earn the living of the whole family. He ascribes his impotence to Mem's intelligence and competence. Here is one extreme example Walker gives us of how the prevailing Eurocentric patriarchal ideology ruins the black men by putting them at the center of the family and allowing them to make any decisions that may show their authority. Once Brownfield realizes his central position in the family might be replaced (because it is actually Mem who supports the family), he is sure to take a hysterical action—even killing—to protect it.

In sum, imprisoned by the economic reality and poisoned by the patriarchal supremacy, the Copeland husbands lose their basic humanity. Their manhood and masculinity is twisted and ruined so much that they act as brutes to their family and their women in particular. To achieve the spiritual survival, they have to undergo a hard struggle for personal growth.

4.1.2 The Hypocrisy in *Meridian's Men*

Alice Walker's second novel *Meridian*, chronologically, develops from *The Third Life of Grange Copeland* as naturally as the younger generation from the older. Like *The Third Life of Grange Copeland*, it also explores the impact of the social conditions on personal life. But, unlike *The Third Life of Grange Copeland* whose emphasis is on the necessity of taking responsibility for one's life, *Meridian* examines the relationship between a movement for social change and the personal growth of its participants. Although much of the story in *Meridian* happens in the heyday of the Civil Rights Movement, there still exists a strong sense of the white supremacist patriarchy influencing, restricting and even distorting the manhood and humanity of black males. More middle class and less physically violent, the black men in *Meridian* are similarly disloyal and despicable in their abuse of women. If the Copeland males are brutes and they torture their women more physically and directly, the male characters in *Meridian* are hypocrites. The tortures they vent on the women are more in mind. They are harder to prevent and express.

4.1.2.1 The Minor Male Characters: The Personalities Twisted by Racism and/or Sexism

In *Meridian*, Walker creates a group of male images composed of a school teenager Eddie, a radical civil rights activist Tommy Odds, an old nationalist professor Mr. Raymonds, and an artist and civil rights activist Truman Held. As victims of sexism and racism, they irrefutably testify to the inveterate impact of the white supremacist patriarchy and/or the black androcentric ideology on black males, and to the arduousness of black men to reach the goal of the spiritual survival.

Although Walker's focus is apparently on Truman, the major male character, the other three are also vividly depicted. Eddie, Meridian's former husband, is an incarnation of the black androcentric ideology. For him, the duty of a married woman first and foremost is to do housework, to play the literal role of a maid to her husband and family. Under whatever circumstances, she should and must do her duty well. He also holds that a wife is a sex object and potential mother. What he thinks is of vital importance in the husband-wife, or exactly man-woman, relationship is the body rather than the mind. On his part, sex is "the act of 'giving in' for the woman and conquering for the man." (Christian, 1993: 89) Failing to have sex with a woman means failing to conquer her, which further means lack of manhood and masculinity. Therefore Eddie seeks masculinity in sex and in his woman and child, and lets his responsibility of husband/father denied.

Mr. Raymonds is another typical hypocrite cultured by the American society. For him, the only oppression or danger black females have suffered and are suffering comes from white men. By keeping a distance from white males, black females are ensured of security. As to black males, since they and black women are of the same color and of the same root, they are certainly in possession of black females, and naturally have the right to do whatever they like to black women. Therefore, no fear of being accused of rape or maltreatment ever occurs to Mr. Raymonds when each day, after Meridian finishes her work and rises to go, "he clasped her in his arms, dragging her away from the door, … attempting to force her to the floor" and taking no notice of Meridian's struggling. (A. Walker, 1976: 112) Such a thing is as natural as a daily routine to him. Mr. Raymonds may "be red in the face from anger" because of Meridian's "talking to a white divinity student." (111) However, he never becomes red or feels even slightly hesitated when he himself is committing the crime of molesting Meridian.

Here through this nationalist professor, Alice Walker exposes to the black race such a fact that even during the heyday of the Civil Rights Movement black males remain unconscious of the urgency of treating black females as equal beings. What they are doing is follow their oppressors' way to treat their own sisters, which will ruin black people as a whole and eventually further enforce the domination of the white supremacist ideology. So the key to reaching the goal of eliminating racism is the unity and solidarity of black people, male and female, and thus, sexism stands out as a vital problem.

If in Eddie and Mr. Raymonds Ms. Walker tends to demonstrate the hazardous and detrimental impact of the black androcentrism on the black race, particularly on black males, in Tommy Odds we can see the twisted response of black people after generations of white racist oppression. As a civil rights activist, Tommy, attacked by the so-called NOTC (niggers-on-the-corner), the black extremists in practice, cannot face the injury in a sober and objective way so that he fails to handle the event properly. He does not accept the responsibility of the black race for reforming the American extant political system, for eliminating the social injustices. Rather, sticking to the logic that being white is being guilty, he turns to the similarly helpless victim Lynne, a white woman "to avenge himself against white oppressors," just as Karen F. Stein (1986: 138) points out that "powerless victims often turn their aggression from their powerful enemies to others weaker than themselves, as a scolded child kicks its dog." Tommy conquers Lynne by means of sex—an accepted means by black masculinists to prove their masculinity and capacity of conquering—taking no notice of the fact that "Lynne … was a good worker. Better—to be honest—than the black women." (A. Walker, 1976: 157) "Revenge was his only comfort." (162) Obviously, driven by the impulse of revenge, Tommy actually loses his consciousness and consequently acts as a brute. His humanity is denied; his manhood distorted. What Walker tends to assume here is that slipping into racial hatred is similarly hazardous and detrimental to survival whole.

To some extent, these minor characters each overlap with Truman in a certain aspect—Eddie, in his understanding and pursuit of sex; Tommy, in his limitation as a civil rights activist; and Mr. Raymonds, in his falseness and inconsistency between words and actions as an intellectual. Therefore, the following analysis is mainly centered on Truman, into whom Walker condenses the typical weaknesses of black males in the Civil Rights era.

4.1.2.2 The Conquering Prince: A Spiritual Tragic Divisiveness

Truman Held is an artist and "the first of the Civil Rights workers." (83) As an educated black male who is struggling for social justice, Truman is "courageous and new," and, "[u]nlike any other black man she (Meridian) had known," he appears to be "a man who fought against obstacles, a man who could become anything, a man whose very words were unintelligible without considerable thoughts." Meridian "felt protective when she was with him." (100) Nonetheless, when they are romantically drawn together by the common goal of struggling for the civil rights, Truman immediately proves to be nothing better than Meridian's former husband. Like Eddie, what he cares about is not her mind but her body. In other words, he is also primarily interested in sleeping with Meridian. In Truman, Walker seems to stress the qualities that he and Eddie, and black males in general, have in common, so as to pave the way for her only centering on Truman when dealing with the personal change.

Brought up in a white society, Truman's favorite culture "was French. … He believed that anything said in French sounded better, and also believed that people who spoke French were better than people … who did not." (99 - 100) Therefore, on the one hand, he has naturally accepted the aesthetic that has the greatest esteem for the Euro-American image of blonde beauty, and denies the value of the Afro-American negritude. But on the other hand, Truman, as a black intellectual and activist, does not admit the whites' definition of black males that sees the black man "in terms of his penis and his propensity to violence." (Christian, 1993: 90) He at once refuses to submit to the lot assigned to black male activists by society to live with the females whom they claim to save but "whose provincial mind" he thinks is deficient in imagination, dreams and wishes, and eagerly runs after Meridian, who, in his opinion, just has the very "provincial mind" but is, anyway, a black woman, to show his revolutionary feelings toward his people. Thus Truman, just as Karen F. Stein (1986: 136) points out, "like the Civil Rights movement he symbolizes, is tragically divided." While acclaiming slogans for social justice, he attempts to escape his black parentage through getting gilded with exotic cultures and sticks to "a patriarchal insensitivity toward women." (136)

Driven by the desire for upward mobility and to be unique, Truman wants "a woman perfect in the eyes of the world," a woman who is well worth his identity, a woman who accepts him as a hero, as a "conquering prince," as an exception, a woman from whom Meridian is evidently different. (A. Walker, 1776: 142) For Truman, only in this way can he be proved of power and insight, as the white males are acknowledged to have. Hence, shortly after gaining Meridian's love, he is busy dating the three exchange white students who come down South to work on voter registration during Freedom Summer and who "read *The New York Times*," and ends up with his marriage to one of them Lynne who has "worldly experiences" and the leisure to be idealistic, and who, more importantly, claims his life, instead of her own, as hers. (143) Meanwhile, however, he cannot resist the temptation to paint huge, big-breasted black women. For, born of blackness, Truman is unavoidably inclined to respect strong black women as "magnificent giants, breeding forth the warriors of the new universe." (168) Since such a woman is far from his "ideal" wife, a woman who "would not mind being a resource for someone else, … a woman [for him] to rest in," as a port for a ship, as a shed for a train, he can only seek an outlet for his passion in art, in the lifeless stone statues he creates. (141) He seems to feel more secure and comfortable to admire an artwork than face the live female activist Meridian. Truman "did not want a general beside him. He did not want a woman who tried, however encumbered by guilt and fears and remorse, to claim her own life." (110) He needs a woman who "had lacked courage, lacked initiative or a mind of her own." (109) Such a woman is virtually an imagined ideal static image created by Truman only in his art. Thus Truman painfully wavers between the two opposite "ideals."

Truman's spiritually tragic divisiveness is also displayed in his traditional male hypocritical separation between "good girls" and "bad girls." "He had wanted a virgin, had been raised to expect and *demand* a virgin; and never once had he questioned this." (142, italics original) After the exchange students have gone back North, Truman once returns to Meridian. But when he finds Meridian is not a virgin at all, "there arose [repugnance] in him for her." (114) So he deserts Meridian and goes "back to the last of the exchange students" Lynne Rabinowitz, a virgin as he expects. Despite his eagerness to find a virgin, Truman "had been as predatory as the other young men he ran with, as eager to seduce and devirginize as they." (142) The first time his demand for sex is refused or, to be more exact, delayed by Meridian, he finds a girl at the party to replace her. After deserting Lynne and being refused by Meridian, he again succeeds in living together with a blonde girl. In so doing, Truman fails to be aware of the contradiction and inequities in his sexual ideology. Surprisingly, this intellectual and activist is never stranded by questions such as "where had he expected his virgins to come from." (142) His view of the opposite sex manifests the fragmentation that a patriarchal society nurtures between males and females. Truman is torn between his desire for courting women and for upholding virginity. As a man conditioned by the Eurocentric patriarchal ideology, he denies women as equal human beings. In his eyes, Meridian, Lynne and other blondes are nothing but sex objects or potential mothers. He oppresses the women who love him in the way any white masculinist does. As an intellectual raised in exotic cultures, he expects his woman to be both innocent and knowledgeable, both a virgin and romantic. In this sense, the "true man" (as his name implies) is anything but "true."

Truman's inconsistency between his revolutionary slogans and liberal education and his maltreatment of and irresponsibility for his women are at once ascribed to his acknowledgement that the white culture values are superior to the black ones, and to his wavering politics of black manhood. His first discarding Meridian for Lynne and later deserting Lynne back to Meridian both result from his interpretation of black manhood. For Truman, since the civil rights activists are struggling for social justice, black males, equal to their white counterparts, also have the right to explore the white woman's body, which is actually motivated by the ideology that the white woman's body is a "holy territory," and that to conquer it means to hold supremacy. Therefore, to display his exceptional identity of an intellectual and activist, Truman determines to run after Lynne, to explore the "holy land" while leaving Meridian pregnant and to have an abortion. In so doing, he never thinks of the essential content of manhood—to be a "true" man, to claim manhood, one must first accept his responsibility for others, for his women in particular. By discarding Meridian impregnated by him, Truman actually denies his manhood rather than realizes it. He does not transcend self-hatred that has tortured and ruined the soul of the black men. In pursuing Lynne and other blondes, Truman demonstrates the fact that he does not escape the impact of the white patriarchal discourse, the discourse in which masculinity is manifested in terms of his penis. In this way, he reduces his manhood to brutality, which proves that he is still driven by racial hatred and conditioned by racism.

Married to Lynne, he becomes increasingly aware of the challenges the Southern society presents to any "deviant" couple. The 1960s South has not yet been prepared to tolerate interracial love and marriage. He and Lynne have to suffer from the Southern exclusion of their deviancy. Gradually Truman's "feelings for Lynne had been undergoing subtle changes." (131) He feels more and more embarrassed in his relationship with Lynne. Nonetheless, it is "the shooting of Tommy Odds in Mississippi" in a demonstration that touches off the rupture of their marriage. This incident appears to force him to accept Tommy's inference that "all white people are motherfuckers." (132) Accordingly, Lynne is guilty of Tommy's loss since she is white. Such logic is obviously a replicate of the white vision that "black people … were 'guilty' of being black." (133) So it naturally leads to racism. As a civil rights activist, Truman certainly knows well about what goal the movement members are fighting for. But to ensure his own comfort in the Southern community, he eventually abandons Lynne. Ironically, Truman's reason for discarding Lynne is just the same as the one for having been attracted by her—"Lynne's intelligence," "her inability to curb herself; her imagination, her wishes and dreams," and "her lack of restraint, which he so admired at first and had been so refreshed by." (140) Lynne's intense idealism based on freedom and security, which attracts him so much before their marriage, now begins to trouble him. For this quality is just what Truman and his people are bereft of. To display his love for black people, he needs to reject Lynne and return to Meridian, who, in contrast to Lynne, symbolizes the myriad aspects of his heritage: the provinciality, the suffering, the impotence, and the lack of freedom. In other words, in the eyes of Truman, Meridian embodies the limits of black people, which is, in effect, absolutely wrong. So his return to Meridian implies that he remains unable to thoroughly cast himself off the restrictions that control the black race for ages.

Thus by depicting Truman's alternatively changing feelings for his women and by presenting other black males' ingrained sexism and/or racial hatred, Ms. Walker tends to expose the fact that the 1960s' black people, especially black men, still get stuck in their oppressors' logic and fail to elevate their own manhood and to get the spiritual survival of black people.

4.1.3 The Brutality of the Males in *The Color Purple*

If *The Third Life of Grange Copeland* focuses on the interactive effect of racism and sexism on black people, especially on degeneration of black males, and *Meridian* centers on the everlasting impact of patriarchal supremacy on black males, then *The Color Purple* examines "black-on-black" oppression as well as incest existing in the Afro-American community. The over thirty years in Celie's life witnesses the brutality of her stepfather Alphonso and her husband Mr. ——, both of whom abuse Celie physically and psychologically, and of Harpo, Celie's stepson, who beats his wife Sofia to "mind" him. The novel is more concerned with the politics of sex and self than with the politics of race and class, and emphasizes the dominating role of black males in the frustration of black women's search for self-identity. Within the contexts of the white supremacist patriarchy black males internalize their oppressors' notion of maleness that acknowledges males as perpetual power and subordinates females to males. Depressed by the impossibility to exert such power and domination in the white society, black men naturally turn to their own community, to their inferiors, to pour out their grievances.

4.1.3.1 Alphonso's Scoundrelism: The Identification with White Power

Due to the generations' oppression by white people, some of blacks are accustomed to the life of servitude to their oppressors. They put aside the liberation of their people and are busy currying favor with their white masters and making a fortune for themselves. To procure their personal purpose, they, in effect, are identified with white power. Alphonso, Celie's stepfather, is one of such examples. As a black, he is a faithful servile follower of the white. As a patriarch, he is a cruel oppressor of his people and a shameless scamp in his family and community.

To take possession of the family property of the widow, Celie's mother, he "lavished all his attention on the widow," who is nearly killed at the sight of Celie's father's body which is mutilated and burnt by the white merchants, and who is now "mentally unstable." (A. Walker, 1982: 181) Quite soon, he succeeds in getting married to Celie's mother and seems to act as husband/father in the life of the widow and her children. Yet in essence, he treats his wife as nothing but a sex object. "Almost at once [after they got married] she was pregnant ··· though her mental health was no better. Every year thereafter, she was pregnant, every year she became weaker and more mentally unstable," until she is "half dead" and eventually dies. (181, 1) Like his white masters, Alphonso never accepts his wife and black women in general as equal human beings. Of course, he cannot take the responsibility for his family. He never cares for his wife's health: By impregnating her every year after their marriage, he ruins her health and eventually causes her death. Nor does he care for his children: He leaves them looked after by his fourteen-year-old stepdaughter Celie, who also has to do all the housework. Here in the family he actually plays the role of a surrogate of his white oppressors.

A servile follower of the whites, Alphonso is as good at abusing black women as the white males are. As his wife is getting too weak to serve him in sex, he turns to her daughter Celie, who even does not understand what it is, rapes her repeatedly and gets her pregnant twice. In the eyes of Alphonso, a female is just a sex object and, since an old one is out of use, a new and young one must be found to take its/her place. In Celie's mother's place, he finds Celie. However, soon after Celie's mother's death, he gets married to a girl of Celie's age and begins beating Celie for whatever reason. More disgustingly, "sometime he still be looking at Nettie," Celie's younger sister, his other stepdaughter. Each time his new wife gets sick as a result of his excessive sexual assaults, he would trouble the two sisters. Poisoned so deeply by the white supremacist patriarchal ideology, Alphonso has not even realized his animal-like action and enjoys his nauseating life by changing his wife, or to be more exact, his sexmate from one girl to another. The only advantage for him to act like a brute is the family property and the land he has captured from Celie's mother through marriage.

Alice Walker examines Alphonso's dehumanization not only in his physically and sexually bullying black women and his stepdaughter Celie in particular but also in his silencing her voice. The novel opens with an admonishment that "*You'd better not never tell nobody but God. It'd kill your mammy.*" (1, italics original) Uttered by the scamp Alphonso after he rapes Celie, this admonishment, as Lindsey Tucker (1988: 83) points out, "establish[es] not only the primacy of a male text, but also convey[s] the essence of patriarchal repression"—silencing the oppressed. By so doing, he deprives Celie of the freedom of communicating even with her mother, only to leave her suffering alone. And the rape itself is also characterized by silencing. Celie describes it in her letter to God like this: "When that hurt, I cry. He start to choke me, saying You better shut up and git used to it." (A. Walker, 1982: 1 –2). When he impregnates Celie, he forces her to stop going to school, saying "you too dumb to keep going to school." (11) In this way, he occupies Celie as his full-time sexmate and expropriates this poor girl from her last pleasure. On Alphonso's part, the black females are anything but emotional beings. So when Celie's babies are born, he takes them away without her consent or even her awareness. He highhandedly arranges everything for Celie, including her marriage. Determined to marry her off to Mr. ——, a widower with four children, he is willing to throw in a cow to sweeten the deal in the same way as he disposes of a used-up head of livestock. To make sure that the evil he brings on Celie is held back for ever and that his silencing her remains efficient after Celie's marriage, he does not forget to tell Mr. —— that "she tell lies." (9) Thus, Alphonso, in effect, denies Celie's every right in her lifetime as a woman and as a human being, for his patriarchal philosophy of life is that "men make decisions and women make adjustments." (Marvin, 1994: 415)

Before the white, this brute, however, acts like a different being. To make a fortune and preserve his position over his people, he fawns on his white masters at the cost of his human dignity. Walker clearly puts it in Alphonso's own monologue:

> Take me, he say, I know how they is. The key to all of 'em is money. The trouble with our people is as soon as they got out of slavery they didn't want to give 'em something. Either your money, your land, your woman or your ass. So what I did was just right off offer to give 'em money. Before I planted a seed, I made sure this one and that one knowed one seed out of three was planted for *him*. Before I ground a grain of wheat, the same thing. And when I opened up your daddy's old store in town, I bought me my own white boy to run it. And what make it so good, he say, I bought him with whitefolks' money. (A. Walker, 1982: 188, italics original)

By paying off whites and hiring a white boy to run Celie's father's store, Alphonso virtually identifies himself with white power and blazes a new path to economic integration with whites, which is finally seen as accommodationist for his own benefit. After making his fortune, he moves into "a big yellow two story house" that looks like "some white person's house" and, like whites, establishes paternalistic relationships with other blacks. (185) When Shug and Celie once meet him, he has a new wife, a "child" "not more than fifteen" whose parents "work for him, … live on his land." (187) Up till now, Ms. Walker has succeeded in producing a vivid image of the servile follower of the whites, who is characterized by atrocity and greed, but has nothing to do with masculine dignity and humanity.

4.1.3.2 Mr. ——'s Cruelty: The Failure as a Human Being

Patriarchy, as a social structure which supports and condones male power and domination, is responsible for Mr. ——'s cruelty to and oppression of his wife Celie. For one thing, Mr. —— himself is a victim of patriarchy. He and Shug, a blues singer, fall in love with each other. But as a result of his father's determined opposition they never get married. He therefore vents his resentment on his women, and thus becomes a typical patriarch himself. For another, the code of patriarchy that accepts women as subordinate beings, as a separate species guarantees Mr. ——'s supposition that a wife is anything but an equal and emotional being. This naturally results in Mr. ——'s enjoying a prerogative of committing all kinds of outrages on his wife and Celie's being deprived of even the basic right of living a normal life.

Their marriage is built on a pragmatic foundation rather than love. From the very beginning, Mr. —— places Celie in a subordinate status. He at last chooses to marry her only because he is badly in need of someone who looks after his children, manages his household affairs and ploughs his fields; because Alphonso recommends to him that "she can work like a man." (9) He accepts Alphonso's offer of Celie as he accepts a commodity, which is observable in the following description by Celie:

> He say, Let me see her again.
>
> Pa call me. Celie, he say. Like it wasn't nothing. Mr. —— want another look at you.
>
> I go stand in the door. The sun shine in my eyes. He's still up on his horse. He look me

> up and down.
>
> Pa rattle his newspaper. Move up, he won't bite, he say.
>
> I go closer to the steps, but not too close cause I'm a little scared of his horse.
>
> Turn round, Pa say.
>
> I turn round, … (11 – 12)

Mr. —— examines Celie in the way he picks out a head of livestock. This is intensified by his last question whether "that cow still coming." (12) Therefore it is understandable that when his son "pick up a rock and laid my [Celie's] head open," Mr. —— treats it lightly by saying "[d]on't do that." (13)

Mr. ——'s notion that women are a separate species, whose value lies only in their labor force and the occasional sexual convenience for their men, is inherent. The first time he gets married, as one of his sisters says, "he just brought her (his first wife) here, dropped her, and kept right on running after Shug Avery. … Nobody to talk to, nobody to visit. He be gone for days." (21) He treats his second wife Celie no better. Although she is a "good housekeeper, good with children, good cook," Mr. —— looks at her "like he looking at earth" and never thinks of buying her a piece of clothes. (21) Not only does he leave all the housework to Celie, but he seldom helps her with the farm work. While Celie is in the field "sweat, chopping and plowing," he is sitting "on the porch, look[ing] out at nothing, sometime look[ing] at the trees out front the house" or "at a butterfly if it light on the rail," and "drink[ing] a little water in the day or a little wine in the evening. But mostly [he] never move." (29) In the eyes of this dehumanized and patriarchy-twisted husband, Celie is a cow, a maid. Beating her is part of his everyday life. When Harpo, his oldest son, asks him why he beats Celie, Mr. —— simply says, "cause she my wife." (21) To him, a "wife" is just another name for a cow, for a maid, for a slave. He teaches Harpo: "Wives is like children. You have to let'em know who got the upper hand. Nothing can do that better than a good sound beating." (37) To get his "upper hand," to conquer and control Celie, which he has already done, Mr. —— would beat her "like he beat the children," as Celie describes it, "Cept he don't hardly beat them. He say, Celie, git the belt. The children be outside the room peeking through the cracks." (23)

In addition to physical tortures, Mr. —— also abuses Celie psychologically. His disregard of his first wife's existence results in her death, but he has no tendency to change in his relationship with Celie. He is still running after Shug. Preparing for meeting Shug, Mr. —— would tell Celie to "wash this, iron that, look for this, look for that, find this, find that." (25) He never thinks it necessary to get to know whether Celie has any different or opposite ideas, or how Celie, as a wife, is feeling. For a maid or a slave has no right to get concerned with her master's affairs. Only when Shug leaves and he needs to satisfy his sexual desire, does Mr. —— remember Celie. But he "never ast me (Celie) how I feel, nothing. Just do his business, get off, go to sleep." (81) Even when Shug is seriously ill and needs looking after, he brings her home without consulting with Celie about it or informing her of it beforehand. Not until "they (Mr. —— and Shug) git halfway up the step" does Mr. —— tell Celie: "This here Shug Avery. Old friend of the family. Fix up the spare room." (47 – 48) But his purpose is clear—he wants Celie to nurse his mistress back to health. No matter how Celie will deal with it, the idea to let his wife look after his mistress itself proves Mr. ——'s cruelty to Celie or his denial of his wife as an emotional being.

Mr. ——'s cruelty and dehumanization is further explored in his intervention in and/or destruction to Celie's spiritual life. He strips her of every possibility of fulfilling her personal values or, exactly, of speaking out her mind. He has been concealing from Celie her sister Nettie's letters. Fully aware that Celie and Nettie depend on each other for survival, Mr. —— of course understands what it means to one of them to fail to get any information about the other. Having been refused by Nettie when he tries to seduce her, Mr. —— determines to get back at her by preventing the two sisters from receiving each other's letters. By so doing, Mr. ——, in effect, like Alphonso, attempts to deprive the two and Celie in particular of the right to communicate. Tortured by the uncertainty of each other's fate and lacking in the encouragement and consolation from each other, the two sisters, especially Celie, are living a dead-alive life. But that's not all. To show his supremacy over his wife and enjoy the satisfaction of his twisted masculinity, Mr. —— restricts Celie within domesticities and never allows her to attend Shug's performance, saying "wives don't go to places like that." (76) To Mr. ——, black wives only deserve attending to household duties and waiting upon their husbands sexually. They are unemotional beings so they have no need of living a cultural and spiritual life. Nor can it be imagined that they will go out to live an independent life. When Celie, encouraged by Shug and enraged by discovering that Mr. —— has been hiding Nettie's letters, determines to go to Memphis with Shug, Mr. —— does everything possible to hinder her. At first he threatens that Celie can leave only walking "over my dead body." (206) Then he tries violence, the most efficient way he believes to deal with Celie—he "reach over to slap me (Celie)." (207) Depressed by the failure of all these attempts, Mr. —— grasps his last straw—hurling insults at Celie: "Who you think you is? he say. … Look at you. You black, you pore, you ugly, you a woman. Goddam, he say, you nothing at all." (213) Right here, Walker successfully presents us how crazy a black patriarch may become to maintain his dominating position in his wife's life.

4.1.3.3 Harpo's Conquest: A Distorted Masculinity

Harpo's distorted masculinity is embodied not only in his persistent attempt of conquering his first wife Sofia physically and his desperate act of maltreating her sexually but also in his hampering his second wife's freedom of action. In this regard, he is a close copy of his father Mr. ——. However, the two cases are different. If Mr. ——'s violence against his wife and his suppression of her freedom are, to some extent, attributed to his first coercive and loveless marriage, Harpo's matrimony is supposed to be better. For Harpo and Sofia get married of their own free will, regardless of the opposition of their parents. Yet, in this androcentric society, even the kind of marriage based on mutual affection cannot escape the fate of failure. Just as Celie concludes, "wherever there's a man, there's trouble." (212)

As a child, Harpo is already taught by his father's personal example that women, as a subservient race, must be obedient to their men, and that a real man does not work. Now that he is not just doing this or that as Sofia tells him to but also Sofia seems to persist in her own way of doing things, he begins feeling threatened, especially from the moment Mr. —— warns Harpo "she going to switch the traces on you" when seeing Harpo help Sofia look after the baby. (36) Their formerly happy marriage is going wrong: Harpo is distressed with questions like how to "get an upper hand" over Sofia and "what to do to make Sofia mind." (66, 37) Eventually he adopts his father's suggestion of beating.

Nevertheless, Sofia is not Celie. Every time Harpo tries to beat her into a submissive wife, she strikes back. As a consequence, he gets himself beaten, for he is not so big as Sofia. Since then, he racks his brains to explore ways of conquering Sofia and is so much distorted that he acts fantastically, even though Sofia is "not mean," "not spiteful" or doesn't "hold a grudge." (66) He tries to eat as much as possible "when he ain't even hungry" to get as big as Sofia. (62) Unfortunately, things do not always turn out the way one wishes. Only "his belly grow and grow, but the rest of him don't." (64) He still cannot conquer his wife physically. Rather, he makes Sofia tired of him: He has not thought of how to create a harmonious and happier life since they got married, but, as Sofia states, "all he think about … is how to make me mind. He don't want a wife, he want a dog." (68) What is worse, Harpo begins to abuse Sofia sexually since he is unable to beat her into minding him. "He git up there and enjoy himself just the same. No matter what I'm thinking. No matter what I feel. It just him. Heartfeeling don't even seem to enter into it." (69) Thus, by letting his twisted masculinity have its own way, Harpo breaks off their marriage and ruins their happy life personally.

Harpo does not change at all after Sofia's leaving. He continues to treat his second wife Mary Agnes in the same way. He orders her around as if she were a slave and persists in calling her "Squeak" to deny her identity. Like Mr. ——,

Harpo restricts Squeak within his juke joint. He does not allow her to sing in public since, as Harpo himself explains, "everything you need I done provided for." (210) In so doing, Harpo holds his father's view that wives are lifelong household slaves, and they should never appear on public occasions, let alone sing in public.

Thus through portraying the male images like Alphonso, Harpo and Mr. —— in the novel, Alice Walker (204) presents us such a stern reality that "man corrupt everything. … [He] in your head, … He try to make you think he everywhere … [and] think he God." To fulfill the womanist ideal, black males need a personal change first.

To sum up, in her first three novels, Ms. Walker explores black males of various circles—the sharecropper, the farmer, the merchant, the civil rights activist, and the intellectual—who live in different periods of the twentieth century (from the early years of the century to the mid-seventies). However different they may be, they share the supremacist patriarchal ideology that distorts and/or denies their manhood and humanity. Nevertheless, not all of them are beyond improvement. Realizing and acknowledging the evils they have brought on their women and children, they come to undergo a personal change, which paves the way for the womanist ideal.

4.2 The Process of Self-improvement: Shaking off the Confines of Supremacist Patriarchy

Ogunyemi (1997: 240) points out that the aim of the womanist philosophy is "the dynamism of wholeness and self-healing that one sees in the positive, integrative endings of womanist novels." In this sense, most of Walker's novels well reflect the author's womanist ideology. At least one of the male characters or the major male character(s) in each novel is/are sure to undergo a personal change after realizing all his/their previous evils, and reaches/reach or tends/tend to reach the goal of self-healing and self-improvement. Walker herself once states: "I believe in change; personal change, and change in society." (qtd. in

O'Brien, 1993: 332) It is such a belief in change that sets her male characters like the title character in *The Third Life of Grange Copeland*, Truman in *Meridian*, and Harpo and Albert in *The Color Purple* attempting to change and improve. If Truman only presents his strong potential for fulfilling the final self-redemption, Grange, Harpo, and Albert do achieve their goal of the spiritual survival and foster the survival whole of the other characters, female character(s) in particular, and/or of the whole black community in general.

4.2.1 Grange Copeland's Second and Third Lives: The Process of Regeneration

After leaving Baker County, Georgia, Grange goes North to Harlem where he begins his second life through hustling and stealing. Although, "unlike some misfortunate Southern migrants, he did not starve," "the North put him in solitary confinement" and makes him exist as an "invisible man." (A. Walker, 1970: 144 – 45) It is the death of the white woman whom he refuses to rescue only because of her racial hatred that awakens him from self-hatred and liberates him "in a strange way, a bizarre way." (153) He understands at last that, if black people want to survive, they must learn to hate the white, their enemy. The common hatred for the white will someday unite the black race. "His aggressiveness, which he had vented only on his wife and his child, and his closest friends, now asserted itself in the real hostile world." He starts to "fight all the whites he met." (155) But soon he realizes the finitude of an individual's power and decides to return to Georgia, to his people. His new life (his third life) begins when he takes up the responsibility of a husband/father in his family.

Back at home, Grange gets married to Josie. With the money from selling her little inn and that he has saved from hustling and stealing, Grange buys a productive secluded farm where he determines to lead an unrestricted, self-sufficient life. He starts out by helping Mem and her children, while his son Brownfield is right on the way to his total degeneration. After Brownfield is sentenced to ten years' imprisonment for murdering Mem, Grange takes his youngest granddaughter Ruth in (Ruth's two sisters have been taken North by Mem's father, only to be degraded). He brings Ruth up by teaching her everything he has learnt from his previous life and telling her stories he has got in the Northern Streets. Their ideal happy life, however, is interrupted by Brownfield's release from the jail: Brownfield insists on getting back Ruth not out of love for his daughter but out of spite against Grange. Determined to free Ruth from the emotional slavery, Grange murders Brownfield instead of giving him custody of Ruth and gets himself killed under the bullets of the white police.

4.2.1.1 Grange's Escape: A Preparation for a Positive Self-concept

Just as Robert James Butler (1993: 19) points out, "avoiding the 'blindness' created by her awareness of injustices done to blacks in the South, she (Alice Walker) is able to draw 'a great deal of positive material' from her outwardly 'underprivileged' background." "Her characters have the fundamental human responsibility of improving themselves and their relationship—they have the ability to change, and change for the better" in spite of the restriction of the social and economic conditions. (Tate, 1991: 513) Grange Copeland is one of such characters.

Grange is set up as a violent antithesis to Brownfield. He demonstrates some of the positive features of the black males in addition to their shortcomings, whereas Brownfield is a terrifying example of how the white supremacist society can physically enslave and spiritually distort black men. If Brownfield's attempt to escape to North ends fruitlessly and manifests his latent incorrigibleness, that of Grange proves his potential for self-transformation. Fully understanding Shipley's real purpose of urging him to get married and settle down in his parents' house and of offering to lend him some money to fix the house, Brownfield possesses the possibility and opportunity of pulling himself out of anyone's control. "His mind raced headlong into the realm of his dream. … He would be his own boss. … As he left the clearing a thousand birds began wildly singing good luck." (A. Walker, 1970: 24) Brownfield seems to have a bright future. But his ideal of being "his own boss" has already confined him to following the pattern of Shipley, the white boss. He would rather become a boss himself and have control and authority over others than cherish the newly-found freedom. This naturally leads to his shortsightedness and the tragic ending of his escape: Arriving at the Dew Drop Inn, he falls in Josie's arms and forgets everything about his dream.

Grange is a husband/father, deep in debt, when he tries to escape from the sharecropper's condition. Unlike Brownfield, Grange is in a dilemma: Staying at home means that he will be undoubtedly trapped in a permanent debt and have no hope for a free life, whereas leaving home and discarding his wife and son will inevitably drive them into despair. Compared with Brownfield, Grange has more disadvantageous elements that hinder him from developing into a free man. Yet Grange's flight turns his self-aggression into the more constructive act of resistance against the norms of the South and initiates a learning process as prerequisite to a positive self-concept. For Grange, the death of the white woman in Central Park takes the role of stimulating his sense of change in the whole novel. Insulted by her words and angered by her extreme racial hatred, Grange gives up the chance of rescuing the white woman. Although the death of the woman is haunting Grange and condemning his soul (because virtually he could have insisted on rescuing her despite her racial hatred), it does liberate him and awaken his value of human life. In this sense, the incident is not all failure. From the moment on, he begins to take a correct attitude toward Margaret's death and acknowledge his own responsibility for her suicide. Also, it is from that moment on, he stops self-hatred and understands the importance and necessity of manufacturing the manhood and self-respect of black men, or the black race as a whole.

Like Grange, Brownfield also experiences such a moment as a turning point. But he lets it slip away. In prison for murdering Mem, Brownfield, amazed at that he can read a newspaper article about his trial, realizes that he has learned to read and write from Mem. This skill he has forgotten just as he has forgotten the good times they shared. Such a revelation could be a turning point, but Brownfield misses it. Although he does "burst into sobs," "… his tears did not soften him, did not make him analyze his life or his crime." (165) He chooses evil. Out of prison, he still holds his previous view that his wife and children belong to him and are owned by him just as he is owned by his white boss. Obviously, Brownfield links his manhood to the ownership of material things. He tries to take possession of Ruth, his daughter—who, in Brownfield's eyes, is just an object—not out of a father's love or responsibility but for the purpose of proving his ownership. Therefore, when Martin Luther King is marching all over America for civil rights, Brownfield still restricts himself in the trap of white masculinist discourse and is still blaming whites for his not doing anything in life. Through the striking contrast between the two images, Walker inclines to stress the difficulty in Grange's regeneration.

Grange's initial change begins with his racial hatred. Instead of hating his wife, his child and even his closest friend, Grange turns to hating the "crackers." He holds that, to free black people's "suppressed manhood," "they must kill their oppressors." So shouting "up and down the Harlem streets," he preaches his new religion—"Teach them to *hate*, if you want them to survive." (153) He even fights with "Italians, Poles, Jews," if only they are white. He wants to vent all his frustrations and evil doings in his previous life on the "crackers." Walker (155) writes about it thus: "… [I]n this fighting too he tasted the sweet surge of blood rightfully directed in its wrath that proclaimed his freedom, his manhood. Every white face he cracked, he cracked in his sweet wife's name." He begins to realize that self-hatred in blacks can only be destructive and self-destructive. It not just ruins black individuals and their family but the black race as a whole. To eliminate racism, black people must unite because "soon he realized he could not fight all the whites he met. … Each man would have to free himself." (155) Realizing the limitation of an individual's power in reforming the American society, Grange determines to withdraw "for the time being" and "find a sanctuary" to defend, protect and keep his life inviolate from the white world which has victimized him economically and poisoned him with hatred. (155) In this sense, Grange's racial hatred acts as a powerful stimulus to his regeneration. After a long learning process it eventually liberates Grange's capacity for self-forgetfulness, for love of something beyond himself. In a word, Grange's second life in the North serves as a preparation for his positive understanding of manhood and humanity. Since then, he begins to seek new ways of changing, the regain of soul.

4.2.1.2 Grange's New Life: The Revival of Manhood and Humanity

Grange's third life witnesses his real change, the regeneration of his humanity and soul. Back in Baker County, "he is able to, as his name suggests, 'cope' with his 'land'" and "build a 'grange' or farm which will nourish himself and others." (Butler, 1993: 201) It is this farm life that endows Grange with the independence and freedom that enable him to take the "fundamental human responsibility" which is absent in his first life, i.e. in his life with Margaret and Brownfield. To show his repentance for his wife and son's suffering and to thank Josie, "the only person in the world who loved him," Grange, on the one hand, marries Josie shortly after his return from Harlem and undertakes the role of husband, providing Josie with the love between a man and a woman which he fails to provide for Margaret. (A. Walker, 1970: 156) On the other hand, despite his son Brownfield's spite against him, Grange manages to assume the role of father by assisting Mem and bringing his granddaughters food and fruits. Upon Mem's murder by Brownfield, he thoroughly embraces the role of "father" in his granddaughter Ruth's life, offering her the love and care which he fails to give to Brownfield in his son's childhood. He not merely provides Ruth with a "snug house" and adequate nourishing food but good schooling as well. (69) He manages to arrange for her to attend school and, more importantly, teach her "the realities of life." (139) His rich experience and wide knowledge of black folklore are an endless resource to Ruth. In the several happy and valuable years they live together, Grange nourishes Ruth's mind and soul. He conceives himself as a teacher who can instill racial pride and individual identity in Ruth, and as a redeemer who can save Ruth from self-hate and helplessness. He devotes himself to preparing "Ruth for some great and Herculean tasks," i.e., to awakening her to the sense of self-identity and the pursuit of a new life. (198) He even steals books—books ranging from mythology through geography to romantic rebellion—from the white library to broaden Ruth's horizons and stir her imaginations. He also informs her with the episodes from the *Bible*, especially those such as the story of Exodus that can empower her with the compelling myth of an oppressed people who triumph over difficult circumstances through the strength of their will and spirit, so that she can avoid the "numbness" which has blighted so much of his own life. On Ruth's sixteenth birthday he buys her an automobile—an image of power and independence—and begins saving money for her further studies at college. In so doing, Grange suggests his affirmation of her growing independence and his understanding of her desire to leave home. In a word, Grange tries to give everything he could gain to Ruth and ultimately sacrifices himself for her secure and happy future. Thus Grange's recovery of the meaningful roles of farmer, and husband and father in particular results in his regeneration. Starting a "third" life, Grange takes a decisive step toward the regain of his manhood and humanity. Simultaneously Grange learns that his freedom depends on relation, not on isolated autonomy.

If love and responsibility are crucial for a person to regenerate, then forgiveness is indispensable. Living with Ruth and redeemed by his relationship with her, Grange realizes that hatred is not productive. Therefore he abandons his hate and seeks to stop the cycle of evil. Bit by bit, he learns to forgive and understands how to improve one's self and soul, as he once explains to Brownfield who is still on the way to dehumanization in spite of his experiences both in and out of prison:

> By George, I *know* the danger of putting all the blame on somebody else for the mess you make out of your life. I fell into the trap myself! And I'm bound to believe that that's the way the white folks can corrupt you even when you done held up before. 'Cause when they got you thinking that they're to blame for *every*thing they have you thinking they's some kind of gods! You can't do nothing wrong without them being behind it. You gits just as weak as water, no feeling of doing nothing yourself. Then you begins to think up evil and begins to destroy everybody around you, and you blames it on the crackers. *Shit*!

> Nobody's as powerful as we make them out to be. We got our own *souls*, don't we? (207, italics original)

It is Grange's first life and his journey to the North that teach him the lesson that he cannot attribute all his failure to be a man to the white man and that too much blaming other men for his own degradation can only make them the power of gods and himself their slave. Forgiveness can save black males and return their manhood. Donna Haisty Winchell (1992: 54) points out that "the willingness to forgive, like the willingness to accept blame, ultimately must be measured in terms of the strength of the individual soul." Both Brownfield and Grange in his first and second lives fail to forgive. They vent their frustrations on their women, only to become the brutes their white bosses think them to be. Their manhood and humanity are denied; their souls spoilt. However, while Grange, redeemed by Ruth and by his own introspection, stops his soul from being completely spoilt by regaining the ability to forgive, Brownfield gets no rebirth and loses his scope for regenerating. Thus through Grange, Walker articulates that the key to survival is to keep some corner of one's soul sacred from the external abuses and destructions.

Grange's regeneration also demonstrates strongly in his attitude toward the white couple that, along with a black couple, come to persuade him to register to vote, and in his gladness to learn on the TV that the marchers consider it possible to change the "crackers"' minds. When he is informed by the two couples that blacks are voting in Green County and will soon run for office, he admires them for such a courageous idealistic belief (though he remains skeptical). Therefore, he gives a watermelon to the two couples, white and black, when they depart, and "when he waved good-bye he waved to all of them." (A. Walker, 1970: 242) Since the young believe that even the "crackers" are likely to be changed, Grange begins to dream that there would be such a day when change occurs to people like Brownfield. Yet his dream never comes true. To prevent Ruth from emotional suffering, Grange is forced to shoot Brownfield to death at the cost of his own life. For Brownfield's purpose of getting Ruth back is clear: Ruth is his daughter, so she is in his possession. Besides, he still can't forgive Grange for deserting him and, in so doing, wants to take vengeance on his father.

Facing the same challenge, Brownfield and Grange end up differently: the former dies physically as well as spiritually but the latter, though physically dead, remains alive spiritually. Grange instills his hope, his new life in his granddaughter Ruth. As Melissa Walker (1991: 118) says, the ending of the novel focuses "on this old man, who, having transformed his own life and proved that it is possible for people to change, has used that life to give Ruth a chance". Through his action, Grange proves his belief: "Survival was not everything. … But to survive *whole* was what he wanted for Ruth." (A. Walker, 1970: 214, italics original) Up to this point, Grange becomes a synthesis of Walker's individual values—being introspective and analytical and capable of transcending the corrupting abuses of any external, destructive forces as he examines himself. He represents Walker's ideal: At whatever costs, all peoples in the world have the right and capability to undertake changes and reach the spiritual survival if they have the courage and imagination to move toward any changes. They may be poor, black, and uneducated, it is true, but they are able to live in spiritual health and beauty with their inner selves blossoming.

4.2.2 Truman's Potential for a Personal Change: A Hope for the Survival Whole

The analysis in 4.1.2 shows that Truman at once has the flaws of black sexists like Eddie and Mr. Raymonds, and the limitations of the civil rights activists like Tommy. He can, in effect, be regarded as a collective image, in whom all the novel's minor characters can find their own shadows. In other words, Truman is an epitome of the black men in the heyday of the Civil Rights Movement. His change or potential for change has a representative significance. Almost all the negative aspects of the 1960s' black men—the traditional middle-class black males' unequal treatment of or discrimination against black women (e.g. in Eddie and Mr. Raymonds), the black intellectuals' possible falseness, meanness and shamelessness (e. g. in Mr. Raymonds), and the civil rights activists' over-correction in their relationship between blacks and whites (e. g. in Tommy Odd)—get overcome through the personal struggle of Truman for his self-improvement. Thus Walker arouses a great hope in the minds of black people through portraying the collective image Truman's self-healing process.

4.2.2.1 Truman's Marriage and His Later Relationship with Meridian: The Attempts to Escape from the Social Confines

In Truman we can see the dual character of the black males in the period of the Civil Rights Movement—the limitations of a social transformation and the potential for a personal change. Therefore, we cannot simply accept Truman's acts such as his first courting the blonde girl Lynne and later discarding her after marriage as irresponsibility or lack of manhood. In a way, they witness Truman's attempts to fulfill his personal values matching up to his exceptional identity.

Different from Brownfield, he is a "new" man, "the first of the Civil Rights workers", and possesses the positive aspect of a civil rights activist—the great courage to withstand the pressure on interracial marriage from both white and black, which is requisite when he decides to marry Lynne. If his desertion of Lynne suggests that he is conditioned by racial hatred, then his marriage to her at least proves his attempt to escape from such confines. Since the first appearance of slavery in the Southern plantation, black people have been inculcated with the ideology of "white supremacy." Having lived under the pressure of their white masters for generations they, on the one hand, get used to their own status of servitude, but, on the other hand, their hatred for the white race becomes deep-rooted. Hence Truman's marriage to Lynne is of political significance. It not only breaks the taboo against interracial marriage in the American society but also proves the possibility of the equal relationship between whites and blacks. Truman's action brings hopes to the elimination of the ingrained Euro-American racism. In this regard, Truman is worth his identity of a civil rights activist. So even though Truman's marriage to Lynne closes with failure, due to Truman's own inherent weakness and the racial pressure from both his friends and the white race, his courage to attempt the firsts needs affirming and deserves somewhat of respect.

Also, Truman's discarding Lynne and return to Meridian, to some extent, suggests that he is likely to face up to his parentage and, accordingly, lays the foundation of his personal change. Depressed by the failure of his marriage to Lynne, Truman withdraws from the struggle for social justice and goes to New York where he sets up a studio and continues with his painting in which he achieves success. A successful painter accompanied by a young blonde girl—after Lynne he again finds a blonde lover—Truman does not feel as happy and content as he expects. Without Meridian, he seems bereft of something. He also feels puzzled: Why does she reject his feelings for her since she has already forgiven his past irresponsibility? Why does she stick to revolution now that "no one is thinking about these things any more"? (A. Walker, 1976: 188) The more Truman thinks about Meridian, the more puzzled he feels. Meridian emerges as a mystery to him. Therefore, now and then, he comes back to her, "whom he imagined as more calm, predictable" and whose "brown strength … would not mind being as a resource for someone else." (141) Being with her, he finds that "he wanted her still, but would not have wanted … to make love to her." (141) As a consequence of these visits, Truman's love for Meridian begins changing. He no longer regards her as only a black female but rather as a lifeboat in his spiritual life. "He knew that in this woman who never seemed to hurry, and whom he was destined to pursue, the future might be short, but memory was very long." (141) Truman's recurrent visits to Meridian symbolize his search for meaning in his own life and for an understanding of Meridian's life, and thus can be regarded as Truman's journey toward mature self-knowledge, on which he comes to understand the meaning of heroism, social activism, self-sacrifice, and moral judgments. This understanding in turn leads to the change of Truman's view on Meridian, which implies his tendency to transcend the white androcentric discourse and achieve oneness with his people. Now he finds that "existing a few days in Meridian's presence was the best that he could do." (143)

On the basis of such a tendency, Truman is able to establish his relationship with Meridian in terms of equality. In the third part of the novel, the two sit discussing about revolution. An atmosphere of calmness and peace prevails. Each speaks out his/her mind freely. By so doing, Truman gets a further understanding of Meridian and of her insisting on the struggle for social justice, which forms a striking contrast with his once pragmatic point of view that "when the time comes, trust yourself to do the right thing." (189) It suddenly dawns on him that the very constant struggle of Meridian separates her from the others who in the end "did what they had to do to survive," who "acquiesced," "rebelled," "sold out," "shot it out," or "simply drifted with the current of the time, whatever it was," and who "didn't endanger life and limb agonizing over what they would lose." (189) In this difference between Meridian and other revolutionaries, Truman discovers a "new" Meridian whom he has ignored before, a great Meridian who devotes herself to the liberation of the black community heedless of her personal safety, and a model Meridian who sets him reconsidering his own history and status quo. By depicting such a discovery Ms. Walker actually presents a positively changing Truman, who casts off the traditional masculinist ideology and determines to go after Meridian and mend his way sincerely. As Alice Walker (191) puts it, "Truman was always looking for Meridian, even when he didn't know it. He was always finding her, as if she pulled him by an invisible string." This "invisible string" is Meridian's personal values and their common goal of social transformation. "But though he always found her, she was never what he expected." (191) The common goal now links them together, but Truman still needs a thorough change in his personality to undertake the task of struggling for wholeness.

4.2.2.2 Truman's Pilgrimage to the South: The Start of Self-healing

Truman's return to the South and joining Meridian in a campaign for the voter registration marks his recovery of manhood and humanity. Following Meridian, he visits the ordinary black people from door to door to awaken them to a sense of franchise, a sense of involvement in the country's affairs. In the encounters with people like Treasure Sisters, and the devoted black family where the woman is dying, Truman gets the firsthand experience of Meridian's genuine concern for black people. Influenced by her true feelings, and touched by his people's afflictions, he throws himself into the voter registration more on his own initiative. For instance, on the visit to a family who earn their living only by selling waste newspapers to "folks with fireplaces" in the wintertime, Truman sees with his own eyes under what conditions the family are living: "In winter the house must be freezing, thought Truman, looking at the cracks in the walls; and now, in spring, it was full of flies." (204) To change such circumstances black people must decide their own destinies personally, and winning the right to vote is the key to arriving at a solution. He patiently interprets for the husband what good voting would bring him and his family: "free medicine for your wife," "a hospital that'll take black people through the front door, a good school for Johnny Jr. and a job no one can take away." (205) Probably, voting won't get all these specific advantages in a short time. But it is the beginning of the use of one's voice, as Meridian adds. From Meridian and from his personal participation Truman gets to understand fully that the significance of his and Meridian's work is to make black people accustomed to using their own voices. What's more, they manage to help these people solve matters of pressing urgency, such as bringing Johnny and his family two bags of food before leaving them, and taking Miss Treasure to a doctor to convince her of not being pregnant.

If Truman's participation in the voter registration arouses his sense of responsibility for the black race as a whole, his encounter with the thirteen-year-old child who is in prison for murdering her baby awakens his sympathy for females in particular and his conscience as a man. After the visit, "Truman lay as if slaughtered, feeling a warmth, as of hot blood, wash over him. *Shame*. But for what? For whom? What had he done?" (213, italics original) It is the first time that he feels such a strong sense of shame. Witnessing the child's innocence, ignorance and suffering in particular, Truman cannot help thinking of his past—what he has done to Meridian and Lynne and what the women have suffered from his misdeeds. He is so tortured by his introspection that that night his "dreams escaped from his lips to make a moaning, crying song." (213) Up to this point, Walker has succeeded in presenting a "true man" who is worthy of the name "Truman." Out of the once selfish hypocrite grows an authentic self. He is "beginning to experience moments with Meridian when he felt intensely maternal" by wiping "her forehead with a cloth soaked in cold water." (213) He also adopts a conciliatory attitude toward Lynne by offering her a brotherly-sisterly love. Concomitant with the personal change of Truman, an atmosphere of forgiveness pervades the end of the novel. In such an atmosphere, Truman accepts one of Meridian's poems as his principle for action:

> i want to put an end to guilt
> i want to put and [*sic*] end to shame
> whatever you have done my sister
> (my brother)
> know i wish to forgive you
> love you
> … (213)

As Karen F. Stein (1986: 136) once points out, "[t]o be 'in process' is to grow, to develop." Truman's pilgrimage to Meridian and to the South is a manifestation of his personal change, his search for truth, which leads to his commitment to black people. "By so doing, Truman accepts his personal duty towards all blacks, discovers his own meaning, and commits his life in love to both present and future generations." (Davis, 1984: 50) At the end of the novel, while Meridian is leaving for still other crusades, she, in effect, leaves Truman struggling to experience self-discovery and rebirth by himself, just as Meridian writes in her poem, "and we, cast out alone to heal/ and re-create/ ourselves." (A. Walker, 1976: 213) Thus far, Truman's destination is indicated. "He climbed shakily into Meridian's sleeping bag" and pulls her cap upon his head. (220) In this way, Truman accepts the long process of Meridian's struggle as his own. Understanding well the source of Meridian's vitality and the ultimate value of his life, he knows that his people "would wait patiently for him to perform, to take them along the next guideless step." (220)

Although Ms. Walker does not make Truman's quest clear in the ending, she does instill hope in Truman, who is likely to heal his psychic split and achieve a rebirth of spirit as Meridian has done. By following Meridian's model and implying that he is now going to see the world from her perspective and to see her within a new context which no longer obscures his vision, Truman virtually transcends the logo-centric discourse, in which men have traditionally exerted power, and further undermines racist domination. Susan Willis (1990: 125) points out, "the transition from Meridian to Truman lifts the book out of its sexual polarization and suggests that everyone regardless of socially ascribed sex roles, must work to deessentialize sex. Now it will be Truman who works for the community and in its care to bring the collective dream into being." In depicting Truman's slow, painful and even uncertain confrontation of self, Ms. Walker manages to emphasize that the hope for social justices "inheres not merely in political change, but in personal transformation" as well. (Stein, 1986: 130)

4.2.3 Albert and Harpo's Self-healing and Samuel's Virtue: The Bright Future of Black Males

The black androcentric discourse is so ingrained in black males that it is consciously passed on from father to son, from generation to generation in the black community, and that it deprives black men of their humanity and soul and causes domestic violence and rupture of marriage. Through the description of its destruction to black females, to black males themselves, and to the black race as a whole, Alice Walker aims at awakening the black race and black males in particular to the detriment of patriarchal supremacy and to a sense of responsibility. Only when black males realize their guilt for black females can they determine to throw off the masculinist stereotypes and undergo a personal change. In *The Color Purple*, as in both *The Third Life of Grange Copeland* and *Meridian*, Walker endows the male characters like Albert and Harpo with the potential for self-redemption.

4.2.3.1 From "Mr. ——" to "Albert": The Cruel Husband's Rebirth

One principle theme of *The Color Purple* is "love redeems, meanness kills." (Prescott, 1982: 67) Mr. —— is saved from total failure as a human being by his irrational but sincere love for Shug Avery. It is his love for Shug that maintains his last bit of humanity. When he and Shug are courting, Albert would allow Shug to put on his pants and he himself wears Shug's dress. This implies his subconscious acceptance of equality between himself and Shug, or between male and female in general. When Shug is sick, he brings her home to be looked after. This does demonstrate his responsibility for love, though it simultaneously denies his wife's existence. It is exactly the responsibility for love and the subconscious acknowledgement of equality between the sexes that breed the potential in Mr. —— for the rebirth of a new natural man, Albert.

Mr. ——'s transformation begins with Celie's leaving him for Memphis and her unexpected leave-taking curse that disempowers him. In the patriarchal context Celie's overt curse undermines Mr. ——'s status as a man, therefore further threatens his existence. Much too stricken spiritually, he gets "shut up in the house …[and] wouldn't let nobody in until finally Harpo force his way in." (231) If Mr. ——'s love for Shug maintains his potential for changing, then it is Harpo's care and love that set Mr. —— confronting his mistakes and commencing his healing process: "Harpo went up there plenty nights to sleep with him" and "made him send you (Celie) the rest of your sister's (Nettie's) letters" so that "[r]ight after that he start to improve." (231) The next time Celie meets him at the funeral of Sofia's mother, he looks "clean" with "his skin shin[ing]" and "his hair brush[ed] back." He consoles Sofia by "whisper[ing] something to her and pat[ting] her shoulder." (229) Within the family, Mr. —— experiences the warmth of being loved and learns how to love the others. To help Harpo's daughter Henrietta recover from the blood disease, he, like many others in the community, tries every means—"He dream up his own little sneaky recipes. For instance, one time he hid yarns in peanut butter"—to feed her yarns that are thought to be able to cure the disease. (259) He comes to realize his guilt for his children's degradation, and tries "to do something bout my (his) children" as compensation for his previous mistakes. (289) As a rule, what is indispensable in the healing process of an oppressor also contains the change of his attitude toward physical labor. Mr. —— is no exception in this aspect. After Celie's leaving, Mr. —— not only begins doing housework like cleaning, cooking and washing but goes in for farm work as well. "He work real hard… out there in the field from sunup to sundown," Sofia informs Celie, "and clean that house just like a woman." (229) By so doing, the formerly lazy, listless and emotionless patriarch turns to a hardworking, vigorous and compassionate senior, to a real man who earns his own living and takes the responsibility for his evils and the suffering he inflicts on his family members.

As bell hooks (1993: 288) puts it, Mr. —— "moves from male oppressor to enlightened being, willingly surrendering his attachment to the phallocentric social order reinforced by the sexual oppression of women." The most significant transformation he fulfills lies in his respect for and understanding of his wife Celie. He gets treating her as an equal being instead of a maid, or an occasional sexual convenience as before. Even Celie herself has to acknowledge that "I don't hate him" and "when you talk to him now he really listen" and "Mr. —— seem to be the only one understand my feeling" when she feels depressed over Shug's absence. (267, 266) Throwing off the imprisonment of the traditional masculinist ideology, Mr. —— emerges as "a natural man," who discards the "unnatural" treatment, such as abuse and oppression, of women. (267) He confesses to Celie his maltreatment of and compassion for his first wife, saying "both of us (he and Shug) messed over my first wife a scanless. And she never told nobody. Plus, she didn't have nobody to tell. After they married her off to me her folks behave like they'd throwed her down a well. Or off the face of the earth." (277) Here we see a shadow of Grange Copeland, a moody introspectionist, sincere and genuine. It is Mr. ——'s understanding and genuineness that win Celie's forgiveness and friendship. Near the end of the novel Celie finally calls him by name and Mr. —— is able to discover "a good company" in Celie. (282) They would spend their evenings together, sitting on the porch, sewing and talking. The scene in which Mr. —— is listening to Celie telling the Adam and Eve story shows how greatly their relationship has changed and improved.

As an autonomous, genuine and human "Albert" revives from that once cruel and abusive patriarchal authority "Mr. ——," he gets a full understanding of love. He once states it movingly, "I start to wonder why us need love. … I think us here to wonder. … The more I wonder, the more I love. … [And people start to love me back.] Harpo seem to love me. Sofia and the children." (290) It eventually dawns on Albert that life is overflowing with love and that only respect and understanding earn love and love in turn intensifies understanding and respect. He comes to acknowledge Celie's independence and integrity as a person by both respecting Celie's previous choice and participating in her work as a helpmate, "patterning a shirt for folks to wear with my (Celie's) pants." (290) He even carves Celie, with the shells he collects and treasures, a purple frog, an emblem of her feelings about men and her impression of her rapist. In this way, Albert reinforces their already established friendship and understanding. It is Albert's company and understanding that comfort Celie when Shug, the only person who has loved Celie except Nettie, leaves her. Walker (278) presents us how well Albert understands Celie's feelings and to what extent they depend on each other: With the words—"I'm real sorry she left you, Celie. I remember how I felt when she left me"—"the old devil put his arms around me (Celie) and just stood there on the porch with me real quiet. Way after while I bent my stiff neck onto his shoulder. Here us is, I thought, two old fools left over from love, keeping each other company under the stars." Thus in the whole healing process of Albert, Walker tends to manifest that it is possible for the most unpromising of black men to change their day-to-day behavior that black women feel to be oppressive. But to ensure such happenings black men must first realize their own evils and have the tendency to undergo self-healing. Only when they discard the traditional masculinist ideology and treat women as equal beings can they achieve their spiritual survival, can they establish a friendly and harmonious relationship with black women.

4.2.3.2 Harpo's Survival: The Regain of Humanity

Compared with his father Albert's transformation, Harpo's change is more believable. For if Mr. ——'s cruelty is inherent and ingrained in the patriarchal supremacy, Harpo's violence seems to be the product of vanity. During the first three years after their marriage, Harpo is happy, whistling and singing all day, with the non-traditional gender roles—Sofia is "out in the fields or fooling with animals. Even chopping wood," while Harpo loves "cooking and cleaning and doing little things round the house." (62 – 63) "It seems so natural to him," just as Sofia once tells Celie. However, Mr. ——'s warning that "she going to switch the traces on you" appears to hurt his so-called male dignity. Since then, Harpo has begun his attempt to conquer Sofia to prevent himself from losing his face. Therefore, Harpo's brutality is not out of any grievances or a loveless marriage—both are the case with his father—but out of the outside force or, to be more exact, out of his father's pressure. In other words, Harpo is forced into maltreatment of his wife. With Celie's leaving, this outside force is collapsed—Mr. —— himself is faced with a spiritual crisis. Harpo's inherent quality naturally manifests itself.

The rehabilitation of Harpo's self starts with his efforts to look after his almost broken-down father in a manner that he would have rejected as "woman's work." Seeing "Mr. —— live like a pig [and] shut up in the house so much it stunk," Harpo does not wait but "force his way in. Clean the house, got food. Give his daddy a bath." (231) In this way, he consciously accepts the responsibility of a son regardless of his father's former irresponsibility for him. He devotes all his energies to his father's recovery. Sofia recalls:

> Harpo went up there plenty nights to sleep with him. … Mr. —— would be all cram up in a corner of the bed. Eyes clamp on different pieces of furniture, see if they move in his

> direction. You know how little he is, … And how big and stout Harpo is. Well, one night I walked up to tell Harpo something—and the two of them was just laying there on the bed fast asleep. Harpo holding his daddy in his arms. (231)

By comparison between the size of Harpo and that of his father, Walker presents the difference of their inner development. For Harpo awakens and matures and is growing into a real human being before his father does. With his father in his arms, Harpo breaks the restriction of gender roles: Like a mother/female, he nurses his father into a healthy being. That Harpo can openly demonstrate his capacity for tenderness proves the revival of his humanity, of his love. His later persuading his father into sending Nettie's letters to Celie suggests the possibility of his respect for women, and of his equal treatment of his wife. On such a basis, he and Sofia reestablish their relationship. Sofia describes it thus: "After that, I start to feel again for Harpo … [a] nd pretty soon us start work on our new house." (231)

Their new relationship is reinforced by Harpo's respect for his wife's decisions. The changed Harpo no longer considers it as a shame to allow his wife to do things of her own will. When Celie asks him whether he minds Sofia going out to work as a clerk at Celie's store, Harpo replies: "what I'm gon mind for? … It seem to make her happy. And I can take care of anything come up at home. Anyhow, … Sofia got me a little help for when Henrietta need anything special to eat or git sick." (288) By working as a househusband and allowing Sofia to work as a storekeeper Harpo has completely repudiated the traditional patriarchal codes and acknowledged Sofia as an equal and thinking being. By valuing her decision as well as her work, he shows his respect for Sofia's human dignity, which consequently earns Sofia's love. Thus another flawed black man succeeds in reaching the goal of the spiritual survival.

4.2.3.3 Samuel's Perfection: A Balanced Complement to Alphonso's Evils

If Alphonso, like Brownfield in *The Third Life of Grange Copeland*, is a downright scoundrel, representing the negatives of the black community and indisputably proving the urgency of self-development of black males, his friend Samuel stands out as a striking antithesis to him and is pregnant with a bright future for the spiritual survival of the black race. He not only acts as "a voice of rationality and caution" but as an emotional and reliable husband/father as well. (Kaplan, 1996: 132) Throughout the novel, Samuel is functioning as a balanced complement to Alphonso: He succeeds just where Alphonso fails; he possesses just what Alphonso lacks. As a womanist, Walker is fully confident of the realization of the survival whole of the black race in the transformation of every individual and the social change. Yet here are still Brownfield, Alphonso and the like who could not find anything of value within themselves except being white men's tools and, consequently, have no courage to imagine a life without the existence of white people acting as a foil. To put it simply, they refuse to change and to uplift their manhood. To bring hope to her people, Walker creates comparatively perfect characters to compensate for the destructive influence of the kind of males like Alphonso. In other words, taking the black community as a whole and one individual as a continuity of another (e. g. Samuel as a continuity of Alphonso), Ms. Walker endows every male individual with the possibility and fulfillment of the spiritual survival. In this sense, Alphonso also gets redeemed and survives in the image of Samuel.

In contrast to Alphonso's evils, Samuel is a synthesis of black males' virtues. He appears as a large, black, kind and gentle man of a kind of ease with which he gets on with women. "[H]e has the most thoughtful and gentle brown eyes. When he says something it settles you, because he never says anything off the top of his head and he's never out to dampen your spirit or to hurt." (A. Walker, 1982: 144) Contrary to Alphonso's abuse and maltreatment of his wife, Samuel is a touching person and natural comforter. The relationship between Samuel and his wife Corrine is an equal one. In a letter to Celie, Nettie describes thus: "Corrine and Samuel have a wonderful marriage." "Corrine is a lucky woman to have him as her husband." (139, 144) It is true, Samuel loves his wife and never treats her as a subservient being. In their husband-wife relationship, one can always sense Samuel's generosity and understanding that an ideal husband is supposed to possess: To solve the trouble that they cannot have their own children, he adopts Celie's son and daughter without any complaint to his wife. Later, even when Corrine, influenced by the Olinka women, began suspecting that he and Nettie might be the children's biological parents, he, instead of getting angry at being wronged by his wife, patiently tells her all the details he knows. As he later explains to Nettie, "[h]e never told Corrine about the man or about the children's 'mother' [before] because he hadn't wanted any sadness to cloud her (Corrine's) happiness." (182) In actuality, Samuel loves his wife so deeply that, when Corrine died, he "is like someone lost." Nettie thus writes, "I don't believe they've spent a night apart since their marriage." (196)

As an incarnation of ideal black males, Samuel presents his kindness and understanding not only in the husband-wife relationship but also in his treatment of other black women like Nettie. Sexually troubled by her father Alphonso, who, Nettie later knows, is only her stepfather, Nettie goes to Samuel for help. Though not knowing her before, he accepts Nettie as a member of his family and manages to offer her a secure life. In this sense, Samuel acts as a substitute for Nettie's father, or to be more exact, for her stepfather Alphonso. As Alphonso's former friend, Samuel plays the role of Alphonso's deputy from the very beginning. He adopts Celie's children fathered by Alphonso and becomes their real father in the social respect. Since Nettie is accepted as the children's biological mother by Samuel at first in place of her sister Celie, Walker obviously intends to create Samuel as an image with a double role in Nettie's life just like Alphonso in Celie's life, to see how "Alphonso" is improved and redeemed in the image of "Samuel." In contrast to Alphonso's never having a kind word to say to Celie, Samuel would like to tell Nettie almost everything about himself and Corrine and about their past to cherish his memory of his dead wife. Furthermore, he would satisfy Nettie's need for a listener: "[He] asked me to tell him about you," Nettie writes to Celie, "and words poured out like water. I was dying to tell someone about us." (197 – 98) In this way, he's involved in Nettie's life as a rescuer both physically and psychologically. Till now, Walker succeeds in portraying Samuel as a rational and reliable emotional being.

Carla Kaplan (1996: 123) once states: "It is our (the writers') power to create a perfect (or nearly perfect) world which realizes the values of intimacy we prize in the private sphere. This perfect world is, ultimately, in fact, the private sphere writ large." "This perfect world" is undoubtedly the ultimate goal of womanists, and is naturally the one Walker is trying to create in fiction. As a member of Walker's would-be "perfect world," Samuel possesses "the values of intimacy" in his "private sphere"—Take the American society as a whole, the black race can be considered as a private sphere or a small sphere. As a missionary sent to Olinka by the white American authority, he fully understands his "big advantage"—"we are not white. We are not Europeans. We are black like the African themselves. And that we and the Africans will be working for a common goal: the uplift of black people everywhere." (A. Walker, 1982: 143) In other words, Samuel has already been prepared for the demonstration of "intimacy" with the Olinka People before he gets to Olinka. Therefore he does not outlaw the celebration of the roofleaf which the white missionary before them would not let the Olinka have. Thus in Olinka, Samuel works not only as a missionary to try to uplift black people there but much more as a black, fused into the Olinka affairs. When the British strip the Olinka people of their land for a rubber plantation and are about to bring the Olinka to the verge of dying, he and Nettie go to their bishop in England to present "the Olinka's grievances." (238) Though the journey ends in failure, and brings no better understanding from the Olinka who don't accept them "as the brothers they sold" because they are, after all, missionaries from the white world, Samuel's passion for the Olinka is clearly felt in this action and in the angry declaration of this "voice of rationality and caution" that, if they are to remain in Africa, their sole source of action is to join the resistance movement and urge the Olinka to do so as well. (243)

To some extent, Samuel's attempt to be intimate with the Olinka cannot be acknowledged as a success, owing to the Olinka's hostility toward the missionaries from the white world in general, white and black, but it does bring them closer to the Olinka people. He and Nettie begin to move away from patriarchal Christianity and open themselves up to African Spirituality. Just as Nettie tells Celie in another letter, "God is different to us now, after all these years in Africa. More spirit than before, and internal. Most people think he has to look like something or someone—a roofleaf or Christ—but we don't. And not being tied to what God looks like, frees us." (264) As for Samuel's change in faith, what his adopted daughter Olivia recalls in *The Temple of My Familiar* may be regarded as a concise summary: "My Father, Samuel, was a missionary also, but by the time we returned to America he had since lost his faith, not in the spiritual teachings of Jesus, the prophet and human being, but in Christianity as the religion of conquest and domination inflicted on other peoples." (A. Walker, 1989: 146) The essence of Samuel's change in faith is apparently a revolt against the authority of Christianity in human mind and a tendency to undermine the white patriarchal domination in the black community, which is the first step toward the spiritual survival of the black race: Only the harmony in the "private sphere" can make the intimacy in the large world possible.

Walker's success in presenting Samuel as an ideal of the black race also lies in her portrayal of the image as a vulnerable man, capable of tears, of being wrong, of admitting failure. Looking back at his life, in the sense that this journey virtually brings him a spiritual uplift, Samuel comes to a somewhat wrong conclusion that his efforts among the Olinka are, a total failure. He tells Nettie, "[i]t all seem so improbable. … Here I am, an aging man … We failed so utterly." (A. Walker, 1982: 241 – 242) Here we see an old man's frankness and genuineness in face of the unsatisfactory ending after years of efforts: The Olinka show indifference to his every attempt to establish an intimate relationship with them. They refuse to accept Samuel and the others, as Samuel has expected, "as brothers." This disappoints and saddens Samuel so much that he could not help crying in Nettie's arms. In so doing he appears as a success as a human being, as well as a success with women who desire a man who is human like themselves. Up to this point, as a continuity of Alphonso, Samuel has fulfilled his mission of improving the former in accordance with a womanist will, and all that characterizes the stereotype of black males has collapsed through the image Samuel. Thus the womanist ideal of a new black man is set up.

If the healing process of both Albert and Harpo reveals Walker's womanist principle that only adopting sexual egalitarianism can black men be humanized, or in other words, if only gender role-sharing can free black males from the imprisonment of traditional androcentric discourse and fosters love and redemption for them, the complement of Alphonso's evils in Samuel, or rather, the perfection of Samuel declares the great hope of the spiritual survival of black males and the black race as a whole.

The fact that Alice Walker is among the first who break the ice lies not only in her audaciously dealing with the taboos in the black community like family violence in *The Third Life of Grange Copeland*, revolutionary violence in *Meridian* and incest and lesbianism in *The Color Purple*, but also in her persistent concern with the fulfillment of the womanist ideal. Ms. Walker never diverges from the womanist concern about the survival whole or spiritual survival of her characters and her people in general even in presenting the black males as flawed characters and the black women as embodiment of submission and resistance in the three novels. A womanist writer, Walker, as she herself explains, "was brought up to try to see what was wrong and right it" and "was brought up to look at things that are out of joint, out of balance, and try to bring them into balance." (qtd. in S. Wilson, 1993: 369) "To see what was wrong" and reveal the typical shortcomings of black men, she portrays these flawed characters. However, her ultimate purpose is not "to reveal" only but to awaken real and unreflective people burdened with the similar flaws to the damage and destruction their actions have caused and "to right" them. Therefore, Walker's male characters are always vested with the hope and power to change and improve. Her female characters, though sometimes seem to be silently submissive, do not lack for the sense of self-dependence and equality. Instead they are saliently marked by the rebellious spirit. Their different destinies eloquently bear out Walker's claim that the only way out for black women is rising to resist against the conventional restraints.

The regeneration, the self-healing process of Walker's black males, is a hard struggle against the codes of both Eurocentrism and androcentrism. Like other black women writers, Walker sets her characters in a white supremacist patriarchal society and imposes upon them the mission to strive consistently to shake off the strong confines and get equality and freedom. But unlike them, she concerns not just the pain and hardship of black females but that of black males as well. In other words, what is unique in Walker's writing is that her male characters are also victims of the double oppression. Therefore they ought to work hand in hand with black women instead of creating dissensions in their struggle for human rights. For Walker's men, this struggle is not merely for replacing whoever is in power but releasing the spirit, the humanity and manhood that inhabit all life. Her ideal is harmonious coexistence of men and women, of blacks and whites, and, in a large sense, of all the inhabitants on this planet, no matter of what sex and color they are.

In these early novels the redemption and improvement are first undertaken by single individuals since it is these single individuals' evils that bring about the breakdown of experience or identity in private lives and further in the public or social life of the community or of the black race as a whole. Walker holds that individuals are responsible for their own growth, their self-improvement, and the enhancement of all their relationships. Only when the individuals take the responsibility for themselves and undergo the process of self-healing an self-freeing struggle, can they make themselves physically and spiritually healthy and redeemed. Only when the black males achieve a sense of the oneness of creation, can they improve their relationship with their women by accepting them as equal beings and work to rebuild their life in the community together with black females. Similarly, to realize their liberation, the female individuals have no choice but first to enlighten themselves and then to improve their relationship with black men. Separatism means suicide and breeds no future. For Ms. Walker, the ultimate and ideal way of redeeming black people, male and female, is unity and solidarity within the black community.

Return is the developmental imperative in Walker's first three novels, where the personal growth is symbolized by the characters' journey, both geographical and psychological: Grange's return to Baker County regenerates him as a human being with a new mode of consciousness which transforms his life and the lives of others (especially Ruth's); Truman's pilgrimage to the South after Meridian implies his inclination to accept Meridian as his model, which marks his transcendence over the sexual boundaries, and his attempt to undergo spiritual development; Albert's apparent psychological return to black roots is primarily a portent of a healing process, which is represented by his love for and understanding of others.

In brief, Walker sees writing as a way to correct wrongs that she observes in the world, so her works transmit such a message that art is able to make people better, which further demonstrates the author's love for her people, both men and women. It is this love for her people that leads to her belief that black men are inherently good and that, through the use of art, their flaws can be removed and their manhood and humanity can be restored to health. In these three novels Walker affirms her male characters' struggle for survival whole and depicts a promising future for her people, i. e., her womanist utopia, the survival whole of the entire people, a state of oneness with all things. In this sense, rather than being a sign of "enmity" toward black men, her characterization of black males is the strongest reflection of her deep love for them and for black people as a whole. Although her characterization of black females is not so well balanced in terms of womanist ideology—Margaret and Mem in *The Third Life of Grange Copeland* and Celie in *The Color Purple* are created to reveal sexual exploitation in black families while the heroine in *Meridian* is more concerned with the racial issues in black communities—they are enabled to construct the same beautiful new world, in which the dominant values are defined in terms of the womanist criteria—love, freedom, equality rather than the color of skin or sex.

However, there are still a few weaknesses in her portrayal of the male images. Walker excessively emphasizes the individuals' survival, which weakens the extension of survival to the group. The influence of her male characters needs widening to the black community. Moreover, black men created by Walker are recovered only to the extent that they buckle down to housework and let women attend to business. They seem capable of goodness only when they become old like Grange Copeland and Albert, or paralyzed and feminized like Truman Held. In spite of these and/or other weaknesses concerning these novels, Walker's great achievement in creating black male and female images can never be exaggerated from the womanist perspective.

Chapter V Over the Racial and Patriarchal Hegemony: Lesbianism and Sisterhood within Black Women

> What particularly distinguishes Alice Walker in her role as apologist and chronicler for black women is her evolutionary treatment of black women; that is, she sees the experiences of black women as a series of movements from women totally victimized by society and by the men in their lives to the growing developing women whose consciousness allows them to have control over their lives. (M. Washington, 1993: 39)

As "black" and "female" are defined as the negative, and "white" and "male" as the positive, black women are always constituted as objects or as the Other. Circumscribed in a negative space, they neither participate in the white and/or patriarchal discourses nor establish their identity outside white and/or patriarchal definitions. For whites, they, together with black men, are social inferiors. For male blacks, they are housekeepers, maidservants or even sexual tools. The social canon forces upon black women such attributes as silence, obedience, and hardworking. They are dis-empowered in the society and, what's worse, many of them passively accept and blindly succumb to the social convention. Therefore, it is all the more urgent for black women to authorize themselves as women and human beings, namely, to realize their rights, dignity and value both at home and outside in the society; yet it is no easy task for black women to reconstruct themselves, to disengage their black feminine identity from the racial and patriarchal ideology.

As an apologist and spokesperson for black women, Walker faces the challenge of rewriting cultural narratives from a new perspective to awaken black women's self consciousness and stimulate their fighting spirit. In the novels since *The Color Purple*, she seems to emphasize the special power of the black women's alliance/bonding based on sisterhood as well as lesbianism. In Walker's womanist texts lesbianism is of political significance. It, spanning the whole spectrum of women's friendship and sisterly solidarity, subverts the established cultural narratives (i. e., masculine cultural narratives) of femininity and desire. Sisterhood, which literally means friendship and companionship between/among women, serves as an effective way to unite black women and support them in their struggle for independence and liberation. Both are therefore among the recurring themes in Walker's novels like *The Color Purple, Possessing the Secret of Joy, By the Light of My Father's Smile* and/or *Now Is the Time to Open Your Heart*.

5.1 Lesbianism: The Sexual Subversion of the Male Dominance

The term "lesbian" came into being in the late 19th century and was not widely acknowledged and used to refer to the female sodomites until around the 1920s. It originates from the Island of Lesbos, the home of the Greek poetess Sappho, whose poetry celebrates the passion and love between women. Ever since its emergence, the concept "lesbian" has undergone a series of changes and developments. Just as Lisa Duggan (1979: 80) points out, "[m]ost of the material…on the subject of lesbianism…focuses on cause or 'etiology,' characterization, adjustment and even 'cure' of lesbianism. The assumption is made that lesbianism is an individual psychological phenomenon, which can be labeled as pathological and isolated from the social context which defines and controls human sexual behavior." Obviously, at the early stage, lesbianism was used as a clinical term to refer to a mental disease which needs to be cured or an abnormal sexual behavior between two women, which has nothing to do with the social environment and women's living status. Then in 1980 the concept got expanded by

Adrienne Rich's use of "lesbian continuum" instead of "lesbianism." In the essay "Compulsory Heterosexuality and Lesbian Existence," Rich (1980: 648) writes:

> I mean the term lesbian continuum to include a range—through each woman's life and throughout history—of woman-identified experience; not simply the fact that a woman has had or consciously desired genital sexual experience with another woman. If we expand it to embrace many more forms of primary intensity between and among women, including the sharing of a rich inner life, the bonding against male tyranny, the giving and receiving of practical and political support... we begin to grasp breadths of female history and psychology which have lain out of reach as a consequence of limited, mostly clinical, definitions of "lesbianism."

For Rich, lesbianism not simply indicates two women's love and sexual relationship but the sharing of woman-identified life and experience between/among a group of women as well. Or rather, it should be interpreted as more a spiritual bonding between/among women than an erotic behavior between two females, for it is closely related to and firmly grounded in the social context. In this sense, lesbianism is both normal and healthy. Rich's definition is undoubtedly inclusive; yet this inclusiveness risks blurring the distinctions between lesbian and non-lesbian relationships.

Almost immediately came a different voice from Catherine R. Stimpson, who claims that "desire must be there and at least somewhat embodied" and "[t]hat carnality distinguished it from gestures of political sympathy for homosexuals and from affectionate friendships in which women enjoy each other, support each other and commingle their sense of identity and well-being." (qtd. in Zimmerman, 1981: 456) By stressing the sexual desire between women, Stimpson limits lesbianism to a physiological phenomenon, eliminating the social, spiritual and psychological or pathological tendency, and naturally stands on the opposite side of Adrienne Rich. Stimpson's definition may be described as exclusive. In this regard, Lillian Faderman, another feminist, goes in between. For Faderman, "[l]esbian describes a relationship in which two women's strongest emotions and affections are directed forward each other. Sexual contact may be a part of the relationship to a greater or lesser degree or it may be entirely absent. By preference the two women spend most of their time together and share most aspects of their lives with each other." (qtd. in Zimmerman, 1981: 457) Like Stimpson, she confines lesbianism to the relationship between two women; unlike Stimpson, she does not think that the lesbian relationship may be fully expressed in the sexual contact. She agrees with Rich that lesbianism connotates sexual and spiritual, or physical and emotional, or physiological and psychological relationships. Nevertheless, Faderman does not take the social context into consideration. The lesbian relationship, in her eyes, is still isolated and personal.

Thus before Alice Walker, lesbian/lesbianism has been defined either as a pathological condition in Freudian psychiatry, or a form of sexual deviancy equivalent of female sodomy, or simply a sexual preference and alternative life style, or the sharing of woman-identified experience and emotions. Diversified as they are, these definitions cross at one point: a lesbian is "a woman who desires and/or wants to be desired by another woman." (Rapi, 1993: 148) This common ground implies that there exists the possibility of intimacy, companionship and/or support between women, which will threat and subvert the male-dominated heterosexual relationship. Charlotte Bunch, an advocate of international attention to women's issues, once states that "[l]esbianism and feminism are both about women loving and supporting women revolving against the so-called supremacy of men and the patriarchal institutions that control us." (qtd. in Kerber, 2002: 277) Here lies the reason why many feminists are themselves lesbians or supporters of lesbianism. Alice Walker is such a feminist or womanist. Her definition of a womanist in 1983—"a woman who loves other women, sexually and/or nonsexually," who "[a]ppreciates and prefers women's culture, women's emotional flexibility… and women's strength," who "[s]ometimes loves individual men, sexually and/or nonsexually" and is "[c]ommitted to survival and wholeness of entire people," and who is "[n]ot a separatist" and "[t]raditionally universalist"—not only presents her political stand but also implies her sexual orientation or at least her emotional inclination to women's (to be more exact, black women's) strength and culture. (A. Walker, 1983: xi) To some degree, Walker's womanism is an extender and a synthesis of the previous definitions of lesbianism, especially of Adrienne Rich's "lesbian continuum." Walker's broadens to a holistic, radical feminist embrace of love of black people, male and female, and of the whole world. Evidently, Walker's aim is to subvert the male dominance so as to build up a harmonious utopia. This is well expressed particularly in her novels since *The Color Purple*.

5.1.1 Lesbian Salvation in *The Color Purple*: Celie's Relationship with Shug

According to Walker and other lesbian feminists, women's subordinance in the heterosexual relationships greatly affects their position in the familial and social lives. Equality and autonomy in sexual behaviors are instrumental in the formation of an independent personality. Lesbians, bonding against male tyranny, enjoy intimacy and affectionate friendship, support and encourage each other, and therefore gain strength and self-confidence. Just as what Charlotte Bunch summarizes, "[b]eing a lesbian means ending identification with, allegiance to, dependence on, and support of heterosexuality. It means ending your personal stake in the male world so that you join women individually and collectively in the struggle to end oppression." (Bunch, 1987: 166) In *The Color Purple*, Celie's change and awakening are attributed to Shug's love and sexual inspiration. Without Shug's help and sexual enlightenment, Celie would have been a sexual illiterate and lived numbly. So it is reasonable to say that Shug is Celie's savior.

5.1.1.1 Celie's Numbness and Voicelessness

Heterosexuality is considered normal and legal because it guarantees patriarchy or male dominance, the canon that highlights men's supremacy. It is a long tradition that women are acknowledged as the non-significant Other, for, according to the *Genesis*, the first woman Eve is made from "a supernumerary bone" of the first man Adam. Thus the woman is simply decreed by the man. He is the Subject, absolute, inevitable, essential, perfect, and autonomous while she is the Object, relative, incidental, marginal, imperfect, and dependent. She is called "the sex," by which it means that she appears essentially to him as a sexual being. Julien Benda (1992: 162) once depicts the difference as follows: "The body of man makes sense in itself quite apart from that of woman, whereas the latter seems wanting in significance by itself. Man can think of himself without woman. She cannot think of herself without man." Therefore, as long as patriarchy exists, there will be everlasting inequality in heterosexual relationships. Male-dominant hegemony determines women's subordinate and oppressed status.

Celie is a typical victim in the heterosexual relationships. She has nothing to do but accept the rules and standards set for women in the patriarchal system. She suffers sexually, physically, and psychologically. She has no power to fight against the patriarchs. Before marriage she is forced by her stepfather to work as a sexual surrogate of her sick mother and is therefore frequently raped by him. Then she is transferred to Mr. —— in the name of marriage. Silent, obedient and even numb, Celie bears the suffering without resistance. Nothing ever changes in her life after marriage except that she now serves a different male at night, and that she deals with the different household chore and works in different fields from morning to night. Actually, the ongoing oppression or sexual abuse imposed upon Celie by the patriarchs (first her stepfather, then her husband) makes her numb and voiceless. She learns to materialize herself so as to live.

Celie's first fear and silence come from her stepfather's threat. As a girl of 14, Celie does not know anything about sexual behaviors. So when she is raped by her stepfather, she is feared and confused. She needs to talk about it to someone; yet he threatens her: "You better not never tell nobody but God. It'd kill your mammy." (A. Walker, 1982: 1) Unaware of what has happened to her body and afraid of hurting her sick mother, she eventually chooses to keep silent and tell nobody but to write to God. Even when his stepfather is fed up with her and decides to marry her off, she says nothing and lets him arrange everything.

She has no right to speak out her own will. She knows nothing about the man she will be married to, even about what he is called. She is treated as a commodity which can be totally exchanged. The condition that lures Mr. —— to agree to marry her is that he can take away a cow for free from her stepfather. Furthermore, he is told that she is a good nurse and housekeeper and can work like a man in the fields. Evidently, what Mr. —— wants is not simply a wife but a slave. Therefore, Celie is destined to suffer from her husband's abuse and bullying after marriage.

After she is married to Mr. ——, Celie even loses her feeling of sadness. In the new family, she is naturally regarded as anything but an equal being. In the daytime she works as a housemaid and field hand. At night she is obliged to satisfy her husband's sexual needs. Moreover, "He beat me (Celie) like he beat the children. Cept he don't never hardly beat them. He say, Celie, git the belt. The children be outside the room peeking through the cracks. It all I can do not cry. I make myself wood. I say to myself, Celie, you a tree." (23) Celie does not think of resistance. She tries to make herself acclimatized to and accept her husband's violence. She sees herself as a tree only because wood could neither feel any pain nor get sad. Nevertheless, this does not alleviate her fear of her husband. She does not dare to mention the maltreatment of her husband to anybody. Thus violence successfully maintains Celie's silence. As a matter of fact, violence is an effective mechanism for men to conquer women. Celie is completely mastered by Mr. ——. She is absolutely in compliance with him and has no intent to challenge his authority. When her sister-in-law Kate tells her to fight against men, Celie does not say anything to her but thinks about Nettie: "She fight, she run away. What good it do? I don't fight; I stay where I'm told. But I'm alive." (22) Seeing herself as a tree (i. e., getting herself materialized), Celie shows no human feelings to others: "Patting Harpo back not even like patting a dog. It more like patting another piece of wood. Not a living tree, but a table, a chifferobe. He (Harpo) look at me (Celie). It like he looking at the earth." (31) Physical materialization results in emotional numbness. In Celie the numbness also extends to her sexual life with her husband. As husband and wife, Mr. —— and Celie do not love or like each other. When night comes and Mr. —— needs to release his sexual lust, Celie has no choice but to cooperate with him. Again she sees herself as an object or supposes herself to be someone else, to be Shug, for instance. "I lay there thinking bout Nettie while he on top of me, wonder if she safe. And then I think bout Shug Avery. I know what he doing to me he done to Shug Avery and maybe she like it. I put my arm around him." (13) In effect, Celie has no sexual desire for her husband and of course experiences no sexual pleasure. What she can do to relieve her pain is make herself an object or just keep absentminded.

Celie's fear and repulse of heterosexuality is ascribed to the incest or exactly her stepfather's rape and her husband's sexual abuse. Her cognition of sex is distorted by the male-dominated heterosexuality. Her sexual experience is thus burdened by contradiction and ambivalence. The materialization and absentmindedness actually help Celie bury her identity and body consciousness, which in turn encourages the patriarch's oppression and worsens her own plight. Celie's psychological numbness and her spiritual voicelessness are the consequence of her suffering in the heterosexual relationships.

5.1.1.2 Celie's Awakening and Independence

If the unfortunate heterosexual experience sets Celie in suffering and bondage and thus becomes a lifelong nightmare to her, then lesbianism offers her an opportunity to shake off the patriarchal fetters and enjoy equality and independence and thus marks a turning point in her life. Perhaps that is why Ms. Walker devises the moving but controversial relationship between Celie and Shug Avery, a blues singer. By depicting the lesbianism between Celie and Shug, Walker explicitly emphasizes the positive effect of the woman-to-woman relationship (including the sexual relationship between two women) in the course of women's growth and liberation. As Trudier Harris once states, "[e]ach stage of Celie's transformation and progress on her journey towards happiness and self-esteem is inspired by Shug." (qtd. in Andrews, 2001: 413) From Shug, Celie learns how to love and be loved sexually and non-sexually, what the outside world is like, how to live an independent life, and what the essence of God is in the white religion. It is Shug who enlightens Celie's life.

In the traditional heterosexual system, women are not only acknowledged as the objectification to meet men's sexual needs but also supposed to be saints and their bodies be shrines. They should be ashamed of their sexual desire. Celie does not enjoy love and even hardly knows anything about sexual desire until Shug appears. Celie's first sight of Shug is from the picture brought home by her new stepmother, a young black girl. On seeing the unique woman in the picture, Celie is firmly caught by her glamorous appearance and begins dreaming of her at night. "Shug Avery was a woman. The most beautiful woman I ever saw. She more pretty then my mama. She bout ten thousand times more prettier then me. I see her there in furs. Her face rouge. Her hair like somethin tail. She grinning with her foot up on somebody motorcar. Her eyes serious tho. Sad some. …An all night long I stare at it. An now when I dream, I dream of Shug Avery. She be dress to kill, whirling and laughing." (A. Walker, 1982: 7) Celie's first notion of Shug is that she is beautiful, rich, confident, audacious and autonomous. Therefore, she admires and adores Shug. This admiration and adoration implies Celie's subconscious longing for dignity and individuality, and sets the scene for her taking good care of Shug when Mr. —— brings Shug home as a mistress. When standing face to face with Shug for the first time, "I (Celie) don't move at once, cause I can't. I need to see her eyes. I feel like once I see her eyes my feets can let go the spot where they stuck." (48) Celie is so captivated that she is willing to do angthing for Shug. She takes up the responsibility without any hesitation of attending on Shug who is so ill, even when everyone hits Shug when she is down.

According to the Patriarchal tradition, Shug is a bad woman, who is casual and flippant about life. As a wife, she keeps connected with Mr. —— as his mistress. As a mother, she leaves her children to her mother and spends little time looking after them. As a woman, she does not stay at home and shows herself much in public. This unconventionality brings her curse and condemnation from the black public, especially from the black males. So, like every other woman, she is underprivileged. Yet she earns her own living through singing and stays independent from the male world. Her blues songs bring pleasure and amusement to her audiences, the majority of whom are black males; for black females seldom have the opportunities to turn up in the entertainment venues. Ironically, these black men look down upon Shug the black woman but cannot do without Shug the blues singer. Smart, unconventional and full of rebellious spirit, Shug clearly knows what she expects in her life and is courageous enough to strive for it. Thus, she lives through the prejudice and pressure in the black communities and develops into an independent professional singer. Audacity, rebellion and persistence constitute Shug's personality, which exerts a great influence on Celie's growth and transformation.

As far as marriage is concerned, Shug is unfortunate. She and Albert are in love with each other and tend to get married. Nevertheless, they are broken up by Albert's father, who discriminates against Shug's sexy figure, singing career, independent life, and scandal-plagued experiences, and regards her as the image of siren like Medusa in Greek mythology. As a consequence, Shug enters marriage without love, which is the same story as Celie's. Therefore, to some extent, Shug empathizes with Celie. She shows sympathy for Celie's plight and fully understands Celie's numb and indifferent attitude towards Albert. This also contributes to the two's later intimate relationship.

With Nettie's departure, Celie is completely isolated. Shug's appearance satisfies Celie's curiosity and offers the opportunity to feast her eyes on Shug's beauty, on the one hand. On the other hand, Shug means a potential companion to Celie. Hence Celie accepts Shug as a friend even though she is Albert's (Mr. ——'s) mistress. During Shug's stay in the home, Celie shows enough fondness and softness to her. "I work on her like she a doll or like she Olivia—or like she mama. I comb and pat, comb and pat." (55) The warmth and affection that Celie lavishes upon Shug are both appreciated and rewarded. Shug composes a song titled

"Miss Celie's song," and sings affectionately before her audiences the first time she goes back to work after her recovery. The song dedicated to Celie expresses Shug's sincere thanks, which is of special significance to Celie. It is the "[f]irst time somebody made something and name it after me (Celie)" and therefore the first time that Celie has the consciousness of self-identity. (77)

Their relationship changes and becomes distinct when Shug talks about sex and teaches Celie to recognize and admire her own female body. The heterosexual tradition that stops women from knowing about or looking into their bodies results in Celie's sexual ignorance in spite of the longtime sexual experience. For this reason, Shug asserts that Celie is still a "virgin" and decides to help her discover the mystery of her body. "Listen, she say, right down there in your pussy is a little button that gits real hot when you do you know what with somebody." Then she encourages Celie to look at it directly in the mirror. "She say, Here take this mirror and go look at yourself down there, I bet you never seen it, have you?" (81) In so doing, Shug manages to overcome Celie's shame and awaken her sexual consciousness. With her increasing knowledge of sex and her own body, Celie comes to know to love herself and gradually shows a woman's charm, which in turn attracts Shug, who eventually expresses her affection for Celie: "If you was my wife, she say, I'd cover you up with kisses stead of licks, and work hard for you too." (115) Shug's love and appreciation make Celie confident. She dares to speak out how she feels and is no longer embarrassed when making physical contact with Shug.

> She say, I love you, Miss Celie. And then she haul off and kiss me on the mouth.
>
> Um, she say, like she surprise. I kiss her back, say, um, too. Us kiss and kiss till us can't hardly kiss no more. Then us touch each other.
>
> I don't know nothing about it, I say to Shug.
>
> I don't know much, she say.
>
> Then I feels something real soft and wet on my breast, feel like one of my little lost babies mouth.
>
> Way after while, I act like a little lost baby too. (118)

Shug's caress gives Celie a new experience and opens a different world to her. Little by little, she is not afraid of her husband and dares to curse him when he is found hiding Nettie's letters. Later, regardless of Mr. ——'s hindrance and opposition, she leaves him for Memphis and starts an independent life. In short, it is lesbianism that ultimately emancipates Celie from the patriarchal chains. The lesbian love between Shug and Celie does not mean control and possession but equality, freedom and mutual trust. Accordingly, it creates Celie's self-confidence and self-possession. When talking about her life without Shug at the end of the novel, Celie says calmly, "I know I can live content without Shug… If she come, I be happy. If she don't, I be content." (290)

According to Andrienne Rich, all women are originally and potentially lesbian because a woman first loves another woman and mothers love daughters. She celebrates the power of maternal love and describes lesbian relationships as invested with the intensity and ambivalence of the mother-daughter bond. In this sense, Shug is to Celie what a mother is to a daughter. For, in essence, what Shug does for Celie is what a mother does for her daughter. On the one side, Shug's company gives Celie warmth she has never experienced before and protects her against Mr. ——'s physical abuse and makes it possible for her to feel safe and secure at home. Together with Shug, she enjoys the unwonted peace of mind: "Me and Shug sound asleep. Her back to me, my arms round her waist. What it like? Little like sleeping with mama." (119) On the other side, Shug's love nurtures Celie's strength and confidence and enables her to reach maturity and establish her self-identity. It is generally acknowledged that the mother plays a pivotal role in the formation and development of the daughter's personality. In accordance with the feminist psychoanalysis, the construction of women's identity is bound up with their psychical and cultural experience as daughters. Nancy Chodorow argues that women, by being daughters, learn to affiliate with others, which is triggered by their initial affiliation with their mothers. In a strict sense, Celie does not enjoy the maternal love of her biological mother, who, ignorant of Celie's being raped, suspects Celie and even shows hostility to her. It is with

Shug that Celie experiences such initial affiliation. With Shug's help, Celie finds all the letters from Nettie, which have been intercepted and hidden by Mr. ——, and ultimately obtains the information about Nettie's life and experience in Olinka so that she gets relieved and makes up her mind to leave Mr. —— and start a new life. With Shug's care and affection, Celie comes to open her heart and dwell on her psychical trauma brought about by the bitter experience. If the event of hiding the letters is the direct cause of Celie's determination to leave, Shug's personal charisma, which keeps attracting Celie toward a free and self-sufficient life, gives her enough courage and power to take the vital step. Celie's open revolt against Mr. —— comes when he stops her from leaving home, and is marked by her angry shout and curse:

> I curse you, I say. …Until you do right by me, everything you touch will crumble. … Until you do right by me, I say, everything you even dream about will fail. I give it to him straight, just like it come to me. …Every lick you bit me you will suffer twice, I say. …You better stop talking because all I'm telling you ain't coming just from me. Look like when I open my mouth the air rush in and shape words. …The jail you plan for me is the one in which you will rot, I say. (213)

The roar and curse is loaded with fear and pain, the nightmare that has tortured Celie during the marriage. After being silenced for so many years, Celie eventually realizes her self-existence and utters her own voice as a dignified and independent self: "I'm pore, I'm black, I may be ugly and can't cook… But I'm here." (214)

Leaving home, Celie is freed of the patriarchal shackles, which enables her to go back to her true self and show her initiative and creativity. Walker thinks highly of black women's creativity and acknowledges it as a potential for an individual's growth as well as an impetus for social changes. As uneducated people, black women can embody their creativity only in their daily activities like singing, gardening and sewing. As for Celie's process for self-identity, Walker takes great pains to present the effect of sewing. If quilting works as a site to fortify her relationship with Shug and lays a good foundation for her later awakening and rebirth, her success in sewing pants guarantees her economic independence and thus helps achieve her self-identity. As Walker (1983: 235) claims in *In Search of Our Mothers' Gardens*, to gain independence and achieve self-identity, a black woman has to "have a room of her own (with key and lock) and enough money to support herself." The economic independence is the prerequisite for and guarantee of an independent personality. Shug knows well that the efficient way for a black woman to get out of the patriarchal control is to make a living on her own. So, as Celie's lover and mentor, she takes the responsibility of teaching Celie how to live independently. In Memphis, she first sings high praise for Celie's skill of sewing pants and gradually builds up Celie's self-confidence. Then she encourages and supports Celie to set up a pants-sewing company, "Folkspants, Unlimited," and start her own business. Celie always designs different styles and/or different patterns for different individuals, according to the wearers' jobs and bodily forms. When Mr. —— asks her what is special about her pants, Celie answers that "[a]nybody can wear them." (A. Walker, 1982: 278) For Celie, making pants is not simply a job and a means of subsistence, but also a creative activity. She likes making pants and is good at pants design. Pants-sewing offers her required scope for imagination and creativity, within which she shows her aptitude for sewing and finds the meaning of life. Meanwhile, by making pants, Celie gets acquainted with more and more people and learns how to communicate with them, men and women. In others' preference and compliment for her pants, she gains pleasure and value of life. In a letter to Nettie, Celie writes: "I am so happy. I got love, I got work, I got money, friends and time." (222) Pants-sewing turns a new page in her life. She can master herself. She achieves the survival whole as well as the social respect. Independence in economy makes Celie independent psychologically and spiritually.

Celie's growth and transformation is also attributed to Shug's subvertive interpretation of the Whites' notion of God. Shug's God is not a white. According to Shug, "God ain't a he or she, but a it. …God is everything. …Everything that is or ever was or ever will be. And when you feel that, and be happy to feel that, you've found it." (202 – 203) For "God is inside you and inside everybody else." (202) Shug's words actually suggest that religion is a kind of mental state and exists as is believed and expected. The religious mind determines the religious belief and the creation of God's image, which further impact the destiny of the religious follower. Celie's former miserable life results from her notion of God: "He big and old and tall and graybearded and white." (201) Shug's animist interpretation brings God from high up in heaven down to the natural world and to the human life. God exists everywhere in nature and in the human mind. Celie, who now feels that she herself is part of everything, not separate from nature, does not think God mysterious and far-fetched any longer. She finally understands that she herself is her own God and that she is sure to harvest happiness with her own efforts. Meanwhile, she becomes caring and tolerant. She even forgives her husband and works together with him in her company. Till now, a new confident entrepreneur grows out of the numb, self-based housemaid.

In *Living by the Word*, Walker (1988: 91) writes: "Women loving women, expressing it 'publicly,' if they so choose, is part and parcel of what freedom for women means, just as this is what it means for everyone else." With the support and guidance and love of Shug, Celie finally grows to be content, fulfilled, self-sufficient, and self-actualized. The ugly, timid, voiceless and marginalized black girl is transformed into a confident, successful, independent and integrated woman. During the course of Celie's transformation, Shug fills the roles of a mentor, confidant and lover. It is lesbianism between Celie and Shug that facilitates Celie's awakening and independence.

5.1.2 Lesbian Healing in *By the Light of My Father's Smile*: Susannah's Survival and Pauline's Transformation

"Human sexuality is a mystical moment in the history of the Universe. All the angles and other beings come out to wonder at this." (qtd. in A. Walker, 1998: epigraph) By citing Father Matthew Fox's words from *Natural Grace: Dia-*

logues on Science and Spirituality, Ms. Walker implies her purpose (or at least one of her purposes) of writing *By the Light of My Father's Smile*—celebrating human sexuality. Accordingly, the novel is accepted as an erotic book by some critics and readers as well, and has aroused so much controversy and criticism that the author's underlying intention—to heal the traumatized women through sexual adjustment (i. e., through lesbian relationship)—is almost ignored. As a womanist, Walker regards it as her ultimate target to actualize harmonious coexistence in human society, to which sexual harmony is an imperative step. In *By the Light of My Father's Smile*, the female characters like Susannah, Magdalena and Pauline are all deeply hurt by their fathers, directly or indirectly, when they are in teenage years. After her sexual affair with the Mundo boy Manuelito is found by her father, Magdalena is badly whipped. Accidentally, the whipping is seen by her little sister Susannah, who is even more shocked. This event haunts the daughters and greatly affects their later sexual orientations. Pauline's first sexual experience is an inevitable consequence of her parents and brother's betrayal and their conspiracy with the raper. Heterosexuality becomes her lifelong trauma. Thus the relationship with the other sex has proved her almost insurmountable obstacle, be she Susannah or Magdalena or Pauline. If escape, or rather, no sex is Magdalena's way out, lesbianism is Susannah and Pauline's solution. Since "sexuality is the place where life has definitely fallen into the pit for women," Walker appears to claim that the active way out, is to affirm, acknowledge, and celebrate sexuality between two women. (White, 1998: 45) In other words, for Walker, lesbianism makes for sexual harmony and is thus an effective cure for the women's psychic trauma. In lesbianism Walker emphasizes black women's resistance, the resistance that leads to reconciliation and harmony within black community.

5.1.2.1 Susannah's Regeneration

By the Light of My Father's Smile is set in the patriarchal society, in which sexual initiative is a shame for a female, who is marked by silence and subordination. Although he himself takes great interest in sex and it would drive him crazy not to make love to his wife, Mr. Robinson the father feels it awkward or unnecessary to explain adolescent sex knowledge to his growing-up daughters. Actually, he cannot bear his daughters' sexual awareness. He accepts it as abnormal, feels uneasy about it and tries to nip it in the bud. His uneasiness exemplifies his sexual hypocrisy, which prevents him from affirming his daughters' bodily development and budding sexuality. Family education exerts great influence on children's later development, including their sexual orientations. The father is supposed to play a more important role in children's enlightenment, of which sexual knowledge is an integral part. In terms of Susannah's growth, Mr. Robinson is more an obstructer than a facilitator. Her psychological block to heterosexuality is ascribed to her father's outburst of anger at her sister's sexual act at the age of fifteen, which becomes her lingering fear.

As a girl, Susannah likes her father. She and her sister live happily. Mr. Robinson is a well-educated anthropologist. He loves his wife and daughters. However, all this is based on one thing, that is, Mr Robonsin is the only one who makes rules in the family. As a convinced patriarch, Robinson follows the traditional patriarchal norm, which strictly defines women's body language and dressing manners, in order that he can cultivate in his daughters the so-called femininity, "a certain set of sensibilities, behavioral dispositions, and qualities of mind and character" as well as "a compelling aesthetic of embodiment," or "a mode of enacting and re-enacting received gender norms" as Butler argues. (qtd. in Bartky, 1998: 321) So Robinson's love for his daughters is conditional on their possession of femininity. Susannah, who is "demure, interested in women's things" and embodies more feminine traits, is his favorite, whereas Magdalena, who is bold and "wild" and runs "like the wind" as the Indian boys, and lacks the so-called feminine qualities, is his worry. (A. Walker, 1998: 18) Therefore, when he finds Magdalena's sexual acts with Manuelito, he bursts into anger and beats her soundly.

Robinson's violence is incomprehensible to the daughters and leaves ineradicable scars on both Magdalena the beaten one and Susannah the one peeping the beating through the keyhole. Since "[h]is profession, as he explained to me

(Magdalena) and Susannah, was based on the forgiveness of other people's sins," why couldn't he have forgiven his dear daughter even if she had gone wrong? (23) Is he still their kindly and amiable father? Is this his way of expressing love? The daughters are feared and troubled. Ever since then, there is nothing like happiness in their life any more. They keep their hearts closed against their father. The event of whipping in effect changes their life contrails.

Averse to their father's punishment, they, as if by prior consultation, express their resistance against their father's hegemony by means of mastering their own bodies. Now that they are two individuals, their ways of mastery are certainly different: Magdalena's choice is no-sex life while Susannah's lesbianism. As the topic in this chapter is the latter (i. e., lesbianism), the following paragraphs will focus on Susannah.

A witness of the whipping scene, little Susannah faces an awkward dilemma. For one thing, she has seen "her gentle, compassionate father turn into Godzilla" with her own eyes and cannot pretend that she knows nothing about it. (27) He is like a stranger to her now. "[T]he twig (symbolizing little Susannah) was bent in that moment of her horror and disbelief" so "severely" that she is worried that "she would never be loved back to her daddy again." (27) She begins to have a suspicion that he has been lying to them and that he does not love them at all. She is not likely to be as close to him as before. Her love and sympathy for her sister keeps her away from her father. For another, as a daughter, she feels guilty while she is estranged from her father and treats him coldly. Hence, for a time, Susannah is in a haze of fear and confusion. Or rather, she has lost herself in the father-daughter relationship. Nevertheless, she turns out to be a strong-minded woman after she grows up. Walker (1988: 91) states in *Living by the Word*, "[i]f you are not free to express your love, you are a slave; and anyone who would demand that you enslave yourself by not freely expressing your love is a person with a slaveholder's mentality." Once she becomes aware of the patriarchal nature in her father's act, Susannah seems to accept her father as a figure who wants to enslave her. So she makes every effort to get herself free and be the master of her own body. That is to say, Susannah's way to regeneration witnesses her growth and transformation in sexuality. She first tries out a man-woman relationship with her Greek husband Petros. Although they get along well with each other, what she senses in the sexual politics—that "sex is not meant to be pleasurable to them (women), only to the men fucking them"—disgusts her and makes her reject him. (A. Walker, 1998: 130) Gradually, she finds their relation "incomprehensibly empty" and becomes estranged from him, especially when she meets Irene, the Greek dwarf in Petros' home village church, and knows about her parentage and suffering. (45) Just as Petros feels it, "his home, his village, his country, was a sad place for her. …she was profoundly disappointed, and had become estranged from him because of that. He blamed the dwarf." (68) Her estrangement from Petros apparently comes from her realization that patriarchy is a universal phenomenon and that men will never be women's partners to overturn the established patriarchal system. Since resistance against patriarchy is the basis of Susannah's personal relations, she decides to put an end to her man-to-woman relationship with Petros and begins to search a new relationship in which men's central position is eradicated. She turns to the woman-to-woman relationship this time.

Talking about the novel, Ms. Walker once says: "I wanted to show how women can grow in a relationship with each other. By no means, am I saying that such a relationship is smoothly sailing. It definitely isn't, but there are some incredible lessons that can be learned." (qtd. in White, 1998: Appendix) Obviously, Walker here refers to the woman-to-woman "relationship" (esp. lesbianism) in the novel. Like in *The Color Purple*, Walker stresses the vital catalytic role of lesbianism in women's growth and development in *By the Light of My Father's Smile*. For Walker, to be a lesbian is a proper and effective way for a woman to resist against men's dominance and struggle for women's discourse rights. As an illustration, she plots Susannah and Pauline's encounter, acquaintance and love.

Susannah gets to know Pauline in the latter's "upscale organic soul food restaurant." (A. Walker, 1998: 135) She seems to have a fondness for her at the first sight and vice versa. Two weeks later, they meet again after Susannah calls Pauline, and their relationship soon develops into a lasting lesbianism. The physical contact with Pauline brings Susannah a fresh, pleasant experience of sex, which liberates her from the patriarchal constraints in sexuality. As women bearing similar pains and sufferings in the patriarchal society, Susannah and Pauline both feel an antipathy against men's domination in heterosexuality and are longing to establish a free and equal sexual relationship through lesbianism. What's more, Pauline's rich experiences, along with her previous lesbian relationship with Gena, enable her to mentor Susannah physically and spiritually. Just as Susannah herself states it later, it is Pauline who takes her "closest to the door of [her] own locked closet" and teaches her "a freer and much deeper expression of sex." (187, 189) Bathed in Pauline's love, Susannah gets a new cognition of sex and reaches sexual maturity. She once says to Pauline gratefully, "[w]ithout our relationship I would never have known how far away I was from what could be. What heights of spirit one might reach through such a physical act." (187) The whipping event ends Susannah's joyous and carefree childhood. Before Pauline's appearance Susannah lives a stifling life. She has trouble in choosing between her sister and her father: While she tends to forgive her father when he tries to win her back and rekindle her trust, her sister always reminds her of what he has done on that wretched day and thus tells her that to be reconciled with her father would be nothing different from "sitting in the lap of a monster." (118) The trouble glooms Susannah's life, which she is used to since childhood and is fully embodied in her dressing. Conversing with Irene, Susannah admits, "… whenever I'm getting dressed, black garments are suddenly in my hand. I seem to feel most comfortable in them." (181) Obviously, Susannah's life without Pauline is dark-colored. Being a lesbian partner, she "cut it (black) off one day without thinking" and "wanted suddenly to be free of it." (181) Therefore, the mutual love between Susannah and Pauline, like that between Shug and Celie, transcends lesbianism and develops into Walker's "evolutionary sex," a sexual relationship that can be established between woman and woman, between woman and man, or even within oneself and can explore and expand one's "bodily love and spiritual awareness." (White, 1998: 45)

Getting out of the dark-colored world, Susannah becomes bold and outspoken. She no longer keeps silent before Magdalena. On the one side, she attempts to interpret to Magdalena their father's care and thought in the whipping event. She explains that "Daddy loved you (Magdalena)" and that the reason he beats her is that "[s]ex scared him" so that "he thought you (Magdalena) might get pregnant." (A. Walker, 1998: 116 – 117) She points out Magdalena's paranoid opinion about their father, who "tried to make it up." (116) She wishes that her sister would forgive him and accept his apology. On the other side, Susannah confesses her dissatisfaction with Magdalena and her reluctance to be in cahoots with her. She accuses her sister of wrecking her life by mentioning their father's violence years ago time and time again. As for their father who is dead now, Susannah would recollect those happy moments they have spent together and his persistent heartfelt apology after the event. Shaking off the spiritual shackles that have been chaining her in those past years, Susannah is now a magnanimous lady. She not only has a very tolerant attitude towards her father's past but also treasures the bond between sisters. Even when Magdalena bites her "arm right through to the bone" she chooses not to blame her by just saying "[w]ell, you didn't strangle me to death. I'm thankful." (122) And she tries to persuade Magdalena to give up hatred for their father.

> We were leaving the mountains, said Susannah; you would have lost Manuelito anyway.
>
> …
>
> We could try to help each other heal, said Susannah. We could heal each other.
>
> …
>
> Don't pin him (their father) to that one moment. He was a human being, like you and me. You just strangled me and took a plug out of my arm, but now you're lying there looking like you're sorry. Are you? (123)

From fear through estrangement to eventual forgiveness, the transformation of Susannah's attitude toward her father witnesses her regeneration, a long journey inward, on which Pauline's affection and enlightenment apparently play a vital role. Accompanied by Pauline and nourished by her love, Susannah becomes understanding and tolerant. Her love is extended to "man, woman, or succulent plant." (115) This is essentially a womanist love, which is physical, and above all spiritual. Pauline describes Susannah's love as this: "it is with courage, with guts, which she fears she lacks, that she falls in love. It could be with anyone. She does not appear to look first at the genital area. Loving comes before that, not after. She is faithful to the person she's with." (127) With her personal experimentation, Susannah goes toward sexual and spiritual healing, and lights up black women's way to spiritual survival. Here Walker sublimes lesbianism to spiritual realm, and regards love and sex as not simply sources of bodily pleasure but of spiritual comfort and self-knowledge as well.

5.1.2.2 Pauline's Autonomy and Self-reliance

In the patriarchal system, men almost hold all the aces in both social and familial relations. They are masters of women's destinies. This is the case with Pauline, whose story of survival is to escape from the heterosexual constraints. Pauline is cheated into a heterosexual relationship and gets married against her will after being impregnated. After marriage, she serves her husband just as a sex object and never enjoys any pleasure in heterosexuality. Like Celie, she has lived a male-dominated life before she becomes a lesbian. Lesbianism brings equality and autonomy into Pauline's life and helps her achieve sexual maturity. With her shift from a sex object to a sexual partner, Pauline becomes self-esteemed, self-confident, self-reliant and self-dominated. So Pauline's autonomy and self-reliance is characterized by the sexual orientation.

A girl born in a poor family, Pauline has to do the housework and take care of her baby sisters and brothers at the early age. Actually she "was a mother from the age of five" as she tells Susannah. (100) In spite that she is not the eldest of the ten children in the family, she considers herself very important at home. For "[t]he older children had my (Pauline's) parents for parents···The younger ones had me (Pauline). ···By the time I was eight I could cook dinner while holding one baby and watching over two more." (100) However, Pauline likes school and "would sneak off to school in the morning." (100) Therefore, when she is around fifteen, her father, one of her brothers and even her mother get her drunk and set her having sex with Watson, a man of twenty-five, in order to keep her away from school. Consequently, she is impregnated and married off to Watson. Thus begins her unfortunate marriage, which forces her into the struggle for a way out.

In the patriarchal system, heterosexuality dominates and women are positioned just as child-bearing tools. They have no choice but to surrender. As a girl, Pauline sees babies drop out of her "mother's body every year, like apples falling to the ground" so that "this old, graying, bent woman" "had to wear a tight band around her lower body to hold her uterus in place." (102, 103) Her mother's suffering and her own disastrous pregnancy awaken Pauline's rebellion against the patriarchal "normality." To avoid being a mother like her mother, Pauline decides to abort the baby. Just at that time, she meets Gena, who tries to find an abortionist for her. Although the baby is born, Pauline develops a lesbian relationship with Gena. Before meeting Gena, Pauline is "almost completely ignorant, though pregnant as anything," and does not know "the wonderful blossoming that good loving means." (130 – 131) It is Gena, a woman "disgusted that so many women thought sex was just for the man," who talks a lot with her about sex, teaches her sexual knowledge, and gets her interested in sexuality. (130) As Pauline recalls, Gena's lesbian love has "nurturing quality"; "Our affair was the kind of affectionate sex that seemed designed to reconnect me to myself, to keep me alive. However, it was passionate enough so that I learned about orgasms. And once I learned that I could have them, and have them easily, I realized that in at least that one area I was free." (132) Lesbianism offers Pauline a new concept of sex. Orgasmic freedom gives her a new birth. Instead of fearing and escaping it, she now enjoys and desires sex. She is no longer depressed but becomes vigorous and optimistic. She can even laugh her suffering off. In a way, lesbianism is a decisive step Pauline makes "on the path to liberation" and self-knowledge. (107) Influenced and encouraged by Gena, she, like Meridian, gives up her three-year-old son Richard and runs away to seek a new life. She goes to night school and studies business at college. After graduating from college, she joins the Navy. Then she gets out and works in restaurants. Having saved enough money, she buys her own restaurant and becomes master of herself. Thus she starts creating a "herstory."

While Gena's sexual love and guidance awaken Pauline's sense of resistance and lead her to freedom and independence, Susannah's fondness and curiosity enhance Pauline's self-confidence and sense of fulfillment. "[A] powerful, bold, opinionated woman," Pauline explicitly shows her sexual orientation and excites affection in Susannah the first time they meet. (106) The second time they are together, she opens her heart to Susannah and becomes her lesbian partner and mentor. Liberated by Gena's sexual feelings, Pauline is convinced that lesbianism is the best choice to go to freedom and equality. Being a lesbian, she no longer worries about pregnancy, which eases the burden of looking after children and offers the opportunity to live a free life. Being a free woman, Pauline learns a lot from her rich experience and becomes proactive and confident in sexuality. She enlightens Susannah on sex, gives her new experience of it, and thus saves her from the fetters of the past. Susannah's transformation brings Pauline a sense of fulfillment. The newborn Susannah is a living proof of the success of lesbianism. For Pauline and for Walker as well, lesbianism essentially implies the unity between women. God helps those who help themselves. Once they rely on themselves, i. e., on the unity and mutual assistance within women, black women will completely break out of the heterosexual hegemony. Bodily autonomy is the first step of women's emancipation.

Economically independent and bodily autonomous, black women become tolerant and understanding and broad-minded. In this sense, Pauline is another example after Celie. In a conversation with Magdalena, she depicts her father as "someone now whom I never knew before. Someone who grieves that his children grew up without knowing who he really was. Someone who wants to make amends. Someone who's fun, actually. Old and cute." (127 - 128) Being the master of her body, Pauline becomes philosophical and has a broad outlook on life. She is now able to treat the people around her in a tolerant way. To look at him afresh, she finds her father a pitiful man of sense: he feels sorry for his absent role in the children's growth; he comes to regret the harm he has done to the children and tries to right his wrongs. Facing such an old confessional father, Pauline finally gets at the Alexander Pope's words that "to err is human, to forgive divine." She forgives her father with all her heart. She tells Magdalena that "[y]ou have to open your heart to them (fathers)… No matter what they've done." (128) Meanwhile, Pauline has a liberal view on her relationship with Susannah. When Magdalena tells her that Susannah likes sex and "sleeps around," she just replies that "[b]ad woman aren't the only women who enjoy sex" and that "your sister is completely loyal to whoever she's in love with." (126) These words not simply reflect the speaker's rationality and magnanimity but convey her confidence and maturity as well.

However, if Susannah seeks equality and placid happiness in lesbianism, Pauline seems more inclined to find some compensation and psychological balance in the homosexual relationships, especially in the one with Susannah. To be more exact, she wants to be master of Susannah to show her own power, for the latter is more educated and has had a happier childhood. Once she fails to satisfy the desire, Pauline betrays her disappointment at and even complaint to Susannah— "what I've learned from our years of mutual cramming is that I can neither have you nor be you. Nor can I have your childhood instead of my own. I'm stuck with who I am, … I'm trying to learn that that's not so Bad." (189) From being mastered by the males to tending to master others (this has actually come true in the fact that she employs her brothers and other male workers in her restaurant), Pauline more or less deviates from Walker's usual intention of creating perfect women images like Celie and Susannah and thus weakens the healing power of lesbianism; yet she embodies part of, if not most of, women who are freed from the heterosexual hegemony, and therefore is more authentic and acceptable.

The development of lesbianism, to a great extent, is ascribed to women's fear of men, their suffering from sexual abuse (including rape and incest) as well as their ambivalence toward the parents. As abused adolescent girls, physically and/or spiritually, Celie, Susannah and Pauline naturally resort to lesbianism to resist heterosexual hegemony and seek liberation and independence. As a black woman writer, Walker is greatly concerned with her black sisters' oppression and restraints in the patriarchal society. She once says, "[i]f you are not free to express your love, you are a slave; and anyone who would demand that you enslave yourself by not freely expressing your love is a person with a slaveholder's mentality." (A. Walker, 1988: 91) For Walker, the freedom to express one's feelings is the basic condition for spiritual survival. Lesbianism not only frees black women from the male-dominated sexual order but works as a bond between black women as well. By knitting them close together, it wins black women the opportunity to release their love and passion freely and thus paves the way for their spiritual liberation. As a matter of fact, Walker places a high value on sexuality in her writings and regards it as a light source in the dark. In the patriarchal society, heterosexuality is acknowledged as the single normal mode of sex. So in *The Color Purple* and *By the Light of My Father's Smile*, Walker chooses lesbianism, which is considered as abnormal according to the patriarchal norm, to disintegrate the sexual "normality." Lesbianism illuminates black women's road to awakening and liberation, and successfully helps black women obtain dignity and confidence and self-identity.

5.2 Sisterhood: The Possibility of Black Women's Autonomy

> Male supremacist ideology encourages women to believe we are valueless and obtain value only by relating to or bonding with men. We are taught that our relationships with one another diminish rather than enrich our experience. We are taught that women are "nat-

> ural" enemies, that solidarity will never exist between us because we cannot, should not, and do not bond with one another. We have learned these lessons well. We must unlearn them if we are to build a sustained feminist movement. We must learn to live and work in solidarity. We must learn the true meaning and value of Sisterhood. (hooks, 1986: 127)

Just as hooks argues, one of the disastrous impacts from patriarchy is women's internalization of the dominance of men in their life. Women or most women, if not all, depreciate and even deny themselves consciously or unconsciously. Or, to put it differently, women, like men, believe that, without men, their life will be meaningless and purposeless and that it is impossible for women to unite and work together for their common interest. In view of the absence of solidarity and mutual trust between women, hooks advocates an all-inclusive sisterhood that could transcend the barriers not just of sex but of race and class as well.

The literal meanings of the word "sisterhood," as is stated in the authorized dictionaries like *Collins Cobuild Advanced Learner's English-Chinese Dictionary, Longman Dictionary of Contemporary English* and *Oxford Advanced Learner's Dictionary*, contain "the kinship relation between a female offspring and the siblings," "a religious society of sisters (especially an order of nuns)," and "the affection and loyalty that women feel for other women who they have something in common with" or "a special loyal relationship among women who share the same ideas and aims, especially among feminists." In a nutshell, the word per se suggests a close relationship between women who are either siblings or live in a community together, especially a religious one, or stand side by side to challenge exploitative and oppressive practices, especially of men. As a political term, "sisterhood" is defined by Maggie Humm (1995: 131) in *The Dictionary of Feminist Theory* as that which

> sometimes called sorority, includes the idea and experience of female bonding, and the self-affirmation and identity discovered in a women-centered vision and definition of womanhood. Sisterhood is based on a clear awareness that all women, irrespective of class,

> race, or nation have a common problem—patriarchy. Feminists believe that women should establish close ties and bonds with other women in recognition that men should not play an exclusive role in women's lives, that women are worth relating to, and that all women share interests.

While Humm's definition stresses women-bonding or close relationship between/among women, Annette Kilcooley (205) seems to focus on the term's concern with women's commonality, stating that "sisterhood was sister inhabited, woman powered and characterized by the pursuit of woman-centered values, aims and objectives. The politics of sisterhood emerged through personal experience and self-recognition in common with each other."

The 1960s and 1970s saw a resurgence of feminist activity, which has been called the women's liberation movement or the Second Wave of feminism, with the first wave usually thought of as being from 1848 to 1920, when women won the vote. The two prominent women's liberation groups are New York Radical Women (NYRW), a feminist group in existence from 1967 to 1969, and Redstockings, a radical feminist group founded in New York in 1969 when NYRW dissolved. They put forward the slogan that "sisterhood is powerful" and called for women to unite to oppose the patriarchal system and achieve liberation from men. From then on "sisterhood" was employed by the feminists as a political term to underscore the cohesive force between women. In this sense, the term is closely linked with the marginalization of women in the male-dominated society.

However, black feminism, as a political and social movement growing out of black women's feelings of discontent with both the Civil Rights Movement and the (white) feminist movement, argues that sexism, class oppression, and racism are inextricably bound together. Now that white feminists strive to overcome sexism and class oppression but ignore race and discriminate against black women through racial bias, black feminists are inclined to underline the particularity of their struggle for liberation. Alice Walker, for instance, asserts that black women have experienced a different and more intense kind of oppression than that of white women. Her womanism is a critical disidentification with what black women understood to be the anti-male sentiments of white feminists and white feminist movements. As is stated in Chapter Two of this book, a womanist, for Walker, is a "woman who loves other women, sexually and/or nonsexually," who "[s]ometimes loves individual men, sexually and/or nonsexually," who is "[c]ommitted to survival and wholeness of entire people, male *and* female," who is "[n]ot a separatist." (A. Walker, 1983: xi) Walker stresses solidarity in her theory, solidarity between black women, solidarity within the black community, and solidarity of all races. This is echoed by bell hooks in the book *Feminist Theory: From Margin to Center*. bell hooks (2000b: 65) argues that, if feminism seeks to make women equal to men, it is impossible due to the fact that the white-supremacist capitalist patriarchy does not view all men equal, and claims that "[w]omen in lower class and poor groups, particularly those who are non-white, would not have defined women's liberation as women gaining social equality with men since they are continually reminded in their everyday lives that all women do not share a common social status." In *Feminist Theory* hooks addresses topics like the goals of the feminist movement, the role of men in the movement, the solidarity among women, and the like, and encourages the long-standing idea of sisterhood but reminds women, black women in particular, to acknowledge their differences from women of privilige while still accepting each other. She offers a new, more inclusive feminist theory and urges feminists to consider gender's relation to race, class and sex, a concept coined as intersectionality. Like Walker, hooks (69) insists on the inclusion of men in the feminist movement and criticizes the anti-male stance of second-wave feminism, asserting that this position "alienated many poor and working-class women, particularly non-white women, from feminist movement." So it is reasonable to say that the particularity of the black feminism lies in its complexity and arduousness. As victims of both racism and sexism, black women require more help and support to win victory in their struggle. Hence by "sisterhood" black feminists not just advocate women's solidarity in and out of the black community but also show their tolerance and inclusion or at least no exclusion of male blacks who are similarly discriminated against in the white society. If the white feminists are more concerned with the connotations of the term "sisterhood" on the ideological level which addresses questions of representations (womanhood/femininity), the black feminists more on "a material, experiential, daily life level which focuses on the micropolitics of work, home, family, sexuality, etc." or on both levels. (Mohanty, 1991: 21) As a political activist and spokesperson for black women, Alice Walker acknowledges sisterhood as an important approach to black women's emancipation. With the aid of sisterhood, the black females in her novels not only shake off the traditional womanthood/femininity but also win their economic independence in the white patriarchal society.

5.2.1 The Transforming Power of Sisterhood in *Meridian*: Meridian's Relationship with Truman and Lynne

> "Mama, why are we brown, pink, and yellow, and our cousins are white, beige, and black?" Ans.: "Well, you know the colored race is just like a flower garden, with every color flower represented." (A. Walker, 1983: xi)

Alice Walker likens the human world to "a flower garden" filled with flowers of different colors, with every color representing a race. Accordingly, each race is unique and indispensable as every color contributes to the beauty of the garden. The black race, like a sort of flowers in the "flower garden" represented by the certain color, is one of the segments composed of humankind. So are the white and other colored races. Therefore the ideal of Walker's womanist, who is "[n]ot a separatist" but a "universalist," is the "survival and wholeness of entire people," that is, the racial equality and the sexual harmony. (xi) By "entire people," Walker includes not only the black race but all the other races of different colors. Solidarity is the keynote of Walker's concept. In a conversation with Sharon Wilson, Walker says: "For white people who have been very keen on staying white… it means then they come in one color and are just one segment that has separated itself from the rest of humankind, and are very isolated in the world because they are a minority." (qtd. in S. Wilson, 1993: 323) To avoid being "isolated" and becoming a "minority," Walker's black female characters consistently rely upon sisterhood to achieve their harmonious co-existence with men (especially black men) and women of the other races (especially the white females). In such novels as *Meridian*, the theme of sisterhood is even extended to the white world. By developing an inter-sexual friendship with her former lover Truman and an inter-racial sisterhood with her white rival Lynne, the title heroine of *Meridian* illustrates Walker's womanism on a new and higher level.

Meridian Hill is an anti-traditional black female image. She is not an "obedient daughter," or a "devoted wife," or an "adoring mother." That is, she is not a "good" woman according to the patriarchal norms. She begins her career with shattering the established images of perfect women in the male-centered society and becomes a staunch fighter against sexism. As a daughter, Meridian is aware of her mother's sacrifice and suffering. Mrs. Hill, in her teens, dreamed to be a schoolteacher, but was forced to give it up due to "marriage and childbirth," which "made her dependent" and "also divided her from her newly emergent self." (Tucker, 1991: 3) She feels that she is "buried alive, and walled away from her own life brick by brick." (A. Walker, 1976: 51) In effect, the stifling marriage and childbirth completely extinguish Mrs. Hill's original idealistic fervor. When "she wanted to teach again" after "her children were older and not so burdensome," she "did not like the new generation of students" and "had no interest in children" in the least. (51) Her life is thus absolutely changed, which not simply "speaks of [her] long-suffering, self-sacrificing motherhood" but demonstrates the intangible impact of patriarchy. (Tucker, 1991: 3) Mrs. Hill's voice, as Tucker (3) states, is now "identified with the god-voice derived from patriarchal discourse." She is turned into an accomplice of patriarchy. She, a victim of patriarchy, educates her daughter Meridian in the light of the patriarchal requirements. Meridian, who does not want to repeat her mother's life, hence becomes a disobedient daughter. She breaches all the male-centered conventions for a "good" woman; she goes against her mother's will, leaves her husband, and abandons her baby son for adoption. With all the burdens unloaded, Meridian is devoted to the Civil Rights Movement and henceforth leads a new but controversial life. Standing out against the patriarchal "normality," she defines her identity in an absolutely different way and sets an example for the downtrodden women.

However, as a civil rights activist, Meridian is not an audacious revolutionary in the eyes of her co-workers. She refuses to kill for the revolution when many civil rights workers resort to violence. During the mid-1960s (especially during the Freedom Summer campaign of 1964), numerous tensions within the Civil Rights Movement came to the forefront. Many blacks in such organizations as SNCC (Student Nonviolent Coordinating Committee) and CORE (Congress of Racial Equality) came to realize that the massive presence of white students in the Movement was not reducing the amount of violence that blacks suffered, but appeared to be increasing it. They began questioning the strategy of involving the white activists in the Movement and got intolerant and lacking in amity with the whites. They even regarded the whites as enemies when they found that the federal government would not respond to the requests to enforce the provisions of the Civil Rights Act of 1964, or to protect the lives of activists who challenged segregation. During the March against Fear in 1966, SNCC and CORE fully embraced the slogan of "black power" to describe their trends towards militancy and self-reliance. They followed the ideology of Malcolm X using a "by-any-means necessary" approach to stopping inequality. Then the murder of Martin Luther King, Jr. in 1968 pushed the Black Power Movement (1966 – 1975) up to its climax. The corollary was that violence and killing became the touchstone of the commitment to the Movement. Meridian's hesitation to kill for the revolution is, as a matter of course, acknowledged by her co-workers as a betrayal of the revolutionary community. In spite of the fact that nonviolence has failed to free black people and that it might be correct to kill for the freedom of her race, Meridian persists in building a fair, just and harmonious society through non-violence, for blood and killing can never bring serenity and peace to a killer, nor real freedom or justice to a community or a race. At this point lies Meridian's agreement with Martin Luther King, Jr., who holds that "in using violence a people risk 'losing…[their] soul.'" (Hendrickson, 1999: 115). Meridian's insistence on nonviolence explicitly expressed Walker's preoccupation with "the spiritual survival, the survival whole of" black people. (A. Walker, 1983: 250)

In the essay written for *New York Times Book Review*, Marge Piercy (1993: 9) argues that Walker "writes with a sharp critical sense as she deals with the issues of tactics and strategy in the Civil Rights Movement, with the nature of commitment, with the possibility of interracial love and communication, …with violence and nonviolence." Set in the Movement, *Meridian* has the idea of nonviolence and interracial love or sisterhood as its pivotal motif and well illustrates Walker's womanist ideal. Meridian's anti-traditional qualities as a woman and unique adherence to nonviolent protest against racism lay the foundation of her later forgiveness and magnanimity in the interracial relationship with the whites, especially with Lynne. Or rather, although Walker punctuates Meridian's fearless challenge to the authority of patriarchy and non-conformist action in and after the Civil Rights Movement, her great success in portraying the black female image lies more in her concern with the development of love, nonsexual love and interracial love in particular. "Sisterhood" in this novel is at once a bond between females and a fellowship between sexes. As Meridian extends sisterhood to her former lover Truman and to her white rival Lynne, Walker's womanist ideal reaches its highest level.

At the time of working for the Civil Rights Movement, Meridian comes across Truman Held. They work side by side and fall in love with each other. Soon they sleep together, which lays bare Meridian's loss of virginity before meeting Truman. At this point, Lynne Rabinowitz, who is a virgin as is expected, turns up and attracts Truman away. Meridian is left pregnant. She has no choice but to have an abortion on her own. In this sense, she and Lynne are rivals. She has every reason to hate Lynne. Or, at any rate, there seems to be no possibility for Meridian to become friends with Lynne. Nonetheless, Meridian acts out the impossibility.

After being abandoned by Truman, Meridian first aborts her child and gets sterilized, and then throws herself into the Civil Rights Movements. With the emergence of the Black Power Movement, which challenged the established black leadership for its cooperative attitude and its nonviolence, and instead demanded political and economic self-sufficiency, she leaves the North and returns to the South to get involved in the voter registration and take nonviolent remonstrant actions. With her commitment to the civil rights of black people, she blots out her personal grievances by degrees and becomes open-minded and magnanimous. She comes to forgive Truman and accept him as a friend instead of a lover. Meridian's feeling for Truman was no longer a sexual but a sisterly love, as she once says to Lynne, "there's not the slightest thing between us. We are as innocent as brother and sister." (A. Walker, 1976: 146) So when Truman goes back to her three years later and begs her "to give him another chance," Meridian refuses him, though she allows him to live in her house. (139) Actually, they have been working together for black people ever since and establish a true friendship between them, which helps Truman to grow into a full-fledged revolutionary. In Meridian's relationship with Truman, the stereotype of traditional women is subverted. Truman's transformation testifies to the great power of friendship and solidarity, which may be interpreted as a variant of sisterhood, the inter-sexual "sisterhood."

If the friendship between Meridian and Truman results from the commonality within the black community, then that between Meridian and Lynne embodies the tolerance and wisdom of black people, black women in particular. The special and embarrassing relationship between the two women decides the difficulty in improving it. The appearance of Lynne puts an end to Meridian's happiness and normal life as a woman. To some extent, Meridian's abortion and sterilization is ascribed to Lynne's involvement with Truman and their later marriage. Moreover, they belong to the different races, which are antagonistic to each other. There ought to exist personal grievances and racial hostility between them. It follows logically that they are implacable foes and should be at daggers drawn. Nevertheless, when Truman asks Meridian why she refuses to resume their intimate relationship, she simply answers, "[f]or Lynne's sake alone, I couldn't do it." Then she retorts, "[w]hat does she have now besides you?" (139) Evidently, Meridian puts herself in Lynne's shoes. In the face of Truman's imploration, what comes to her mind is not wreaking vengeance on Lynne but persuading Truman to reflect on Lynne's future life with his absence, saying "[s]he (Lynne) was that when she decided she'd rather have you than everything." (139) For, as a woman, Meridian knows what a hard life an abandoned wife would face; as a black, she can imagine how the black males would treat an isolated white woman. When it comes to racial conflict, Meridian is rational and intelligent. She is aware of the risks of separatism and racial hatred. She supports racial solidarity and advocates a sense of community and fellowship between blacks and whites. In this sense, she is an incarnation of Ms. Walker's womanism. In Meridian, Walker's sisterhood is successfully magnified by means of taking in the white women.

As Hendrickson (1999: 111) states, "[W]hen Walker began to write *Meridian*, the Civil Rights Movement, which offered the hope of 'Freedom Now!' and the ideal and practice of nonviolence and 'Black and White Together,' had been declared dead. Many young blacks had given up on white Americans and on nonviolence, because of their experience of white racist violence and intransigence in the Civil Rights Movement." They adhere to black power and emphasize black autonomy. Whites are excluded in the black community. Lynne is thus placed in such difficult circumstances, especially after Tommy Odds is attacked by his so-called NOTC, the black extremists in practice, because some of them once find the three friends (Tommy, Truman and Trilling) being together with Lynne. It is undoubtedly logical that Tommy and Truman ascribe this event to Lynne's presence, or to be more exact, Lynne's color—Lynne was guilty "because she was a white woman." (A. Walker, 1976: 133) Hence Truman becomes estranged from her and eventually leaves her during her pregnancy. Forsaken, Lynne lives in solitude. She is not welcome in the black community because of her whiteness. Neither is she welcome in her mother's home, for her history as an exchange student is accepted as a betrayal to her own race. She has nobody to speak her mind. The birth of her daughter is the solace to her. They have depended on each other for survival before the baby is unfortunately killed in an accident. Just when Lynne is put in a desperate situation once more, "it was Meridian who was, miraculously, there." (172) Then Meridian busies herself with attending to Truman and Lynne alternatively. "She had spent a month shuttling between his lovely bright uptown to Lynne's tiny hovel downtown. Between them they had drained her dry." (172) As Meridian herself recalls, she spends the days "dashing in and out of subways, cooking meals, listening to monologues thickened with grief, being pulled into bed—by Lynne, who held on to her like a child afraid of the dark." (172) The loss of the child finally brings together the original rivals, the two women of different colors. There appear such harmonious scenes in the novel: "Meridian, would sometimes, in the afternoons, read poems to Lynne by Margaret Walker, and Lynne, in return, would attempt to cornrow Meridian's patchy short hair"; "Sometimes they talked, intimately, like sisters, and when they did not they allowed the television to fill the silences." (173) Meridian's company brings Lynne sisterly love and warmth. Lynne is moved and changed. She eventually clears up the past grudges against Meridian and opens her heart to her. They become friends and sisters, which is undoubtedly Meridian's contribution. As the only figure that comes to comfort Lynne, after the baby's death, Meridian is Lynne's savior. She works as Lynne's life support and emotional anchor. She pulls Lynne out of the depths of despair and helps her start a new life. When the time comes for them to say goodbye, Lynne expresses the depth of her gratitude to Meridian, saying "[t]hanks, Meridian, for everything. I honestly don't know what I would have done without you." (174) For Lynne, affection and gratefulness thus far weaken her personal rivalry with Meridian, while, for Meridian, the target she is striving for—harmony and solidarity between races—is much closer as her relationship with Lynne is improved.

If her child's death plunges Lynne into deep sorrow, the hard life thereafter makes her "exhausted," "a great deal changed" and palpably cynical. (145) When she pays a visit to Meridian about a year later, she is full of grumbles. She complains about black separatism, accuses Truman of ruining her life, and blames Meridian for her attraction to Truman. Lynne has already accepted Meridian as a friend, a shoulder to cry on. She weeps and says, "You're the only one I can talk to about it (being raped by Tommy). The only one who would believe it wasn't my fault that it happened." (153) Although she, talking with Meridian, shows plainly her envy and jealousy of Meridian, Lynne trusts Meridian deep in her heart. Together with Meridian, she appears casual and relaxed. As soon as she enters Meridian's house, she unburdens herself, flops "heavily onto the couch" and eats whatever she likes. She weeps, laughs, and cries out her bitterness, undisguised and off-guard. Meanwhile, Meridian manages to be a good listener and conveys her sympathy and understanding to Lynne on the one hand; and on the other hand she tells Lynne her reservations about the latter's comment on and accusation against Truman and the black males. Moreover, Meridian's repeated explanations to Lynne of her relationship with Truman shows that she cares much about how Lynne feels and that she is afraid of Lynne's misunderstanding. She values her friendship with Lynne or, in a broader sense, the friendship between black and white women. All in all, in the relationship between Meridian and Lynne, Walker tends to highlight the possibility of improving the inter-racial sisterhood. While the company and consolation Meridian offers to the grief-stricken Lynne show Meridian's kindheartedness and tolerance and bring Lynne the hope for a new life, her dignity and wisdom are fully embodied in her patience in listening to Lynne, in her argument about the perplexing sexual relationships Lynne maintains with the black men, in her determination to change black males, and in her teaching Lynne how to respect blacks and look at them in an objective and impartial way. This leads to a rational statement that, through the development of the inter-racial sisterhood, Walker pays a tribute to black women's goodness, brightness, generosity and wisdom.

Meridian is accepted as a semi-autobiographical work. The title heroine, like Walker herself, is an inflexible womanist, who sticks to harmony and solidarity of all races, men and women. Meridian is ready to die for black people's freedom; yet she is reluctant to kill for revolution. As a persistent fighter for womanism, she is characterized by tolerance, magnanimity, kindheartedness and wisdom. Her success in developing the harmonious relationships with both Truman and Lynne pushes the impact of "sisterhood" to a unique and unprecedented level, and thus well illustrates Walker's womanist ideal.

5.2.2 The Salvation Power of Sisterhood in *The Color Purple*: The Black Women's Awakening and Independence

Women, especially black women, are marginalized in the male-centered American society. Subjected to the oppressors, they have no freedom and selfhood; they are imprisoned in the life of their fathers/husbands. To change their marginal roles and shake off the patriarchal fetters, black women have to unite and bond together. The sisterly solidarity and affection gains black women courage and power so that they can strive for what they have been deprived of in the male-dominated world. "Sisterhood," as a slogan for women's alliance, thus becomes a recurring theme in feminist (including black feminist and womanist) writings. If *Meridian* is Ms. Walker's first attempt to manifest the power of sisterhood—the transforming power—in women's growth, *The Color Purple* marks the author's culmination in reflecting this theme. With its power of salvation highlighted, "sisterhood" is here no longer confined to two women but extended to a female group, which works as a community where black women seek solace and comfort, get support and encouragement, and share happiness and sufferings. In this novel, sisterhood embodies the fellowship between sisters within a family, between women within a race and between inter-racial women as well. Through developing sisterhood, the female characters, especially black women represented by the heroine Celie at once achieve their economic independence and construct their self-identities as autonomous individuals.

5.2.2.1 Celie's Maturity and Regeneration

Sisterhood exerts a dominant influence on Celie's growth. The sisters, with or without kinship to Celie, offer their support, care and love to her, and thus help her rise to freedom and independence. In the novel Celie develops three kinds of sisterhood respectively with her sibling Nettie, with her stepson's wife Sofia, and with her lesbian partner and spiritual mentor Shug Avery. Actually, Walker traces Celie's awakening to her relationships with the other black women like Nettie, Sofia and Shug.

Nettie is Celie's full sister. She spends her childhood with Celie and knows very well of her suffering. Nettie is luckier than Celie in that she, thanks to Celie's protection, escapes from her stepfather's sexual harassment and therefore has the opportunity to continue her study. Smart and literate, she is Celie's spiritual support in the family. She makes every effort to help Celie. The first time their stepfather takes Celie out of school, due to pregnancy, Nettie "stood there at the gate holding tight to my (Celie's) hand" to try to keep Celie at school. (A. Walker, 1982: 10) Then when Celie is completely stopped from schooling, Nettie tries her best to promote Celie's literacy. Just as Celie describes it, "[n]o matter what happen, Nettie steady try to teach me (Celie) what go on in the world." (17) After Celie gets married and is bullied by her stepchildren, Nettie tells Celie to fight and teach them a lesson, saying "[d]on't let them run over you." (18) As the first to tell Celie to fight, Nettie is an enlightener to Celie in terms of rebellion. Forced to leave Celie and travel to Africa, Nettie promises that she will keep writing to her. Although Mr. —— secretly hides all Celie's letters from Nettie and makes the sisters lose touch with each other, Celie firmly believes that Nettie never stops writing to her and that she will hear from Nettie one day. Nettie and her supposed letters are propping Celie up.

With the hidden letters found, Celie gets good solid information about Nettie. Learning that she is alive and kicking somewhere in the world, Celie "begin[s] to strut a little bit. " (154) The news about Nettie strengthens Celie's conviction for survival. Form then on she looks forward to the new life when Nettie comes back to her. Nettie is her only reason and support for survival. She "mean[s] everything in the world to me (Celie)." (124) Early in the first letter to Celie, Nettie manifests her great concern over her sister, warning that "[y]ou've got to fight and get away from Albert." (131) Nettie's other letters constantly bring Celie hope and courage for survival, which enable her to fight against Mr. —— and challenge his authority, as well as information about the outside world, which broadens Celie's mind. Nettie tells Celie that "[t]he world is changing" and "is no longer a world just for boys and men." (167) The implication is that girls and women should not be excluded; they are part and parcel of the human world. This undoubtedly sows the seeds of Celie's reaction against Mr. ——'s tyranny. Moreover, Nettie offers Celie her new interpretation of the Bible and God:

> Think what it means that Ethiopia is Africa! All the Ethiopians in the bible were colored. It had never occurred to me, though when you read the bible it is perfectly plain if you pay attention only to the words. It is the pictures in the bible that fool you. The pictures that illustrate the words. All of the people are white and so you just think all the people from the bible were white too. But really *white* white people lived somewhere else during those times. That's why the bible says that Jesus Christ had hair like lamb's wool. Lamb's wool is not straight, Celie. It isn't even curly. (140 – 41, italic original)

This, along with Shug's view on God, negates Celie's inherent understanding of the image of God and removes her invariable awe to Him. Now God, for Celie, is simply an old white man, who never cares about black women's suffering. The collapse of the image of God brings Celie back to reality; she comes to see that God help those who help themselves. Celie no longer writes to God; instead, she turns to writing to Nettie and begins struggling for a free and self-reliant life. In this sense, Celie's independence and autonomy is attributed to Nettie's enlightenment and guide; the sisterhood between Celie and Nettie plays an important role in Celie's awakening.

Sofia is a free-spirited black woman who puts equality first in her relationships with men including her father, her brothers and her husband Harpo. The first time she is brought to meet Harpo's father Mr. ——, Celie sees them—Sofia and Harpo—"marching, hand in hand, like going to war," with Sofia "in front a little." (32) Sofia, though pregnant, does not show any fear or embarrassment to Mr. ——, who questions her about her baby's father and opposes their marriage. This leaves a deep impression on Celie; she senses something unusual in Sofia. Mutual love brings Harpo and Sofia together; they get married regardless of Mr. ——'s objection. After marriage, Sofia lives an equal and happy life; she goes on her own way no matter what the family members (especially Mr. —— and Harpo) think and say. All this is not merely abnormal but impossible for Celie. Jealousy wells up in her heart. "Beat her" is Celie's answer when Harpo asks her "what he ought to do to her (Sofia) to make her mind." (38) However, Sofia is not Celie. Instead of being beaten to obedience, she fights back, though she loves Harpo. "They [are] fighting like two men." (39) As she later describes it to Celie, Sofia will "kill him dead before I (Sofia) let him beat me." (42) Sofia's words echo what Nettie tells Celie to do to Mr. ——. The voice of agreement resounds somewhere deep in Celie's heart. Her jealousy is unknowingly replaced by admiration, the admiration for Sofia's courage to express her disebedience to her husband and to any man who tries to control her. With her emotional identification with Sofia's action, Celie feels guilty that she has advised Harpo to beat Sofia, and confesses it to her, admitting, "I say it cause I'm a fool. …I say it cause I'm jealous of you. I say it cause you do what I can't." (42). Celie's confession wins Sofia's understanding and forgiveness, which marks the turning point in their relationship. The two women thereupon have a heart-to-heart talk about their miserable past. The similar experiences draw them closer and spontaneously strengthen the bond of their relationship.

Sofia's is literally a story of struggle. She tells Celie, "All my life I had to fight. I had to fight my daddy. I had to fight my brothers. I had to fight my cousins and my uncles. A girl child ain't safe in a family of men." (42) After hearing about the maltreatment of Celie, Sofia encourages her to fight, too, saying, "[y]ou ought to bash Mr. —— head open." (44) If Nettie's encouragement merely stays in words, Sofia sets an example for Celie by her action. Although Celie does not fight back as is expected, Sofia's action at least gets her to see that it is possible for a black woman to fight for her freedom and independence and thus to live a different life, or rather, to refuse to play the stereotypical role of a wife. She longs to become Sofia's soul mate, though she still takes a wait-and-see attitude toward Sofia's struggle. Therefore, when Sofia suggests making "quilt pieces out of these messed up curtains," Celie gets so joyful that "I (Celie) run git my pattern book." With Sofia's forgiveness and their relationship removed, "I (Celie) sleeps like a baby." (44) Quilting is a cooperative activity; and in the novel it symbolizes the reconciliation between Celie and Sofia, and the forming of their alliance or sisterhood.

As a staunch fighter for her own right and equality, Sofia not only rebels indefatigably against the patriarchal conventions but also refuses to surrender to the white hegemony. Although she chooses to leave her family at last because she is disappointed in and tired of Harpo, (who, according to Sofia, only thinks about how to make Sofia mind since they get married) and is put in prison because she does not agree to go into service of the mayor's family at his wife's request, her efforts tell Celie that black women's struggle for equal rights has still a long way to go and that their hope only lies in the consistent rebellion since silence and obedience will never prick the oppressors' consciences. To some extent, Sofia awakens Celie's rebellious consciousness or makes her question her own invariable passiveness. It is the sisterhood between Sofia and Celie that enables Celie to imagine and then experience an absolutely new life.

"Walker is very careful to balance women who find themselves weakened by their position with women who are strong to rise above their unfortunate circumstances." (Bates, 2005: 52) In *The Color Purple*, Shug is created as a strong woman who shows courage in adversity and walks out her own way. By portraying Shug, the author manages to maintain a balance between the weak and the strong. Shug is an incarnation of beauty, passion, confidence and ability, a perfect symbol of glamour. All that Shug possesses is just what Celie lacks. What she brings to Celie are novelty and uniqness, by which Celie is enthralled at first sight. From the outset Celie regards Shug as a goddess, if not a friend or sister, rather than as a rival. She attends to Shug wholeheartedly and helps restore her to physical health, which in turn wins Shug's affection and help. The relagionship between Celie and Shug is at once the lesbian partnership and the sisterly friendship. As the case stands, Shug is portrayed as Celie's spiritual mentor. She breeds Celie's sexual consciousness, arouses her instinct to love and to be loved, and helps her grow out of self-negation into self-awareness.

Like Sofia, Shug carries on a constant struggle against patriarchy. But, unlike Sofia, she is tactical. Different from Sofia's radical physical rebellion, Shug's is a moderate spiritual defiance, which is more feasible and effective. She takes singing as her weapon and works Celie over inside. The "Miss Celie's song" composed by Shug makes Celie first aware of her own existence as a human being and arouses her appetite for self-identity, which spontaneously leads to Celie's intrinsic change, a shift in her attitude toward life in general and Mr. —— in particular. Charles Darwin (1958: 2) once points out that "[i]t is not the strongest of the species that survive, but the one most responsive to change." That Celie is able to live through Mr. ——'s tyranny is ascribed to her awareness of being oppressed and her subsequent struggle for change. If Shug's enlightenment and encouragement pave the way for Celie's change and rebellion, the fact that Mr. —— has been hiding her letters from Nettie is the immediate flashpoint in her breaking the patriarchal cage and pursuing independence and self-respect. At the moment that she knows the truth, Celie feels so angry that she wants to kill Mr. ——. However, Shug convinces her that a better way to solve the problem and shake off Mr. ——'s confinement is not violence but economic independence and spiritual emancipation. She therefore encourages Celie to earn a living by making pants and gain economic independence from Mr. —— on the one hand; on the other hand, she instills the black animism into Celie's mind so that Celie realizes the racial supremacy in the white's version of God and deveolps her own interpretation of God and religion. Based on this, Shug easily persuades Celie to leave Mr. —— after the hiding-letters event and go to Memphis with her to start a business. As a sister/friend, Shug is Celie's keen supporter. She herself even gets alienated from Mr. —— and leaves him at last because of his abuse of Celie. In this regard, it is Shug's fellowship that gives Celie courage and power to leave her husband, go out of her past and begin a new and different life. Or rather, Celie's change and growth result from the sisterhood between the two women. Bathed in Shug's affection and friendship, Celie successfully develops into an able, confident and independent woman.

Celie is lucky, though she has been accepted as a sexual tool since she was 14 and deprived of all the basic rights as a woman. For she has such courageous and kind-hearted sisters as Nettie, Sofia and Shug, who offer her warmth, care and love, and guide her through the numb, ignorant and submissive state to self-confidence, self-respect and self-reliance. Sisterhood helps Celie grow into maturity and attain rebirth, and thus achieves her spiritual survival.

5.2.2.2 The Other Women's Survival

The Color Purple is largely concerned about black women's survival, physical and spiritual. Around the heroine Celie the author portrays a group of women characters, whose stories are interwoven with Celie's growth. Sisterhood, as a strategy for black women's emancipation, manifests itself not simply between two women but in the women's alliance, which is successfully established among the black females including Sofia, Squeak (Mary Agnes), Shug and Celie. In other words, the minor characters like Sofia and Squeak also experience personal transformations under the support of the female community. They, like Celie, get strength and possibility from sisterhood to achieve independence and self-identity.

Quilting is a symbol of women's alliance. Sofia and Shug first appear together when Celie and Sofia are working on a quilt and Shug donates "her old yellow dress for scrap." (A. Walker, 1982: 61) That the three women contribute to the same quilt, a nice pattern called "Sister's Choice," forms the first harmonious scene in the novel. This foreshadows the meeting at which Celie, Shug, Squeak, Sofia's sisters and even Harpo and Mr. —— discuss about how to rescue Sofia when they know about what torture and maltreatment she suffers in prison. Sofia's suffering affects the hearts of those present partly because she has a close relationship with them and partly because they have the same color and belong to the same race. They make concerted efforts to think up schemes to take Sofia out of prison and come to an agreement that the only workable way is doing everything possible to prod the warden into making Sofia work as a housemaid for a white lady. They finally decide to send Squeak to the warden as they make it certain that he is Squeak's white uncle. Although Harpo and Mr. —— also participate in the discussion, the women play a decisive role in the action. For one thing, the women dress Squeak up as a white lady so that she is allowed to see the warden, and teach her how to make the warden do what they expect him to. For another, the whole plan is carried out by Squeak, a member of the women's alliance. She frees Sofia out of the inhuman torture at the jail even at the expense of her own body—Squeak is raped by the warden, her white uncle. "Poor little Squeak come home with a limp. Her dress rip. Her hat missing and one of the heels come off her shoe." (100) For a woman, being raped is a burning shame and therefore the most intolerant thing. However, Squeak feels her sacrifice is worthwhile because she demonstrates the value of her existence in the event of rescuing Sofia. She begins to have a sense of identity. Back home, she first implies her willing to have Harpo's true love and then directly expresses her demand for being called by her real name "Mary Agnes" instead of the nick name "Squeak." Mary's transformation well illustrates the truth that those who help others help themselves. The success in freeing Sofia out of prison brings Mary self-confidence. She comes to realize her significance to others and begins to have a positive attitude toward life. She no longer feels herself inferior and becomes courageous enough to sing on the stage. Mary's survival is not just the fruit of her own struggle but the embodiment of the positive influence from the women's alliance as well. Thanks to Shug's encouragement, Mary begins her singing career. She is first brought "before the crowd" at Harpo's by Shug. Later on, she follows Shug to Memphis and sings and lives as a confident and independent individual. Meanwhile, the fact that Mary agrees to make her effort to help Sofia demonstrates her tolerance and kindheartedness. Mary sleeps with Harpo after Sofia leaves him, and once slaps Sofia out of jealousy so that Sofia knocks "two of Squeak's side teef out." (87) As a matter of fact, she takes Sofia as her rival. Even so, Mary does not hesitate to see the white warden regardless of the consequences. Sofia hence accepts Mary as her friend and sister. She offers to take care of Suzie Q, Mary and Harpo's daughter, so that Mary has the opportunity of leaving for Memphis and keeping her mind on singing. Mary is another black woman after Celie who develops within the women's alliance and benefits from black sisterhood. She testifies her worth, embodies her personality charm and wins economic independence as well, and thus ultimately establishes her self-identity.

Sisterhood plays a pivotal role in black women's emancipation. This is the case not only with the submissive, vulnerable women like Celie and Mary but also with the audacious, free-spirited women like Sofia and Shug. Sofia is first described as a strong and fearless woman warrior who dares to defy both sexism and racism. She temporarily extricates herself from the former through leaving Harpo and giving up her marriage. However, confronted with the white hegemony, she has to accept her failure. The individual strength is limited, after all. After "sassing the mayor's wife" and refusing to work as her maid, Sofia is put in prison and given a twelve-year sentence. (89) She not simply works "all day long from five to eight" in the prison laundry, but suffers from the jailor's maltreatment as well. (93) The first time Celie and the other family members visit her in the jail, they are profoundly shocked: "They crack her skull, they crack her ribs. They tear her nose loose on one side. They blind her in one eye. She swole from head to foot. Her tongue the size of my arm, it stick out tween her teef like a piece of rubber. She can't talk. And she just about the color of a eggplant." (92 – 93) The inhuman torture conquers Sofia and leaves her a changed person. She says to Celie, "[e]very time they ast me to do something, Miss Celie, I act like I'm you. I jump right up and do just what they say." (93) To survive, Sofia has no choice but to be obedient, though she "dream[s] of murder sleep or wake." (94)

Although Sofia succeeds in freeing herself in a family of men through fighting single-handedly, there is no possibility for her to cast off imprisonment and see a ray of hope without the help of the women's alliance. For one thing, the loving concern of the women's alliance brings Sofia warmth and solace. Shug comes "special to see Sofia" from Memphis on hearing that she is taken into custody. (94) Seeing Sofia in a blue and dirty prison state, Celie offers to comb her hair, change her clothes and give her a good scrub. Even Squeak disregards previous enmity and looks after Sofia's children. For another, the wisdom and efforts of the women's alliance get Sofia out of prison. To rescue her, Celie, Shug, Squeak, and even Mr. —— and Harpo rack their brains to find a sure way. Since prison break and jail delivery are risky in case Sofia might be found soon and taken back to prison, they decide to employ the scheme of convincing the warden that the severest punitive measure to Sofia is to make her serve a white woman. As Sofia's rival and the warden's nephew, Squeak is accepted as the best candidate to go to the warden. "Say you living with Sofia husband and her husband say Sofia not being punish enough. Say she laugh at the fool she make of the guards. Say she gitting along just fine where she at. Happy even, long as she don't have to be no white woman maid." (98) Squeak does everything as is expected and, accordingly, Sofia is made a "white woman maid" and saved from the current physical suffering.

Seemingly, the women's alliance helps Sofia just in the sense of realizing her physical survival; her struggle against racism is fruitless, for she ultimately becomes a housemaid for a white lady. Nevertheless, taken as a whole, the prison record is an asset to Sofia; it makes her realize the importance of united strength. The scheme design and implementation not only eloquently tells the intelligence and magnanimity of the participants but also spontaneously bonds them. Out of prison, sent to serve a white lady, Sofia cannot live together with her children;

yet she is not worried about them because Squeak and one of Sofia's sisters help look after them. Therefore, Sofia soon returns to what she was, getting "her color and her weight back" and "look[ing] like her old self." (105) Robust as before, she is ready to help those who help her, especially Squeak. Their relations are improved and they get on well with each other. When Squeak wants to go out singing, Sofia offers her a hand, saying to her, "[g]o on sing, …I'll look after this one (Squeak and Harpo's child) till you come back." (211) She is effectually so devoted that the child does take to her. As a result, a fortress-like friendship is being established between Sofia and Squeak, and, by extension, between Sofia and her friends and relatives, who provide strong backing to Sofia and her fight against racism. Furthermore, Sofia is now a wise and calm person. She knows that only those who live may fight for and see the day their other rights will be realized. So she does what she is told to by the white master, just to live (or rather, to fulfill physical survival), though she is never willing to do so and "all time think[s] bout killing somebody." (105) Sofia is clear that physical survival is the premise of spiritual survival. She seems to be awaiting opportunities to fulfil spiritual survival. We do not know how long Sofia will wait, for till the end of the story there is no opportunity arising; but we do know that Sofia grows mature, experienced and sophisticated. Now that she knows well that the whites are so powerful that isolated struggle is doomed to failure, she is sure to fight back in the near future in a united, intelligent way.

If Sofia's story tells the black women's difficulty of survival in a white society and their sensibility to choose to protect lives threatened by the white power, Shug's manifests the greatness of a black woman who earns her living all alone and bravely says "no" either to the male or to the black. Instead of the outflanking tactics Sofia has to adopt, Shug marches forward courageously and almost meets with no failure in her singing career. She is a winner in life and therefore an ideal model for black women to be casual, careless, lighthearted and fun. She is wealthy and seems to do anything by nature. She travels and sings all over the country. "She make so much money she don't know what to do with it. She got a fine house in Memphis, another car. She got one hundred pretty dresses. A room full of shoes. She buy Grady (a young man Shug loves and lives together with after leaving Mr. ——) anything he think he want." (114) A uniquely independent woman, Shug is also a friend in need and a spiritual mentor of the other black women. She guides Celie and Squeak to awakening and independence; she supports and encourages Sofia's struggle against the patriarchs. What's more, she contributes to Harpo and Mr. ——'s transformation by taking Squeak and Celie away to the North. Apparently, Ms. Walker tends to portray Shug as the fittest survivor in the sexist and racist Amerian society. Nevertheless, even Shug's survival depends on sisterhood within the black women.

The first time she is brought to Mr. ——'s home, "Shug Avery sick and nobody in this town want to take the Queen Honeybee in." (45) Even her parents would not like to take her home. In her letter to God, Celie writes that "[s]he sicker than my mama was when she die."(49) "Mr. —— be in the room with her all time of the night or day. He don't hold her hand though. She too evil for that." (49) Deadly sick, Shug becomes passionless and irritable; she sleeps less and loses her appetite. She appears somewhat desperate and even Mr. —— is at his wits' end. Just at this crucial moment Celie reaches out to her. She makes every effort to comfort and tend Shug: she washes her body, eats before her to whet her appetite, elaborately cooks the dish for her, combs her hair and pats on her head, and what not. It is all worth the effort, and Shug regains her self-confidence and musters up all her strength and courage to face the disease. With Celie's considerate care, Shug recuperates rapidly. In the meanwhile, she comes to accept Celie as her bosom friend. The longer the two black women stay together, the deeper their friendship and sisterhood grows. They open hearts to each other, talking about their personal topics, and become devoted to each other. To some extent, Celie saves Shug's life, offering Shug warmth, love, care, harmony and dedication of mankind. To put it another way, bathed in the sisterhood between herself and Celie, Shug gets the courage to live and catches the meaning of life. In this sense, not only Shug's physical survival but also her spiritual survival is attributed to Celie's friendship.

In the male-centered American society, the oppressed black sisters receive little care or concern from the family and the society. No one but themselves can fully understand their depressed plight. The care, love and support they offer to one another help to ease their physical pain and arouse their innermost feelings. In *The Color Purple*, Ms. Walker highlights the salvation power of sisterhood through depicting the transformation of each black female figure and her eventual self-confidence in meeting the varied challenges in life.

5.2.3 The Enlightenment of Sisterhood in *Possessing the Secret of Joy*: Tashi's Individuation Journey to Wholeness

In her fifth novel *Possessing the Secret of Joy*, Alice Walker "shifted her authorial emphasis from the external conditions of society to the internal psychological development of the individual." (Moore, 2000: 111) Specifically, in portraying the heroine Tashi, the author highlights her individuation journey to wholeness, on which Tashi is accompanied and enlightened by the female characters like Olivia, Lisette and Raye, along with her husband Adam. Sisterhood is still the author's focus here. Like in *The Color Purple*, the female characters play an important role in the heroine's life. Olivia, like Nettie or Sofia, is Tashi's spiritual support. She accompanies, cares about and channels Tashi. Lisette is to Tashi what Shug is to Celie. She is both Tashi's rival and enlightener. Lisette not simply shakes Tashi's marriage but throws light upon her gender perspective through the mouth of Pierre. Raye is Tashi's friend and doctor of soul. She offers Tashi psychological guidance and therapy and paves the way for her eventual personal wholeness. Therefore, emphasizing the heroine's psychological development, the novel depicts the sisterhood both within and beyond the race (i.e., the black sisterhood and the white-black sisterhood).

Olivia is Celie's daughter by her stepfather. She is taken by her adopted parents to Olinka, where she gets to know Tashi, who later gets married to her brother Adam and becomes her sister-in-law. The two black girls play and grow up together. They are family and friends. A firm sisterhood is established between them, though they have different cultures and customs, which result in their different outlooks on life and Tashi's pains and sufferings. Olivia objects strongly to the traditional customs of the Olinka people like face-tattoo and female circumcision, accepting them as signs of ignorance and backwardness and as inhuman torture on the Olinka women, while Tashi has them as symbols for her national identity and her unique way to support the Olinka people, and therefore persists in following the tradition. Thereofore, to prevent Tashi from going back to Olinka for the female circumcision, Olivia begs her and even cries like a lover. Tashi thus depicts,

> I listened to Olivia trying to control her breathing as she held on to the rope bridle. She was crying…
>
> She was like a lover.
>
> Tell me to do anything, and I will do it, she said.
>
> Tell me to go anywhere, and I will go, she said.
>
> Only, don't do this to yourself, *please*, Tashi.
>
> …
>
> We've been friends almost all our lives, she said. Don't do this to us. (A. Walker, 1992: 21, italics original)

No matter how Olivia begs her, Tashi determinedly returns to Olinka and has M'Lissa carrying out the surgery. "The operation she's had done to herself joined her, she felt, to those women, whom she envisioned as strong, invincible. Completely woman. Completely African. Completely Olinka. In her imagination, on her long journey to the camp, they had seemed terribly bold, terribly revolutionary and free. She saw them leaping to the attack." (63) For all that Tashi "care[s] about is the struggle for our (her) people," and the face-tattoo and female circumcision are her only possible way to support the Olinka people. (22) However, in the train of the surgery comes Tashi's trouble. At first, she has to endure the physical sufferings. This is Tashi's own narration: "I am like a chicken bound for market. The scars on my face are nearly healed, but I must still fan the flies away. The flies that are attracted by the odor coming from my blood, eager to eat at the feast provided by my wounds." (45) Although Tashi is now "accepted as a real woman by the Olinka people," we cannot sense her expected happiness and fulfillment in the depiction. (120) That's not all. When Adam finds her and takes her back home to America, Olivia surprisingly finds Tashi's lamentable change: "It was heartbreaking to see, on their return, how passive Tashi had become. No longer cheerful, or impish. Her movements, which had been graceful, and quick with the liveliness of her personality, now became merely graceful. Slow. Studied. This was true even of her smile; which she never seemed to offer you without considering it first. That her soul had been dealt a mortal blow was plain to anyone who dared look into her eyes." (65) The female circumcision not simply slows Tashi's pace but also numbs her soul. In a word, she is completely changed from body to soul. This is the beginning of the disruption of Tashi's personality. On the one hand, she deems to have become a true Olinka woman and maintained her Olinka identity after the female circumcision. She feels as if she had fulfilled her mission as an Olinka woman and therefore rests content with it. On the other hand, the scar has deprived Tashi of the basic rights as a woman, including having sex and giving birth to babies. She never enjoys sex as a normal woman. She suffers from difficult births, due to which her first child is retarded—"[s]ome small but vital part of his brain crushed by our ordeal"—and the second time she gets pregnant she is forced to get aborted. (60) Besides, she emits an odor, which is exclusively hers and makes her embarrassed and self-abased so that, just as her son Benny depicts, she "bathed constantly, as if to rid herself of any scent whatsoever." For "[t]o smell like herself seemed beyond her ability to accept." (94) Tashi is a victim of the age-old custom. Her personal suffering overwhelmingly demonstrates the social benightedness in Olinka. But as an Olinka woman, she seems to have no choice but to identify with her people. Tashi dangles and struggles between reason and emotion, between reality and dream.

Since Tashi's return to America after the mutilation surgery, Olivia is never away from her. She gives her care and support at any time Tashi needs. Their sisterhood is well illustrated in Olivia's constant company and selfless assistance both in the Tashi's daily life and psychological development after the female circumcision, particularly after Tashi is put in prison for killing M'Lissa. Tashi narrates in the novel, "I am dressed in cool white cotton from head to foot; Olivia shops for me in the tourist boutiques." (103) As a tender, loving and faithful friend and companion, Olivia looks after every bit of Tashi's life, including her daily necessities and psychological needs. Sentenced to death, Tashi's days are numbered. Olivia makes every effort to accompany Tashi and racks her brain to meet Tashi's wishes. She knows well that the female circumcision is Tashi's lifelong regret. To make up for it and alleviate the pain, she manages to get a similar female clay figure playing with her genitals, which Tashi likes best but is forbidden to be in possession of. Tashi relates,

> Olivia has crept up behind me as we all stand to be dismissed. She pushes a small paper bag into my hand. When I am in my cell again I open the bag and extract a small doll made of clay. It has been years since I saw another like it, quite by accident one morning in M'Lissa's hut. She found me playing with it, and boxed my ears, claiming the thing I held—a small figure playing with her genitals—was indecent. I was too young to ask why, therefore, she had it in her hut. A note from Olivia read: This is a replica. There are women potters here who make them." (109)

The small doll bears Olivia's care and hope as well. Olivia hopes to enrich Tashi's life and help her achieve self-realization. So she does. "Within the prison she (Tashi) is permitted freedom. Her days are busy. There are visits from women's groups and the foreign press. …Through it all, she flourishes, her alert face kind and reflective, ... Each morning she works with me (Olivia) on the AIDS floor, feeding, bathing or simply touching the patients." (245) The sincere sisterhood eventually cheers Tashi up. Now she possesses a healthy body and mind, from which flows vigor and strength. She not only spends her last days looking after the

AIDS victims but also becomes considerate and understanding. When Olivia firmly believes that she is innocent and asks why she confesses, Tashi tells a white lie, saying "[y]ou are right, Olivia, that I did not kill M'Lissa," (250) so as to cater to Olivia's emotion and concern. Till now Olivia's unremitting care helps enliminate the hostility of Tashi, who opens her heart to Olivia as a friend and sister: "it would kill me to get any older. There is nothing more of this life I need to see. What I have already experienced is more than enough. Besides, she says soberly, maybe death is easier than life, as pregnancy is easier than birth." (250) Moreover, with these words, Tashi, who comes to know love, tends to ease the grief over her death of Olivia and her other family members and friends. To some extent, Olivia is Tashi's emotional restorer. Olivia's love and care give Tashi courage and strength to accompolish her individuation journey. Throughout the individuation process Olivia accompanies Tashi and helps and witnesses the evolvement of her personality from disruption to wholeness.

Another important female figure in Tashi's life is the Frenchwoman Lisette, Adam's mistress. Lisette is Tashi's doom. If the female circumcision is an inducement to Tashi's split personality, Lisette is a determinant of Tashi's eventual spiritual disruption. The female circumcision severely undermines Tashi's sexual life with Adam after marriage. Tashi's pain results in Adam's fear of making love, which by and by alienates him from her. With Adam's alienation and particularly after her failure in giving birth to a healthy baby, Tashi becomes irritable and oversensitive. She loves Adam and their son, but she can neither satisfy her husband's sexual needs nor bring her son up to be a normal mental person. Thus, as a wife and mother, Tashi is a complete failure. She becomes a useless woman according to the traditional American notion. She has already had a strong sense of crisis. With so much at stake, she is informed of Lisette's pregnancy with Adam's child. The information is the last straw that breaks the camel's back. It gives Tashi such a fatal blow that "she flew into a rage that subsided into a years-long deterioration and rancorous depression. She tried to kill herself. She spoke of murdering their son." (125) Tashi is on the brink of collapse. On the very day she gets the information about Pierre's birth, she begins to collect all sorts of stones—"[l]arge oblong stones from the roadside; hearvy flat stones from the riverbank; sharp jagged shale stones from the fields"—so that she would strike him with the stones one day they meet. (143) Although she knows it is neither Adam's intention nor Lisette's fault, Tashi cannot help harboring bitter hatred against Lisette and her son Pierre.

Comparatively, Lisette's conduct is worth respecting. In portraying the white female character, Ms. Walker seems to overstep racial lines. She endows Lisette with such merits as thoughtfulness, tolerance and broadmindedness. Lisette is one of the rare positive images of white women in Walker's works. From the outset, she heartily sympathizes with Tashi's past miserable experience and endeavors to foster good relations with her. In spite that Tashi refuses to meet her, Lisette never stops caring for and helping her. Tashi herself later recollects, "How she tried to know me. Tried to visit me. Wrote me letters. Tried to interest me in French cooking—sent me cookbooks and recipes. Sent me clippings about wild mushrooms and where to look for them. …Sent me her son. And how I refused her. How I thought she knew me too well." (159) Lisette accepts Tashi as a relative. She is not just trying to communicate with Tashi but to figure out how to treat her mental illness as well. The Old Man, Tashi's first psychotherapist, is Lisette's uncle, who is introduced by Lisette herself. Thanks to The Old Man's psychological counseling and the admonishment that "[y]ou yourselves are your last hope," Tashi realizes her own psychological problems and has the courage to envisage her psychological fear of blood. (53) In childhood Tashi witnesses her sister's bleeding to death while being circumcised, which has been branded deeply in Tashi's heart, though she, as a little girl, does not understand it fully. With the aid of The Old Man, Tashi begins reminiscing about what has been done to her sister by M'Lissa. She spontaneously paints "[t]he picture of a fighting cock," which helps her remember, "as if a lid lifted off my (her) brain, the day I (Tashi) crept, hidden in the elephant grass, to the isolated hut from which came howls of pain and terror. … and I knew instinctively that it was Dura being held down and tortured inside the hut. Dura who made those inhuman shrieks that rent the air and chilled my heart." (71, 73) With a flashback to the past, Tashi comes to understand the root of her fear of blood and thus embarks on a journey to remedy. In this sense, Tashi's eventual realization of personality wholeness is largely attributed to Lisette.

In the meantime, throughout the treatment process, Lisette keeps up correspondence with Adam and gets well informed of Tashi's therapeutic effect. She worries when Tashi is not in compliance with the doctor, and delights as long as there appears a little progress in the treatment. When she learns of Tashi's nightmare of tower, Lisette is trying to interpret it so as to help her out. Pierre writes to Tashi that "[t]he tower question obsessed my mother since the day she heard of it, and she read many books trying to figure out what it could mean." (160) Lisette not just cares about Tashi genuinely and resorts to every means to help her but trusts her completely as well. When she herself is ill and about to die, she sends her son Pierre to live with Adam and Tashi and attend university in America. Pierre grows up with the story of Tashi's circumcision. He is interested in her nightmare about tower. Everything he studies, trivial or important, is more or less related to Tashi's suffering. He inherits both Lisette's looks and merits like tolerance and warmheartedness. He takes the initiative to write to Tashi, expressing his sincerity to help her. He reads books to make out what the tower is in Tashi's nightmare and helps her analyze the brutal patriarchal truth of the African tradition. Accordingly, Pierre walks Tashi out of the sequela of the female mutilation and works as a spiritual guide on Tashi's individuation journey to wholeness.

With her healthy personality regained, Tashi comes to understand Lisette and her care and worry: "Suddenly I see Lisette very clearly. She is sitting by a window in front of which there is a desk. She is thinking of me as she looks into a thick brown book in front of her, and her white brow is puckered in a frown." (172) The more Tashi thinks of Lisette, the more sorry she feels for her previous indifference and even hostility to Lisette. On the eve of her execution, she writes to Lisette, "Now it occurs to me to wonder how you died. If I had been able truly to understand that you would die, and cease to write to me and to exist, I would have paid better attention to you before you died." (276) So far Tashi has fully accepted Lisette as friend and sister, knowing that Lisette is "someone who has seriously thought about me (Tashi)." (272) She is sure to meet Lisette in the heaven, explaining, "[b]ecause through your son, to whom my suffering became a mystery into which he submerged himself, we have already met on earth." (276) As a continuation of Lisette's life, Pierre is actually created as replacement of his mother. He has been a gift to Tashi and a link between the two women. His relationship with Tashi is an extension of that between his mother Lisette and Tashi or their inter-racial sisterhood in a broader sense. His success in healing Tashi and the development of their relationship foreshadow the bright prospects of Walker's womanism.

Raye is a middle-aged Afro-American woman, introduced by The Old Man as Tashi's psychotherapist after his death. "She radiated a calm, cheerful competence that irritated" Tashi, who dislikes and rejects her also because Raye, as a black woman, is "whole" and not circumcised. (113) Tashi's emotional repulsion against Raye is, in essence, a simple manifestation of envy. In the eyes of Tashi, what Raye possesses—competence and wholeness—is just what she lacks. Raye's existence seems to declare Tashi's fault in getting herself circumcised and totally negates what Tashi has been adhering to, for all that Tashi has lost and been suffering is rooted in the so-called "female initiation into womanhood." The female mutilation is Tashi's eternal irritation. It has deprived her of the right to live as a normal woman, yet she has no courage to face up to it. Therefore, when Raye, the uncircumcised black woman, appears and compels her to talk about it and admit its evil, Tashi feels irritated or, to be exact, humiliated. Nevertheless, the sense of humiliation lays bare Tashi's regret and envy, which she herself does not realize, and which betray Tashi's unconscious negation of the Onlinka ritual. As a matter of fact, Tashi is touched deep in the soul by Raye's personal charisma. This lays a foundation for her later opening her heart to Raye.

As a doctor of soul, Raye is dedicated and worth respecting. Before sitting side by side with Tashi, she has made a detailed study of her files and is therefore well informed of her mental block. To remove the "boulder" (using Tashi's own words), she determines to expose Tashi to the evil of the Olinka ritual through goading persuasion. As a follower of Carl Jung, Raye believes that Tashi's self is now tyrannized by the negative manifestation of Persona (i. e., the conformity archetype), or, to put it in specific terms according to the novel, her submission to the Olinka culture and traditions. To help Tashi out, she has to awaken her to the harm of the ancient customs, the female mutilation in particular, so that Tashi will consciously free herself out of the national restraints. Raye therefore is another enlightener in Tashi's individuation process.

Raye's endeavor tells success. Despite the initial repulsion, Tashi is finally willing to talk with Raye. She begins with the story of the Olinka people's Leader, who was Jesus Christ to Olinkans, and their remembrance and love of him. As is expected, the narration brings Tashi little by little to the fact that it is this respectful god who mutes and even enslaves Olinka women by getting them circumcised. This is done in the name of resisting whites' aggression and preserving the national identity. Tashi tells Raye, "from prison we received our instructions" from "Our Leader" that "we must remember who we were," that "we must fight the white oppressors without ceasing," that "we must return to the purity of our own culture and traditions," and that "we must not neglect our ancient customs." (115) There appears nothing wrong with these instructions. Whoever is an Olinkan is supposed to follow them. Olinka women (including Tashi) are of course no exception. The problem lies in that, as far as Olinka women are concerned, the so-called patriotism or national identity can only be embodied in female mutilation: "From prison Our Leader said we must keep ourselves clean and pure as we had been since time immemorial—by cutting out unclean parts of our bodies." (119) With these instructions kept in mind, Olinka women spontaneously choose to suffer from the unbearable genital circumcision to meet men's needs.

Fully aware of the sexual hegemony in female circumcision, Tashi casts off the fetters of the conformity archetype in her personality. Her true self stands out. She does not mind any longer that she will be accepted as a traitor by the Olinka people when she kills the tsunga M'Lissa. She speaks out for the right of Olinka women. She struggles to eradicate the traditional hindrances to Olinka women's freedom and equality. At this point she stands closer to Raye. Their relationship has already gone beyond that between doctor and patient. They are friends or, exactly, sisters. In effect, from the very beginning, Raye treats Tashi more than a patient. She shows sympathy for her suffering; she encourages her to open her heart; she helps her to understand the evil of the traditional ritual and the necessity of striving for freedom and equality. In a word, Raye awakens Trashi to her own twisted belief and illumines her individuation journey to wholeness.

If she emphasizes care and love in the relationship between Tashi and Olivia or Lisette, Ms. Walker highlights the incentive function in depicting the sisterhood between Tashi and Raye. Both exert a guiding and enlightening influence on the realization of the self in Tashi's personality. The novel ends up with Tashi's execution. The author designs a scene, where a banner with the "huge block letters"—"RESISTANCE IS THE SECRET OF JOY"—is held and unfolded by Tashi's family and friends on the execution ground. The words on the banner summarize Tashi's life experience well and truly. Resistance does bring joy and adds meaning to Tashi's life. It is resistance, resistance against the ancient Olinka culture and traditions, that finally sublimates Tashi's soul. Through resistance Tashi eventually accomplishes her individuation process to wholeness.

5.2.4 The Spiritual Guidance of Sisterhood in *By the Light of My Father's Smile*: Susannah's Emancipation and Autonomy

By the Light of My Father's Smile is also characterized by the portrayal of a group of women figures—Pauline, Magdalena, Susannah and Irene. They each have a different relation with Susannah: Pauline is her lesbian partner; Magdalena her biological sister; and Irene her intimate friend. They impact Susannah's growth, to varying degrees. If Pauline and Magdalena, as is analyzed in 5.1, change Susannah's sexual orientation, Irene guides Susannah to self-recognition. Susannah has long been puzzled by her relationship with the people around, especially with Mr. Robinson (her father), Magdalena and Pauline. She loses herself both in the father-daughter relationship and in the sisterhood and the lesbianism. She cannot express her true feelings to her father. Life for Susannah is a constant struggle to win either Magdalena's or Pauline's heart. She enjoys relaxation neither with Magdalena nor with Pauline. The relationship with Irene first tells Susannah comfort and equality, which further breed her emancipation and autonomy.

Irene is a dwarf bastard. Her mother was raped and impregnated; and when giving birth to Irene she died. Therefore, Irene is received as "God's punishment for her mother's sin. She was given at a very young age, as a servant, to the church." (A. Walker, 1998: 52) She lives a miserable life there and never leaves the place before meeting Susannah. Irene thus describes her early days to Susannah: "In the old days, when I was young, it (leaving) was forbidden. I was beaten if I left. Dragged back. There was no place to go, either. My mother was dead. Nobody wanted me." (57) Compared to Irene's unfortunate parentage and tragic life, Susannah is the fortune's favorite. "She had been born into a family that wanted her, loved her." (58) She has basked in her parents' love and care and received a good education. Normally, Susannah should be grateful to her parents or at least have no complaint about them. However, "she had somehow discovered a rejecting power in herself, even in childhood, and had used it to shut her father out." (58) Actually, after seeing her father beating Magdalena, Susannah regards her father as a monster and rejects whatever he offers, including his love and care. She hates him and never thinks of forgiving him. This not simply upsets her father but also perturbs Susannah herself. Into adulthood, she could feel her father's love in a more tangible way; yet she cannot but reject him. After conversing with Irene, she comes to realize that rejecting her father is not of her own accord; she loves him all the time and is willing to forgive him deep inside; her feelings toward her father have long been controlled, consciously or unconsciously, by her sympathy for her sister. Susannah is deeply touched by Irene's free and easy way of looking at what she experiences: Irene even does not complain about her misfortune in the least; what she keeps doing is try her best to make life purposeful and meaningful. Besides doing the routine work in the church, she learns "other people's languages," including German, Italy, Spanish, Japanese and Latin, and keeps contact with the outer world chiefly through TV. (55) Knowing everything in the world, Irene is intelligent and strong-minded; she has her original views on things and finally lives a free and unrestrained life. In contrast, Susannah finds herself narrow-minded; she has no independent opinion and always goes with the tide. She never lives at her own will. Compassion for Magdalena holds back Susannah's true feeling to her father. Susannah is thus trapped between two feelings—grievance against her father's wrongs and guilt for not forgiving him. This, in essence, is a manifestation of tension and stress and lack of self-confidence. Irene's positive attitude toward life awakens Susannah's self-recognition and desire for freedom, and makes it clear that forgiveness is a powerful catalyst for Susannah's transformation and emancipation.

Susannah encounters with Irene in Petros' home village church. The moment their eyes meet, Susannah feels "as if she and the dwarf shared a moment of recognition." (49) Irene's "look appeared to scorch Susannah." (49) The "hot gaze" seems to tell a story of "ancient, indelible grief," which immediately excites Susannah's curiosity about the aging Greek dwarf. (50) So, although Petros implies that Irene is hard to communicate with, saying that "no one actually talked to Irene" and Irene "wouldn't speak English," Susannah determinates to go to Irene and get to the bottom of her life. (50) So she does. Consequently, she has a good talk with Irene, which not only gives her the needed information about Irene's life but also proves that Irene speaks several languages including English. The talk shortens the distance between the two women. Soon they meet again and unknowingly become friends. They love and help each other like sisters; their relationship has nothing to do with sex. Thanks to Irene's help, Susannah develops a proper understanding of her relationship with her father, her sister Magdalena, and her lesbian partner Pauline.

As the consequence of women's struggle for a homosexual order to subvert the patriarchal sexual order, lesbianism helps women achieve independence and dominance against the patriarchal background. For patriarchy, as Lerner (1986: 98) once defines, is "the manifestation and institutionalization of male dominance over women in society," and this kind of dominance is built on the basis of heterosexuality. The homosexual order in lesbianism breaks the established heterosexual order and subverts the patriarchal dualism. However, there appears a new dualism in lesbianism, the dualism of the active and the passive. Thus inequality and oppression still exist in lesbianism. Susannah is keenly aware of the frequent disharmony in her relationship with Pauline: Pauline is attempting to be the dominant; she wants to control everything. Even when they are making love, she tries to steal something from Susannah. Pauline herself also admits that she likes to control Susannah because she is jealous about Susannah, because Susannah seems to have everything that she wishes for: the trips to Mexico in childhood, the parents who never betray their children, the chance to enjoy discussion about primitive art and culture, and the like. That Pauline means to find some compensation and psychological balance in her relationship with Susannah disappoints the latter and sets her in a long ambivalent state. Susannah is also the passive side in her relationship with Magdalena. As a witness to her father's violence, Susannah feels obligated to take sides with her sister. She regards it as an act of betrayal to share a normal close relationship with her father. So she persists in her refusal to accept her father's love and becomes estranged from him, though she feels sorry and tends to forgive her father time and time again. What's more, each time Susannah wants to forgive her father, Magdalena will do something to stop her. Even so, Magdalena is never grateful for what Susannah has sacrificed and suffered from—she takes Susannah just as a tool to take revenge on her father. There exists a similar awkward situation in the father-daughter relationship. Susannah appears totally indifferent to her father but never stops loving him. She refuses him firmly and decisively each time her father expresses his care for her and tries to communicate with her, though she has been longing for his care and love. Hence, Susannah's emotional life before meeting Irene is characterized by dilemma and awkwardness.

Fortunately, Irene appears and offers Susannah not only a model but also a hand. On the one hand, Irene's experience eloquently tells Susannah that there are racism and sexism in the world outside America. Irene sets up an example for Susannah through her own active and optimistic attitude toward life. She teaches her how to master her own life. On the other hand, Irene helps Susannah analyze the causes of the disharmony in her relationship with Magdalena, Pauline as well as her father, and makes Susannah understand that neither blind compliance nor absolute predominance results in harmony, and that equality is a must in a long-term and stable relationship. For the passive in a relationship, equality never comes spontaneously. It requires the autonomy of the passive and the coordination of the active. It means both a struggle and change. Irene is Susannah's spiritual mentor. She guides Susannah to self-recognition and ultimate escape from bewilderment in her emotional life, which is well represented in the dream in which "there are two women, each of whom offers her food. She begins to eat the food, happily. Enjoying it. When the first woman sees this, she slowly begins to pour salt over everything. Susannah turns hopefully to the food offered by the other woman. That woman calmly pours a fine stream of sand." (A. Walker, 1998: 199) When Susannah tells Irene the dream, Irene thus interprets, "Pauline was the woman pouring sand, ... you were able to sense something wrong there. Magdalena was the one pouring salt. In itself, salt is a condiment; it belongs in food. That is why you hardly noticed until it was too late." (202) Magdalena's dominance does more harm to Susannah than Pauline's, not only because hers, just like too much salt in food, is hard to notice, but also because its impact extends to the relationship between Susannah and her father. Irene further explains to Susannah, "[a]t many different points you might have reconnected with your father, but there was a shaker of salt right by your elbow. Before you knew it, in all kinds of ways, Magdalena had unpalatably overseasoned your food. A word here, a whisper there. … [she] feed you such distortions and lies!" (202) Irene's interpretation seems to enlighten Susannah all of a sudden. She comes to get at the fact that both Pauline and Magdalena attempt to play a dominant role in her life simply out of jealousy or even hatred as far as Magdalena is concerned. For Magdalena takes Susannah as an accomplice of her father, who kills her happiness. Having found the crux of the problem, Susannah decides to change her passive state in the relationships. She no longer yields to Pauline or Magdalena; she no longer keeps silent; she speaks out how she feels and what she thinks. In other words, she becomes autonomous. With the return of her inherent autonomy, Susannah becomes lenient and magnanimous. She begins to redefine her father's fault and dares to face her feelings to her father. She eventually understands her father and determines to forgive him, though he has already died.

If lesbianism leads Susannah to physical autonomy, sisterhood (i. e., her relationship with Irene) contributes to the fulfillment of her self-recognition and spiritual autonomy. Irene is the leading light, which guides Susannah to spiritual survival.

5.2.5 The Assistance from Sisterhood in *Now Is the Time to Open Your Heart*: The Females' Rebirth

An eternal subject in Ms. Walker's novels is (black) women's struggle for emancipation, physical and/or spiritual, and their eventual salvation, which cannot do without the assistance from sisterhood. In this sense, *Now Is the Time to Open Your Heart* is no exception. Along with the protagonist, a black woman named Kate, the author portrays some other female characters like Lalika and Missy. Different in parentage, education and careers, these women are all lonely hearts in the modern world. They are eager to find a spiritual home, where they could open their hearts to each other and get themselves out of psychological perplexion. The spiritual renewal and transformation is their common goal and the thought-provoking theme of the novel.

Kate Nelson is a black author of fame and wealth in her fifties. A "compact, muscular woman with good skin and screamy white teeth, a woman no longer sure there was a path through life or how indeed to follow one if there was," she finds some subtle changes in her body. (A. Walker, 2004: 15 – 16) "She had felt it begin to shift beneath her feet. Or above her feet, because the change had started in her knees. In her fifty-seventh year they had, both of them, mysteriously, out of the blue, began to creak." (11) The physical changes affect Kate's life. She begins dreaming of a dry river every night. "Her pens as well seemed to go empty on her. An unusual number of them, though practically brand new, refused to scratch more than a few pale lines. No matter that she banged them in frustration on the desktop. Her eyes dimmed. Nor could her new reading glasses often be found." (14) She is greatly perplexed by the old age and feels uneasy, insecure and even panic-stricken. She is eager to escape from her present state. A voice from her inner world keeps saying: "You must find a real river somewhere in the world—forget the dry one in your dreams—to travel down." (14) So she complies with her inner calling and starts out her journeys—first to the Colorado and then to the Amazon—to search for her river of life.

Kate has experienced several marriages. She is especially hurt by her first marriage, and could not forget the scene that "her first husband and their child had given her" "a serving dish" as a gift "for Valentine's Day," and her intense agitation it gave rise to: "At the time of the gift she'd stuffed her disappointment. ... A lump had risen in her throat. Of sadness. Of disappointment. Anger that she had entered the unromantic era of life, so soon! That her child was in cahoots with her father in giving her this awful gift, this mirror in which she saw herself as someone whom time was passing by." (27) She comes to realize the role she has played in her husband and child's life and "saw how they ceased to really see her. They saw instead a service, a servant." (28) A housewife whose worth lies only in the details of housekeeping, Kate is expected to be everything but an independent individual with thought and desire. She has no self. To live is to serve and look after her husband and child—this is the life her family set for her.

"[S]he's gazed into their greedy eyes and saw the rest of her life being sucked away. And she had swallowed and swallowed." (28) As a matter of fact, the gift, like an alarm bell, awakens Kate from emotional numbness. She begins reevaluating her past and meditating on the meaning of her own life, and determines to free herself out of the tiring housework with monotonous regularity. She leaves her husband and child and means to live the rest of her life for herself. Subsequently, she goes through several marriages, and, as all of them end up with failure, she resists marriage. Now Kate lives together with her male lover Yolo, a painter much younger than her. She is attracted to Yolo by her admiration of his paintings. "The moment I stood in front of any one of his paintings, she [Kate] elaborated, my bird nature became activated. I felt I could fly!" (20) Yolo's paintings inspire passion and vitality in Kate, which enable her to commence a long journey. She believes that the dry river inside her is surely connected "to a wet one somewhere on the earth," and feels that she is "being called." (21 – 22)

Determined to follow her inner voice, Kate leaves "her house heading directly into her journey" to the Colorado, with nobody driving her to the airport, "[n]o long cuddles near the ticket counter, no second thoughts about whether they (she and Yolo) would be all right. It was like her to want it this way. No fuss." (16) To Kate, the journey is a farewell ceremony to the past, to the chained life in the household chores. What she is trying to do is go forward with her burdens—her resentment, belief, attitude, or responsibility—discarded so as to make it possible to reset her life. Therefore, she must break off relations with anybody, including her lover Yolo, and put her heart and soul into the journey with a rafting group consisting of women members. Kate senses that women share common psychological disturbance, which will easily draw them together. "Her journey now was to be with women. Only women. Because of women. And partly because she had seemed to feel, and to wonder aloud, about the possibility that only women, these days, dreamed of rivers, and were alarmed that they were dry." (16)

Floating on the river with the women partners, Kate feels that "[t]he savage rushing of the river seemed to be inside her head, inside her body." (22) As a matter of fact, there is "an internal roar as of the sound of a massive accumulation of words, spoken all at once, but collected over her lifetime, now trying to leave her body." Having restrained within the confines of a home for so long a time, Kate has a strong desire to open up to others and share her innermost thoughts and feelings in an un-protected way. The torrents of the river-water and the vast expanses of the nature immediately excite her and help open her spiritual journey. She begins throwing up, which indicates her pouring out words from the heart. "All the words from decades of her life filled her throat. Words she had said or had imagined or had swallowed before saying to her father, dead these many years. All the words to her mother. To her husbands. Children. Lovers." (23) All the scenes of solitude, disharmony and even brutality in her past life flash constantly before her eyes. Kate eventually says exactly as the mind dictates and tells her women partners about the unforgettable in her past life.

To revive means to cast off one's old self and take on a new one, to which opening one's heart is an indispensable preliminary. Kate's time to open her heart comes when she gets concerns and care from her women partners: "The women were gentle with her. Placing all her small belongings—toothbrush and paste, soap, eyeglasses—within her reach." (28) Kate feels it "luxurious to be out camping with a band of mature women" and "reveled in the intimacy engendered by their distance from everything and everyone." (38) She gets relaxed, feels secure and breathes freely so that she says out her psychological disturbance—anger, grievance, sadness and disappointment. "As her body gave up the last of its bitter memories…, she experienced a lightness" that enables her to face up to reality, her aging in particular. (36) She feels "no stirring within" any longer. (42) At night around the campfire, she is frequently "flooded with gratitude" while seeing her partners safe and hearing their "humorous stories of their surprise, their fright." (43) The common concerns narrow the distance between Kate and the other women, and harmonize their relations. They talk about getting older and some other problems that perplex female seniors, and exchange their opinions on dyeing hair as well as their sexual life. They live in a family of warmth like sisters. Sisterhood helps Kate shake off the fetter of the family completely, draw a period for the past, and restore her true self. Bathed in moonlight, she feels the kinship with her women partners as well as with the moon and the river moving through her body, and finds herself integrated into nature in the canyon. Obviously, Ms. Walker, as a womanist, never forgets her ideal of harmony, harmony among humans, and between humankind and nature.

Ms. Walker writes a lot about herself in Kate—the life experience, the identity as a writer in her fifties, the concern about the sexism and racism, and the belief in shamanism. *Now Is the Time to Open Your Heart* was produced in the author's fifties, when she was likewise troubled by mental confusion. In portraying the heroine, the author tends to explore her own psychological disturbance and find the way out. In an interview in 2003, Ms. Walker called a spade a spade, saying that "[i]t was a pleasure to relive some of my own discoveries about life in the person/character of Kate," who epitomizes the author's different 'isms—environmentalism, ecologism, Buddhism and Shamanism, etc. As a black woman, Kate, like the author, particularly takes stock in shamanism as her spiritual savior. She has had an experience with plant medicines and already read everything she could find on the probable result of taking them. She even has visited a local shaman before her second journey, to get informed of the "Grandmother medicine," a magical plant in South America which is said to get people with inner problems remedied. So, when she encounters the other Medicine Seekers at the airport, Kate recognizes them "immediately as Medicine Seekers" and joins them on the journey to the Amazon. (A. Walker, 2004: 50)

Traveling to the Amazon, Kate "undergoes a shamanic initiation that transforms her understanding of indigenous healing as well as indigenous comprehension of the planet," stated Ms. Walker in the same interview in 2003. "[E]nlightenment of any sort required a lot of regurgitation," which, in the case of Kate, is facilitated by the "Grandmother medicine." (A. Walker, 2004: 52) After waves of intense nausea and vomiting, Kate has a strong sense of consanguinity. She feels "[i]ndigenous to the Americas" and finds that, only in North America, nowhere else, could she, a "so-called Black person—African, European, Indio—exist" and that "[t]his old medicine surely must care for, belong to" her. (53) The continuous internal cleansing also helps Kate flee "the frightened animal aspect of herself" and gradually open her heart. (63) After several sessions with Grandmother, Kate begins recounting stories both about her own and her people's past to the shaman healer Armando, and expressing her bewilderment, grievance as well as indignation to him. Psychological disturbance results from long-term lack of communication. With her thoughts, feelings and experiences poured out, Kate settles into a peaceful calm. In practice, the goal of shamanism is to open the heart of human beings. As Walker expressed it in the 2003 interview, only if "the heart opens and we are able to feel each other as we feel ourselves the whole world" will escape from "the danger of being destroyed by war. War created by people whose hearts are so closed they cannot feel or even know what they are doing." Her heart opened, Kate becomes positive, caring and communicative. She is now able to help Armando and actually has become "someone to whom the others turned." (A. Walker, 2004: 85) What she concentrates on is "her inner peacefulness." "She began to have the feeling that it was this inner peace that attracted peace around her." (104) Therefore, as far as the heroine is concerned, "Now Is the Time to Open Your Heart," the title of the novel, seems to indicate the moment of her enlightenment and transformation.

As a womanist, Walker never fails to set in the company of women her heroine's journey to spiritual survival. *Now Is the Time to Open Your Heart* is no exception. Although there are male members like Rick, Hugh, Armando (a shaman) and Cosmi (Armando's apprentice), Kate appears to be on more intimate terms with the female members, Missy and Lalika, who are likewise troubled by mental confusion. As misery loves company, the three women feel kinship with one another.

Lalika is a black woman in her mid-thirties from Mississippi, who has a criminal record. She killed a man who "had raped her and was trying to rape her friend," and was thus sent to jail with her friend, where they suffered from every insult and had no moment of privacy at all—they were beaten by the patrolmen and raped repeatedly by the jailers and inmates, and had been watched day and night from a surveillance camera; and what is more disgusting is that "[t]he beatings and brutal rapes had been preserved on video and marketed by two of the guards." (105) Lalika is stuck in the bitter memories ever since then. To extricate herself from the past nightmares, she joins the Medicine Seekers and becomes one of Kate's partners. At first Kate keeps distance from Lalika due to her infamous past. However, finding her weeping alone one day, she feels sympathy for Lalika and becomes concerned about her pain.

Forlornness is Kate's first impression of Lalika. In effect, "Kate had never heard a voice so forlorn." (86) So she offers Lalika what she needs most—company. She begins accompanying Lalika on her own initiative. They are found sitting together like sisters, shoulders touching. Then the intuition of a woman tells Kate that there is a sad story behind Lalika. Together with the shamans, Kate convinces Lalika to take the "Grandmother medicine" so that she opens her heart. Lalika finally tells her miserable story to Kate. She even begins dreaming of the future: "If I survive this journey, she told Kate, I will shave my head. Then, until I'm used to being bald, I will wear this little crocheted cap. It has many tears woven in, Lalika said thoughtfully, but if I live, the sun will dry them." (107) Though a bit miserable, it proves that Lalika gets herself relieved from pain and loneliness. That the sun will dry the tears woven in the cap simply implies that she believes that a bright future is right ahead. Sensing the marked changes in Lalika, Kate sheds tears of joy. "Catching a tear as it slid down her own cheek Kate leaned forward and pressed it into Lalika's design. There will be the tears of two of us, then, she said. Lalika burst into tears." (107) The scene is "so like women to create their own rituals, ··· their own little markers of transition, their own ephemeral celebrations." (107) It is both a celebration of Lalika's rebirth and of the establishment of the women's friendship. In the sweet and heartwarming atmosphere sisterhood is once again highlighted.

Missy is another female victim of sex assaults in the group of the Medicine Seekers. She has been suffering from self-accusation and self-guilty of incest since she was old enough to understand sex. Missy and her mother lived with her grandfather after her father joined the army and left them for ever. Her grandfather was a clown who was good at amusing kids. While playing with his granddaughter, he would "be wearing his clown clothes and his clown nose," out of which Missy got great fun. (156) And every time when they had fun together, he would cheat the little girl into sex, which the infant Missy never knew and just interpreted as playing. Although she and her mother left her grandfather when Missy came to understand what he had been doing to her, both the mother and the daughter "couldn't leave off feeling love for him." For "except for what he'd done to" Missy, "he was the greatest guy" they had ever known. (155) As an adult, Missy is actually put in a dilemma. On the one side, she feels guilty of what she has done with her grandfather and is afraid to have sex with anyone, including her boyfriends and her husband. "It just felt like the wrong thing to do." (156) On the other side, she does not hate him in the privacy of her thoughts. Missy was "used to him physically" and "missed snuggling and cuddling and lying on the sofa on a rainy afternoon watching cartoons," although she "didn't want him messing around my (her) private parts"; she and her mother, "were so used to him"—his jokes, pranks and dependability; she as well as her mother "*missed him terribly*" after leaving his house. (155, italics original) Thus her grandfather is both a devil and angel in her life. She wants to get rid of the painful memories but cannot help missing him.

Compared with Lalika and Kate, Missy is more miserable and therefore more pitiful. She is completely destroyed by her grandfather. To start a new life, she needs to remould herself thoroughly, which is almost impossible without the care and company from the group of seven. As a matter of fact, Missy is set in the center of care. When she, after taking the "Grandmother medicine," "seemed to die," both the shamans and the Medicine Seekers, male and female, gather around her in a circle, Armando "singing over her," Cosmi "fanning her," and Kate sitting beside her and looking after her. (154) They watch her and wait for her to come to herself. Missy wakes up and eventually opens her heart and tells the "scary parts" of her story to the group members, as they are the first people who disturb her solitude. A sweet and harmonious picture unfolds before readers: "Lalika took one of Missy's hands. Kate took the other. Hugh and Rick placed their hands on her knees. …Armando coming up behind them. …Cosmi, who walked behind him, to join them." (157) Thus, as the story progresses, the male-female relationship gradually reveals hope and vitality. Missy's revival is not simply her own victory over the old self but the group's transcendence of the gender divide as well. This coincides with Walker's constant pursuit of unity and harmony between sexes. Ms. Walker surely declares her persistence in the womanist ideal while emphasizing the power of sisterhood in women's emancipation.

"Now Is the Time to Open Your Heart," the title of the novel, calls for Kate and the other women's explorations of the unknown territory in their later years. Only with their hearts opening will the senior women mollify their internal disturbance, remove their anger and hatred, and enjoy peace and harmony. When asked about what inspired her to write the book in the 2003 interview, Ms. Walker explained,

> My friend Gloria Steinem often comments that for a woman over fifty the territory is largely unexplored. This is true. I was amazed to discover in my own life that there seemed to be as much if not more life after fifty than before. After all, it is after fifty that women return to a balanced sense of self they may not have felt since they were ten. … If we are lucky and are able to follow our inner directives, we find our fifties to be a perfect time to explore this previously unknown territory that is in fact the entryway to the next half of our lives. …So in *Now Is the Time to Open Your Heart* I set out to chart such a journey, the adventures of Kate Nelson Talkingtree. (http://www.penguinrandomhouse.com)

Thus through depicting Kate's experiences and adventures on the two journeys, to the Colorado and to the Amazon, Ms. Walker effectively penetrates into the women characters' inner world and explores their spiritual sublimation, or rather, the women characters' spiritual survival or rebirth, which eloquently proves the great power of sisterhood.

Chapter VI Toward Cosmopolitanism: Humanity and Harmony in the Later Novels

> [T]he greatest value a person can attain is full humanity which is a state of oneness with all things. (O'Brien, 1973: 205)
>
> Walker's interest in the South is not restricted to the time after slavery was introduced: Just as her concern for her racial roots extends to Africa, so her compassion for the Southern earth extends to the remnants of the original Indian population. The ancient burial mound "Eagle Rock"—it also features in the novel *Meridian*—symbolizes for her oneness with nature, communication with one's body, and peace. (Nowak, 1993: 180)
>
> The South, then, signifies for Walker a measure of humanity and of the importance of a life in which dreams bridge past and present. (184)

Since she created her womanist utopia (i. e., the "survival and wholeness of entire people, male *and* female"), Alice Walker has expressed her support for different 'isms—environmentalism, ecologism, vegetarianism, Buddhism and Shamanism—on different occasions, in different works. (A. Walker, 1983: xi, italics original) As what all these 'isms share is humanity and harmony, or "oneness with all things," including humankind and nature, it is obvious that Walker, in actual fact, has been committed to extending and perfecting her womanism, which now not simply transcends binary oppositions of male and female, and of white and colored (esp. black), but strives for universal equality and harmony as well. In other words, Walker tends to blur the boundaries between genders, among races, and even across all species so that her womanism develops into cosmopolitanism, to a certain extent.

In the literal sense, cosmopolitanism is the ideal that all human races belong to one single community, based on a shared morality, where individuals from different places (e. g. nation-states) build relationships of equality and mutual respect, and live in proximity and interact with each other, despite their various ethnic, and cultural and/or religious backgrounds. That is to say, cosmopolitanists believe that all humans come under the same moral standards. The boundaries between nations, states, cultures or societies are therefore morally irrelevant. In Alice Walker's ideology, cosmopolitanism, dominated by humanity and harmony, is de facto an epitome of her different 'isms, of which her later novels—*The Temple of My Familiar*, *By the Light of My Father's Smile* and *Now Is the Time to Open Your Heart*—are best illustrations.

6.1 The Pursuit of Harmonious Union in *The Temple of My Familiar*

Unlike Walker's early novels, which are limited to the black community and focus on racism and sexism and their joint effect on black women, *The Temple of My Familiar* expands its scope of concern to include the whole human world and nature, and explores the male dominance over women, the human dominance over nature, and the white dominance over colored people respectively. The novel is set not simply in a district or a province or a country or a continent but a world or the earth as a whole. Through a series of loosely related stories, representing 500,000 years of human history, told by a vibrant creature Miss Lissie with a thousand pasts, the book defines the present state of human affairs and presents a world which includes all people, be it descendants of whites, blacks, Native Americans or Asians. It is therefore a revision of "the Western representation of reality," emphasizing the connection and equality within the human world as well as between humankind and nature. Ms. Walker pursues a harmonious union of men and women, of the white and the colored, and of humankind and nature through overthrowing the male-dominated white culture which has controlled the Western world for thousands of years.

6.1.1 Disharmony from Male, White and/or Human Supremacism

Supremacism believes that some particular group or race is superior to all others and has a privilege to dominate, control and subjugate the other groups or races in religion, ideology, culture as well as in their mutual relations. Specifically, it expresses itself as male supremacism, white supremacism and human supremacism, which contribute to the discordant relationships between men and women, between the white and the colored, and between humankind and nature respectively. With the purpose of realizing a harmonious union of all humans and nature, Walker deals with all the three manifestations detailedly in *The Temple of My Familiar*.

6.1.1.1 Men's Dominance over Women

Men's dominance over women may be dated back to the ancient Greek times when Aristotle declared that "women are merely tools" and "they are property at the free disposal of men." (qtd. in Stiff, 1995: 5). It also has its origin in Christianity: according to the Bible, the first woman Eve is created from one of the first man Adam's ribs to make him happy, as he feels lonely in the Garden of Eden and needs company. So it is God's truth that woman serve man and meet his need. It is not exaggerated to say that patriarchy goes hand in hand with the Western culture, which underscores women's passiveness, weakness, irrationality, and so forth.

While it is a universally acknowledged truth in the Western culture that men are superior and women inferior, Ms. Walker attempts to show the opposite, or to prove that it is not women's inherent characteristics but the oppressive patriarchal dualism that imposes the inferior qualities on women. In *The Temple of My Familiar*, this is chiefly manifested in the narrations by the women characters, including Lissie, Zede, Olivia, Fanny and Carlotta. Through the narrative fragments, the author presents a vivid picture of the black women's past and present—their life and history, including love, marriage and suffering. In one of Zede's narrations, her mother Zede the Elder does holy work. She, along with other women, makes the costumes for the male-priests, year in year out. The garments they have made are so "resplendent" and "so gorgeous" that it is hard to believe that they are "made by human hands." (A. Walker, 1989: 47) The annual ceremony, whose center the male-priests are supposed to be, will not do without the women's needlework; yet they are not respected as is expected but "considered inferior and kept out of the secrets the men felt it necessary to have." (48) As a matter of fact, the men are afraid of the women and regard their intelligence and creativity as a threat to men's superiority. Little Zede (Carlotta's mother) finds, "[t]he priests of our (Zede's) village lacked any sign of joy. They always seemed, from their sour expressions, to be hurting and as if they had given up something that now plagued them with anxiety. Of course they were feared, if not respected, and of course the fear looked like respect." (46) The men therefore suppress the women in case their superiority is replaced by these creative, intelligent women. However, the men fail to prevent the women from telling the younger generation the story about priests. As the story goes, in the remote antiquity, men worshiped women as priests while they found out that women had the ability to give birth, and did not know where the babies came from. Then, as soon as they discovered, many years later, "that the life that woman produced came out of a hole at her bottom," the men "began to operate on themselves" to make "a hole through which life could come" so that they took the place of women to be priests. (50 – 51) The story tells the truth that men are essentially inferior to women and their seeming superiority is actually artificial. This is why the men in Zede's village fear and suppress rather than respect the women's exquisite craftsmanship in needlework. In this sense, men's dominance over women manifests their lack of confidence and their anxiety over identity.

If Zede's narration is chiefly about what she is told, Miss Lissie's is what she has experienced in her many lifetimes. Her miserable experience in one of them epitomizes the varied tribulations of black women as slaves in a patriarchal society. In this narration, Lissie is a black girl, whose father died of heart attack when she was just two years old. By law her mother and the four children become the property of Lissie's father's brother, who "already had more wives and children and slaves than he knew what to do with." (61) As it is normal at that time, the mother and her children are sold into slavery by Lissie's uncle, in spite of her mother's "begging, pleading and calling for mercy." (62) They are sold to the black slave traders, who then sell them to the white men, who, before paying the blacks, inspect them thoroughly—looking at their ears, their eyes, their teeth and even their genitals, and making them "hop up and down to test the strength" in their legs. (63) Then they are "taken to the holding pen, which was like a cellar underneath the fort" and "was already crowded with depressed and frightened people." (63) The food shortage and the dirty environment soon make Lissie's mother and many others fall ill and meet with death. Having stockaded for days, Lissie and all the other living beings "were forced onto the ship bald, branded, and naked" and "packed as if" they "were sardines." (69) In the whole process of trading, Lissie, her mother and many other female slaves are treated as draught animals. Exposed to strangers (male strangers in particular) in a state of nature, they are inspected with the thoroughness beyond imagination, leaving not any inch of their skins unexamined. In "the embarrassed and helpless presence" of their children, the mothers, having lost their dignity as well as freedom, are particularly put in a living death. (65) Furthermore, each woman is "raped by the crew on board the ship" time and time again. (68) Suffering physically and spiritually, Lissie is not deeply saddened by her mother's death. Accepting it as extrication, she even "envied" her mother and "pitied" herself, for she "did not know how to ask the strangers or even her sisters and brother to kill" her. (65) As men's property, women simply have no chance of mastering their own lives or protecting their children. What a woman can do is place herself at the mercy of her husband or his brother (after his death) or any man who'd like to buy her as property or slave. In the novel, the author points out, "[t]o sell women and children for whom you no longer wished to assume responsibility or to sell those who were mentally infirm or who had in some way offended you, became a new tradition, an accepted way of life. As did the idea... that a man could own many women, as he owned many cattle or hunting dogs." (64)

In another narration, Miss Lissie looks back on one of her worst lifetimes sorrowfully, in which she is "permitted to marry a man I (she) myself (herself) actually picked and loved, and there was peace for a time, a beautiful 'rightness' about the world." (88) Nevertheless, the peace is immediately broken—Lissie is deserted by her husband only because she was "born without a hymen" and "there were no bloodstains to show the villagers" after their wedding night. (88) Thrown out of the house by her parents, she becomes "the lowest sort of prostitute for the men of the village, including the husband I'd (she'd) loved, until I died of infection and exposure at the age of eighteen." (88) In a patriarchal society, men always adopt dual criteria—they are eager to seduce and devirginize girls, to sleep with as many women as possible, but they look down upon the girl who has already lost virginity and therefore the girl they choose to marry must be a virgin. Since virginity is a constant prerequisite for good girls, Lissie's tragedy is inevitable. This inevitability not only conveys Walker's sympathy for the victim but also uncovers the absurdity of the patriarchal thinking that judges women's morality by a mere biological fact.

Fanny is another important narrator in the novel. In a letter to her ex-husband Suwelo, she gives an account of what she talks about with her half-sister Nzingha. Hers or, exactly, Nzingha's is a narration of the latter's mother's suffering. Nzingha's mother was "a brilliant fighter" against "white supremacy and colonization." (254, 260) Although "she saved my (Nzingha's) father's life" and "many people's lives" as well, she is completely forgotten after "the people took back the country." (254) "This was true of all the women: they were forgotten," as the men turn back to the traditional values to define women's role, even though they "always suspend traditional behavior during wartime." (256) In men's eyes, as Nzingha describes it, "[a] woman was for breeding, a woman was for sex"; and in Nzingha's native language Olinka, "the word for woman is the same as for seed granary." (256) This is the way Nzingha's father treats her mother. Sent "off to Sweden to further his studies," Nzingha's father leaves Nzingha and her mother in the little hut for several years, not knowing how they live and what they want. Back home, he appears displeased with his daughter and becomes alienated from his wife, though he comes home "regularly after that." (256) Later, he takes Nzingha away from her mother and leaves her alone at home. He seems to forget "how she'd saved his life or how heroic she was." (254) He never thinks about how his wife feels. He is just the sort of man, who "can always run on and on about the white men's destructiveness" but "cannot look into" his own family and his own wife and children's lives and "see that this is just the destruction the white man has planned. Meanwhile, the women are starting to crack from the white man's blatant success and the lack of their men's support." (253) When Nzingha is sixteen, her mother dies, "after a lingering illness." (258) The reason for her death the villagers describe is that she is "very tired" and "very lonely. There was not enough for such a woman to do, now that there was peace, and black men ruled the country." (258) Nzingha's mother dies more from mental fatigue and psychological emptiness than from physical illness. Her husband's indifference and negligence are the leading cause of her death, while the patriarchy or the government of men is the accomplice. Through the tragic death of Nzingha's mother, the author seems to warn women, particularly black women, about their doomed fate in a male-dominated society and aims to awaken their consciousness of resistance.

Men's dominance over women is a long-standing tradition. It works from ancient times to the present. In *The Temple of My familiar*, it reveals itself in the lives of the black women of three generations. Besides the aforementioned ones, there are also Celie and Carlotta. The former belongs to the first generation while the latter to the third. The story about Celie (the heroine in *The Color Purple*), retold by her daughter Olivia in this novel, is such a typical illustration of the black women's misery that a repetition of it is needed, though some details have already been done in the previous chapters dealing with *The Color Purple*. Raped and impregnated by her stepfather, Celie is forced to leave school and give birth to two babies, Olivia and Adam. Then, her babies given away by her stepfather, she is married off to a widower, who has several children left to her to raise. Her husband treats her as a servant, a laborer, a sexual object, anything but a woman and wife. He beats her only because she is his wife. Celie is beaten so frequently and so heavily that she has to imagine herself as a tree. For Celie, or for the women of the first generation in general, men are masters and devils. They have absolute authority to dominate women physically and mentally. Women have no choice but to obey and/or serve their fathers/husbands. As one of the representatives of the third generation, Carlotta lives a comparatively free life. A women's literature teacher, she has a steady income and can live an independent life. However, after her husband Arveyda leaves her for her mother Zede, she is badly hurt and gets lost. Living a life without a man, she feels so lonely that she tries to change her dressing style to attract men. She is once a female impersonator, putting on the outward garb that would draw men's attention. As a female intellectual, Carlotta also lives for men or, to be exact, men's attention is the backbone of her life. Seemingly, she is free to choose what she wears and how she lives; but, essentially, whatever she chooses results from men's effect or rather men's dominance over her thought or even her soul. Later, she tells Arveyda, "I wore the kind of shoes you'd asked me to wear, though they hurt and you'd left me for my mother, who always wore flats"; and "even if they destroyed my feet and crippled my legs, I know I wasn't giving them up. I liked the way men looked at me in high heels. The look in their eyes made me forget how lonely I was. How discarded." (294) Arveyda's leaving takes Carlotta's confidence away, so she wants to regain it in men's admiring look. Unfortunately, in the eyes of men like Suwelo (Carlotta's lover), "[t]hree-inch heels are designed to make a man feel like all he needs to do is push gently and a woman is on her ass." (244) Carlotta does attract men's (Suwelo's particularly) attention to her, wearing "sweaters that followed every curve of her luscious body," "[s]weaters that dipped," "[s]kirts that clung," "[s]hort skirts," "[e]arrings" as well as "[f]alse eyelashes sometimes"; yet Suwelo thinks it her special way of seducing him and naturally links Carlotta with the pornography he delves into while his wife is away on an extended trip to Africa. (244) He is attracted to her only physically. Catering to men, the modern women like Carlotta actually live under the yoke of men's admiration or interest, which consequently masters women's minds.

Men's dominance over women is universal. Not only black women but also all women in the world, including the white, suffer from men's tyranny. In the lifetime when she is sold as a slave, Lissie notices that a place, which she later knows as "the fort's brothel," is "inhabited by variously colored women of all ages, many yellow or light brown and some almost white," who suffer from forced pregnancy and miscarriage due to the endless rapes by the white men. (66) The scene bears a striking resemblance to what happens to the women in the prison where Zede and her daughter once stayed:

> Most of the women who'd borne children for their captors were dead, but their captors were not. They raped each new batch of slaves and made slave wives of the ones they preferred, ignoring the old and battered ones for whom they no longer felt lust. These women produced children. This placed the guards in the curious position of being masters over their own and each other's offspring, and where there used to be harmony in their power over so many helpless people, now there was hatred and disgust. Each captor... begat a favorite son, and this son he did not want either to acknowledge or to have mistreated by any other person in authority other than himself. Then, too, there was the inevitable rape of his daughters by buddies trained not to care about her resemblance to him. Sometimes he did not recognize it himself. A hell. (122)

Rapes are the most brutal violence and the greatest pain men inflict on women. What they ruin is not simply the raped but the children born by the raped, especially the girls. It is not uncommon that a girl is raped by her uncle or father, even if he knows the kinship. As a matter of fact, the white rapists never regard women or colored women as human beings. Hence they are supposed to take no responsibility for their own natural children born by the women they raped. In their eyes, the children, like the mothers, are also nonhuman. Ironically, while denying the women and the children, the white men deny their own humanity.

This is probably what the author implies or declares. Just as Nzingha points it out in the novel, "[m]en are mangled by the system," which they themselves "help create." (253) While oppressing women, they get themselves distorted. In condemning the patriarchal system, Ms. Walker directs the spearhead at the existing governments in the world, which are "unnatural bodies, male-supremacist private clubs" and sanction men's oppression of women. (272)

6.1.1.2 White Dominance over Colored People

White dominance over colored people has as its premise white supremacy or white supremacism, a racist ideology centered upon the belief that white people are superior in certain characteristics, traits, and attributes to people of other racial backgrounds and that therefore white people should rule non-white or colored people politically, economically and socially. The concept is also a deep-rooted Christian tradition. In Christianity, God is described as a white Father who has absolute authority of creation and history and plays the role of Life-giver and Lawgiver. The white are therefore His permanent Chosen People, who represent His will and enjoy His privilege. White superiority is, to some extent, the core of Christianity. The spreading of Christianity is, in essence, the dissemination of white dominance over the other ethnic groups, which is adequately embodied in racism and colonialism. In *The Temple of My Familiar*, the author denounces white dominance over colored people, particularly over blacks through the narratives of various witnesses like Fanny, David, Jesus, Lissie, Zede and Nzingha.

Racial segregation is the primary guarantee of white dominance over colored people, particularly blacks. Fanny originally teaches at a college but now works as a masseuse "in her own little parlor down the street from the college." (292) Asked about why she takes up the new job, Fanny explains, "I took it up so that I would be forced to touch people, even those I might not like, in gentleness, and be forced to acknowledge both their bodily reality as people and also their pain. Otherwise," "I am afraid I might start murdering them." (293) Fanny's homicidal urge is rooted in the injury afflicted upon her in childhood by Tanya's grandmother. Tanya, a white girl, is one of Fanny's playmates living in the neighborhood. Fanny, as a black girl, is never allowed to play at Tanya's house. They usually play together "outside in the backyard." (328) One day while playing, Fanny kisses Tanya "on the cheek," as kissing or being kissed is "the common greeting and the common good-bye" of black people. (329) This is seen by Tanya's grandmother, a traditional white lady, who sticks to the belief that blacks are dirty, vulgar and graceless, in a word, inferior. She keeps warning Tanya not to being kissed by any black. For the whites like Tanya's grandmother, a physical contact with any black is beyond the permission of white civilization and being kissed by a black girl is indeed an insult. To defend her granddaughter's or even her people's dignity, she rushes at Fanny and "slap[s]" her and "knock[s]" her down so that, when sitting up, Fanny holds her head between her hands and says that she sees stars. This incident hurts little Fanny badly and sows seeds of grievance in her heart. Notably, the scream—"If I ever catch you putting your black mouth on Tanya again, I'll knock your little black head off—has engraved itself on Fanny's memory. (330) Fanny's hatred for Tanya's grandmother has unwittingly developed into the aforementioned homicidal urge, an extreme way of the weak to voice their protest against the white domination.

The extreme expression of white dominance over the other ethnic groups is that the white never treat the colored as human beings and that they can torture them in any way they could imagine, including killing them. Jesus, Carlotta's father, is an Indian, whose village has been occupied by the white invaders. He stays in his hometown while all the other members from his tribe run away. The reason for Jesus' not leaving the village is that he is "the protector of the sacred stones of the village," the "three simple, ordinary-looking rocks" kept "in a certain area of the villager's center" "for thousands of years." (72, 73) These stones are accepted as a symbol of his people's home. If they were moved, his people would never find their home and "would remain dispersed forever." (73) Jesus regards it as his mission to keep the stones in their original place. Therefore, he hides in the jungle nearby in the daytime and goes back to the village furtively at night "to restore the stones' position," and wash and brush the stones clean, for they are usually kicked by some sullen idle soldiers or dirtied by the blood spilled from the beaten or by some food dropped. (73) In a large degree, Jesus seeks solace in protecting these stones. It is probably the only reason for him to continue his life. That is all. However, what the white invaders seem to do is just drive away and exterminate everyone, though Jesus' act neither conflicts with their aggression nor disagrees with their belief nor affects their normal life. "At last they captured him" and enslave him. They send him to "fell and uproot the trees and vines" in his hometown. (73) For Jesus, who has a special attachment to his home town, felling the trees is "a torture comparable to being cut down himself"; yet he does not dare to revolt; as a slave, he has nothing to do but be obedient. (74) Even so, he fails to escape the doom. When Jesus is found sleeping with Zede, the guard, who has chosen her to sleep with him, cut off Jesus' hair, "slowly, coldly, methodically, as if he had been thinking of doing it for a long time." (74, 75) Then he has Jesus killed brutally—with his genitals removed, Jesus "had been violated in every conceivable way." (75) Colored slaves are nothing but private property of white people. Everything in the slaves, including their lives, belong to their white masters, who enjoy the privilege to dispose of the slaves whenever and wherever possible, which is thoroughly reflected in the guides' brutal and inhumane acts. Jesus has no freedom, no right, no dignity before his white masters. He is not only deprived of his homeland and enslaved in his lifetime, but also mutilated and trampled on after his death. He even fails to die a full-body death. His body is exposed to the flies for days before his tribesmen sneak into the hut and have it wrapped. Thus the white make their dominance over the ethnic people like Jesus last till after death.

Slavery is always the typical manifestation of white dominance over blacks. The ways the black slaves are treated are usually incogitable. In one of her lifetimes, Lissie, as a slave, has the experience of being branded. She recalls that she and her fellow slaves are "branded with pieces of hot iron shaped into configurations," dreamed up by the slave traders to serve as marks. (67) Slaves are recognized by such brands. If anyone dies, her brand is checked and she is "marked off the record book." (67) Using the established method of marking and recognizing animals on Lissie and her fellow slaves, the slave owners actually accept them as property instead of human beings; so they naturally disregard the great pain the slaves have to suffer when the metal is pressed "to the skin of a buttock or upper arm," and the "swelling and burning," which "continued for days afterwards." (67) What they care about is not what the slaves suffer and how they feel but how they themselves could gain the maximum profit with the minimum wasting in the slave trading. Meanwhile, they never forget to seize every opportunity to rape the female slaves, the non-human beings in their racist eyes. In so doing, they only express the belief that sexual conquest can bear witness to the white men's superiority but do not realize that they inevitably equate themselves with animals. As a matter of fact, sexual attacks on the enslaved females are almost a must for the white masters. None of the women slaves can escape from the doom. Lissie is raped and gives birth to a girl, who is taken away by the mistress of the plantation as a slave companion to her baby. Enslaved once, Zede clearly remembers the horrible experience under the heel of the white slave owners. She, like any other woman slave, has been chosen by a guard to sleep with him, and "would often hear their slave women screaming or sobbing prayers into the night." (74) She is haunted by the nightmare of being raped by the guards one by one and being forced to stay with Jesus' corpse in a hut for days: "That night the other men, the guards, one after the other came to the little hut in the forest in which they placed me," Zede recalls, "At dawn, as I lay bleeding, they brought his body and threw it in with me. Then they nailed shut the door, which was the only opening." (75) Zede "was broken" and hurt so utterly by the incident that she "could trust no one" and "could never again reach out to love." (75)

Compared to the visible physical pain analyzed in the previous paragraphs, the spiritual dominance of the white men is more dangerous and threatening as it is usually invisible and irresistible. David, Mr. Hal's father, is an odd jobber and gofer "on the Island." He "used to help unload the yacht," on which white people sail over from the mainland, and thus gets to know a white boy called Heath. (133) They become friends soon; yet their friendship is just like that between Tanya and Fanny. Heath often goes to David's house, stays there and eats with the family while David "could never get closer to Heath's house than the back doorsteps." (133) Even so, they maintain their friendship till into adulthood, "seeing each other for holidays and summers, for many years." (133) Then Heath and his wife come to settle down on the Island, and things begin changing. As a grownup, Heath is a racist, who often makes some insulting remarks to David's face, which makes David quite uneasy. Their so-called friendship begins to "walk that fine line between anger and fear": David is irritated by Heath's racism but "feared him as a white man." (134) Later, Heath encourages David to make furniture, and helps him open a furniture shop on the Island and market his products on the mainland so that the latter not only gets "out of farm laboring" but also "lived well" with his family. Their relationship finally undergoes a subtle change. (134) When he realizes that they or just Heath might be gay, David tries to protect himself by retreating into "his old-time know-nothing niggerisms" but fails. (135) One day Heath goes to David. Before the latter "knew anything he was being hugged drunkenly" and is thus forced to respond to Heath. (135) What is even worse is that the scene is seen by David's wife. Mr. Hal recalls,

> He was never the same person after that. He was gloomy. He seldom smiled. He continued to see Heath, though, and I can still remember the sullen bitterness of the fights they had. Fights that were full of a few well-chosen cruel and cutting words, and much drinking. Because, with time, my father drank as much as Heath. Whenever my father read about a lynching of a black man by whites and that they'd cut off the man's privates and stuck them in his mouth, he said he understood the real reason why. Whether he ever did so or not, I'm sure this is something he must have wanted to shout at Mr. Heath. That he understood there was something of a sexual nature going on in any lynching. (136)

Heath's success in fondling David sexually in the shop is attributed to his superior identity as a white man. As a racist, Heath believes that he has the privilege to do whatever he likes—hating, insulting, and embracing or caressing—to David, who, as a black, has no choice but to surrender. He never considers David's will and feeling just because he is black. He thinks it his favor to David to keep an intimate relationship with him. On David's part, it is the last thing to revolt, though he regards Heath's intimacy as an insult to him. What he could do is continue to meet Heath on the one hand, and deplore and torment himself on the other. What tortures him is that he fully understands the injustice and immorality in the incident but he has not strained every nerve to react against Heath's indecent assault and has indeed responded to him. Thus through kidnapping David morally, Heath dominates him once for all. Although he "murdered" "that part of himself" and "tried to bury" it "away from other people and from himself," David has lived in "prejudice against 'funny' men" ever since; "what happened to him that day remained a burden on his soul" till his death. (137)

Cultural conquest is more likely to thrive, as it is deceptive, unobservable and high-sounding. The Westerners habituate themselves to disseminating white ideas and values in the name of knowledge transmission. In the novel Nzingha is sent to Paris to further studies. In the "cold place," "[n]othing seemed to move" the natives "from the heart" and "[n]othing whatever made them smile"; there are no smiles, no warmth, no courtesy. (264) Not just the living French whites like the waiters in restaurants take superior attitudes, but also the Louvre, with "all the booty from other countries on display," smells like "a grave." (264, 265) Everywhere in the gloominess are sensed the white arrogance and superiority, which are specified in the white culture that creates its own ideology through willfully distorting the African beliefs. In an art history class, talking about "the *Greek* foundations of Western civilization and art," the professor makes reference to "Perseus slaying Medusa." (267) Medusa is "a symbol of fertility and wisdom" in African culture. She "is the *mother* of Christian angels. She is Isis, mother of Horus, sister and lover of Osiris, Goddess of Egypt. The Goddess, who, long before she became Isis, was known all over Africa as simply the Great Mother, Creator of All, Protector of All, the Keeper of the Earth. *The* Goddess." (167, italics original) However, the Goddess and Great Mother in the African culture is deformed and depicted as a gorgon, in the white myth, whose head is severed by Perseus, a son of Zeus and Danaë, to rescue Andromeda. In a slide the professor vividly presents Medusa's miserable situation—with "two snakes floating about the corners" of her mouth, her face is "horribly contorted," and "[t]he rest of her rather large, womanly body is still on its knees." (167) As a symbol of evil, Medusa is severely punished; her kneeling down in front of Perseus implies her final surrender to him, which indicates both the European conquest of Africa and the male conquest of the female in the Western culture. Through imparting lots of information of this kind to the world, the Westerners virtually declare the victory of Europe over Africa, of men over women, and thus consolidate and amplify the white male supremacy. Along with the teaching in class, the Frenchmen also attach importance to the formative influence of surroundings. Hence they built Notre-Dame "on the site of a shrine to Isis, who was later called the Black Madonna." (168) The replacement of the shrine to Isis by Notre-Dame conveys the similar message that Europe is victorious and formidable and therefore superior and dominant. Just as Nzingha understands it, Notre-Dame was built for the same purpose as the Louvre—"it had been built to colonize the spiritual remains of a goddess, as the Louvre had been built to colonize the material remains of devastated cultures." (268) The cultural colonization embodied in the two buildings eloquently proves that cultural hegemonism and Western-centrism are deeply rooted in the white culture; so the ethnic harmony cannot happen overnight.

In depicting the miserable sufferings of the characters, male and female, Ms. Walker mercilessly exposes and castigates the evils of racism and colonialism, and expresses her deep sympathy for the ethnic minorities, including blacks and Indians. As her permanent concern is the tragedy of the disadvantaged groups like colored people, the author tends to awaken the awareness of rebellion of colored people as a whole. She appears to believe that the collective rebellion is the most effective way for colored people to shake and smash the white dominance, and build the ethnic harmony in the human society.

6.1.1.3 Human Dominance over Nature

Human dominance over nature has anthropocentricism or human supremacy as its premise, which also has its origin in both religion and philosophy. In religion, it is deeply rooted in Christianity. According to the Bible, God created the first man in His own image and thus entitled humankind to the unique power over "the fish of the sea, and over the birds of the air, and over the cattle, and over the wild animals of the earth, and over the creeping thing that creeps upon the earth," that is, over all the other species and nature as a whole. (Huang, 1998: 6) Therefore, humans have a good reason to believe that they are born masters of all the creatures in the world, and that they are endowed with the supremacy over nature. Meanwhile, the concept of human dominance over nature may be traced back to the ancient Greek philosopher Protagoras' view that "[m] an is the measure of all things." (Plato, 1956: 157) Then in the Age of Enlightenment, the French philosopher Descartes definitely pointed out that "[h] umankind is superior to animals and plants" and "[h] umankind is the master and ruler of nature." (Lewis, 1992: 69). Hence humans accept it as their divine mission to dominate and harness nature for their own sake. They take from nature whatever they want and never consider protecting nature so that the ecological environment is severely destroyed. In *The Temple of My Familiar*, Alice Walker details humans' crimes against nature, including maltreatment of animals, deforestation and environmental damage.

For anthropocentricism, animals' value lies in their bodies only. Humans can take any part of any animal's body without any consideration or hesitation if only it is needed. Like earth and rocks, animals have no feeling of pain. Or even if there is, it is out of humans' consideration, due to animals' inferiority and subordination to humankind. At the beginning of the novel, Zede recalls her hard life with her mother Zede the Elder, who "made her living selling her incredibly beautiful feather goods." (A. Walker, 1989: 4) As a little child, Zede is often "sent to collect the peacock feathers used" in her mother's designs. (3) She still remembers the scene that "the fat, perspiring woman who owned the peacocks held them in ashen, scratched hands and tore out the beautiful feathers one by one" while the beautiful peacock "emitted a sound as if a soul in torment." (3) The "painful plucking of feathers" is repeated by the man "who kept the parrots and cockatoos." (3) Understanding the birds' "mournful cry," Zede gets puzzled by the peace and indifference of those who pluck feathers from the living birds. Once she "paid a visit to the old woman who specialized in 'found feathers' and who was poorer than the others but whose face was more peaceful. This old woman thought each feather she found was a gift from the Gods, and her incomparable feathers—set in the spectacular headdresses of the priests—always added just the special flair of grace the ceremony required." (3) Regarding feathers as God's gifts, the feather pluckers like the old woman wittingly ignore the birds' suffering. In their eyes, the birds are just sources of feathers. Their pain is not worth caring at all. What the feather pluckers do care is the beauty and grace the feathers offer to the priests' headdresses. Furthermore, Zede notices that, in order to make as much money as possible, they usually pluck feathers before they get mature—"[e]ach was plucked while still relatively green"—so that the feathers they supply are of "poor quality." (4) As an anti-antropocentrist, Ms. Walker is keenly aware of the jeopardy of animals. Through the mouth of little Zede, she exposes humans' cruelty and cold-bloodedness in the feather-plucking and expresses her disgust with humans and sympathy for the birds.

Human dominance over nature also finds expression in their savage acts like deforestation and environmental damage. It is often inextricably interwoven with white and/or male dominance. It is so in Jesus' story narrated by Zede: "They (our captors) made him (Jesus) work with the rest of us, clearing the forest with a machete. The men used machetes and pickaxes and saws to fell and uproot the trees and vines, and the women used hoes and rakes to complete the slaughter of the earth." (72) By giving life to the earth, Ms. Walker accepts the exploitation of the earth as "slaughter," which indicates her denunciation of men's brutality and her deep affection and great concern for the earth. The author's distress is mirrored in Jesus' feeling—"cutting them (the trees) down was for him to be a torture comparable to being cut down himself. They were sobbing all the while, Jesus and his tree." (73) Mary Ann, a rich gringa, is another witness to humans' damage to nature and a mouthpiece of the author's thought. She believes nothing her parents do is right. She shows aversion to her parents by going to their dinner table, unclothed or in slovenly attire. Like Zede, she acknowledges humans' exploitation of nature as "slaughter" and describes her parents "as people who had personally assassinated six rivers and massacred twelve lakes, because they manufactured a deadly substance that was always swimming away from them." (79) To meet their economic greed, humans make every effort to exploit the natural resources, even at the cost of the balanced ecological system. Hence some areas become uninhabitable today. Back to Africa, Olivia, Fanny's mother, witnesses the grave consequences of the ecological damage there: "the climate has changed drastically. It rains only sporadically now, and in large areas of the country there is severe drought." (162) The American historian Lynn White (1967: 1205), in his essay "The Historical Roots of our Ecological Crisis," attributes the modern exploitation of nature to humans' abuse of this "dominion," asserting that "Christianity is the most anthropocentric religion the world has ever seen." Indeed, as Olivia finds it, the Europeans have robbed the whole African continent of much of its sustenance. Millions of its trees have been shipped to England and Spain and other European countries to make benches and altars in those grand European cathedrals; its minerals and metals have been mined and its land has been growing rubber, cocoa, pineapples and all sorts of crops for the benefit of the European invaders.

The Australian eco-feminist philosopher Val Plumwood points out that the assertion that men's power over nature is part of the patriarchal dualistic thinking, which defines a definite boundary between the superior and the inferior, or the ruler and the ruled, of which nature belongs to the latter. In her recent lifetime, Lissie, as a child, is taught that the religion (i. e., Christianity) "is a thing that causes people to try to eat up the earth, since we were taught 'everything is for man,' while man was never asked to be for anything in particular." (A. Walker, 1989: 194 – 195) As the inferior in the binary relation, nature, like women and colored people, is set as the oppressed and exploited. As the superior, human beings entitle themselves to the permanent privilege to trample on nature. Consequently, there lies a desperate world as is depicted in Lissie's words to Suwelo: "You have your poisoned rivers and your poisoned air and your children turning into critters before your eyes. You have your leaders that look like empty cartons and the politicians who look drugged. You have a world that scares everybody to death. You can't go nowhere. You can't eat anything. You can hardly make love. And that's just today." (190) In agreement with the external damage, there appears inanition, insensitivity and despair in human mind. Here, through the mouth of Lissie, Ms. Walker voices her own fear for the future of both nature and humankind: "my fear is not that we people and the earth we're on will die. ... But it looks like it will take a long time and death will be painful and slow." (191)

In deploring the humans' crimes—maltreatment of animals, deforestation and environmental damage—against nature, Ms. Walker ascribes the deterioration of the living environment of mankind to anthropocentrism and human dominance over nature. Through the mouths of different characters living in different periods, the author tends to illustrate the universality of human destruction of the natural world and express her deep affection and great concern for nature. Walker's real concern here still lies in the tortuous life and tragic fate humans have to face.

6.1.2 Harmony from Equality and/or Unity

With the expansion of her womanist concern to the survival and wholeness of the planet and every creature on it, Alice Walker attaches more and more importance to harmony, harmony within the human race, and harmony between humankind and nature. Harmony is virtually the highest state and ultimate goal of Walker's womanist utopia. In *The Temple of My Familiar*, Walker is committed to the harmonious union within all creatures on the earth. While exposing and criticizing all the savage acts and evils caused by the male/white/human supremacy, the author concentrates on the targeted improvement of the awkward relationships of the so-called superior with the alleged inferior. She emphasizes equality and unity where others see binary oppositions, and blurs the boundaries between men and women, between humankind and nature, and between the white and the colored. Just as Rudolph P. Byrd (1983: 126) once points it out, "Walker believes that in the artist's search for forms and examples appropriate to her needs and goals it is imperative that she looks beyond the boundaries of her own race, sex, and the culture."

6.1.2.1 The Equality and Unity in Man-Woman Relationship

Equality and unity are the premise of a harmonious human relation, which nourishes mutual understanding and respect between genders. In *The Temple of My Familiar*, Walker redefines the relationship between men and women by putting emphasis on equality and unity, which could eliminate the split and confrontation between the two sexes, the consequence of men's dominance over women. Neither men nor women are supposed to surrender to the opposite sex, physically or spiritually; neither men nor women could separate from their opposite sex. Walker once admits frankly that her writing is both a means of survival and a way of healing herself. Similarly, the characters in her novels are in search of healing and wholeness. This is echoed by Donna Haisty Winchell (1992: x), saying that Walker's female characters "achieve psychological wholeness when they are able to fight oppression," whereas her male characters "achieve psychological health and wholeness only when they are able to acknowledge women's pain and their role in it." It is no exaggeration to say that *The Temple of My Familiar* abounds with such characters. They, like Miss Lissie, Mr. Hal, Suwelo and Fanny, tell different stories about themselves or about their other familiar, few of which actually take place in the present of the novel but concretize the characters' transformation and/or wholeness.

Peace is so dear to humans largely because it is hard to get. A fancy woman as she is, Lissie has not experienced peace so often as she has "known oppression" in her lifetimes. (A. Walker, 1989: 83) "[T]here are only moments—at most, days—of peace" so that "these blessed periods are a vacation, in a sense, from life," and they exist only in "dream world" of Lissie's memory. (83) In her dream memory, Lissie and her parents and the tribesmen are pygmies living in the jungle. The "children live with the mothers and aunts;" the fathers and uncles live nearby, separately. (84) It is the duty of the aunts and mothers to search for food. They often get so tired after a day's work that they have the children "sent to their cousins," living in different trees from theirs. Different from Lissie's tribesmen, these cousins are not pygmies but apelike humans, big "and black and hairy, with big teeth, flat black faces, and piercingly intelligent and gentle eyes." (84) It is fun for Lissie to visit them not only because they—both the fathers and uncles and the mothers and aunts—"lived together as a family," and "played with and looked after the children," but also because there "was such safety around their trees." (84, 85) The secure and harmonious life comes from the unity of the men (the fathers and uncles) and the women (the mothers and aunts). They take it their joint duty to take care of the children and protect the family. "They seemed nearly unable to comprehend separateness; they lived and breathed as a family, then as a clan, then as a forest, and so on. If I hurt myself and cried, they cried with me, as if my pain was magically transposed to their bodies." (85) What's more, "the cousins ate only plants" and never eat meat or kill animals. (85) They are kind to Lissie and like dressing her up with leaves, "skins from dead animals, moss, tree bark." (86) The family pattern, based on equality, unity and mutual care, and the way of life characterized by vegetarianism and simplicity—these are Lissie's favorite (as well as the author's ideal). As a matter of fact, Lissie in this lifetime is Walker's model of an audacious black woman, who strives for love, freedom and unity. When she grows up, she lives together with her true love, one of her playmates. She refuses to live separately with her mate like her tribesmen and wants to look after her babies together with their fathers like her cousins; so she and her mate run away "to stay with the cousins," who consider it natural for lovers to live together. Unfortunately, good times don't last long. There suddenly comes "days and nights of terror"—Lissie's tribe and the cousins' tribe as well are attacked by some invaders and they are "driven into the most remote reaches of the forest." (87) The peaceful life is destroyed and there is not trust among them any more. Notwithstanding this is Lissie and the tribesmen's misfortune as well as a human tragedy, the family pattern of cohabitation comes into vogue for a time as Lissie recalls it:

> It was this way of living that gradually took hold in all the groups of people living in the forest, at least for a very long time, until the idea of ownership… This very thing had happened before, and our own parents had forgotten it, but their system of separating men and women was a consequence of an earlier period when women and men had tried to live together—and it is interesting to see today that mothers and fathers are returning to the old way of only visiting each other and not wanting to live together. This is the pattern of freedom until man no longer wishes to dominate women and children or always have to prove his control. (87 - 88)

According to Lissie, the disruption of cohabitation contributes to men's "idea of ownership." Therefore to restore the harmonious family pattern, men must abandon their thought of dominating and controlling women and their children.

Miss Lissie's present lifetime is also characterized by peace and harmony. Her relationships with her husband Mr. Hal and with her lover Rafe, Suwelo's great-uncle, are both based on mutual understanding and mutual respect. Lissie and Hal grow up together and gravitate "toward each other, 'cause that's where life felt safest and best." (42) They are actually childhood sweethearts. Their marriage grows out of true love—he loves her who loves him. After marriage they get on well with each other and share everything, good or bad. As Mr. Hal recalls it, they "cried and kissed each other a few million times and whispered all our (their) little failings and hopes and secrets to each other." (99) They first live in her mother's house; but soon they have their own house and move out. It is in their own house that they enjoy the happiest time in their marriage. Then Lissie gets pregnant and Hal witnesses the process of her giving birth to their daughter Lulu. The pain Lissie suffers from the childbirth hits Hal hard—"I (Hal) was dying from the pain Lissie was feeling"—so that he feels guilty: "I (Hal) couldn't stand the thought that I was causing her this pain. That making love with her caused this sad, pitiful behavior of hers." (108, 107) Hal's love for Lissie makes it "[t]oo much [for him] to risk putting her in that kind of pain again"; he swears not to impregnate her any more and thus extinguishes his "desire for her, for sex with her." (108) Although he delivers each of her four other children after that, Hal fathers none of them. However, this does not affect their relationship. On the contrary, as Hal himself describes it, he seems to love Lissie much more. They develop a firm relationship based on mutual understanding and "each other's company." (117) They love "each other with true devotion." (112) They know each other as fully as he/she knows himself/herself. When one makes a self-portrait, what he/she practically paints is the other. Their marriage is practically a union of spirit instead of physical dependence. One regards the other as an independent individual, who has freedom to think his/her own thought and live his/her own life. Lissie approves of Hal's painting while Hal never interferes in Lissie's privacy.

Lissie's harmonious relationship with Rafe is owed to his understanding and tolerance as well as her honesty. Lissie tells Rafe all her lifetimes—"[n]one of my (her) selves was hidden from him"—and Rafe "affirms" even her "hateful" and fearsome parts, that is, the part as a white man and the part as a lion. For Rafe, white people are "the most pathetic people who ever lived. Ruling over other people" "automatically cuts" whites "off from life" and gets them isolated. (368) He not simply forgives Lissie for what she has done in her lifetime as a white man, but also shows sympathy for her isolation in ruling over colored people. He takes her to zoos many times just to help her face up to her past. Once when Lissie carries a large mirror to the zoo so that the lion in the cage has "the first and only look at himself he'd ever had," Rafe does not think it strange but helps her "carry it and hold it up outside the cages." (370) He loves "the total" her, past and present, man and woman, white and black, (wo)man and beast, and fears "none of them." (370) In her last words left to Suwelo, Lissie concludes,

> So, loving Rafe and being loved by Rafe was the experience of many a lifetime. And very different from being loved by Hal, even when our passion for each other was at its height, Hal loved me like a sister/mystic/warrior/woman/mother. Which was nice. But that was only part of who I was. Rafe, on the other hand, knowing me to contain everybody and everything, loved me wholeheartedly, as a goddess. Which I was. (371)

Lissie's lover and husband both possess the ideal qualities of good men—Rafe's acceptance and elaborateness and Hal's tolerance and considerateness. Here again the author emphasizes men's important role in improving the man-woman relationship.

Suwelo is a black professor of American history, who takes no interest in any women writers, black or white, and never reads African history from the perspective of black females before he goes to Rafe's funeral in Baltimore, though Fanny attempts to advise him to do so. All the time he holds the grudge against Fanny, as she has divorced him. He feels "abandoned, rejected" because Fanny is the woman he has "loved for a good portion of my (his) life." (141) Furthermore, in the early days after marriage they are happy, or rather, he is pleased: Fanny busies herself with going to the office, doing the marketing, and cooking the freshest food. Everything seems to go on well till one day she asks him to do the marketing, using the cart, which reminds him of women. As a man growing up in a patriarchal society, Suwelo thinks it women's duty to shop or cook; so he refuses Fanny without hesitation. It is this refusal that sounds an alarm to Fanny, who is formerly "skilled at driving, swimming, running even," but whose "running knees rusted," "swimming arms creaked," and "driving eyes clouded over" after marriage. (164) Sensing Suwelo's privilege and her own passivity in their marriage, Fanny becomes "a woman who periodically fell in love with spirits" and begins longing for freedom. (183) She finds that marriage does not fit her or both her and him. The reason for Fanny's decision to end their marriage is not that she does not love Suwelo any longer but that she does not feel free in marriage. As Suwelo admits it, "I couldn't bear the thought of a loss of autonomy or freedom causing her to lose her magic." (282) Their eventual separation results from the husband's desire to dominate the wife and the absence of equality within the couple. Annoyed and frustrated as he feels, Suwelo cannot deny the fact that "separate spaces increased our (their) harmony." (282) During his stay in Baltimore, he is lucky enough to get to know Lissie and Hal. He recounts their divergence of marriage and Fanny's persistence in divorce, while Lissie and Hal tell him stories about Lissie's various lifetimes. Their stories and their anatomization of Suwelo's story get him enlightened so that he comes to understand (black) women fully and realize his inclination to dominate Fanny and the underlying inequality between them. Back home from Baltimore, Suwelo has a heart-to-heart talk with Fanny, who is persuaded by her father to harmonize her relationship with Suwelo. He takes in Fanny's words—"harmonizing is possible" and it "has nothing to do with the question of whether or not we (they) sleep together," but "it takes two to harmonize." (318) Suwelo seems to have a better understanding of Fanny by calling her "a womanist," though his tone is of some bitterness. This is indeed the case. Fanny is portrayed by Ms. Walker as a womanist. She is broad-minded enough to forgive Suwelo's "affairs with other women," "with Carlotta in particular," and tells him that she does not "feel particularly betrayed as an individual." (320) She values a spiritual union more than the physical intimacy in her relationship with Suwelo. Spiritual survival is what she is striving for.

At the end of the novel, Suwelo and Fanny are building on their homestead a house "modeled on the prehistoric ceremonial household" of the Ababa tribe, "a house designed by the ancient matriarchal mind and the first heterosexual household ever created." (395) By designing such a house, Ms. Walker explicitly expresses her affirmation of female wisdom and her belief in heterosexual harmony. Indeed, it is with Fanny's efforts that the former couple develops a spiritual union at last, though they haven't resumed their matrimonial relation. Moreover, they become friends with the other couple, Carlotta and Arveyda, who are still in marriage but live apart. Not only do the couple or the former couple live harmoniously within, but also "[t]hey are a collective means by which each of them will grow"; "they all vaguely realize they have a purpose in each other's lives"; and "[t]here is palpable trust" among them. (394) Living apart and free, Suwelo and Fanny, and Carlotta and Arveyda return to the lifestyle of their ancestors, a lifestyle in which neither sex seeks dominion over the other and only equality and unity are in action.

Walker not simply adheres to the free will of individuals, male or female, be it the cohabitation in Lissie's dream memory or the separation in present life, but also emphasizes the spiritual union and mutual understanding in the tribe/community. On the one hand, to realize the survival whole of entire people, each individual, male or female, is supposed to have freedom and equality in his/her physical and spiritual life. On the other hand, any individual could not live absolutely in solitude; they have to cooperate and communicate with each other, and therefore unity is indispensable. With this in mind, the author juxtaposes the free love between men and women in the prehistory clan with the spiritual union in modern times throughout the novel, and thus unfolds a harmonious picture of human life characterized by equality and unity.

6.1.2.2 The Equality and Unity in the Relationship between Humankind and Nature

Alice Walker is a nature-lover. In *Living by the Word*, she proclaims, "I love you (nature). I love your trees, your sun, your stars and moon and light. Your darkness, your plums and watermelons and water meadows. And all your creatures and their fur and eyes and feathers and scales." (A. Walker, 1988:

96) For Walker, everything in nature is so sweet that it would be hard "not to see the sunrise every morning, the snow, the sky, the trees, the rocks, the faces of people, all so different." (O'Brien, 1994: 58) Her celebration of nature is embodied in her literary writings, including *The Temple of My Familiar*, *By the Light of My Father's Smile*, and others, which illustrate the author's firm belief in the equality and unity of the human and non-human worlds. According to Walker (1999: 307, 310), "all of creation is of the same substance and therefore deserving of the same respect"; human beings are "connected to them (the animals) at least as intimately as we (they) are connected to trees." Obviously, Walker yearns for a world where humans and nonhumans are equally divine, a world where humans and nonhumans get along with each other harmoniously, and there is no human dominance permitted. Interviewed by Winfrey, Walker points out, "Here is no heaven. This is it. We're already in heaven, you know, and so in order … for the earth to survive, we have to acknowledge each other as part of the family, the same family." (qtd. in Day, 1990: 133) Only when humans identify themselves with the members like animals and trees in the earth family, could they treat nonhumans equally and protect the earth home tirelessly. The author's love and worship of nature and her ecological awareness are fully expressed in *The Temple of My Familiar* through the stories and/or experience of such characters as Lissie, Shug, Fanny, and Ola.

On the tape left to Suwelo, Miss Lissie tells him the "dream memory" of her other lifetime, when he—Lissie is a man in this lifetime—and his mother's tribe live "at the edge of an immense woods." (355) His mother's familiar is a lion, who "also had a family of his own." (355) They usually visit each other and develop a harmonious relationship. The animals neither fear the tribeswomen nor have the thought of eating them. In those days, the women "met other animals in much the same way people today meet each other." (356) The tribeswomen and the animals share the same dwelling place, use the same water, and eat the same foods. Although it is not the case with men's group, the men imitate the women and their familiars, and try to tame dogs into their companions or friends. Their positive efforts to improve their relationship with animals indicate Walker's optimism about the realization of harmony between humans and nature, between men and animals specifically, and thus bring hope to the whole world, human and nonhuman. Similarly, Lissie's lifetime of being a pygmy is also characterized by harmony between nature and humankind. In this lifetime, Miss Lissie lives in a forest that "covers the whole earth." (84) The trees are like cathedrals. They serve as apartment buildings at night, while in the daytime Lissie and the other children play under them, just as city children play on the street in the present day. They are sometimes left "in the care of the big trees" when their aunts and mothers go out foraging. (84) In the eyes of the children, who know "every branch, every hollow, and every crevice of a tree," the tree is the safest place. (84) It can protect them from whatever danger threatens them. Through Lissie's dream memory, Walker presents readers a peaceful and harmonious picture of humans and nature, which provides a sharp contrast with the "Sound and Fury" of the modern world. In so doing, the author underlines the possibility of direct communication between human and non-human beings, and the great urgency to improve the relationship between humankind and nature. For Walker, humans are not superior to nature, animals or plants; humans and non-humans are equal beings; they should coexist as parts of a spiritual union rather than as a binary opposition.

Shug, one of the main characters in *The Color Purple*, is an animist and nature worshipper. She continues to propagate her animism to her generation as well as the younger generation in *The Temple of My Familiar*. Olivia still remembers the great blues singer Mama Shug's "real high standards" in choosing friends: "if you stepped on an ant in Mama Celie's presence and didn't beg forgiveness, you were just never invited to her house again." (169) This "sensitivity to animals" Mama Celie learns from Mama Shug. In fact, Celie, like the other black people in the South, would mistreat animals, particularly her dog. She appears vicious and unfeeling, though the dog "worshiped her" and serves as "her absolute slave." (311) She never looks into the dog's eyes, which are always "wounded, pained, saddened, completely expressive." (311) This makes Shug, who loves animals as much as she loves people, furious so that she is frequently found fighting with Celie for the dog. To protect the dog, Shug even takes him to Memphis and teaches him to rebel. So the next time Celie wants to beat him, the dog bites her, which seems to awaken Celie's conscience and nurture the seeds of her kindness. She begins to "feel for *everything*: ant, bat, the hoppy toad flattened on the road." (312, italics original) Shug's behavior also conveys Ms. Walker's idea that animals are as equal as human beings and that humans are supposed to take active measures to restore their relationship with animals and return peace, justice and widespread happiness to animals, and to the planet as a whole. The author expresses her suggested attitude through Fanny's statement: "I live on Earth, I love it; I see that it really needs me, whether it knows this or not." (281) Loving and respecting nature is, at heart, loving and respecting humans themselves. Nobody has any reason to abuse animals and wreak havoc on natural resources.

Talking with Fanny about the female fighter, the prototype of the protagonist in one of his plays, Ola digresses to tell the story about Sandino and the monkeys, which is liked best by the woman. As the story goes, Sandino, a man in a guerrilla band, is an animal protector. The guerrillas are once hiding in a forest, where live a lot of monkeys. They usually capture the little monkeys and eat them. To prevent them from killing the pathetic monkeys, Sandino makes "impassioned speeches," pointing out "that it was the monkeys' screeches that always saved the men from the surprise of enemy attack" and that the monkeys are their little brothers and loyal companions. (305) He holds that the guerrillas should feel grateful for the monkeys' alerting and reward them with protection instead of killing. By appealing for thanks and reward, Sandino accepts the monkeys as emotional creatures, which deserve humans' equal treatment. Here lies the reason why the woman fighter likes Sandino. As Ola concludes it, "even though he was as famished as the rest of his men, he held to the vision of the future he wanted to have, a future that would include even the monkeys." (305)

In nature, Ola and the woman fighter and Sandino are fused as one. Their behavior and/or standpoint show(s) the distinctive animistic consciousness Ms. Walker has ever expressed since *The Color Purple*. Interviewed by John O'Brien (1993: 332), Walker admits that she inherits this belief from her ancestry:

> If there is one thing African-Americans have retained of their African heritage, it is probably animism: a belief that makes it possible to view all creation as living, as being inhabited by spirit. This belief encourages knowledge perceived intuitively. It does not surprise me, personally, that scientists now are discovering that trees, plants, flowers, have feelings … emotions, that they shrink when yelled at; that they faint when an evil person is about who might hurt them.

Fanny is another animist the author creates in the novel. She grows up in the care of two old ladies, Celie and Shug, and spends a lot of time playing with Mama Shug. The earliest gift she could remember is a red bird from the two ladies and the first word she could speak is "bird." She is greatly influenced by what she sees and hears. Since "[t]he bird, any bird, it turned out, was precious to my grandmama Celie, just as turtles and elephants were precious to her friend Shug," Fanny naturally develops into a nature lover. (154) To be more exact, she becomes an incarnation of Shug's gospels (i. e., an animist). Taking "all creation as living, as being inhabited by spirit," an animist would like to integrate himself/herself into nature and regard birds and animals as friends and companions. This is the case with Fanny. Her wish is to live in nature and have animals and birds as her neighbors. For a while after marriage, she and Suwelo live in a yurt overlooking "a valley of sheep ranches and vineyards." (275) Each morning they are woken up by the rising sun. There is forest all around their dwelling place and they share "the land with deer, squirrels, rabbits, raccoons and birds of all description," like hawks, owls and vultures. (275) Here Fanny finds her desired tranquility and expresses her love and worship of nature to the full. "It really is special," as Suwelo later recalls it, and they "often found bits of chiseled flint and an occasional potsherd." (275) For Walker, being close to nature is, to some extent, establishing a settlement that deserts civilization and returns to primitive life. As a womanist, Walker fully understands the obstacle to the harmonious relationship between humankind and nature, and the interaction between the racial oppression and the exploitation of nature. In the foreword to Marjorie Spiegel's *The Dreaded Comparison* (1996), a book comparing the African slave trade in the period of slavery to the abuse of animals in the present day, Walker protests, "[t]he animals of the world exist for their own reasons. They are not made for humans any more than black people were made for whites or women for men." In the eyes of Walker, animals should not be oppressed by humans, just as women should not be tyrannized by men, and blacks should not by whites. The establishment of the harmonious relationship between humankind and nature depends on humans' endeavor as much as the harmony between genders rests with men's or as the harmony within races with whites'. Therefore, in Walker's world, or in the world of *The Temple of My Familiar*, blacks, men and women, and particularly the black women are depicted as those who are more sympathetic with animals, plants, and nature as a whole. The novel abounds with the harmonious scenes—extending from the past to the present—of black people living together with animals or integrated into nature. They nurture hope for the bright future of the human-nature relationship, though they are destroyed from time to time by whites' aggression against blacks or men's oppression of women.

As an animist, Walker holds that all creatures in the world have the right to live as human beings. She is aware that the whole natural world is imperiled by the so-called human civilization and that humans never stop killing animals, felling trees, abusing natural resources, polluting environment, etc. As a writer, Walker chooses to state her position through literary creation. Since *The Third Life of Grange Copeland*, she has been taking it as her mission to voice concern and support, in her literary writing, for the voiceless—blacks, women, and later animals and plants. Through the mouths of such characters as Shug, Lissie, Manuelito, a young Mundo man in *By the Light of My Father's Smile*, and Kate, the protagonist in *Now Is the Time to Open Your Heart*, Walker explicitly defines her animistic ideology, accusing white men of their maltreatment of nonhuman beings and of their dominance over the whole natural world. In this regard, *The Temple of My Familiar* plays a vital role in reflecting the author's constant creative intention: Walker tends to foster humans' sense of responsibility to protect nature and respect life so that a harmonious relationship will be established between humans and other species on the planet. The stories and/or standpoint of such characters as Lissie, Shug, Ola and Fanny either present harmonious pictures of humans' coexistence with nature or at least bring hope to the future harmony.

6.1.2.3 The Interdependence between Whites and Blacks

Committed to the harmonious coexistence of all the races, Alice Walker asserts that human races of different colors are like different flowers in a garden, each of which is an individual existence and contributes to the diversity and abundance of the world. None can be excluded, be it blacks or any other colored race. The harmony of the world cannot do without racial equality and the mutual assistance and interdependence within races. As a womanist, Walker shows contempt for separatism; she advocates universalism, which emphasizes the survival whole of the universal beings, human and nonhuman, and dissolves the boundaries not simply between humankind and nature, but also between men and women as well as between the white and the colored. In *The Temple of My Familiar*, the author, as always, explores the way for racial integration and harmony in concert with her concern for the female and natural destinies under the oppression of patriarchy. Through depicting mutual assistance between Zede and Mary Ann Haverstock (later changed into Mary Jane Briden) and the spiritual and cultural connectedness of both a white family and a black tribe, Walker unfolds a harmonious picture of interdependence between the white and the black.

Mary Ann was born into a manufacturer's family. A white as she is, she stands on the side of the blacks and befriends "los politicos extremistas in Norte America." (A. Walker, 1989: 79) However, she is always misunderstood by the "negros radicales," whatever she does. (79) A black girl even tries to murder her when a black radical, the girl's boyfriend, is put in prison by the white. Frustrated by the attack, Mary leaves the black ghetto and returns to "her parents' estate," where she does not become "competent" as is expected by her parents but "a scarred, drugged, disheveled mess." (79) So they send her to "La Escuela de Jungla," a school for the retarded and handicapped, the managers of which care only about making as much money from people like Mary's parents as possible and attend to the "students" by no means. Mary Ann and the other "students" "lived in huts like the poorest campesinos, and they were drugged and shut in most of the time"; "sometimes the little alumnos-prisioneros would die of the loneliness and poor food, the awful boredom and the dirt." (77, 80) Working as a maid in the school, Zede gets to know Mary and grows to like her as the girl is "a naturally sweet person who had no understanding of how to be rich in a world like this one." (80) Witnessing her suffering in the school, Zede feels pity for Mary, who "was very dirty, barefoot, and wearing rags" when Zede first sees her, and eventually writes a letter to Mary's parents, alerting them to her "fate" at the school. (78, 80) Mary's parents soon come to the school and take their daughter back home. Thanks to Zede's letter, Mary Ann is freed. As a black woman, Zede has experienced the nightmare of being sold into slavery and raped by the white guard. Besides, Carlotta's father is killed by the slave owners. In this regard, there is a blood feud between Zede and white people. It makes sense for her to seize opportunities to take revenge on the white; so what Zede does for Mary Ann is seemingly contrary to common sense. This is actually Walker's stroke of genius. In the case of Zede lies the author's firm belief that forgiveness is the first vital step toward reconciliation, or simply, that virtue is its own reward. Sure enough, Zede reaps the rewards in next to no time. Mary Ann goes back to rescue Zede and Carlotta. When asked "how she had found the courage to do what she did" for the mother and daughter, Mary explains that "while clearing herself of the drugs on which she'd leaned for years she had had a religious conversion of a sort," which "had been based on something" that "Christ was reported to have said," "[s]omething about 'the least of these'";

she explains that it is "the least of these" referred to by Christ that reminds her of Zede and Carlotta, and helps her to adhere to her politics, "for as a radical she had tried to stand with 'the least of these.'" (81 – 82) In emphasizing Mary's revelation from Christianity, Walker seems to imply that there is no absolute opposition between the white and the black, and that the racial integration will work in practice, though it sounds rather contrived. Indeed, Mary Ann has strived for the white-black integration and tried to help "the least of these." The reason why she is once discouraged and disheartened is that the people she has helped before are those she does not know, those she has no "reciprocidad" with, those "who could not see that she, too, suffered, or even believe that she could." (82) Reciprocidad and mutual understanding are the basis and guarantee of repairing racial relations. In other words, it is the business of both whites and blacks to improve their relationship, and the unilateral endeavor, whether the white or the black, hardly bears fruit. Mary Ann's rescue of Zede and Carlotta is more out of personal gratitude than political stance. Zede's help and understanding rouse the love, care, kindness, and compassion in Mary, extinguished by the black radicals' ridicule and misunderstanding. Zede's luck is a good illustration of the saying that God helps those who help themselves. Mutual assistance is what Ms. Walker advocates in her utopia of racial unity.

The Temple of My Familiar witnesses a major innovation in both theme and characterization of Alice Walker's novel-writing. It arouses the attention in the academic field not only through its extended concern for nature but also through the ideal white images like Eleandra Burnham Peacock, Eleanora Burnham, and Mary Ann Haverstock (Mary Jane Briden). As a matter of fact, Mary Ann is the first white positive character in Walker's novels, an epitome of New Whites. For one thing, she is a conservationist and does not approve of her parents' exploitation and destruction of nature. For another, she is a political activist for racial equality and shows great respect and admiration for the culture heritage of the ethnic minorities, particularly of the African. In the portrayal of the white girl/woman Mary Ann, Ms. Walker apparently pins her hope on white people's awareness of the interdependence between whites and blacks, or between whites and colored people in general. To exhibit the dualism of the white-black relations, the author designs a two-phase life for Mary Ann, the phase of striving for physical survival (i. e., Zede's and her own, and that of the black race), analyzed in the previous paragraph, and the phase of spiritual wholeness and cultural connectedness.

After rescuing Zede, Mary Ann Haverstock leaves the ship *Recuerdo*—the symbol of her old life—sinking into oblivion, and boards *The Coming Age* and starts her second phase of life, during which she establishes herself in Africa and makes efforts to bring its culture heritage to light again. In order to get a fresh start, she changes her original name into a new one "Mary Jane Briden," which sounds close to Africans. Mary Jane decides to find something African in her great-aunt Eleanora Burnham, an English upper-class woman who has spent years in Africa. Eleanora tells her great-niece Mary Jane about her own aunt Eleandra Burnham Peacock, who "was a disgrace to England, and even more to the family," for she "had a liking for Arabs" and Africans as well. (210) The common interest in Africa or Africans of the three generations of aunts and nieces immediately narrows the distance between Mary Jane and her great-aunt and great-great-aunt on the one hand, and, on the other, offers sufficient proof that not all whites are racists and supremacists and that there is hope to establish a peaceful and harmonious relationship between whites and blacks. Walker's emphasis on cultural connectedness evidently does not exclude the white, even though it is just a bond between generations of the same family.

It is Eleanora's muttering—"I hated Africa. The heat, the bugs, the leeches, the niggers."—that excites Mary's curiosity. (210) She goes to visit the library, to which Eleanora has sent not only her papers, but also her baskets, bowls, sculptures and cloths. In the section of the library called "Eleanora Burnham Room," Mary gets dozens of photographs of Africans taken by her great-aunt, which eloquently proves that "[f]ar from hating Africa and the bugs, leeches, and niggers, as she'd claimed, Africa had been the great love" of Eleanora's life. (212) Mary Jane is deeply touched by what she reads in these photographs:

> Almost without exception the Africans were interestingly, often spectacularly, dressed, and this especially surprised and pleased her (Mary Jane). The women's hairstyles, with their interwoven cowrie shells and feathers, were fabulous and made them look, at the same time, serene, regal, and wild. And the cloth of which their robes were made... glistening as if shot through with golden thread. In these photographs she saw Africans whose eyes, skin, clothes *shone*. With richness and intelligence and *health*. Finally, it was the shine of health that captivated Mary Jane, for she realized that so degraded had Africa become in the mind of the world that a healthy African, like the ones she saw in the photographs, was practically unimaginable. (217, italics original)

To these photographs Eleanora obviously has given over her intense feelings. If she, as is claimed by herself, had hated Africans, she would never have got such great reaction shots, which completely subvert the image of black savages in the white mind. Eleanora's photographs not simply have faithfully recorded the Africans' costume and hairstyles but also have accurately captured their spiritual appearance and inner wisdom. The "kindly" eyes of the Africans tell "a special bond" between the photographer and the photographed. (217) The Africans feel love and honor from Eleanora and spontaneously deliver their love and respect for her with their grateful eyes. Here Walker underscores affective interaction in the white-black relationship. Although she says nothing about the African women in the pictures, Eleanora fails to hide her true feelings. Gazing at the photographs, she lets the tears spill "over her red and swollen lower lids." (217) With years gone, these African women are still in Eleanora's mind, or rather, she still remembers something about them; she seems to be missing them. By depicting such a touching scene, Walker successfully offers proof of ethnic harmony. The direct link between Mary Jane and her great-aunt and great great-aunt is M'sukta, an African woman who is the last of her tribe—"the Balawyua, or the Ababa." (233) The only picture that looses Eleanora's tongue is a painting, instead of a photograph, of M'sukta, "wearing the beautiful robes of her tribe," "painted against a gray stone interior of what might have been a cathedral." (217) Different from describing the other pictures, the author highlights the background in the painting, which implies the heroine's confined, monotonous life and attracts Mary Jane's attention to the story behind.

It is from the diary by her great great-aunt Eleandra Burnham Peacock, kept in "Eleanora Burnham Room" in the library, that Mary knows about M'sukta. As the diary records it, M'sukta lives in a "medium-sized room," with windows high up in the wall as well as a strange smell, in the Museum of Natural History in London. On the surface, she lives a delicate life characterized by her tribal culture.

> She was dressed exquisitely in cloth made from hundreds of the strips that decorated the pegs by the door of the hut, which I (Eleandra) now saw copied many of the colours, motifs, and symbols that covered the mud walls. Her hair was in dozens of mid-back-length plaits; on the end of each one was a bit of seashell. Her small feet were encased in colourfully beaded slippers of soft leather. She came towards us (Eleandra and her cousin) with holding her spindle and carrying a large basket of cotton from which she was making thread. (223 – 224)

Every detail in M'sukta, from what she wears to what she does, is filled with a strong ethnic flavor. The entire meaning of M'sukta's life lies in incarnating the tribe's culture and ancient way of life. "The museum lets her live here" so that she is preserved and exhibited as a rare treasure. Whenever there comes a visitor, she will sit in her splendid garb and begin a demonstration of weaving the tribal cloth, one aspect of her village's way of life. She never cares about who the visitor/audience is. There is nothing like interest, curiosity, or even communication in her life. She has no freedom at all. What touches Eleandra so deeply is that M'sukta, like animals encaged in zoos, is afraid of visitors/audiences. Indeed, on the part of the museum, M'sukta, as the last of her tribe, is nothing but one item of its rare collection; she is never treated as a live human being with thought and feelings and desire.

For Eleandra, M'sukta is pitiful and mysterious. In order to help her out, Eleandra decides to invest time and energy in studying M'sukta and her people. The more visits she pays to her, the more puzzled she becomes. She finds that everything in M'sukta is different so that none of the things—history, geography, science, literature and language—she has learned works before M'sukta. Eleandra is especially interested in the ancient saying of M'sukta's people—"ME TAO ACHE DAKEN SOMO TUK DE," meaning "THEY CANNOT KILL US, BECAUSE WITHOUT US THEY DIE"—etched in the mud wall of the compound (a replica of part of M'sukta's village in the museum). (229, capitals original) She endeavors to figure out what happened to M'sukta's people and why they would have this thought as their life guide, and eventually gathers an understanding of the tribe and its history. M'sukta's tribe had been a matriarchy from time immemorial. Then the people were always under siege for one reason or another, and finally all the tribe was sold into slavery or killed, leaving alive only M'sukta and a young boy, who were taken to the Museum of Natural History by an English commander in the name of passing on "the history of her people's ancient way of life." (233) Soon the boy died and M'sukta is left alone in the museum. The life in the museum is indeed a torment and ordeal for M'sukta. She is deprived of nearly everything that a normal human being should have—family and friends, freedom and dignity, and feelings and soul. In the eyes of the white visitors, she is just a performer or even a stage property. It is her only job to feed the visitors' curiosity by demonstrating her tribe's ancient way of life. However, on the part of M'sukta, there is no alternative but to be obedient. Staying in the museum is the only chance for her to survive. Surviving means having the possibility to remember. For the life of M'sukta's people "is to remember forever; each head granary is full," namely, full of the tribal history and culture. (231) To win the possibility of remembering and cultural transmission, M'sukta has to endure. As M'sukta tells Eleandra later, it is the ancient saying of her people that keeps M'sukta hanging on. She accepts it as her ancestors' gift to her. It is even more important to her than singing or weaving, though singing helps her hear and remember her own language, and weaving her tribal cloth has the magic of setting her in the presence of her people. Till now, Eleandra seems to understand M'sukta and her people, a people who believe that they can never be killed by the white because whites and blacks are dependent on each other.

While the photographs and the diary work as links from Mary through her great-aunt to her great great-aunt, the story about M'sukta juxtaposes the cultural transmission of the black tribe (i. e., M'sukta's people) with the spiritual connectedness of the white family (i. e., the three generations of aunts and nieces). M'sukta's life and belief are thus interwoven with the thoughts and experiences of the diarist (Eleandra) and her readers (Eleanora and Mary). As a junior and great-niece, Mary Jane Briden is supposed to take up where her great-aunt leaves off. She gives up the estate—which Eleanora leaves to her—"to fund an anthropological group," which Eleanora Burnham has been fond of, in Africa, and is about to embark on her own journey to Africa. (234) The white woman Mary's coming journey foreshadows racial integration in culture.

Alice Walker never gives up her optimism about racial unity and integration. In this regard, she anchors her hope more on white women than white men. Beginning with Lynne Rabinowitz in *Meridian*, Walker is persistently trying to create positive, strong-minded white woman images in her novels. If Lynne is more or less disappointing due to her self-abandonment and Eleanor Jane in *The Color Purple* is similarly dissatisfactory as she is a weak softhead who cannot go without Sofia, Mary Ann Haverstock (Mary Jane Briden) in *The Temple of My Familiar* gives full expression to the author's boldness in characterization of white women. A bold, witty antiracist, who is grateful and sympathetic and has a strong sense of justice, Mary incarnates Walker's ideal of new white women through her two-phase life experience. Her struggle for physical survival and her pursuit of spiritual wholeness and cultural connectedness present a warm harmonious picture of mutual assistance and racial integration between whites and blacks, which reasonably illustrates Walker's womanist manifesto that a healthy and harmonious world can neither do without the racial and ethnic diversity nor without the cultural and spiritual connectedness.

As the first novel in the second stage of Walker's literary career, *The Temple of My Familiar* not only maintains its focus on the equality and unity within black community but also extends its thematic concern to the interdependence between whites and blacks as well as the equality and respect between humankind and nature. By exposing the great damage done by humans to nature and condemning the brutalities inflicted upon women and colored people by white men, Ms. Walker determinately stands on the side of the inferior—women, colored people and nature—and appeals for the return of humanity in the superior—men, whites and humans as a whole. The author underlines equality and unity and interdependence in the relationships within the human community as well as between humankind and nature. She persists in pursuing the survival whole of the entire people, but by "entire people," she exclusively refers to the black race no more. In this novel (and the later novels as well), Walker's survival whole is expanded to cover the whole world, human and nonhuman. Her ultimate goal is to foster humans' sense of responsibility to protect nature and respect life (human and nonhuman). *The Temple of My Familiar* successfully builds a harmonious world characterized by equality and unity and interdependence.

6.2 The Humanistic Concern in *By the Light of My Father's Smile*

Alice Walker is always concerned with the living status of the inferior, women and colored people in particular. She is an advocate of creating living conditions in compliance with humanity and pursuing liberty, justice and democracy of human beings. Humanity or humanistic concern is therefore the focus of *By the Light of My Father's Smile*, her last novel in the past millennium. The book is "A Story of Requited Love, Crossing Over, and the Sexual Healing of the Soul," in the words of the subtitle. The story is centered on the Robinsons, Mr. Robinson's violence, its negative effect on his two daughters, their rebellions, the father's confession after death, and the reconciliation between the father and his daughters. The plot develops around the father-daughter relationship, which turns from rebellion to reconciliation, from antagonism to forgiveness, from disharmony to harmony. The characters, both the father and the daughters, undergo a dramatic transformation in their lives, which witness the absence of humanity and its eventual regression. The novel is undoubtedly an addition to the author's womanist writings.

6.2.1 The Absence of Humanity

Humanity is "the quality or state of being humane," viz., "of being kind to other people or to animals," as is defined in Webster's Dictionary. (Merriam-Webster Online) If one lacks humanity, he/she shows a propensity for violence, cruelty, resentment, prejudice, and indifference or disregard in deeds and/or words. *By the Light of My Father's Smile* abounds with such instances in the relationships between sexes, and between whites and colored people. The major characters either fail to show humanity in their behaviors or suffer from inhumane treatment. As a matter of fact, it is Ms. Walker's consistent way to portray her characters (usually the male ones) as devils or set them (usually the female ones) in a predicament before giving them opportunities to change or survive.

6.2.1.1 Men's Domination over Women

The male-female relationship contains the basic binary opposition in a society, which legalizes male domination. Sexism is thus perpetuated as part of the social structure and women are always the consequent victims. *By the Light of My Father's Smile* is not deficient in this kind of women victims. Magdalena is destroyed by her father's whipping, which further transforms her sexual orientation and results in her later distorted life. Pauline's misfortune begins with her parents and her brother's betrayal while Irene has to confront a miserable life since her birth is the consequence of her mother's being raped, which is believed to be a sin. Walker's concern is extended from Afro-American women to women of other races like Asians, Africans and Europeans. She explores the miserable lives of the women group affected by the patriarchal conventions as a whole. All the sufferings manifest the absence of equality and humanity in the relationship between men and women, especially in the father-daughter relationship. By depicting the sufferings, Walker tends to awaken men's conscience and nurture the seeds of kindness.

As is mentioned in the previous chapter, the central incident in the novel is Mr. Robinson's violence against his eldest daughter Magdalena and her extreme response, which affects not just her own life but her sister Susannah's as well. Here Walker apparently focuses on the father-daughter relationship in order to show how the father's domination directly or indirectly ruins his daughters. She once said in an interview with John O'Brien, "all along I wanted to explore the relationship between parents and children: specially between daughters and their father (this is most interesting, I've always felt; for example, in 'The Child Who Favored Daughter' in *In Love and Trouble*, the father cuts off the breasts of his daughter because she falls in love with a white boy; why this, unless there is sexual jealously?), and I wanted to learn, myself, how it happens that the hatred a child can have for a parent becomes inflexible." (qtd. in O'Brien, 1993: 335) Walker's interest in the father-daughter relationship relates to her memory of her father, which she thus depicts in *In Search of Our Mother's Gardens*: "My father expected all of his sons to have sex with women. …My sister was rarely allowed into town alone…Naturally, when she got the chance, she responded eagerly to boys. But when this was discovered she was whipped and locked up in her room." (A. Walker, 1983: 328) Haunted by his father's different attitudes towards her brothers and sister, Walker persists in exploring the father's discrimination against the daughter and its negative effect on the daughter's development.

Mr. Robinson and her wife Langley are both Afro-American anthropologists, who could receive no funding from any institution; so they go to their church and "explained what we (they) heard about the Mundo," "a tiny band of mixed-race Blacks and Indians," to persuade the church into supporting them financially. (A. Walker, 1998: 14) In return, Mr. Robinson has to work as a Christian missionary. (154) Hence he and his family—his wife and their two daughters—

come to a rural area in Mexico in the early 1940s, in the name of preaching Christianity to the Mundo people. However, Mr. Robinson is "an atheist" or, "[m]ore accurately, an agnostic," as his spirit levels with Manuelito's later in the novel. His soul-stifling deception underlies the family tragedy. A pseudo preacher, "sucked into the black cloth" of Christianity and preaching the message of his puritanical Protestant sponsors, Robinson mistakes his pretended identity for the real one and stands as a spokesman of whites both at home and before the Mundo. Stuck in his lie, he not just believes that he has "brought the Truth" to the Mundo people, who he thinks "grasp it," but also expects that he will cultivate his daughters into demure and sweet ladies according to the white standards, and thus deprives them of their nature in the name of care and love. (155)

As a little girl, Magdalena is bold, wild and curious. She likes playing with the Mundo boys, running about the village, jumping over boulders recklessly. They "discovered birds' nests together, abandoned trails, poisoned wells, vulture feasts, rattlesnake beds, a valley of bluebells early in the spring." (24) She likes doing anything that expresses her nature fully, and leads a free and easy life before the whipping incident. The Mundo people like her so much that they call her "Mad Dog," which is a symbol of cleverness in their culture. Nonetheless, in Robinson's eyes, she lets herself loose and her behaviors are not in conformity with the puritanical norms. He feels embarrassed and anxious when he finds her boldly staring at men's zippered pants. For the father, what interests Magdalena is "men, and what was concealed by their trousers." (15) Sticking to his absolute authority in the family, he just takes everything for granted and never troubles to ask his daughter or his wife for the reasons. The truth is, Magdalena is fascinated by nothing but zippers: her father once gave her a small round purse with a golden, hidden zipper, but she got it lost on the way to Mexico; it is hence a great pity for her. After all, it is far less common for Magdalena to receive gifts from her father. Robinson's misunderstanding grows with each passing day, however. When Magdalena is at puberty, he begins "to keep her from her friends," even though she "would weep and rage over her homework in the room." (18) In so doing, Robinson attempts to prevent his daughter from sleeping with boys. What he is worried about is that she might get pregnant one day and bring dishonor onto him. He holds that Magdalena "cannot be called Mad Dog" any more as she "is the daughter of a minister." (19) It never occurs to him that it is the parent's duty to educate the daughter about sex and teach her to protect herself. He seems to accept that Magdalena is getting fallen, and monitors her wardrobe as well as Susannah's to make sure that their dresses are long enough and their necklines are high. Robinson thus looks upon his daughters (especially Magdalena) as his private property. He interferes in their life in the name of care and love. His misunderstanding and interference prepare the way for the later crisis in the father-daughter relationship.

As a matter of course, Robinson beats Magdalena violently when he notices her have sex with Manuelito. He does not stand to have his name fouled. He burns with such a frenzy of rage that he decides to teach her a good lesson. The beating is therefore a prerogative expression of his anger at Magdalena's disobedience and his despair at the eventual failure in controlling her behaviors. On the part of Magdalena, she does not understand the violence of her father, who explains to her and her sister that his profession is "based on the forgiveness of other people's sins." (23) She thinks that he should forgive her or, to be exact, feel happy for her since she has experienced so much pleasure, as she later says to Susannah, "I knew I was wild. Disobedient. Wayward and headstrong. But I did not understand his violence, after I had just experienced so much pleasure. So much sweetness. If he had known, if I could have told him, I felt he should have been happy for me. If in fact he loved me, as he often said he did." (26) What Magdalena does not understand is her father's dishonesty and hypocrisy. She begins questioning his love for her. The whipping incident not just completely destroys Robinson's image in her daughter's mind, but also leaves the punished indelible traumas and becomes her lifetime nightmare. What she could not forget is both the beating itself and the fact that her father whips her with the belt, her gift from Manuelito. She harbors resentment against her father and regards it as her only purpose to take revenge on him, because "[h]e'd taken the moment in my (Magdalena's) life when I was most secure in its meaning. The moment my life opened, not just to my family and friends, but to me myself. The moment when I knew my life was given to me for me to own. He took that moment and he broke it into a million bits. He made it dirty and evil." (116) She does everything to remind her father about what he has done to her so that he lives in torment for ever. She refuses sex and numbs herself by gluttony during the rest of her life; she shows hatred for her mother, who promises to leave her father but allows him to return to her bedroom within a month; she becomes indifferent to her sister, who is shocked by the beating but does not keep so far away from her father as is expected. Magdalena neither forgives her father nor allows her mother and her sister to be intimate to him. In the attempt to isolate her father, she gets herself isolated and her family members hurt. In this sense, the beating incident ruins both Magdalena's life and the family's happiness.

The whipping incident is actually a watershed of the family's life. It leads to great changes in the other family members' life as well. Robinson's violence shocks Langley so much that she screams out her wrath—"*We were beaten in slavery*"—"weeping as if her heart would break." (31, italics original) "She cried every night and would not let me (Robinson) enter the bedroom"; she loses confidence in her husband, who seems to have become a monster; she sniffs at him as if he "were disagreeable garbage." (31, 32) Consequently, she "became so weak from her grief" as well as her wrath and disappointment that "she stumbled." (33) She has no intimacy with him. Their happy life comes to a halt at least for the time being.

Langley's response—a mixture of wrath and grief—is at once a strong protest of a wife and mother against the patriarchal tyranny in the family and a special manifesto of a mother's divine right to protect her daughters. It unleashes a firestorm of condemnation to Robinson, the patriarch, who knows clearly about the miserable history of black slaves. As an anthropologist and modern black father, Mr. Robinson is supposed to defend his daughter(s) and the black women in general from any harm, let alone the harm from himself. It is the duty of Robinson and the whole generation of black males to prevent from recurring the similar whipping incidents in the period of slavery, as is described in the literary works like *Uncle Tom's Cabin* (1852) and *Roots: The Saga of an American Family* (1976). Liberated from slavery, black men ought to struggle for justice and nonviolence not simply in society but also in the black community as well as within their own families. Robinson's behavior is essentially the consequence of unconsciously imitating the white slaveholders. As a patriarch, he is privileged in the family, like the white race in the whole society. When the behavior of Magdalena (who is just a woman or the other sex to Robinson) is not to his liking, he naturally resorts to violence, which is, in the eyes of the perpetrators, the most effective way of conquest. It is not the first time for Ms. Walker to create the black fathers, and expose and criticize their evils and vices in their own families. Early in *The Color Purple*, she portrays the shameless black father Alphonso, who rapes her stepdaughter Celie and gets her impregnated twice. Nevertheless, Mr. Robinson in *By the Light of My Father's Smile* is quite different from the stepfather and businessman (Alphonso). As an anthropologist and the biological father of Magdalena, he does love his daughters; and he even makes an agreement with his wife before marriage that "we would never lay a hand on our child." (31) We have every reason to believe that such educated men as Robinson will be sane enough not to take violent acts in the family; yet he is no better than any other black man. Similarly, Robinson's doing is commanded not by reason but by something called instinct, which he admits:

> There was something in me, I found, that followed ideas, beliefs, edicts, that had been put into practice, into motion, before I was born. And this 'something' was like an internalized voice, a voice that drowned out my own. Beside which, indeed, my own voice began to seem feeble. Submissive. And when I allowed myself to think about that submission I thought of... the way Langley, Magdalena, and even the all-accepting Susannah sometimes looked at me. In dismay and disappointment. (30)

Obviously, in the case of Robinson, Walker tends to emphasize that the eradication of violent acts—which, like bad habits, are inveterate—is more a problem in behavior than in cognition, and that black male intellectuals, disguised in the rational coat, are more dangerous and more disappointing.

Susannah is another victim of the beating incident. She has been living in dilemma ever since. Or rather, she has to make a choice between her father and her sister. As the witness of the incident, she cannot turn a blind eye to what Magdalena has been suffering. She is forced to turn her sympathy for Magdalena into her alienation from Robinson. As a docile, obedient daughter, Susannah feels sorry for her indifferent attitude toward her father. She loves him and knows well of his love for herself. She has to conceal her true feelings about him, however. The concealment gradually develops into a habit. Her heart gets closed in the end. Just as Robinson's spirit recounts it, Susannah is "not even aware at the time of my death that she missed me... She did not cry at my funeral. She was a stoic spectator... looking down at me, the father who gave her life, with the passivity of one who has borne all she intends to bear. She did not even bother to smirk as platitudes about me—most of them absurd—filled the church around her." (3) Besides the compulsory choice, the incident casts a shadow over the girl's knowledge of sex. She spends most of her time ascertaining her sexual orientation and struggling between heterosexuality and homosexuality. A writer and independent woman in economy, Susannah feels insecure and gets lost in both heterosexuality and lesbianism. She is in a passive state in the relationships, especially with Pauline or Magdalena, as is discussed about in the previous chapter. Although she, with Irene's help, walks out of the psychological shadow, Susannah has no chance to compensate for her guilt toward her father or restore the intimate relationship with her sister. Her life is thus permanently marked with tragedy.

In *In Search of Our Mothers' Gardens*, Ms. Walker (1983: 330 – 331) expresses her dissatisfaction with her father and brothers: "I desperately needed my father and brothers to give me male models I could respect, because white men…

offered man as dominator, as killer, and always as hypocrite. My father failed because he copied the hypocrisy. And my brothers—except for one—never understood they must represent half the world to me, as I must represent the other half to them." Her father and brothers' failure to be male models in her life contributes to Walker's concern with the daughters' destiny in the male-dominated society.

In *By the Light of My Father's Smile*, Walker also describes the sufferings of the other women characters victimized by their fathers and brothers. In order to prevent her from going to school, which she likes every much, Pauline is got drunk by her father and one of her brothers and left to be raped when she is only fifteen years old. Impregnated, she is married off to the rapist, who is a "penniless" "ne'er-do-well." (A. Walker, 1998: 101) After that, she, "sick as a dog, big as a house," "had to do what her husband anted"; her "life was finished." (107) Although she "taught herself to make pies" to make money later and "saved enough money to run away," Pauline never frees herself from the psychological trauma and fails to develop normal sexual relationships with either a male or a female. Sensitive and vulnerable, she is disgusted with men and jealous of women, who seem a little luckier. The family members' betrayal is Pauline's lifetime pain, which dooms her emotional life to failure. As a rape victim, Irene's mother receives no compassion or care from her father and brothers, who "chose not to believe this" and beat her. (51) "No one ever again spoke to her." (52) She dies after giving birth to Irene and leaves her struggling in the world alone. Accepted as "God's punishment for her mother's sin," Irene is deserted at a very young age, working as a servant in a church and bearing cynicism and hardships in life all alone. (52) Nobody wants her; nobody loves her. Her father and brothers do not regard her as their family member and take no notice of her suffering. She is "chained" to the church till her old age when her father and all of her seven brothers die. Irene's miserable life is also ascribed to nobody but her irresponsible father as well as her indifferent brothers, though she, as the only inheritor that lives, eventually inherits their immense fortune.

Children's healthy development cannot do without fathers' care and love. The patriarchy-centered culture fosters fathers' neglect of their daughters' health, physical and psychological. In fact, the fathers in *By the Light of My Father's Smile* have the prerogative to decide their daughters' fate. They are the devils, who take the responsibility for their daughters' lives of pain and misery, and destroy the probable harmony in the father-daughter relationships. Consequently, all the father-daughter relationships in the novel are characterized by the absence of humanity. Walker's condemnation of the incompetent fathers manifests her longing for the ideal fathers who work as male models in their daughters' lives.

The husband-wife relationship is another habitat of the male domination. Susannah's husband Petros comes from Greece, where women live in such "ancient, indelible grief" that, even "when they smiled," they "seemed to smile through tears," where the word "passion" therefore "denoted suffering," where women "stepped aside with deference when men passed." (50, 46) As a male brought up in this men-centered society, Petros is always frowning upon women. "Whatever a woman was, was never enough, or right enough, for him." (7) He quarrels with Susannah only because she likes wearing high heels, which makes him look quite short, though for some time he feels "only pride to be stepping out with Susannah," who is unique and full of novelty in his eyes as she, unlike the locals wearing black, is "dressed completely in white, her hair lifted off her neck in one thick, coiled braid that accentuated her height and her elegant, gliding walk." (47) Petros gets married to Susannah not out of true love but out of curiosity or, to be exact, out of vanity. He accepts her not as his equal half but an object to gratify his pride. When he feels stressed and hurt because of her tall stature, he is naturally irritated since he has been raised to master women (including his wife). In the case of Petros, Walker highlights the universality of patriarchy and its negative effect on the husband-wife relationship.

In the novel, males' domination over females is also demonstrated in the patriarchal conventions existing in different races. As a womanist, Walker effectually goes beyond races. She shows solicitude not only for the Afro-American women such as Magdalena, Susannah, and Pauline, but also for women in Africa, Asia as well as Europe, among whom are the Greek woman Irene and her mother. As a matter of fact, Irene and her mother's experiences are not uncommon in Greece, where women have been treated inhumanely since the ancient time. Irene tells Susannah about its history of stoning women into silence, saying "they stoned a great many, before they got their vaunted 'democracy' in these parts." (55) Not far from Irene's church is "one of the stoning pillars," whose base "was still pink from blood" a hundred years ago. (55) However, stoning women is not the unique invention of the Greek men. There are similar recordings of "the size and shape of the stones to be used" in the religious books in some other cultures like the Asian—"[s]ome are of a special size and shape to break the woman's nose, others to crack her skull. There had been many recent stonings in Saudi Arabia and Iran; a few brave women and men had risked their lives to tell the world about them." (55)

The women in Africa are as tragic. The Nuer women "in the unmapped wilds of southwest Ethiopia," for instance, are forced "to wear disks the size of dinner plates in their bottom lips," "in the presence of the men." (164) In this way, they are prevented from speaking "in the men's presence" and from eating "as fast as the men" so that the latter "ate most of the food." (164) For the people there are short of food; they must satisfy men's needs first in order to maintain their health and their superiority to women. Here also exists the convention that women "wear heavy iron collars around their necks," which "weigh ten pounds or so" and obviously impose restrictions on their movement. (164) To these sexually-prejudiced conventions not only the male missionaries to Africa from the so-called civilized world turn blind eyes, but also the local women themselves get accustomed—"[t]hey have no memory or record of a time when they did not wear disks and did not wear iron collars"; or rather, "they are enforcers" themselves since "they had originally dreamed them up and were not oppressed by them," according to the missionaries' understanding. (165) Moreover, the missionaries accept the conventions as part of "the tribal culture"; they do not deplore them but would like to have them existing to keep "the tribe unique." (165) They choose to ignore the miserable conditions of women—"the lips and the necks of the women are raw and infected." (165) These conventions and the willingness and permission to keep them definitely take men away from humanity.

Walker explores the essence of sexism in the European culture in the concept of "ladies first," through the mouth of Irene: "It is because, in the early days, if we were permitted to walk behind the man, we would run away. If we were kept in front, they could keep an eye on us. Later on, as we became more tame, they hated to think a woman they desired would only think of running away, and so they invented chivalry. Gallantry. The lifting over puddles, the landing into carriages." (62) What is lamentable in the concept is that, with the prevalence of the so-called chivalry, women have internalized men's thought and are willing to be enslaved. From the example of "ladies first," Walker expresses her worry about women's insensitivity to their own mental slavery and aims to awaken women's liberal consciousness.

In conclusion, men's domination over women is still a universal problem both within families and social communities. The harmonious relationship between men and women still has a long way to go. It depends both on men's reformation and on women's self-awakening and constant struggle.

6.2.1.2 The White Dominance over the Colored

The white and the colored constitute another binary opposition in the human world, in the Western society in particular, in which whites are dominant. Racism is also a large obstacle to Alice Walker's womanist utopia and therefore another main concern in her literary writings. As a womanist, Ms. Walker knows fairly well that "the politics of sex as well as the politics of race and class are crucially interlocking factors." (B. Smith, 1985: 169) Her exploration of sexism is always juxtaposed with that of racism. *By the Light of My Father's Smile* is no exception. In the novel, the author lays bare the white supremacy over blacks and other minor races such as the Gypsies and American Indians. Her purpose is not to make a simple didactic/moralistic judgment but to present the racial and cultural dualities and dilemmas faced by the colored people.

In the modern society, the white achieve their domination over the colored mainly by locking the latter into the bondage of ideas and politics that shackle their national life, the harmful psychological constructs that blind the colored (especially blacks) to their subjection to a universalized white norm. Mr. Robinson is a black anthropologist, who is marginalized in the white world and fails to obtain his academic funding from any institution. An atheist, he disguises himself as a Christian missionary, seemingly for the purpose of defrauding the church and getting its funds. Nevertheless, he is so indulged in his preaching among the Mundo about the white stuff he hardly knows and cares, that is, he is so stuck into his own lie, that he ultimately makes himself believe it. Oblivious to his own slavery, Robinson now stands in whites' shoes and naturally shifts the burden the white society puts on him to his family and the Mundo people. He not only attempts to remold his daughters according to the white norm, which consequently ruins their chances of happiness, but also to regenerate the Mundo people, the inferior or degenerate race in the eyes of the superior. The moment he tries to save Mundo people's souls in the name of God, he gets his own lost, and internalizes the white colonialist ideology and is thus unknowingly changed into a spokesman for the Western culture, which ideologically justifies the self-ascribed racial and cultural superiority of the Western world over the non-Western world.

In the remote Mundo community, Robinson blindly enjoys the illusory superiority over the locals and turns up his nose at the Mundo people, with whom he shares the same African ancestors. As a "whitened" black stripped of psychological health and one of the incalculable victims of the white racist culture in the Western world, he, ironically, identifies himself with the white colonists and takes it his mission to impose the Christian doctrines on the indigenous people regardless of their religious feelings. Robinson's preaching is essentially an activity of colonization. Like the white colonists, he, in the name of civilization, attempts to conquer the Mundo ideologically. He watches their lives and studies their customs, and draws conclusions that suit himself, not paying much heed to the facts; he even imagines the custom that doesn't exist at all so as to testify his racial and moral superiority over the Mundo people. Like the so-called civilized people, he never studies himself. Hence he never realizes his internalization of the white supremacy in his refusal to know about his black brothers. Just as his spirit later admits it, "[t]hey (the Mundo) were so gentle, but they were so poor. When you see that people are so poor it is hard to believe they know what they are doing." (112) The logic Robinson follows is that being poor means being ignorant and uncivilized. Having American citizenship, he positions himself as a rich man, though he has to beg the church for financial aid. Therefore, from the very beginning, he, like white people, characterizes the Mundo as the inferior and acts as their savior to deliver them from ignorance and endow them with civilization. In the meantime, as an imitator of the white behavior patterns, Robinson considers himself an upper-class black and is learning to train his daughters accordingly; he feels sorry for his wife because she cannot read *Times*, which is a popular magazine with the upper-class people in America. As a matter of fact, Robinson is portrayed as an embodiment of paradox: An African descendent himself, he discriminates against the ethnic minority, the Mundo; a victim of racism, he practices the racist moral principles and beliefs both within the family and among the Mundo. The paradox in Robinson is ascribed to the whites' success in enslaving the colored and thus declares the spiritual crisis in the black community.

Despite the abolition of slavery in America early in the 1860s, modern blacks still suffer from racial discrimination. Pauline's father works in a meatpacking plant and holds a dirty job with low pay. As an experienced worker, he trains new comers, but the trainees soon rise "above him at the plant" only because he is black. The discrimination and injustice irritate him so much that, after he gets home, "he vented all his wrath and self-pity on our door that was hurt heavily and full of misery just as our lives," as Pauline recalls it. (97) Such brutal black males are common in the other Afro-American literary works. They are not born monsters, however. Physical poverty and spiritual pressure contribute to black males' insecurity, irritability and even mental contortion. Since they could do nothing but to surrender to the white domination, they naturally pass on their wrath and hatred to the objects like a door and even to their wives and children. Pauline thus describes her father:

> But my father's stereotypical belligerence, hostility, maudlin and abusive bullying were not all there was to him. There was a whole other side, ... When he was in his right mind, ... After he'd bathed and napped and had a good dinner; after he'd reviewed our report cards and found them satisfactory; after he'd forgone a first drink and lured my mother into their back bedroom, he was a father full of funny stories and play. He was a father who loved to repair things, a father who played the guitar. (98)

Relaxed and fully rested, and satisfied, physically and spiritually, Pauline's father appears normal and energetic. He becomes a warm and responsible father who loves his children and likes to do some housework. It is obvious that racism is the root of every sin in the Western world.

In the novel, in addition to the Afro-Americans, Walker also shows her concern for the other ethnic minorities such as the Gypsies and the American Indians. The history of the Gypsies is one of slavery as well. They have been enslaved in Europe "for four hundred years," "[b]ought and sold, humiliated and beaten, killed even, for sport"; the exploitation of their labor usually lasted till their death. (141) The Gypsies are not so free, "forever flying in a new direction," as they are thought, "but more like hamsters, always tramping the same long, well-remembered track." They have never been allowed to settle down; they have always been driven on; so they have to move on to escape from being driven. (141) They are forced to lead a vagrant life, a life no better than black people's. They are "cut off from everyone else in Europe, more cut off than the Jews, even after hundreds of years." (142) They are accepted as non-normal humans and the inferior and therefore singled out for discrimination. The European whites are undoubtedly the superior and the white domination plays a decisive role in the life of the Gypsies.

The American Indians or the Native Americans came to the Northern American Continent much earlier than the Anglo-Saxon whites. Although they were warm-hearted, hospitable and welcoming, and helped the early European settlers a lot, they are also discriminated against in the American society. They are uglified and accepted as the synonym for the ignorant, the barbarian and the backward. They have suffered from slavery as well and still live a hard life. Their thralldom goes hand in hand with the formation of the United States of America as a nation. The US history is actually one of violence and genocide, to some extent, as the European immigrants have been plundering land and property from the natives from the outset. They classified the Natives as their property, which could be evidenced by the early American Constitution where the African slaves and the aboriginals were inscribed as private property. As a multiracial nation, where the European whites have the highest proportion of the population, US is characterized by binary oppositions, including the superior and the inferior, the human and the subhuman, the civilized and the barbarian, the white and the non-white, and follows the traditional Western ideology, which underlines the dominant position of the European whites and the subordinate/marginalized position of the other races. The Vietnam War in the 1960s resulted from the US concept of dominance practiced worldwide. In the novel, Manuelito, together with the other American young men, is sent to fight in Vietnam, where he kills the parents of a little girl and thus ruins her life. Orphaned, the girl has a breakdown and becomes a prostitute after growing up. She later dies of AIDS. Like Manuelito, the American soldiers bring about a disaster to the Vietnamese people; yet it does not prevent the American government from awarding the so-called war heroes, when the War ends, including Manuelito, who is awarded a Purple Heart as well as a Congressional Medal of Honor from Ronald Reagan. As a man of conscience and an inferior citizen in the American society, Manuelito has been haunted by the girl's misfortune ever since. As a matter of fact, he is disturbed not so much by the tragedy itself as by the sense of insecurity hidden in the double standards of American value (i. e., racism). In the eyes of racists, race is a sociopolitical rather than biological category. So prejudice and inequality are the corollary of racial differences and the reasonable excuse for the white colonial intrusion.

The white dominance is also expressed as west-centrism, which regards Western/white culture as the standard/center of all other cultures and supports the white colonialist ideology. The west-centrism takes the center-margin structure as its basis. In this structure, the Western is the self, the center and the superior while the non-Western is the other, the margin and the inferior. According to this principle, the process of colonization is a process of civilization. If violent occupation was the main route of the early colonizers, then cultural conquest is a preferable and idiomatic way in the postcolonial period. The colonists go to the alleged barbarian land to disseminate their so-called civilized culture, including their religion Christianity, in the name of cultural study. With the spreading of the Western cultural values, the quintessence of the tribal culture is furtively displaced or the whole culture is assimilated or killed. In the novel, Walker expresses her disavowal of such cultural study, through the conversation between Susannah and Irene.

> I think it is ridiculous and ultimately insulting to study people, said Irene. I think you would only need to study other human beings if you were worried you were not human yourself.
>
> Susannah laughed. I've often thought what a European trait studying other people is. (184)
>
> Irene, said Susannah, ... as you know, generally speaking, white people almost never study themselves. As white people, they prefer to study us and write about how we don't quite measure up.
>
> They can't believe how out of synch they are, said Irene. They can't figure it out and they're afraid to find out how different they are from the rest of the world's peoples. Rather than risk humiliation and have to own up to an inferiority complex, they've spent the last several millennia trying to prove there's something inferior and wrong about everybody

else. (185)

Through Irene and Susannah's comments, Walker offers a quite subversive interpretation of the whites' cultural study. She believes that white people study the other peoples only because they are not confident enough; they are trying to find the inferiority in the other peoples only because they themselves feel inferior to them. Walker epitomizes the character of the cultural study in her negation of the white colonists and their culture. In so doing, she exposes the hypocrisy and arrogance hidden in the superiority of white people and definitely stakes out her position facing the white cultural conquest.

The white dominance over the colored people or the ethnic minorities abounds in *By the Light of My Father's Smile*. It is embodied in the physical exploitation and spiritual enslavement of both the colored individuals and the ethnic groups. So racism is another universal problem, which gives rise to the absence of humanity in the Western world. In fact, it works together with sexism to block the realization of the harmonious human relations. Through the novel, Walker still means to raise the colored people's equal awareness and highlight the fact that, to build an equal harmonious society, humans, male and female, white and colored, have to unite and make concerted efforts.

6.2.2 Humanistic Concern

Alice Walker is a practical humanist and writer with a strong sense of social responsibility. She is constantly concerned with the life and fate of the vulnerable groups in the human world, in the American society in particular. She holds that a good writer should be, first and foremost, a compassionate person who is responsive to common people's sufferings and committed to the construction of an equal, democratic and harmonious social order. Like Virginia Woolf, she believes that the main function of writing is to inspire readers to improve society. Walker is virtually a brave political writer and social activist. In her novels and other literary writings, she has decried such inhumane practices as incest, domestic violence, black female genital mutilation, racial enslavement, colonial aggression, and cultural intrusion. In real life, she has participated in the Civil Rights Movement and the anti-war demonstrations; she has sided with Fidel Castro and secured Cuba's independence from "American imperialism"; she has made an address to explicitly oppose Present Bush's bombing attack against Afghanistan after 9/11. As a universalist, Ms. Walker is extending her womanist ideal to the global community and never fails to show her humanistic concern for the vulnerable groups, including women and blacks, in her real and fictional worlds. In *By the Light of My Father's Smile*, she voices her belief that love and forgiveness will work to construct a harmonious relationship between genders and among races, viz., among "entire people," which is well illustrated in the improvement of the father-daughter relationships and in the Mundo's admiration for inner natural instincts and their pursuit of wholeness and reconciliation with those they hurt after death.

6.2.2.1 The Father-Daughter Reconciliation

In *By the Light of My Father's Smile*, fathers' tyranny and androcentrism put strains on the father-daughter relationships, particularly the relationship between Robinson and his daughters, as is analyzed in the previous section. In the light of Walker's common narrative mode, the strained relationship is certain to be restored and love and forgiveness have always been the way out. Hence in the novel works humanism, which rejects hegemony and violence and calls for love and forgiveness, focusing on human interests, values and dignity, and affirms human ability to improve their relationships through the use of reason and ingenuity as opposed to submitting blindly to tradition and authority or sinking into cruelty and brutality. It is Robinson's love and Magdalena and Susannah's forgiveness that bring about reconciliation between the father and his daughters. It is reasonable to say that the novel is a "family tale of love, passion and forgiveness."

Mr. Robinson is not portrayed as a villain in the novel, though he does violence to his daughter and ruins his family's happiness. He has always loved his wife and daughters. Before having children, he agrees with his wife on not hitting or slapping their children. When Magdalena and Susannah are little girls, he is a good father who loves his daughters and is loved by them. Even after he is irritated by Magdalena's act and gives her a good beat, he never stops loving her. Immediately after his violence, he recognizes his error and admits that, by beating Magdalena "to the point of actually drawing into blood," he has turned himself "into a monster." (30, 31) As a matter of fact, Robinson begins confessing his sin the moment he throws away the leather belt. And he keeps confessing his sin till his death; even when he becomes a ghost, he still struggles for his daughters' forgiveness.

Since the beating incident goes against his agreement with his wife and hurts her badly, Mr. Robinson's penitence begins with his begging for his wife's forgiveness, for which he strives a month or so. Every night, as soon as the girls are asleep, he makes his way to her wife's bedroom door, which is locked inside by her, and pleads on his knees. Robinson feels so sorry for his precipitance that he makes every effort to make amends. After his wife's death, he frequently goes to see Magdalena, who teaches at a university. If his daughter happens to be out, he would keep waiting, sitting on her stoop "like a stray cat." (69) Robinson's persistence improves his relationship with Magdalena a little, in spite that she still bears a grudge against him. "Over time I (Magdalena) came to expect his surprise visits. He would take me (her) out to a restaurant, any restaurant I liked, and he would order anything I wanted." (70) Sometimes they, the father and the daughter, even exchange good-natured banter with each other. However, Mr. Robinson fails to restore his relationship with Magdalena during his lifetime. He dies with regrets and could not rest in peace. Worried about Magdalena's life distorted by her hatred for him, Robinson's spirit goes to her residence to watch over her. Knowing about her reunion with Manuelito after many years of separation, he stands at her door to stop anyone from bothering them. He even sinks to his knees and, "as wind, began a gentle breathing of apology upward and over the transom of June's locked door." (83) Robinson's soliloquy near Magdalena's residence effectively conveys his regret. "All your life you have the necessary illusion that you know all there is to know about heartbreak. I hate to be the one to tell you about the heartbreak you experience after you die. ... I had beaten her for loving his young body! If I were not dead already, I would have killed myself." (83)

Meeting Manuelito's spirit, the dead Robinson eventually opens his heart and says out his guilt and true feelings plainly. To help him understand Magdalena fully and reconcile with her easily, Manuelito then tells him about the Mundo attitude toward sex and the Mundo fathers' special blessing—"happily looking down on" their children like the moon, which is not full but "has waned and then reappears, as a smile in a dark face, in the sky"—for their daughters as well as sons, who enjoy sex. (210) We could sense Robinson's deep guilt after learning about the Mundo custom:

> I finally got it. That this was what my poor daughter had been singing about, all those years ago! "Por la luz... por la luz..." (by the light, by the light) I could still hear her despairing cry. There had been an element of pleading in her song that I had ignored. She had been begging me to see, to witness, the light that she had found. To love and bless what she loved. But I refused. I had brought her to a culture and a people I'd claimed to respect. She had fallen in love with them, and been betrayed when I myself stopped short. When I myself, in her eyes, had regressed. (210)

Understanding what Magdalena was expecting from him and how deeply he has hurt her, Mr. Robinson makes a sincere apology to Magdalena after her death, following the Mundo ritual—that parents kiss their children's five places to bless them—and kissing "not only her palms and the arches of her feet" "but also her knees" to bless her. His sincere apology and real repentance win Magdalena's forgiveness; Robinson finally reconciles with his eldest daughter successfully.

If it fuels resentment and revolt in Magdalena against her father, the beating incident brings Susannah disappointment and bewilderment. It completely destroys the perfect image in her mind of "her gentle, compassionate father," who seems to have turned into a monster. (27) She feels quite disappointed at this change and becomes alienated from his father. "[S]he had somehow discovered a rejecting power in herself, even in childhood, and had used it to shut her father out." (58) This Robinson of course apprehends and tries his best to remedy. He frequently offers Susannah her favorite candies, notwithstanding her constant refusal. He is invariably patient with her and never criticizes or takes offence at anything she has done. Even when he knows about her love affair in high school, he does not scold her as he has done to Magdalena. He chooses to have a heart-to-heart talk with her about contraception, just as any considerate father does. What Robinson keeps doing sets Susannah in a dilemma. She is at a loss as to how to balance her relationship with her father and that with her sister. She thinks it a betrayal of Magdalena to be close to her father on the one hand; and on the other hand, she is greatly tortured by showing indifference to her father, especially when he endeavors to please her. By struggling to "suppress the love she had felt for her hapless (yes) father," Susannah feels "herself betray her own love," which is accepted among the Mundo as "the greatest crime one can commit against oneself." (170, brackets original) Therefore, it is much easier for Robinson to restore his relationship with Susannah, who, in practice, never hates her father really but fully understands her father's awkward situation. For Susannah, Robinson, to a large extent, is a captive of the church or Christianity, which is the true fact. As a pretended missionary, he has to spread the Christian doctrines among the Mundo, which gradually obscures his own belief. In the meantime, he feels guilty of what he has done to Magdalena, for he even does not know what goes wrong with her—he himself does not believe what he compels his daughters to follow, either.

Susannah feels sympathetic with Robinson and is touched by his sincerity to make amends. She seems to have already forgiven her father at the bottom of her heart. She appears callous and insensitive to Robinson's attempt only because of the pressure from Magdalena. After his death, Susannah comes to realize how pitiful her father is, "trying to win me (her) back, trying to rekindle my (her) trust." (118) Having lost any opportunity to reconcile with her father, she is burdened with guilt and regret. She once persuades Magdalena to forgive their father, saying: "Try to imagine the father I love, why I love him. Why Mama loved him. Why you loved him before he humiliated you. Don't pin him to that one moment. He was a human being, like you and me." (123) After Magdalena's death, Susannah steps out of her sister's manipulation and has the chance to cry out her true feelings: "Daddy, Daddy, I'm sorry. ... I didn't know what it meant to give you up. I didn't know what it meant not to forgive. And now it is too late!" (171) The cry declares Susannah's growth as well as independence. "Susannah felt herself complete the process of becoming an adult. She was grown up. She could handle her own life. Magdalena ceased to be a manipulative and mangled psychic twin, stuck to her by pain." (171) Spiritually freed, Susannah feels relieved, light-hearted and peaceful; she feels "more sane than she'd felt in a long time"; she completely forgives her father as any sane daughter does. (171) In spite of the span of a long time, the father-daughter relationship gets restored at last. Living in the other world, Robinson is sure to feel Susannah's forgiveness since he always watches over her soul. Directed by Manuelito and singing the Mundo initiation song he crosses over the river to realize the wholeness of life.

The father-daughter reconciliation truly comes only after the relationship between the sisters (exactly, the sisters' ghosts) is improved, or rather, after Magdalena realizes that she herself is the tort-feasor in her relationship with Susannah. At the deathbed of Susannah, she thinks to herself, "Susannah's had been a life that, to my regret, and because of my own need to cause her suffering, I knew little about, no matter that the Mundo thought the dead knew everything." (213) Edified by her ex-lover Manuelito and his understanding of the Mundo custom and belief, Magdalena becomes sensible, open-minded and tolerant. As a sister, she realizes her gross negligence of Susannah's life and feelings. She feels guilty of hurting her sister so deeply. She therefore, on her own initiative, comes to Susannah, the moment her sister is dying, and has a long easy talk with her, which is in essence her special way of apology. And Susannah expectedly accepts Magdalena's apology with pleasure, saying, "Magdalena, ... you are here because you are sorry you deliberately led me astray such a very long time ago. That is all the legacy I need." (218) The reconciliation of the relationship between the two sisters concludes the conflict and enmity within the family, which are replaced by harmony and eternity.

Interweaving with the main thread of the Robinson story is Pauline's suffering caused by her family members headed by her father. Compared with Magdalena's or Susannah's, Pauline's forgiveness for her father comes more abruptly. Ms. Walker gives less than one page to Pauline's changed attitude to her father. She sets Pauline talking with Magdalena about fathers. Different from the latter's loud complaint about her father and denial of his love, Pauline expresses her compassion for and understanding of her father: "My father was very tired and confused. He had to pretend he wanted all ten of the children who kept him chained to a table in meatpacking plant." (127) As Pauline explains it to Magdalena, the crux of their poverty and her father's predicament lies in the Christian belief that it is sinful for parents "to stop the births" and that "God would judge them harshly" if they do so. (127) The failure to support his family leads to the impatience and irresponsibility of Pauline's father. With the increase of the number of his children, he begins to find some other way out and perhaps it is his best choice to marry Pauline off for one reason or another. In this sense, the father himself is a victim and is thus worth forgiving: "You have to open your heart to them, eventually, ... No matter what they've done." (128) Despite the abruptness of Pauline's change, Walker does succeed in portraying another kind, rational and magnanimous black woman and thus gives readers a clearer picture of her womanist utopia.

If forgiveness is pivotal in the women characters' reconciliation with their fathers and their eventual peaceful minds, it is not the case with Irene. Strictly speaking, Irene's father is absent in her life. For Irene, he is just a symbol or nothing at all. He never fulfills his obligation as a father. Her only connection to him is the "immense fortune" he leaves to his sons who leave to Irene since they all have died. However, Irene never hates him. She actually ignores his existence. Her father is never in Irene's life, or vice versa. She has no contact or conflict with him, and no love or hatred for him. Hence nothing like forgiveness is needed for him. Irene seems to be living well without him, except for her similarity to Gypsies. Like Gypsies, Irene is a rootless wanderer, who never lives a steady and secure life. In Irene or Irene's relationship with her father, Walker not simply praises the daughter's indomitability but condemns the father's irresponsibility as well. The father-daughter relationship without relation seemingly conveys the author's misgivings about the harmonious coexistence of genders and of classes.

Although Alice Walker has always been criticized for her portraying black men as brutal and violent patriarchs since the first novel *The Third Life of Grange Copeland*, her black male characters are not simply oppressors or devils; instead, they are as victimized as their daughters and wives. As passive receivers, they have themselves whitened unknowingly. Hurting their families, they get themselves hurt. Through depicting the different attitudes of both the father (Robinson) and the daughters (Magdalena, Susannah, Pauline, and even Irene) toward the father-daughter relationships, the author explores the most effective and applicable way to reach reconciliation between fathers and daughters and bears witness to the restoring effect of love and forgiveness. Love and forgiveness triumph and the daughters get reconciled with their fathers. What Ms. Walker stresses in this novel is the old English saying that "to err is human, to forgive divine." Except the occasional subtle skepticism, the father-daughter relationships in the novel appear to hold great promise on the whole. The reconciliation between Robinson and his daughters particularly proves Ms. Walker's adherence to the womanist principles, which highlight harmony and humanity within families as well as in the human community.

6.2.2.2 The Spirituality in the Mundo Culture

Traditionally referring to a religious process of re-formation which aims to recover the original shape of man, oriented at the image of God, modern spirituality emphasizes subjective experience of a sacred dimension and the "deepest values and meanings by which people live," often in a context separate from organized religious institutions. (Sheldrake, 2007: 1 – 2) Typically including personal growth, a religious experience, a belief in a supernatural (beyond the known and observable) realm, a quest for an ultimate/sacred meaning, or an encounter with one's own "inner dimension," spirituality, as opposed to the Western reason, is characterized by super-nature, sacredness, emotion and humanness. (Waaijman, 2002: 315) In *By the Light of My Father's Smile*, Walker presents a great example of spirituality through the depiction of the Mundo culture, which lays emphasis on sparking human beings' real nature in this life and has faith in wholeness and reconciliation or harmony in the afterlife. Appealing to her rich imagination, the author offers opportunities for both those who have hurt others and those who are hurt in this life to make amends and receive comfort in the afterlife, and thus builds a spiritual paradise, where forgiveness and reconciliation work.

Magdalena is a child of nature. Active, optimistic and adventurous, she likes "expressing her own nature" and lives a free and unrestrained life. (A. Walker, 1998: 18) "She was all over the place, sticking her nose everywhere." (92) She is even found having sex with the Mundo boy Manuelito. Her behavior is so much at odds with the white norms represented by Robinson that he calls her "a tramp" and punishes her severely. (29) Nonetheless, the Mundo people like her very much. She is nicknamed Macdoc, meaning "mad dog," which "is considered wise because it has lost its mind" in the Mundo culture. (92) The Mundo people "have visions" rather than thoughts and hold that losing one's mind is an effective way to attain visions. They even "take herbs once a year to lose their minds all together." For the Mundo people, losing one's mind is a way of escaping from living "too much in your head," "a way of reminding you to stay in your emotions," "a way of saying" "that craziness has value." (93) By affirming the value of craziness, they simply highlight the inner natural instincts of human beings, which advocate freedom and individuality and thus benefit the personal development.

Thinking highly of sensibility and emotions instead of sense and thoughts in an individual, the imaginary Mundo culture underlines equality, and peace and harmony between genders. By employing the word "Mundo," which means "world" in Spanish and Portuguese, the author seems to imply that what she outlines about the Mundo community is an ideal model for the whole world. In the Mundo culture, men and women are close relatives. Men cannot do without women, and vice versa.

Anyone can see that woman is the mother
of the oldest man on earth
is it not then a prayer
to bow before her?

Anyone can see that man is the father
of the oldest woman on earth
is it not then a prayer
to bow before him? (161, italics original)

Hence men and women are equals, differently beautiful. When it is born, a Mundo child is kissed by both its father and mother in such five places as ears, eyes, nose, mouth and "the place where life begins." (162) And when a Mundo man or woman dies, his or her intimates are supposed to kiss the same places. Kissing the five places is the Mundo's way of expressing blessings. That a Mundo's life begins as well as ends with the same kissing manifests the Mundo's respect for the sanctity of life. As a matter of course, the Mundo respect sex as well. In their eyes, sex is natural and automatic; it is not just a way of releasing human nature but also a process of producing life. Therefore sex should be celebrated instead of being inhibited.

When one prepares to make love

for the first time
mother arrives singing
father is there
sweetgrass and
feathers are brought
eggs are eaten
one is kissed in all five
places
the sweet breasts
are thanked
one is sent to the loved one
blessed. (162, italics original)

The Mundo regard sex as holy as life is and the first sex is the holiest moment in a Mundo man or woman's life. The lovers are blessed by both parents. The community holds a ceremony of "joining lovers together," sweetgrass burnt to cleanse themselves and their surroundings, and eggs eaten "in the hope that the union would be fertile, not just in children, but in ideas, creativity, bountifulness for the tribe." (163)

The Mundo believe that "spirituality resides in the groin, in the sexual organs, [n]ot in the mind." (111) The Mundo parents teach their children (especially the boys) sexual knowledge as they grow up and become aware of sex, so that they can avoid getting pregnant. They neither sniff at nor punish the children who have already had sex, even though they are girls; instead, the Mundo fathers will be happy when their children enjoy sex. So they still like Magdalena and accept her as a good girl after the beating incident. Treasuring the harmonious relationship between men and women, the Mundo recognize sex as a most important approach to the male-female harmony and put a particular emphasis on the father's role in his life. "The week or so before the marriage of their children, the Mundo believe it is right for the young man to invite the young woman's father into the space that will be her home. It is important that he see what view she will have, so that he can imagine the growing spaciousness of her heart; it is important that he see where she will live; where she will be loved; where she will lie." (206) If the father's inspection of his daughter's new home before her marriage shows his concern for her future life, including her sexual life, then the invitation reflects the fiance's acceptance of his future wife and the fiancee's position in her new family, in the future husband-wife relationship in particular. The initial respect paves the way for the equal and harmonious relationship after marriage, which is the Mundo's constant goal and basic standard as well. The reason that the Mundo do not drive Robinson—whom they accept as a liar and a hypocrite—away and permit him to stay with them "for so long" is that he is "always making love to" his wife. (152) Manuelito tells Robinson, "[s]ome of the people they sent to us would not touch a woman. They did not like a woman's long hair; they did not like her laughter or her breasts; they did not like her smell. We knew those men would lead us straight off the face of the earth. But you loved woman, ... At least, you loved Señora Robinson. You seemed to know that it is when making love that we make life." (153) The Mundo have the tradition of worshipping Goddess, so they believe in women in their secular life. They hold that women "are less likely to identify with the priests." In turn, a priest, who likes women or at least his own woman, is worth trusting. However, as Manuelito points it out, Robinson becomes "confused" when his "own daughter followed in your (his) footsteps." (153) Here, in fact, lies the hypocrisy of the Western culture or its double standard towards men and women.

In the Mundo culture, women are closely connected to the nature, specifically to the moon. They share the rhythms of the moon, that is, their "tides," their "blood tides, connect with the moon." (208) "A woman, living in nature, is full when the moon is full." "And if a lot of women live together, they and the moon are full at the same time; when the moon releases and begins to wane, that is when they release their blood. ... during this time, a man may not make love to a woman. She feels somewhat irritable, somewhat messy," and "just naturally does not want to be bothered!" (209) Similarly, men are connected to the moon as well. The crescent moon, in the shape of "a bowl or a boat," resembles the smile in a dark face of a man, who is waiting for "the good lovemaking that is to come," as this is the time that women "are totally receptive." (210) It is by following this natural law that the Mundo men and women get along with each other peacefully and harmoniously, since sexual harmony is part and parcel of the good relationship between men and women. Meanwhile, the crescent moon is also compared to a smiling father who stands high up and looks down happily at the young men and women who are meeting and making love. That is why the Mundo girls and boys sing "by the light of my father's smile" as they go to meet their lovers; that is why the Mundo marry only when the moon "has waned and then reappears, as a smile" "in the sky." (210) And that is why the Mundo not simply maintains a peaceful male-female relationship but stay in harmony with the moon and the whole nature as well.

The Mundo pursue a total spiritual consummation. They do not want to be left with any regret. Wholeness and reconciliation with those they hurt are their ultimate goal, which they usually reach in their afterlife. The Mundo are taught the initiation song, even when they are too young to understand it, which promises that they "will continue to sing, to live, on the other side" till their "tasks are done." (95)

Anyone can see that the earth
is a grandchild of
the moon
and the moon is mother
of the night sky.

When you die
this is the song
that will carry
you beyond the river
it is your small craft

it is your horse. (95, italics original)

The Mundo believe that there is an afterlife. And the best luck for them is coming to "the other side, singing" their initiation song. (112) With the song, the dead smoothly make the transition from this life to the afterlife and have a feeling of self-assurance on the path of death so that they could complete what they "are required to do," that is, make amends for what they have done in this life and get reconciled with those hurt and attain wholeness: "The dead are required to finish two tasks before all is over with them: one is to guide back to the path someone you left behind who is lost, because of your folly; the other is to host a ceremony so that you and others you have hurt may face eternity reconciled and complete." (148) That Manuelito teaches Robinson the Mundo initiation song is a warm picture of one such ceremony. The beating incident also hurts Manuelito badly, who spends his youth searching for Magdalena and gets married to a woman he does not love in the end. It is impossible for him not to have hated the man who has ruined his life; yet he chooses to forgive Robinson and guide him to his reconciliation with his daughters. In this way, Manuelito is approaching to his wholeness.

The Mundo believe neither in heaven nor in hell or eternal damnation. What they do believe is that it is unavoidable and therefore horrible to hurt others or to be hurt. Each of the Mundo lives a life of "[f]orgiving or not forgiving"; each of them is sure to "have a little bit of time, a window of opportunity, so to speak, in which to make amends, to say goodbye, to bring love back to a love-forsaken heart" in the afterlife. (149) "The Mundo's Story," Manuelito explains, "was created to help us heal the wounds we make while we are alive." (150) The Mundo thus live in two worlds—the world of this life and the world of the afterlife. To have enough time to do their healing is the Mundo's purpose of connecting these two worlds. Once they forgive or complete their healing, they become whole and leave with wholeness. For the Mundo, "there is no difference between ghost and angel, angel and spirit." (149) Anybody, be it ghost or angel or spirit after death, has to make amends and do the healing work. Only when they finish the "two tasks" can the Mundo dead reach their consummate life. Then they disappear, with nobody thinking of them any longer. For the Mundo "are happy to leave whole." (149)

While they are oppressed and marginalized in this world, the Mundo dominate the other with their tolerance and generosity. After death, Robinson, the missionary from the Western world, is found at a loss before meeting Manuelito's ghost. He is shuttling between his daughters' lives, worried about their choices and sorry for their (physical and spiritual) suffering. He does not know how to make amends for what he has done to them (especially to Magdalena) till Manuelito's death, i. e., his ghost's appearance. It is Manuelito's ghost that sits side by side with Robinson and teaches him the Mundo way of penance that helps him restore his relationship with his daughter and thus relieve him of the lifetime guilt; it is Manuelito's ghost that enlightens Robinson with the essence of the Mundo culture—its respect for women (or its concept of equality between men and women) and its sacred attitude toward sex and life—that underlines human nature. What Manuelito does for Robinson is a good illustration of the Mundo culture, where love and forgiveness always spark. He illuminates Robinson's mind. In this sense, Manuelito or the Mundo culture as a whole works as Robinson's guide and spiritual mentor, who helps him understand the true meaning of love and face eternity with peace of mind, and thus successfully leads him to his spiritual wholeness. Robinson's ghost, the soul of a Christian missionary, is ironically saved and conquered by the ethnic culture, a low and vulgar culture in the whites' eyes. The role reversal eloquently proves the charm and spiritual connotation of the Mundo culture.

Set in the Mundo culture, the novel deals with humanity, centering on the human relationships like the father-daughter and the white-colored, and the Mundo's attitudes toward sex and women as well as their pursuit of harmony even in the afterlife. Love and forgiveness take effect, particularly in the improvement of the father-daughter relationship and in the presentation of spirituality in the Mundo culture. Throughout the novel, the author constantly conveys the idea that "to err is human, to forgive divine." She definitely approves of the positive efforts of the characters—Robinson, Susannah, Pauline, and others—and of the Mundo people to forgive and make amends so that their relationships will be reconciled with anyone hurting them or being hurt by them. As a womanist, Ms. Walker never gives up her struggle for an equal harmonious world. And, as a writer, she takes writing as her forum where she delivers her womanist ideas and outlines her womanist utopia. In this sense, *By the Light of My Father's Smile* is characteristically in Alice Walker's writing style.

6.3 The Quest for Harmony in *Now Is the Time to Open Your Heart*

Ms. Walker, still focusing on human survival and keeping her abiding concern for the oneness of the universe, seems to concentrate more attention on the characters' internal struggle and development instead of their external transformation in *Now Is the Time to Open Your Heart*. The work uncovers the life confusion and frustration of modern people, men and women, the white and the colored, the rich and the poor. Kate's search for the river of life is interwoven with Yolo's experience in Hawaii. Male and female figures of different races cluster together with Kate on the journey to the Amazon, carrying their own bewilderments, while various kinds of injustice and oppression unfold and leap to the eyes of Yolo. The whole novel is inundated with different crises—social, ecological as well as spiritual—in modern society, resulting from anthropocentrism, Eurocentrism (or ethnocentrism) and androcentrism, which, constitutive of traditional Western moral thought, are the constant target for Walker's womanist attack. In other words, Alice Walker's first novel of the new millennium continues to set the pursuit of harmony and humanity as the ultimate goal of its major characters.

6.3.1 The Origins of Disharmony in Nature and the Human World

Binary opposition in Western ideology determines the disparity between men and women, between whites and colored people (blacks particularly), and between humankind and nature. Inequality and oppression go hand in hand with caste system, which tacitly approves the superiority of men to women, of whites to blacks, and of humankind to nature. In the Western hierarchical society, women, blacks as well as nature are doomed to be victims of cultural hegemonism and power politics. In *Now Is the Time to Open Your Heart*, Walker explores men's tyranny over women, whites' oppression of colored people, and the destruction of nature by human beings, which contribute to the disharmony in nature and the human world, a corollary of anthropocentrism, Eurocentrism and androcentrism.

6.3.1.1 The Impact of Anthropocentrism

Holding that human beings are the most significant entity of the universe, anthropocentrism interprets the world in terms of human values and experiences, and emphasizes human supremacy or human exceptionalism. It is considered to be profoundly embedded in many modern human cultures and conscious acts, and accepted as a major concept in the field of environmental ethics and environmental philosophy. According to anthropocentrism, it is a matter of course for human beings to become the master of the nature. As a consequence, anthropocentrism becomes the root cause of problems created by human action within the ecosphere. *Now Is the Time to Open Your Heart* is suffused with brutal scenes of environmental disruption, which back up the author's denunciation of human hegemony in the universe.

As an anti-anthropocentrist and environmentalist, Ms. Walker holds that humans and nature are equal beings. Living creatures including animals and plants, in Walker's eyes, have spirits and souls like human beings. She loves trees and was once found talking with trees, which she actually accepts as relatives. When she lived in California, she found most deforestation and saw "the loggers' trucks, like enormous hearses, carrying the battered bodies of the old sisters and brothers down to the lumberyards in the valley." The sight, the "endless funeral procession" (in Walker's words), caused Walker's distress and painful emotions—the feeling of living "in a beautiful neighborhood that daily lost hundreds of its finest members," "mournful but impotent beside the avenue that carried them away"—and left her an indelible memory. (A. Walker, 1988: 119) Ever since she has been indignantly denouncing what humans have done to nature.

In *Now Is the Time to Open Your Heart*, Walker enumerates such ecological problems as deforestation, vegetation deterioration, and occupation of animals' habitats, some of which appear in Kate's dreams, some of which are what the characters, including the heroine, witness on their journeys. In effect, Kate dreams a lot of dreams in the novel, before her journey and on the journey to the Amazon. For instance, one day, after taking the "Grandmother medicine," she falls asleep and dreams about one of her ancestors. When the ancestor tells Kate about what happens to a tree after its death, she "thought of clear-cutting. Clear-cuts she had seen along the Klamath River in northern California. The landscape that had been so lush and powerful was left bare and desolate; the young trees coming up had no shade to protect them from the blistering sun that baked the earth to ash." (A. Walker, 2004: 96) The scene is obviously taken from the author's bitter memory of the tree felling and logging in northern California. Like Walker, Kate regards trees as emotional creatures, which could treasure and inherit their parents' history and tradition. She feels sorry for the young trees, which, having lost their parents' shelter, are exposed to the burning sun, "would never know the grandeur of the parents and grandparents" and therefore would never "guess what their true nature," and feels guilty of the human crime. She even has the feeling that she herself becomes one of the killers, finding "her dress changed into a buffalo skin." (97) Yolo is another witness of what humans have done to the forest. Once in Hawaii, when he gives his girlfriend Alma "a fragrant wood" as a gift and describes it as "something precious, tall and straight, perhaps endangered," Alma says that the wood is just the same as sandalwood and that some of the islands there were covered with sandalwood trees, which could be smelt far out to sea. (75) However, the forests, as Yolo now sees, "were completely destroyed. No trees at all are left. They went to Asia, Europe, America. They were made into incense, matchboxes, doodads." (75)

The felling of the sandalwood trees brings about the loss of the surrounding forest and thus destroys the pleasant living environment of the locals.

In the mad chase of temporary benefits, human beings not simply undermine their own happy home but endanger the animal world as well. Resting in her hut a few steps from the Amazon River, Kate could hear the rainforest, which she thought was "alive" but "would be silent." Nevertheless, it "was the loudest thing she'd ever heard. Like trains, planes and the New York City subway at rush hour." (53). And "every sound she heard that was not made by the vegetation, giant trees and tree-sized vines, groaning as they rubbed against one another, was made by creatures." (53) Humans invade and occupy animals' habitat in the name of development and construction. Kate hears the cry of a jaguar, "which sent a ripple of fear through their little camp" and conveys the information that "most of them want to run." (54) Where there are humans, there will be destruction and killing. "Humans were now in the position of deer or antelope or buffalo or polar bears." (63) With human mining and cutting, the forest is not a secure shelter for animals any longer. In front of those invaders, animals have no choice but to cry. They want to escape but nowhere could they go. "There wasn't any longer a safe place for any of them." (63) The narrations and descriptions overflow with the author's compassion for the animals' plight and her condemnation of human acts as well.

For Walker, human greed and selfish motives are the source of all crises in nature, like the environmental crisis, the survival crisis as well as the extinction crisis, and, backed up by anthropocentrism, appear to be more and more rampant. Anthropocentrism is a joint product of the theory of binary opposition and the hierarchic thinking. Therefore equality and reconciliation are the only way to solve the problems that afflict nature. In other words, only when they treat nature as an equal being and develop a harmonious relation with it could humans love and treasure nature and protect the natural world authentically; could they stop mastering nature and free themselves from anthropocentrism.

6.3.1.2 The Impact of Eurocentrism

The hierarchic thinking and binary opposition similarly work in the human society, from which derives ethnocentrism, or rather, Eurocentrism or Western-centrism, which refers to the notion of European exceptionalism, a worldview centered on Western civilization. Eurocentrism developed during the height of the European colonial empires since the Early Modern period and became prevalent in the discourse of political correctness and cultural relativism during the 1990s, especially in the context of decolonization and development aid and humanitarian aid offered by industrialized countries ("First World") to developing countries ("Third World"). It emphasizes white supremacy or white exceptionalism. According to Eurocentrism, it is a matter of course for whites to become the master of humankind. As a consequence, Eurocentrism becomes the root cause of racial inequality and social injustice, which pervade *Now Is the Time to Open Your Heart* and evidence the author's accusation of whites' hegemony in the human world.

As a black in the white world, Ms. Walker has "watched as her parents and each of her siblings struggled to withstand the punishing blows of racism and knew full well of the price they had to pay to hold fast to their dignity." (White, 2004: 177) In practice, she witnesses every kind of racial discrimination and thus has abundant experiences at her fingertips so that she writes about blacks' sufferings with facility and conveys the message that colored people, sold, enslaved, abused and even killed, are never treated as human beings in the white-dominated society. In *Now Is the Time to Open Your Heart*, Walker exposes the whites' crimes at once through the complaint of the oppressed and the confession of the oppressing. Yolo is a mixed-blood, whose "mother was mostly Anglo-Indian," and whose "father mostly African." (A. Walker, 2004: 56) He has long been discriminated at home and has never enjoyed a secure life in the country, about which he and Kate have a common feeling: "We're considered second-and third-class citizens of a country whose government never wanted us. Except as slaves. We understand by now the world will be blown to bits, doubtless by this same government, before people of color get their fair share. We can't afford health insurance, nor will it even ever be applicable, the way things are going.

Nobody but us wants to be Black." (56 – 57) Traveling to Hawaii, Yolo wants to get himself relaxed. Nevertheless, what he sees is just what he attempts to escape from. The Hawaiians are also oppressed by the American whites. Instead of conquering the indigenous population with armed forces as what they did in the past, the Americans now embrace nonviolence—they sell so much "ice" (known as "crystal methamphetamine") to Hawaii that it "swamp [s] the island." (112) Consequently, "many of the young people are addicted to it" and have their brains "fried." Alma's son Marshall is one of the victims. He "starts using on a dare" and dies of the drug use, though he "hated being hooked." (112) In so doing they not only plunder Hawaiians economically but also paralyze them spiritually; in so doing, they virtually reach their expected goal of dominating Hawaii for good.

Among the Medicine Seekers is Rick, a young man from a wealthy white family. His psychological confusion results from his knowing of his family business—"selling drugs to oppressed people." (152) Having taken the "Grandmother medicine," he opens his heart to his group mates, telling them how guilty he feels of what his family keep doing to the oppressed people and how uneasy when he finds that he is, in fact, invisible to the people around, including his driver. Unlike most American whites, Rick is a man of conscience. He knows that what one possesses and enjoys ought to be based on his/her labor and diligence, and that it is sinful to profit by others' toil. Feeling "instinctively that we had too much of everything: food, clothes, money," Rick accepts himself as a sinner and his family (especially his father) as invaders, who are like "those Roman emperors in the movies, setting off to conquer, to eat up, the earth." (161) He is soberly aware that all his family property—the hotels, the restaurants, the office buildings as well as the elected officials—comes from business speculation and drug smuggling. That "[d]evouring everything seems to be in our genes" is Rick's summary of his family tradition. (161) In spite that they have such a big and profitable business, it is impossible for his family to get respect from the people around. They have nothing but a luxurious life, no heart, no soul, no dignity, nothing. They are nothing but the well-dressed whites. They are invisible to the oppressed. Notwithstanding, they still persist their old ways. Hence Rick could do nothing but confession. Although Rick's confession can compensate for no sins his family have committed, it does light a light of hope, a light of conscience, and a light of love.

Walker's condemnation of Eurocentrism is also embodied in the history of Hugh Brentforth's lake, part of Hugh's property, which was taken from the Indians. As Hugh recollects it, "[i]n the early days of moving west," the white settlers "could settle as much land as" they "could control simply by taking it from the Indians … and keeping them off it" for ever; and "[e]very rancher …has a similar story to tell." (124) The past of a rancher is imbued with whites' invasions and Indians' sufferings. The story of Hugh's lake witnesses how the Indians protect their water source and their ancestors' bones—the spirit of the people—through worshiping the spring, and how the white invaders eventually destroy the underground lake and thus cut the link between the living and their ancestors in the name of energy development. The rivers and waters are sacred to the Indians, partly because it is the source of life, partly because it separates "from any disturbance" their ancestors' bones, which are buried underneath the underground lake. They "would just bend over, put an ear over to the ground," "poke a reed in the ground, and drink." (125) "They knew every river, every stream, every rock, every tree." (125) They respect nature and its laws. They never think of digging for water. The old Indian in Hugh's recollection would show up "with a plastic jug" and carry no more "water from the spring" than he needs: "After coming all that way, wherever it was he came from, he didn't even fill up the jug." (127) Therefore, the "pitiful little spring that just keep bubbling up no matter how dry it gets." (127) The coming of the whites brings disasters not only to the Indians—"[t]he decades of genocide against them (Indians) had left survivors with a deep fear of being seen"—but also to the spring, the underground water. (128) The "energy development company" first digs out "an underground lake," "the source of the spring." (129) Then "the lake lasted for several months" and "dried up." (130) The diggers continue their digging and dig out the "bones of the old man's people from thousands of years ago." (130) Thus they destroy the Indians down to the ground, from present to past, from life to soul.

Eurocentrism is likewise expressed in whites' indifference to the colored people's suffering. The novel begins with Kate's listening to "the dharma talk." (4) The teacher is "a prominent professor at one of the country's most famous universities," "a middle-aged man of southern European descent," who "had grown up in an upper-middle-class home, had had educated and cultured people as parents and as grandparents, had studied and lived in Europe as well as in the East." (4) In a word, he is a typical Euro-American intellectual. What he says and holds represents most of American whites' ideas and beliefs, deriving from the European culture and therefore publicizing its supremacy. His talk that "hot" revolutions (i. e., revolutions "with guns and violence") "attempted in Africa, Cuba, and the Caribbeans" are doomed to failure lays bare his sense of superiority to blacks and his indifference to their sufferings. Taking the stand of American colonialists, he believes that rebellion is wrong and supports the so-called "cool" revolution, which essentially implies that the blacks in these areas have no alternative but to subject themselves to the colonialists. Never suffering what those marginalized and exploited suffer, he and his class, as Kate interprets it, could easily "dismiss the brown and black and yellow and poor white people all over the globe who worried constantly where their next meal was coming from" and "[h]ow they would feed, clothe, and educate their children." (4-5) What Kate says is just what Walker wants her readers to see. As a matter of fact, the white teacher's talk eloquently proves the American exceptionalism, which emphasizes the unique mission of the US to transform the world and its superiority over other nations.

In *Now Is the Time to Open Your Heart*, Ms. Walker mercilessly exposes and castigates the hypocrisy and ugliness in the American society, which are an inexorable outcome of Eurocentrism. The hazard of ethnocentrism amply justifies the principle that equality and brotherhood are the basic premise to create a harmonious society. In other words, only when whites acknowledge themselves as an equal instead of a superior race to any colored one, could they stop mastering humankind and free themselves from Eurocentrism; could the human world escape from violence, chaos and wars, and enter a new era of harmony and enjoy humanity.

6.3.1.3 The Impact of Androcentrism

In terms of gender, the hierarchic thinking and binary opposition manifest as androcentrism, the practice, conscious or otherwise, of placing males or a masculine point of view at the centre of a culture, a history, or the worldview. Androcentrism can be understood as a societal fixation on masculinity whereby all things originate. Under androcentrism, masculinity is normative and all things outside are defined as other. Masculine patterns of life and masculine mindsets are accepted as universality while female ones are considered as deviance. In short, androcentrism highlights male supremacy or male exceptionalism; or rather, men enjoy the privilege of mastering women. Androcentrism is thus another obstacle on the humans' way to humanity and harmony. In *Now Is the Time to Open Your Heart*, the female characters—Kate, Lalika and Missy—are all victims of androcentrism in a large part. They suffered from the male tyranny either within families or in the society, and are therefore put in mental confusion.

White (2004: 173) once questions, "[h]ow can a family, a community, a race, a nation, a world, be healthy and strong if one half dominates the other half through threats, intimidation and actual acts of violence?" Indeed, equality between husband and wife is a prerequisite for a "healthy and strong" family. Kate fails in forming such a family through her first marriage. Although there are no "acts of violence" in her family, Kate still has the feeling of being threatened or intimidated. She becomes more and more invisible in the family except as "a service, a servant." (A. Walker, 2004: 28) Her husband and their child are so used to her role of housewife that they give her "a serving dish" for Valentine's

Day. With more years gone, Kate even finds that "they ceased to really see her." (28) Unable to stand to face the suffocating invisibility, she decides to leave her husband and the family. But when she tells him her decision, he gets "angry enough to kill." (33) They are "hiking in the mountains when she told him; she was just ahead of him on a particularly rough part of the trail"; all of a sudden, her husband "shoved her in the back." (31) "She scrambled to keep her footing on the narrow ledge. She might have fallen to death." (32) When she turns back, she finds him "staring at her as if she'd turned into his worst enemy." (32) He does not care whether she would fall off the cliff; but he does care if his authority in the relationship is shaken. Therefore he gets exasperated and leaves her alone in the mountains, "a hundred miles from home," with "no money, no credit card, no driver's license," when Kate says out what she feels about their marriage—"I have lived with you for nine years. … I have carried in my body two of your children. … I have cooked thousands of breakfasts and lunches and dinners for you. … I have sat up with you when you've been sick. … I have helped you care for your parents. … I have shared my body with you whenever you wanted it, whether I felt like it or not." (33) Kate, like thousands or millions of women, is the inferior and victim in this marriage. She has no thought, no ideal, no desire, no impulse, no freedom, no independence; in a word, she does not have her own life. She is an appendix, a servant, to her husband. Her worth lies only in service and sex. Obedience is her first duty. To live her own life and "be New Age" (in Yolo's words), Kate has no alternative but to get divorced, even though she is a mother of two children. The husband's dominance and the wife's invisibility eventually ruin the supposedly healthy and strong family. Afterwards, Kate experiences several other marriages but all end up with failure. As a new woman intellectual, she keeps resisting the patriarchal tradition and striving for a free, equal, and dignified life; yet she has to sacrifice her marriage. Ms. Walker seems to imply that the harmonious relationship between men and women cannot dispense with men's awareness and endeavor.

Like Kate, Missy is also badly hurt within the family. But unlike Kate, whose sufferings are mainly spiritual, Missy, tricked into incest with her grandfather, is tortured both physically and spiritually. Fate appears to be more unfair to Missy. She is raped in her infancy when she knows nothing about sex by her grandfather, one of those closest to her. Her grandfather "used to tickle" her and make her laugh; and "then the playing would run off into sex; but it was still like playing. He'd started playing with me [Missy] so early I never knew there was a cutoff point. I was actually waiting for the tingle." (156) Having accepted it as playing, little Missy begins having a crush on her grandfather. Even when she grows up and tries to "stop playing with" him, realizing what they did is wrong, she cannot really hate him. As a matter of fact, Missy gets so accustomed to their relationship and so dependent on her grandfather that she could not help but miss him, physically and emotionally, though she knows it is beyond morality. Thus Missy is caught up in great agony. Meanwhile, since she understands what they have "done was wrong," she is afraid to let herself have sex with anybody, including her boyfriends and her husband; she thinks it is "the wrong thing to do." (156) In this sense, Missy is thoroughly destroyed by her grandfather. However, all he did to her has been done in the name of love; perhaps this is the most horrible part of the story: no revolt from the victim, and no violence from the abuser; everything took place on the premise of the parties' own will. All this thus forms the cruelty of the story and makes it the cruelest of all the atrocities men, driven by androcentrism, have committed. If the incident about Kate shows Walker's sympathy for black women and conveys the author's hope for their bright future, grief, distress and despair permeate the one about Missy. For Walker, Missy's story is more dangerous and more alarming.

In a patriarchal society, women are groaning under injustice both within families and outside. Lalika commits murder against her own will, as is mentioned in the previous chapter. A victim of rape, she is put in jail, where she suffers beatings and gang rapes. She is watched round the clock and filmed while being beaten and raped, and the video of the beatings and rapes is put on the market. The patrolmen and jailors never treat her as a person with dignity. As a black woman, Lalika has no dignity in the eyes of the white males. She is just a plaything, a sex object. The patriarchal conventions acquiesce in any male savage acts, which abets the criminal activities of the patrolmen and jailors. Simone de Beauvoir points out in *The Second Sex* that one is not born a woman, but becomes a woman, "the Other." The theory of binary opposition and the hierarchic thinking in the Western tradition determine women's role as "the Other," the subordinate, the inferior, while men are of course defined as "the One," the dominant, the superior. They are masters of women's fate both within families and in the society. In the case of Lalika, the patrolmen and jailors in nature fear nothing with patriarchy at their back; they are even above the law, let alone conscience, morality or humanity. Lalika's tragedy is essentially the failure of a nation's moral orientation. In the account of Lalika's suffering, the author not simply accuses the male brutes of cruelty and obscenity but also lays bare the social evils in the American society. This is a call to conscience in the final analysis, for, as a womanist, Ms. Walker believes that self-improvement is a feasible way of bettering a nation.

By depicting the miserable experiences of the women differing in parentage, education and careers, Ms. Walker demonstrates the normality of androcentrism in the American society and tends to grab society's attention to women's plight in the modern world. On the one hand, women themselves must wake up from numbness and disorientation, and strive for their own freedom, justice and dignity. On the other hand, men are supposed to free themselves out of androcentrism and put the other sex on an equal footing. For Walker, the equal and harmonious co-existence of men and women is the basis of a harmonious society. Therefore, she has always stressed that womanism should not be just about trying to awaken women to their survival crisis but also to empower them in a positive sense, the latter half of which depends on men's conscience and awareness. It is in this sense that the author writes about women's adversity in *Now Is the Time to Open Your Heart*.

6.3.2 The Construction of a "Survival Whole"

The term "survival whole" or the "spiritual survival" was first put forward by Alice Walker in her elaboration of womanism in *In Search of Our Mothers' Gardens*, as is mentioned in the third chapter. By "survival whole," Walker originally emphasized the oneness of her people, men and women. As is analyzed in the previous chapters, Ms. Walker never stops struggling for her womanist utopia—the survival whole of the black race. What's more, she continuously extends its connotation, from the survival whole of black people through that of colored people and that of the whole human race to the survival whole of the cosmos (i.e., the harmony of humankind and nature). In *Now Is the Time to Open Your Heart*, the author not simply uncovers various crises and social problems arising from anthropocentrism, ethnocentrism and androcentrism, but, more importantly, concentrates on constructing a harmonious relationship between men and women, between whites and colored people, and between humankind and nature, viz., the survival whole of the cosmos.

6.3.2.1 The Harmony between Humankind and Nature

Now Is the Time to Open Your Heart bears witness to Ms. Walker's strong sense of environmental protection, the spontaneous overflow of her love for nature. The special feeling for nature, as Alice Walker explained in an interview in 2006, "comes from the way I was brought up. I was born and raised way, way, way in country. We rarely saw other people. We saw more trees than people and more animals than people. And so I became very close to earth and to the knowledge that without a healthy environment we cannot be healthy people." Walker loves nature or "the earth" also because she "had parents who knew what to do with the earth and who respected it and could grow anything there on the farm." She "thinks that that's part of my spirituality, is just—it just is me. It is how I came into the world, understanding how divine earth is." Nature is part of Ms. Walker's life. She loves it, and respects or even worships it. On the part of Walker, nature is sacred and inviolable. She holds that human beings, living in nature, cannot do without the boon from nature. Hence to establish a harmonious relationship with nature becomes the only choice for human beings to maintain a healthy, sustainable environment and ensure a happy, healthy, prosperous and peaceful life.

Kate's new life begins with her integration into nature. As a woman in her fifties, the protagonist is at a loss, facing the problems associated with old age. She always dreams of a dry river and has the feeling that her life is coming to its end. She falls into a depression at one time but ultimately refuses to embrace her destiny. She trusts and obeys her instinctive impulse to go to nature in search of "her life, i.e., the river." (A. Walker, 2004: 14) Hence Kate's journeys—one to the Colorado, the other to the Amazon—which would bring her from "death, being dead, back into life." (28) On the Colorado, "under a huge canopy of stars," Kate feels "like a queen, the flashing, roaring river silver in moonlight." (28) Relaxing in the arms of nature, she recalls her past, her invisible state in the first marriage in particular, and is overcome with a feeling of nausea. Kate is to nature what a daughter is to a mother. Before nature, the gentlest mother, she can't refrain from pouring out her grievance about the injustice her husband did to her. Therefore the nausea and sickness carries a symbolic meaning in the novel, which implies Kate's unbosoming her sorrows and complaints. So after the "heaving sickness past, her nausea gone, her bodily fluids replaced," she feels a sense of relief and "the lightness of being in the open space." "Her walls the canyon's walls, …her floor, the river beach. Her view, the heavens. It was, this freedom she was in, the longed-for cathedral of her dreams." (29) Extricating herself from the boring past and integrating into nature, Kate now enjoys the peace of mind. Listening to the murmur of the river, breathing the fresh air in the canyon, and enjoying the bizarre picture in the sky, Kate dissolves her soul in nature at last. The rare peace draws a gentle conclusion to her boring past. Integrating into nature, she imagines "a return" and has an eagerness to start a new life: "She saw herself flying back home" like "a large black bird," "[t]ransformed." (30)

Nature is dear to Kate, partly because it brings her psychic harmony, partly because it could heal her physical discomfort. Once on the Colorado, Kate feels a little dizzy. Just then she finds a straw "stuck in one of her waterproof sandals," she "bent to pull it out" and, following the "voice of her body," "put it into her mouth." (31) She chews it and "[i]mmediately her stomach calmed. The dizziness left her." (31) In the novel, everything in nature, large or small, is souled and affectionate. For Kate, the straw's healing of her dizziness is its expression of love for her. So she accepts it as a friend and "from then on looked for it along the banks of the river and felt concern for its health," even though she does not know what its name is. (31) By such a trifle, Ms. Walker communicates the idea that all things in nature are equal to human beings and need respecting, and that a harmonious relationship between nature and humankind needs care and love and something in exchange.

Not long after returning from the Colorado, Kate is on the journey to the Amazon to extricate herself from the past bewilderment completely. "Although she was widely published and to some extent a public figure, she had the idea most of the time that she was unrecognizable and therefore incognito." (67) Coming into the rainforest on the Amazon, exposing herself to nature, Kate naturally has a strong sense of self-identity:

> I am an American, Kate thought. Indigenous to the Americas. Nowhere else could I, this so-called Black person—African, European, Indio—exist. Only here. In Africa there would have been no Europeans, no Native Americans. In Europe, no Africans and no Indians. Only here; *only here*, she said, as waves of vomiting continued past the three hours and into the evening, I will bear this as long as it takes. This old medicine surely must care for, belong to, me. (53, italics original)

As a black woman, Kate is both an outsider in the white American society and a foreigner as well in Africa and Europe. However, she finds a sense of belonging, intimacy, and home here in the rainforest, in the "Grandmother medicine" in particular. Nature offers Kate peace and security and thus becomes the end-result of her soul. Each time she merges herself into nature, Kate feels easy and comfortable. "Now she rested in her hut a few steps from the river and listened to this Being, the rainforest." Nature is so intimate to her. She is curious about every creature and every thing in nature. To Kate, every creature has thoughts and feelings. She could always hear them "chatting, talking, whistling, singing." (53) "And everything was in motion." Listening closely, "she could distinguish slithering, sliding, jumping, hopping, ambling, crawling, flying." (53 – 54) Kate is attracted to every sound and every motion in the forest. She feels their spirit with her heart that it brings her peace and harmony. Here Ms. Walker simply implies that a soul-to-soul communication is the only effective way to construct a harmonious relationship between humankind and nature.

United with nature, Kate becomes more broadminded and philanthropic. Every time she takes the "Grandmother medicine," she asks "for help for the humans of the planet and for the coming generations and for the animals and plants and rocks." (62) She is developing into an animist cosmopolitanist. In Kate's world, there is no discrimination but respect, no hierarchy but equality, either between races or species, or between humankind and nature. Regarding herself as one of such equal beings in nature, Kate keeps pursuing "knowledge of how to act in the world for the highest good of all." (62) What she expects from the "Grandmother medicine" is at once healing and acceptancy. Taking energy and liveliness from nature, and getting healthy, physically and mentally, Kate hopes to be accepted by the Grandmother and possess its Spirit, and thus becomes a useful person and lives a meaningful life. She is ready to help others and appealing to environmental protection. Like Kant, Walker blends virtue and happiness into the highest good in Kate, holding that one can enjoy happiness in compliance with the principle of doing goodness.

Kate goes to "search for Grandmother" because she is "afraid of growing old." (200) The "seven hours with Grandmother" in the Amazon helps her to understand what Grandmother tends to teach her: "If you go to another planet you will by your presence contribute to its loss of integrity. You will spend all of earth's resources trying to change a place that worked very well without you. Because you are vain, you will think you are bringing something useful. You are not." (200, 202) She comes to realize that integrity is best, viz., "what is integral to you will always be superior to what is tacked on, simply because it is yours." (202) Now that her hair or skin or eyes are integral to her, it is not worthwhile to make any effort to change herself; now that any endeavor of mankind to change is certain to bring destruction to integrity, as the human history shows, Kate decides to embrace aging—what time and tide offer to her. Back home from the journey she becomes acutely aware that "[a]ge is power" instead of a burden. At the end of the day, Grandmother gives Kate power and courage to face the reality. In practice, Kate feels that she herself is Grandmother now. Or rather, she thinks that "there is no separation between" Grandmother and herself at all. (201) On the part of Kate, Grandmother is a symbol of nature and eternity. "Grandmother Earth" is the highest authority "on this planet." The inseparability between Grandmother and Kate, or, by extension, between nature and humankind is a guarantee of safety on the planet. Thus she retrieves her dignity and self-respect, and becomes a new woman who is greeting the new life. At the end of the novel, Kate lives in a house painted by Yolo into blue, "the color of healing" as well as "the color of water and space and eternity." (207) As is said by the shaman Armando, if someone lives in any community "in a blue house," he/she "you will find is somehow different." (207) Kate is different and unique in the sense that she is now inseparable from Grandmother, which "is inseparable from spirit," and fulfils a "lifting" of her own spirit. (207) According to Armando, Kate has reached such high level that the blue house is not a house but "a big cake" for her soul; so seeing the blue house is just like taking "a big delicious bite." The soul, "awake enough to eat the color," is normally "a healthy soul"; hence Kate's is a healthy one. With a healthy soul, Kate is likely to develop a healthy and harmonious relationship with her neighbors and with other Beings in the universe as well. Kate's experience and transformation thus awaken humans' awareness of the interdependence between nature and themselves. Her attempt, along with her group mates', to go to nature for spiritual healing proves a social normality in the modern world and foreshadows the bright future of humans' relationship with nature, the fulfillment of the survival whole of humankind and nature.

6.3.2.2 The Harmony within the Human Community

To develop a harmonious relationship with nature, humans are supposed to improve their own internal relations, i. e., the one between sexes and the one among races. This is Ms. Walker's belief and dream, which are expressed in *Now Is the Time to Open Your Heart*, through the mouth of Mother Earth: "The biggest problem is thinking the fate of the world rests on you (humans)"; "All that is required" for "[t]he 'saving' of the planet" is "that everyone becomes as one mind." (77) In other words, the unity and concerted effort of all human beings is the premise and guarantee to save our happiness, to maintain our comfort, and to realize our peace of mind. Unity means harmony, which needs equality and mutual understanding and respect. To accomplish the great goal, Walker centers on the optimization of the relationship between Kate and Yolo, between the members in their respective circles, as well as the blending of their circles into a whole.

The improvement of the relationship between Kate and Yolo begins with their separation, which takes place twice in the novel. The first is when Kate goes to the Colorado. Left alone at home, Yolo could not help missing her, the woman who is "some years older than him" but makes "no pretense of being younger," the woman who is "not much of a housekeeper," yet the woman who would bring him joys and happiness whenever and wherever possible. (19, 16) Indeed, Yolo has a mixed feeling of Kate. On the one hand, he finds that she is not a good woman according to the patriarchal conventions. She never feels it her duty to do housework. She even does not want to be bound in marriage. On the other hand, she is a woman of wit, humor and knowledge. She has "a quaintness of expression, a drollness of thought, that she seemed to garner directly from her dreams. She might awake laughing anytime whether day or night and expose him to frolicsome goings-on, pithy sayings, the oddest *bon mot* from perhaps a century or so ago." (17, italics original) As a man brought up in the edification of patriarchy but accepting the thought of equality between men and women, Yolo struggles in his awkward relationship with Kate, not knowing what to do—to accept Kate or to conquer her. The former promises a harmonious relationship while the latter will force her to leave him for ever, the thought of which would make him die. Alone with his thoughts, and putting himself in her shoes, Yolo begins understanding why Kate gets herself in a puzzle about aging. Energy is Yolo's first impression of Kate: "He recognized her immediately when he saw her again. And what he recognized was her energy, which seemed to precede her. As if her spirit were thrusting itself forward, into the unknown; dazzled, charmed, challenged, hopeful, happy to be energized by the mysterious." (19) However, as the years go by, the marked energy starts to disappear, which easily and naturally disturbs Kate, the pushy woman who is always proud. In the meantime, Yolo finds it hard for him to be away from Kate. In practice, he realizes that he cannot do without her admiration for his paintings. It is even flattering to be affirmed and accepted by the energetic and acknowledgeable woman. He enjoys that feeling and gains confidence and gratification.

Leaving Yolo and joining the group of women, Kate leaves the constraints of work and family, and puts down the heavy burden of responsibility so that she gets fully relaxed and opens her heart to her fellow travelers. Back from the journey, she is turned to an energetic and open-minded woman who "could leave a gentle, indelible message of self-love to all humans everywhere." (47) Kate's love has now transcended the erotic Utopia based on heterosexuality, and develops into philanthropism, to a large extent. Although it "is the one change I (Yolo) would never have guessed," Yolo, understanding Kate's pursuit, is willing to accept the change and respect Kate's choice. Actually, neither of the two is ready to face the change; yet they are gentle to each other and encourage each other to welcome the change. They are on the threshold of a challenge and test of their present relationship. If they step over it, they will enter a new and harmonious period of their relationship. So they must summon up courage to reach the tipping point, though they cannot bear to part: Yolo asks Kate to give him time to adjust to the life without her around while Kate, lying "in his arms," "savored and grieved the richness, the sweetness, the sharp edge of intimacy she would be leaving." (47, 48) Their reluctance to leave each other verifies the effective improvement of their relationship through the first parting, and forebodes the eventual harmony between them.

The second time they separate at the airport: Yolo goes to Hawaii and Kate to the Amazon. In Hawaii, invited by Jerry, one of Marshall's brothers, who got to know Yolo in Marshall's funeral, Yolo enters a circle of men hosted by a Mahus woman Aunty Pearlua. Besides the aforementioned injustice the Hawaiian blacks suffer uncovered by Marshall's death, he learns about the enslavement of women in Aunty Pearlua's version of the Mahus' myth. As the story goes, the Mahus now living in Hawaii are mixed-blood people. They are decedents of the first Hawaiians, the "small dark people," who "were wiped out and intermingled with the tall Tahitians." (122) "Mother rule was the dominant way of life" in the time of original Hawaiians. The Mahus saw "the overthrow and enslavement of woman, and the consequent ruination of her children, which was so horrible" that they "decided that until woman was restored to her rightful place" they "would live her life." (122) That is, they "would live openly as women"; they "would live openly the feminine part of" their nature, which "is sometimes the dominant nature with which" they are born, "whether as 'men' or as 'women.'" (122) The Mahus also vowed to protect children. "That is why most Mahus that you see are teaching, feeding, or in some way," "taking care of children." (122 - 123) So what Aunty Pearlua tells is not just a myth or history of the Mahus but their reality as well. What the Mahus men insist on doing is partly out of their loyalty to their ancestors and partly out of their respect for women and love for children. On the one side, they show their protest against the white conquerors who overthrew and enslaved their queen, and demonstrate their resolve to restore their own power. On the other, living as women in itself is an affirmation of femininity, of which motherhood is part and parcel. In the white patriarchal society women, colored women in particular, are never treated as equal beings. Their children never have an equal chance to be fed up, to be educated, and to be employed. The Mahus men, adhering to their ancestors' vow, mean to build an equal and peaceful relationship within their own community, and thus bear hopes for harmony within the larger scope.

In the circle there are also two Australian aboriginals. They tell the story of how the English colonists occupied their motherland and put the natives in depression. For many generations, many young men have "die[d] of despair," thinking that "they have lost the future." (134, 137) They are "found dead on the beach or in the outback or in the towns." (135) Unable to "forget that once upon a time we (they) were one with our (their) land and with our sea," they are "addicted to petrol sniffing" in order to "avoid the anxiety" of their loss of intimacy with their motherland, and escape from "the society that has slaughtered their people and taken their land." (135) Unfortunately, that is not the way out but turned out another loss, the loss of their lives. Thus a new proposal is put forward by Aunty Pearlua, who believes that it is "time for men to take another hard-to-keep vow in favor of children." (170) She suggests that the men in the gathering "should resign from participation in any addiction whatsoever, even from drinking coffee and black tea"; she suggests that "the example for the youth" should "be clean" and "extreme" and that there should be "[n]o drugs, no alcohol, no 'recreational' sex, no caffeine, and no tobacco." (170) Then Yolo witnesses the heated debate on the proposal. Almost all the men in the circle disagree with Aunty Pearlua, though they cannot deny the would-be benefit of the proposal. They hold that it is impossible for men to keep away from some addiction. Even Jerry, whose brother Marshall died of drug taking, asserts that "we can't stop smoking or fucking around or beating our wives and kids either." (171) Most of the men would rather grumble about the lateness of the proposal by making a list of "if only" than take any concrete effective actions to resist drugs or any addiction. This is the social norm Walker is working to change. She puts what she wants to declare in the mouth of Aunty Pearlua, who stresses that drug resistance is "not a protest" but "a strategy," a "strategy for survival," in the sense that, through this strategy, "we can make of our bodies exactly what it is our young people need to see. Health and well-being. *Freedom*." (171, italics original) Aunty Pearlua appeals to the men to give up addiction and resist the white economic aggression, just as they choose to live as women to protest the American violent occupation. She explains that, since the Mahus have been saying no to the plan "laid out for woman and her children, a plan that enslaved and humiliated them before eradicating the divine in them entirely," the men in the gathering have no choice but to refuse the plan the white conquerors lay out for the Hawaiian children. (171) She points out that to resist addiction is to keep healthy and that "[h]ealth is our culture"; so "anything that interferes with it is our bondage." (172) Aunty Pearlua is portrayed as spokesperson of the native Hawaiians. She is not only concerned with the survival of the Hawaiian women and children but also devoted to the protection of Hawaiian culture, which does not stay in words, but is put into reality, into her daily life. She and her sister Aunty Alma are working together to keep something real in Hawaiian culture alive. "She has taught generations of Hawaiian women the true hula, the dance of the traditions and of the soul," while her sister is committed to the purification of the human body. (173) For the sisters, the native Hawaiians need both physical health and spiritual well-being. If the traditional culture is an integral part of the national civilization and is worth preserving and cherishing, body purification provides basic security for a people's health and survival. Only the nation in physical and mental health makes it possible to establish a harmonious relationship within and without. The sisters' work and endeavor have set a positive example for the younger generation and foretell a promising future for the Hawaiian people. In the meantime, what Yolo sees and hears in the circle and in Hawaii refreshes his knowledge of racism and sexism in the American society—before going to Hawaii, Yolo knew little about the living situation of the natives—and sets an orientation for his future life.

If Yolo is just an onlooker of what the Hawaiian blacks suffer and endeavor to change during his stay in Hawaii, Kate is a real participant in the healing of her group mates' psychological perplexion in the Amazon. She not only undergoes throes in her psychological transformation but also accompanies the other group members and encourages them to get out of their psychological predicaments. Actually, the group is characterized by mutual help and care. For one thing, all of the members are guided and looked after by the shamans—Armando and his apprentice Cosmi—after they take the "Grandmother medicine" and begin throwing up. The two shamans not only offer psychological comfort and counseling, but also look after each of the members. For another, the group mates help and take care of each other. When anyone in the group, male or female, white or colored, feels nausea and vomiting or have diarrhea, which are the normal reactions after taking the medicine, the other members will look after him/her and keep his/her company. They are also good listeners when anyone chooses to open his/her heart. For "[a] sick person has no history and no nationality." (90) What he/she deserves is tolerance and care. Since "[t]he inner spirit is never enslaved," everyone will make a remarkable recovery and return to his/her natural state. (91) Everyone is worthy of attendance and respect. After the tough but fruitful days spent together, Kate and the group mates—men and women, of different colors and different races, with different backgrounds and different experiences, from different places or different countries—develop a lasting friendship. They are free and equal before Grandmother, in the arms of nature, and will keep the sense of freedom and equality, back home, in their future life. They succeed in building a harmonious relationship within the group of males and females from different races and will struggle for a harmonious society and, to a larger extent, a harmonious universe, which is Ms. Walker's ultimate goal.

Yolo and Kate's paralleled journeys draw a successful conclusion, which is symbolized in their meeting at the airport, their starting place. On their way home, they sit in their car, which is "perfumed and transformed into a magic carriage," "like a king and a queen" or "like best friends." (184) They are "happy to be homeward bound, happy to be safe and together." (185) Driving in silence, they are looking forward to their happy future. Both of them have undergone great psychological changes and become placid, tolerant, straight-out and easygoing. Back home, they share their thoughts and feelings as well as what they have heard and seen. Yolo tells Kate his encounter with Alma and the death of Alma's son Marshall while Kate describes how she began to "have dreams that diagnosed the illnesses of others" after taking "the amazing plant, Bobinsana." (187) They talk like bosom friends instead of lovers. Their relationship goes beyond sex. "Neither of them said anything about sex, nor was there any movement that suggested making love." (187) They talk continuously day and night as long as they are awake. Yolo tells Kate about Aunty Pearlua and her circle, and his vow to stop smoking; he also tells her how bad he feels while not smoking. Kate does not complain but comforts him when she finds him smoking again. "Smoke it and enjoy every puff," she says to him. Smoking does not smell bad to Kate, not just because her grandfather was a smoker but, more importantly, because smoking has a symbolic meaning to her: when smokers pull in the air, pull out the smoke, "air and smoke mingled, and this symbolized oneness. *Being of one mind*. That is peace. The material and the spiritual come together in smoke." (193 – 194, italics original) Like air and smoke, Kate and Yolo are "of one mind" now. "They sat in silence, gazing at the moon and the slow arrival of pale, barely perceptible stars," and feel safe with each other. Accepting each other as "the whole other side of life," they decide to hold a wedding. (194)

Yolo and Kate's wedding not just indicates the marriage of the two lovers but that of their respective circles and that of humans and nature as well. With the date for the wedding set, they spend many days searching for the perfect place for wedding. They eventually find "a paradise," "a campground," "with small bungalows and an indoor cooking and eating area," "a large firepit, circled by springy grass that would be great for sleeping and storytelling around the fire at night," and, "most marvelous of all," "the most amazing, pure, deep, languidly flowing river," which is "visible from every place on the land." (196) They invite all those they have got to know on their journeys. Yolo's circle includes Aunty Alma, Aunty Peralua, Alma junior, Marshall's two brothers (Jerry and Poi), and the two Australian brothers, while Kate's friends are Lalika and Missy, who tell Kate that they have got boyfriends and will bring them together, and Hugh, who has "got a beau" and will bring him to the wedding. (196) For Walker, the harmony between nature and humans is as important as that between sexes. She designs an eco-wedding for Yolo and Kate so that natural beings and human beings gather together, and get on well with each other, regardless of classes, species, races or colors. In this sense, the wedding is a gathering of men and women—of different colors, from different places of the earth—and a celebration of gender harmony and ethnic unity on the one hand, and a festivity of insects and birds (which can be imagined) and/or fishes (e. g., salmons), by the fire, on the grass or in the river, on the other hand. The wedding thus highlights Walker's higher ideal—the survival whole of the universe.

Now Is the Time to Open Your Heart is both an expose of the vices and evils in the white-dominated patriarchal society, and a paean to the unremitting endeavor of modern people—male and female, white and colored, rich and poor—to blur race and gender distinction, to wipe out tyranny and hegemony of any kind, and to restore the earth—nature and humankind—to its original harmony. Although it is chiefly the same old story of the struggles and achievements of the inferior and/or the oppressed, the novel juxtaposes the major characters' internal development with their external journeys and thus has their way out of psychological perplexion emphasized. That their mental growth goes hand in hand with their physical closeness to nature declares the decisive role of nature in humans' well-being and survival, and the possibility of humans' harmonious coexistence with nature. And that Kate and Yolo walk into marriage after their journeys presents a strong case for the promising future of understanding and respect between sexes. Moreover, some male whites like Hugh and Rich are also among the Medicine Seekers. Their confession of the misdeeds of their family or ancestors manifests Walker's rare optimism about the propertied class and the white race, and surely her prediction of justice and equality within human beings. All in all, the novel bears rosy prospects for peace, justice, equality, and harmony between men and women, between whites and colored people, and between humankind and nature, namely, for the survival whole of the universe.

Chapter VII Within the Black Folklore: The Common Bond between Hurston and Walker

> The passion with which native intellectuals defend the existence of their national culture may be a source of amazement; but those who condemn this exaggerated passion are strangely apt to forget that their own psyche and their own selves are conveniently sheltered behind a French or German culture which has given full proof of its existence and which is uncontested.
>
> —FRANTZ FANON, "On National Culture" (qtd. in Berlant, 1993: 211)

> More than any other black author at work today, Alice Walker has been concerned about grounding her work in a matrilineal tradition of black writing, paying homage to the exuberant imagination of Zora Neale Hurston. … And it was Walker who, … resurrected Hurston's work and reputation from the grounds of obscurity. Walker's patient work established Hurston at the structural center of a tradition of African-American women's writing, and indeed, within a larger tradition of Black letters. (Gates, 1993b: ix)

> Like Hurston, she (Walker) incorporates elements of traditional folklore into her fiction, but elements of the Gothic, of the Southern black migration novel, of the romance, and of the nineteenth-century sentimental novel also appear in her fiction. (Gates, 1993b: x)

Indeed, it is almost an instinctive behavior of a native intellectual to protect his/her national culture. As Afro-American writers, Zora Neale Hurston (1891 - 1960) and Alice Walker are imperceptibly entrusted with the mission of protecting and transmitting the black folklore through their literary writing. While Hurston, as the greatest author in the Afro-American women's literature and one of the distinguished representatives during the Harlem Renaissance, foreran the Afro-American writers in exerting the black folklore in literary creation, Alice Walker stands as her firm and faithful follower in this aspect. Although living in different eras and representing the two remarkable periods of the Afro-American women's literature in the twentieth century respectively, they are virtually identical with each other not only in sex and color but also in family backgrounds and life experiences. The black folklore has always been in the blood of Hurston and Walker, who spent their childhood in the black community of southern America, and becomes part and parcel of their spiritual life and literary creation. As an anthropologist, Hurston was keen enough to sense the unique negritude in the black folklore, which she wittily incorporated into black women's literary narration, and accumulated rich experience for her literary daughters. A black "new woman," Walker similarly treasures the black cultural heritage and thinks highly of Hurston's admiration for blackness and the black folklore. Having her fiction deeply rooted in a matrilineal inheritance, she takes great pains to describe the real life scenes of the black underclass, reflect black people's joys and sorrows in their daily life, and sing high praise of their positive and optimistic attitudes toward life. As a matter of fact, Walker not simply echoes but also revises Hurston in both language and text, and, consequently, has developed a strong bond with Hurston in literary writing. In this sense, Walker is the deserved inheritor of Hurston's literary craftsmanship and theme, and of the Afro-American women's literature in general.

Folklore or folk culture refers to the body of expressive culture shared by a particular group of people, which encompasses the traditions common to that culture, subculture or group. It is well-documented that the term was coined in 1846 by the Englishman William Thoms (1803 – 1885) to replace the contemporary terminology of "popular antiquities" or "popular literature." (Fenton, 2005: 19) The term consists of two component parts—folk and lore. While "lore" is easier to define as its meaning has stayed relatively stable over the last two centuries, the concept of "folk" proves somewhat more elusive. The former simply means the knowledge and traditions of a particular group, frequently passed along by word of mouth, including folktale, folksong, custom, beliefs, etc. The latter (i. e., folk) is "a flexible concept" which can refer to any social group—ranging from a nation, a village to a single family—of two or more persons with common traits, who express their shared identity through distinctive traditions, though it originally applied only to rural, frequently poor, illiterate peasants when Thoms created the term "folklore." (Dundes, 1969: 13) Accordingly, there exist a lot of divergent opinions on the concept of "folklore," among which Ralph Boggs' is comparatively applicable to the discussion about Walker's and Hurston's fiction. In an essay titled "Folklore: Materials, Science, Art," Ralph Steele Boggs (1901 - 1994) (1943: 3) defines folklore as "a body of materials, the science which studies these materials and the art which applies these materials and scientific conclusions about them to practical ends," explaining:

> As a body of materials, folklore is the lore, erudition, knowledge, or teachings, of a folk, large social unit, kindred group, tribe, race, or nation, primitive or civilized, throughout its history. It is the whole body of traditional culture, or conventional modes of human thought and action. It is created informally in a group of persons for themselves, but has been accepted widely enough to have attained considerable currency, and over a sufficient period of time to have acquired traditional traits, such as anonymity of authorship and historic-geographic patterns of variants of basic forms. (3)

According to Boggs, folklore is characterized by currency and tradition. Therefore transmission is a vital part of the folklore process. Without communicating the folk artifacts like beliefs and customs within the group over space and time, they would become cultural shards relegated to cultural archaeologists. These folk artifacts are usually transmitted from region to region and from generation to generation informally by word of mouth and imitative action, as a rule anonymously and always in multiple variants. The folk group is not individualistic but community-based. It nurtures its lore in community. Hence folklore is a function of shared identity within the social group.

In line with their existence forms and social and communicative functions, folkloric materials may be roughly classified into four groups—the "literary," the "linguistic," the "religious," and the artistic, notwithstanding it is really not an easy job to demarcate one group from the other three as each is always "overlapping and intertwined" with any other. (张玉红, 2008: 19) This classification is instrumental in analyzing and examining the common bond between the two representative Afro-American women writers, since the folkloric materials employed in their fiction coincide well with the four groups.

7.1 The Literary Folkloric Materials in Hurston's and Walker's Fiction

The literary group of folklore mainly includes oral traditions such as myth, tales, legends and jokes. As a primitive cultural form, it reflects the customs, habits, thoughts, beliefs, wisdom as well as the living state of a nation or an ethnic group, and supplies abundant cultural materials and nutrition for artistic and literary creation. An important component of the black folklore, the black literary group contains black people's ideas, beliefs, values and their passion, love and understanding of life. It is the product of black people's collective intelligence and the basis and source of the existence and development of black culture. The materials often come from common people's daily life but never exclude some fantasies with tricksters, devils or even God as their characters. These tales and legends at once reflect the social reality of a certain period and manifest black people's humor and wit, and their craving for a happy future.

7.1.1 Hurston's Original Version of the Literary Folkloric Materials

Zora Neale Hurston majored in anthropology at university under the supervision of Franz Boas, father of American anthropology. She made several expeditions to the southern America, Haiti and Jamaica, collecting black folkloric materials. Thanks to these folklore-collecting expeditions, Hurston not only developed a strong consciousness of black cultural identity and took it as her own responsibility to preserve and perpetuate the authentic black folkloric heritages, but also completed her anthropological works written in literary style—*Mules and Men* (1935) and *Tell My Horse* (1938). In the meanwhile, Hurston incorporated the black folkloric materials into her fiction-writing and thus developed her unique folk literary style.

As a native Southerner, Hurston had been soaked in the black folk culture since childhood and therefore, had the folkloric materials at her fingertips. A glance of her fiction (including short stories) will lay it bare that Hurston attempted to dutifully represent the Afro-Americans' daily folk life and the black folk culture. Among her four published novels, three—*Jonah's Gourd Vine* (1934), *Their Eyes Were Watching God* (1937) and *Moses, Man of the Mountain* (1939)—cover a great number of black folkloric materials, with *Seraph on the Suwanee* (1948) as an exception. While her first two novels are both set in the rural South, the cradle of the Afro-American culture in the New World, her third novel is set in Africa, the wellspring of black culture of the African diaspora including African Americans.

Jonah's Gourd Vine abounds with folk tales and legends. The hero John Buddy (John Pearson) is an inherent story-teller, whose duty seems to transmit these ancient stories among African Americans. Finding a job on Mr. Pearson's plantation, John gets his neck out of the yoke of his stepfather for the first time and becomes enraptured with unusual joy and contentment for the time being. Every evening after work, he gathers together with the girls, sits in the doorway and tells tales of Br'er Rabbit, Br'er Fox and Raw-Head-Bloody-Bones, which are principal tricksters in the African American folktales. The scene that John and his workfellows sit together and share stories is overflown with warmth and harmony, and mirrors their satisfaction with the present life. Later, John leaves Mr. Pearson's plantation and comes to a saw camp, where he continues to amuse himself in his free time by listening to and telling stories. Whether on the plantation or in the saw camp, story-telling is always a popular recreational activity for John and his workfellows. As a matter of fact, the Afro-Americans accept story-telling as part and parcel of their daily life so that they are ready to allude to tales or legends in their daily conversations. This is well illustrated in the conversation between Lucy Potts and another girl in her school. When she laughs at John, who uses "Marse" (Master) before the name of Alf Pearson, the white man who offers him a job, the girl boasts that "Ah calls 'em anything Ah please." (Hurston, 1995a: 15) What the girl says irritates Lucy, a kind and honest girl who feels sympathy with John. She immediately refutes the girl, saying "youse talkin' at de big gate now." (15) Here Lucy uses the allusion of "talking at the big gate," which, coming from a black folktale, means talking against a powerful figure behind his/her back. As the tale goes, two blacks are talking about their white master; and one tells the other that he has cursed the master and that all goes well. The listener believes it; so the next time he gets annoyed at his master, he curses him and consequently gets a good beating. Confused, he goes back to the boaster and asks why the boaster is not beaten by the master while he is. What the boaster says is quite beyond his expectation, for he is told that, when the boaster curses his master, the cursed sits on the porch while the curser stands at the gate. The tale not simply conveys the message of racial inequality in the American society, but embodies black people's wit and humor and their self-entertainment in daily life. At the time of first meeting John, Lucy is just eleven years old. That a eleven-year-old girl could blurt out the allusion which properly expresses herself provides sufficient evidence for the fact that the tale is widely known in the black community and very familiar to every black, old and young. Hence the novel is pervaded by the rustic charm of the Afro-American southerners' life.

In addition, *Jonah's Gourd Vine* reveals the identification of the Afro-American folk culture with the African culture in the detail of naming John's daughter Isis after the Egyptian fertility goddess. In fact, the author has already named after the goddess a character in her short story "Drenched in Light" (1924) before Isis in her first novel. For the Egyptian goddess Isis is an intelligent and creative deity, whose words carry the power of healing. Using her magic to trick Ra, the creator, into telling her his "secret name," Isis elevates herself to the position of the most revered goddess of Egypt. As magic is central to the entire mythology of Isis, arguably more so than any other Egyptian deity, Isis is worshiped as the most important and most powerful magician in the universe in Egypt, and as the ideal mother and wife as well as the patroness of nature and magic. Hence Isis is accepted as the friend of slaves, sinners, artisans and the downtrodden. In naming her characters after such a respectable goddess, Hurston implies her revolt against the male supremacy and her affirmation of black women's talent and wisdom.

For Hurston, who was steeped in the black folk culture, telling and listening to tales and legends is an indispensable part of her life, and therefore she is thoroughly at home in employing the narrative strategy to reinforce the theme of negritude in her fiction. In this regard, her second novel *Their Eyes Were Watching God* is more remarkable. In spare time the Eatonville residents like gathering on Joe Clarks' porch and tell "lies" for relaxation and amusement. As the heroine Janie depicts it, "[t]he store itself was a pleasant place if only she didn't have to sell things. When the people sat around on the porch and passed around the pictures of their thoughts for the others to look at and see, it was nice. The fact that the thought pictures were always crayon enlargements of life made it even nicer to listen to." (Hurston, 1995d: 215) Through "crayon enlargements of life," the downtrodden Afro-Americans find joy and fun in their hard life, and make their life interesting and endurable. The porch sitters, for instance, often play jokes on Matt Bonner and invent a lot of funny stories about his yellow mule. When it is lost and he is searching for it, a porch sitter jokes with him, saying: "De womenfolks got yo' mule. When Ah come round de lake 'bout noontime mah wife and some other had 'im flat on de ground usin' his sides fuh uh wash board." (216) When the mule is overworked and dying, Joe Starks shows his sympathy with it and buys and sets it free. More amusing stories are invented:

> New lies sprung about his free-mule doings. How he pushed open Lindsay's kitchen door and slept in the place one night and fought until they made coffee for his breakfast; how

> he stuck his head in the Pearson's window while the family was at the table and Mrs. Pearson mistook him for Rev. Pearson and handed him a plate; he ran Mrs. Tully off of the croquet ground for having such an ugly shape; he ran and caught up with Becky Anderson on the way to Maitland so as to keep his head out of the sun under her umbrella; he got tired of listening to Redmon's long-winded prayer, and went inside the Baptist church and broke up the meeting. He did everything but let himself be bridled and visit Matt Bonner. (221 – 222)

As is commented by Dolan Hubbard (1994: 56), the "creative capacities of blacks are not dependent on living in trembling and fear of white man—nor do the tales use white oppression as a point of departure." The Eatonville residents sweeten the bitterness of destiny. Facing difficulties and hardships in life, they cannot help but laugh. It is their humor and laughter that add interest and fun to their hard and monotonous life.

It is the "creative capacities" that enable black people to invent stories about God or fantasize heroes like Big John who might help them out of plight. In the eighteenth chapter, Tea Cake (whose prototype is the black folk hero Stegolee), Janie and some villagers choose not to believe the Indians' rumor that there will come a hurricane. They stay at home rather than run away with the Indians. However, as the world darkens and there emerge some abnormal natural phenomena, they get panic-stricken. In order to embolden themselves as well as kill time, they gather in Tea Cake's house and tell the folktale of Big John. "Big John de Conquer," an African prince, is sold into slavery; yet he is so smart and witty that he always outwits his white master and escapes his punishment by making mischief. He is acknowledged both as a trickster in black folktales and as a folk hero deeply loved by black people. John "had done everything big on earth, then went up tuh heben without dying still atall. Went up there picking a guitar and got all de angels doing the ring-shout round and round de throne. Then everybody but God and Old Peter flew off on a flying race to Jericho and back and John de Conquer won the race; went on down to hell, beat the old devil and passed out ice water to everybody down there." (Hurston, 1995d: 302) God therefore likes

John very much. With so much at stake, the villagers begin asking Tea Cake to play the guitar because "God would rather to hear a guitar." (302) The insertion of the folktale about John not just indicates the villagers' wish that there would turn up God or an immortal defending them at the dawn of the disaster but brings insight into their psyche of panic and helplessness as well. In the meantime, the narrative strategy of story within story efficiently promotes the plot of the novel. What is worth mentioning here is that the episode of Janie's shooting Tea Cake might originate in a popular blues "Frankie and Johnny," which ends up with the death of Johnny, who is shot by his girlfriend Frankie.

In the ninth chapter, Hurston exerts the black myth of God's creation of man in describing Janie's tough situation:

> When God had made The Man, he made him out of stuff that sang all the time and glittered all over. Then after that some angels got jealous and chopped him into millions of pieces, but still he glittered and hummed. So they beat him down to nothing but sparks but each little spark had a shine and a song. So they covered each one over with mud. And the lonesomeness in the sparks made them hunt for one another, but the mud is deaf and dumb. Like all the other tumbling mud-balls, Janie had tried to show her shine. (247)

Patriarchy is the mud in the angels' hands. It tightly wraps up Janie, who is as small as a spark. Janie's life is just a struggle against the patriarchal oppression and a process of searching for self and getting invigorated. Here Hurston takes the method of story-telling to hint at the heroine's personality traits instead of praising her courage and strength. The narration turns out to be characterized by tactic words and profound meaning.

Rewriting the story of the Book of Exodus of Moses and the Israelites from an Afro-American perspective, *Moses, Man of the Mountain* is also characterized by an abundance of folktales. Mentu, an old stableman, is created as an inexhaustible supply of tales. Spending a lot of time together with Mentu early in his childhood, the hero Moses is bathed in the black folk culture. As a child, Moses is intensely curious about the mystery of Nature and asks Mentu a great many questions, which are always answered in the form of tales. For instance, when asked why "we have nights between days," Mentu answers, "Well, He [God] is still working on the world and He must hide His hand from us humans. That is why things grow at night. Most things are born in the mothering darkness and most things die. Darkness is the womb of creation, my boy. But the sun with his seven horns of flame is the father of life." (Hurston, 1995b: 374) Among the tales told by Mentu, the most far-reaching should be the one about the Book of Thoth, the quest for which becomes one of the three missions Moses has to accomplish during his lifetime.

> There is a book which Thoth himself wrote with his own hand which, if you read it, will bring you to the gods. When you read only two pages in this book you will enchant the heavens, the earth, the abyss, the mountain, and the sea. You will know what the birds of the air and the creeping things are saying. You will know the secrets of the deep because the power is there to bring them to you. And when you read the second page, you can go into the world of ghosts and come back to the shape you were on earth. You will see the sun shining in the sky, with all the gods, and the full moon. (387)

It is such mystery and enchantment in this story and many others that attract both story-tellers and listeners, and make story-telling a most popular form of entertainment of common black people, children and adults alike. Thanks to the fascinating narratives (folktales, myth and legends), Hurston's novels are varnished with a distinctive color of black folklore and become models for her literary daughters like Alice Walker. Perhaps that is why Hurston's works have possessed immortality not only in the Afro-American women's literature but also in the American literature as a whole.

7.1.2 Walker's Repetition and Revision of Hurston's Text

In *The Signifying Monkey: A Theory of Afro-American Literary Criticism*, Henry Louis Gates, Jr. points out that, as far as the relation between texts is concerned, what the literary critics attempt to explore is, in essence, how an antecedent text is repeated and revised. The "repetition and revision" is "Signifyin(g)" in Gates' theory. (Gates, 1988: xxiv, capital & brackets original) For Gates, "all texts Signify upon other texts, in motivated and unmotivated ways"; by repeating, imitating, revising or rewriting a theme in the antecedent text, a descendant writer intends to "imply either homage to an antecedent text or futility in the face of a seemingly indomitable mode of representation." (xxiv, xxvii) As Hurston's veritable adherent, Alice Walker not only admires and respects the black folklore, but also disseminates and eulogizes it in her literary writing. Like Hurston, she absorbs a mass of black folktales and legends into her fiction so that it is brimming with strong smack of black people's everyday life. Following Hurston's folk literary style, Walker's works are filled with respect, admiration and worship, and thus establish a firm "mother-daughter" relationship between the two black women authors.

Early in her second novel *Meridian*, Walker has already imitated Hurston in employing the narrative strategy of story within story. In Saxon College, where Meridian studies, there is a large magnolia tree called "The Sojourner." The tree was planted by Louvinie, a slave on the Saxon plantation. As the legend goes, Louvinie is good at making up and telling stories, as her parents were both good story-tellers. The girl slave's specialty is telling gothic tales. The Saxon children adore her. They always follow her wherever she goes and beg her to tell them all the scary, horrible stories that she knows. Louvinie is pleased to do so. She usually tells stories that make their hair stand on end. When the stories she remembers from Africa become boring, she begins making up new, American ones to attract her audiences. One day, Louvinie, begged by the children, agrees to tell a horrible story as usual. The new story is her "masterpiece of fright," an "intricate, chilling story of the old man whose hobby was catching and burying children up to their necks and then draping their heads—which stuck up in rows, like cabbages—with wriggly eels dipped in honey." (A. Walker, 1976: 43) Nevertheless, before she finishes her story, the youngest of the Saxon children with heart disease, about which Louvinie knows nothing, is frightened to death. Flying into a fury, Master Saxon clips Louvinie's tongue out at the root. In her hometown there is such a curse: "without one's tongue in one's mouth or in a special spot of one's own choosing, the singer in one's soul was lost forever to grunt and snort through eternity like a pig." (44) So Louvinie pleads for her tongue and takes it back at last. She then buries it "under a scrawny magnolia tree on the Saxon plantation." (44) Unexpectedly, the tree burgeons and outgrows all the other trees around it and becomes a luxuriant tree, which is named "The Sojourner" later. The tree is believed to possess magic. The slaves claim that "the tree could talk, make music, was sacred to birds and possessed the power to obscure vision. Once in its branches, a hiding slave could not be seen." (44) For a long time, the exuberant branches and leaves of The Sojourner are a sanctuary for slaves who either escape from the white masters' beating or pour out their grievance and seek consolation. Hence blacks have accepted it as their Mother Tree. In the novel, a black gamine, who was nicknamed The Wild Child, died in a car accident. Out of humanity and compassion, Meridian and her schoolmates spontaneously organize a funeral for the girl, but the president issues an order that the students are not allowed to conduct the funeral inside the chapel of the college. Ashamed and irritated, they carry the casket of The Wild Child "to the middle of the campus and put it down gently beneath The Sojourner." (47 – 48) They are determined to hold the funeral there. Walker's careful arrangement of plot tactfully puts the injustice inflicted upon The Wild Child in parallel with the legend about Louvinie (her tragedy in particular). If the legend relates the miserable past of black people in the period of slavery, the president's refusal to admit The Wild Child to the college chapel veritably reflects the harshness in black people's present life. Both the past and the present demonstrate the monstrous crimes committed by white Americans. As the victims of racial discrimination, Louvinie and The Wild Child, or, to be exact, their souls show empathy for each other and are bonded closely. The Sojourner's "heavy, flower-lit leaves hovered over it (the casket of The Wild Child) like the inverted peaks of a mother's half-straightened kinky hair"; and "The Sojourner herself, ever generous to her children, dropped a leaf on the chest of The Wild Child, who wore for the first time, in her casket, a set of new clothes." (48) The Sojourner is at once a witness of black people's sadness and misery and a symbol of their indomitable fighting spirit. Meanwhile, linking the past and the present, The Sojourner carries the historical and cultural traditions of the black race. However, some of the students are infuriated by the college authority so much that they have lost their minds: "in a fury of confusion and frustration they worked all night, and chopped and sawed down, level to the ground, that mighty, ancient, sheltering music tree." (48) With the falling-down of The Sojourner, the new blacks are cut off from their long history and traditional culture. The students' destructive behavior not simply exposes the extremity and parochialism of some black political activists in the late period of the Civil Rights Movement, but also reflects the severe reality of the endangered black cultural heritages. By depicting the students behavior after the funeral, Walker properly shows her great concern over black people's destiny.

Oral transmission is the salient feature of black traditional culture. Slavery and illiteracy result in the prodigious memory and ready tongue of the Afro-Americans. Each black, a boy or a girl, grows up, listening to the stories told by his/her parents or by some other seniors; each black, a man or a woman, gets old, telling stories to their juniors. Story-telling is a staple of black people's daily life. In *The Temple of My Familiar*, talking about her mother Zede the Elder, an industrious woman skilled at needlework and earning a living by making the costumes for the priests, Zede relates the legend about priests to Arveyda. As Zede recounts it, the earliest priests are women and they are made so by men instead of themselves. The story goes that, in the beginning, there is only a woman, and "in the process of life and change she produced a being somewhat unlike herself," who turns out to be a man. (48) As the man grows up, he becomes "anxious to discover whether there existed, somewhere else, more of his own kind." (48) He then leaves the woman, finds some other beings who look like himself and live with them. The "first men were so new to each other... they had no self-consciousness about how they looked, beyond the dangling evidence of maleness, the elongated clitoris. They had no concept of dress" and are "infuriated with" their "relatively newness" while the women are "interested in high fashion" and are occasionally "host to a man, whom they played with, especially sexually." (48 – 49) All of a sudden, one of the men finds out a secret that the women could give birth to babies. Immediately all the men imagine a huge woman, "larger than the sky, producing, somehow, the earth," whom they accept as a "goddess." "And so, if the producer of the earth was a large woman, a goddess, then women must be her priests, and must possess great and supernatural powers." Naturally, the "men both worshiped and feared the women." (49) It is a long time before "the men grew sick of the women they worshiped" and "made an important discovery about women's ability to produce life." (50) However, when they discover women's secret of giving birth, they immediately operate on themselves so that they could give birth to babies as women do. For men hold that, once they could give birth, they would become priests in place of women. Unfortunately, the operation fails and men "died like flies. This is why, even today, there is a certain sadness a family feels when a boy decides to become a priest." (51) The legendary position of black women sharply contrasts with the hard life of Zede the Elder and her own female generation. Women in the legend are virtually the typical traditional female images—symbolizing ability and wisdom—in the black culture. They live a carefree life except the brief birth pangs, and men are insignificant to them. But the women of Zede's mother's generation, despite their intelligence and talents, have to slave for their families. They make fine clothes not to dress themselves up but to trade for their life necessities from the priests, who are not women any more. Life for Zede the Elder and her generation is all about children and husbands. The ready legend for the characters in the novel both proves Walker's familiarity and love of the black folklore, and demonstrates her unique insight of choosing literary materials. By containing tales and legends in abundance in literary writing, Walker expresses her intense identification with Afro-American traditional culture and her great admiration for the antecedent texts, particularly Hurston's. What penetrates through her literary career is a literary daughter's remembrance of her literary mother.

Alice Walker not simply repeats and imitates Hurston's texts, but also revises them innovatively. In *By the Light of My Father's Smile*, the author, on the one hand, surpasses the geographical boundaries and focuses on the Mundo tribe in Mexico. On the other hand, she builds up a transcendental world, based on the belief that the soul never dies, where those who die with everlasting regret can speak and communicate and continue to fulfil their wishes unfinished in their earthly life. Troubled by the psychic trauma he caused to his daughters during his lifetime, the soul of Mr. Robinson cannot be at peace. His spirit, watching over his daughters, suffers their suffering and worries their worries. Then he meets the spirit of the Mundo man Manuelito, who dies in a car accident. To help Robinson fully understand Magdalena and what she did at the age of fifteen rather than forgive her just out of pity, Manuelito or, more exactly, Manuelito's ghost relates him the Mundo story of woman and the moon. As the story goes, "a woman's tides, her blood tides, connect with the moon." (A. Walker 1998: 208) "A woman, living in nature, is full when the moon is full," and she releases her blood "when the moon releases and begins to wane." (209) The Mundo women take the period when they "release their blood" as "a big moment" that they share with the moon. (209) The Mundo believe that "there is a period of recovery from the 'big moment' that women have had with the moon," and that "there is a period" when women just naturally do not "want to be bothered" and "sexual contact must be avoided." (209) So men become "somewhat gloomy" during this period. (209) But, just when the whole moon is dark and "men have given up hope, the moon appears again." (210) In the eyes of the Mundo people, the moon now "appears as a smile! Very tentative at first, but pretty soon, a wide grin! For by now the women are totally receptive. It is a good time to make love!" (210) Here lies the connection between men and the moon:

> The crescent moon... is the moon smiling its light on the good lovemaking that is to come!

> The moon, while forever a woman, for just a little while becomes, also, a man! ... If you are in love, and going to meet your lover, to make love, you think of the moon as a father, happily looking down on you. For Mundo fathers *are* happy that their children, the girls as well as the boys, enjoy what your (Robinson's) culture calls sex. And that is why a young girl sings, as she goes to her lover, just as does a young boy: "by the light of my father's smile!" And that is why no one among the Mundo would marry when the moon is full, but only when it has waned and then reappears, as a smile in a dark face, in the sky! (210, italics original)

With the story ending, a light breaks in upon Robinson. He comes to get at the fifteen-year-old Magdalena, who always sang "by the light of my father's smile" and wished her father's blessing, and the grown-up Magdalena, who hates him and refuses to forgive him.

Having really understood his daughter, Robinson is anxious to find an opportunity to make amends for his wrong and say apology to Magdalena. He finds a way out in the Mundo belief told by Manuelito that one "will continue to sing, to live, on the other side" at least till his/her "tasks are done." (95) The genuine, good-hearted Mundo people believe, "[t]he dead are required to finish two tasks before all is over with them: one is to guide back to the path someone you left behind who is lost, because of your folly; the other is to host a ceremony so that you and others you have hurt may face eternity reconciled and complete." (148) In the Vietnam War, Manuelito killed the parents of a little Vietnamese girl, "whose spirit died the moment" they were murdered. (95) The girl later declined into a street girl and is infected with AIDS. He feels guilty and waits for a chance to make amends all along. After knowing that she is dying, Manuelito goes to Vietnam, "bringing back something she has lost," something "she most wants to take with her into her death," viz., her soul. (195) In so doing, he helps her die without regret and thus fulfils his own last wish. Witnessing the whole process of Manuelito's wrong-correction, Robinson decides to disregard the identity of a pretended Christian missionary and express his sincere blessing for Magdalena, who is dead as well. He kisses her hands, feet and knees according to the Mundo custom and is eventually forgiven by Magdalena and gets reconciled with her. That Robinson's wandering soul finally rests in peace makes the novel conclude with a perfect ending. The Mundo tales create a good opportunity for the characters' transformation and, in the meantime, avoid the abruptness of the plot caused by the insertion of folktales. Moreover, the author is not limited to tale-telling only; she gets the stories fused into the plot of the novel and properly represented in the characters. Both Robinson and Manuelito succeed in fulfilling their unfinished wishes after death and thus help the Mundo legend come into reality in the transcendental world of the novel. Apart from strong smack of everyday life, the novel creates a wonderland, where fantasy and reality are intertwined. In *By the Light of My father's Smile*, the author practically develops her unique creative style, which is fantastic but not authentic. The magic realism is both characteristic of Walker's later literary works and the revision of Hurston's folk literary style.

7.2 The Linguistic Folkloric Materials in Hurston's and Walker's Fiction

The linguistic folkloric materials consist of sermons and vernaculars, along with proverbs and idiomatic expressions. Blacks were labeled a special species early when they were sold to the American Continent as slaves. In the eyes of whites, they were vulgar, barbarous, slow-witted, illiterate and uncultivated, and belonged to the second-class citizens in the American society. They were not allowed to participate in any social activity. Therefore, churches were the central meeting places for blacks. At the scheduled time, black believers gathered together in churches, praying, caroling, and listening to sermons. In the religious practices, they got acquainted with each other and developed close relationships gradually. Churches thus became the only places where black slaves had voice and expressed themselves in their own ways. In churches originated the black sermons, which are characterized by the dynamic communicative modes like extemporaneous singing and chanting, and the call and response between the preacher and the congregation. Just as the black scholar Hortense Spillers (1978: 4) points it out, "[t]he thrust of the sermon is passional, repeating essentially the rhythms of plot, complication, climax, resolution. The sermon is an oral poetry not simply an exegetical, theological presentation, but a complete expression of a gamut of emotions whose central form is the narrative and whose end is catharsis release. In that regard the sermon is an instrument of a collective catharsis, binding once again the isolated members of community." Indeed, black slaves found the end-result of their wondering souls in the black sermons, which embody black people's ideas, feelings as well as value orientations. Meanwhile, the black sermons provide rich aesthetic elements for the spoken language. Deprived of the opportunities to learn to read and write, the enslaved Afro-Americans chiefly resorted to the oral form to express themselves and communicate with each other. So with the popularity of the black sermons, black vernacular absorbed a great deal of the rhythmical and poetical expressions and were more widely used in black communities.

7.2.1 The Black Sermons

As Dolan Hubbard (1994: 14) asserts it in the essay "Toward a Definition of African American Sermon," the black sermon "is the agent for historical location. As the tap root of blacks in American discourse, the sermon historicizes the experience of blacks in America. The sermon as agent provides a link between generations of black families and makes it possible for the culture of black America to be transmitted over time and for members of the community to adapt to changing external circumstances." Through sermons, black preachers attempt to open up a neutral territory between the sacred and the secular, where the underprivileged Afro-Americans could find spiritual consolation and enjoy transitory relaxation. In this sense, the sermon works as mental nourishment of the black population. It is both a kind of gist of black culture and the embodiment of black emotions. By way of sermons, not only the black cultural values are transmitted from generation to generation, but also the aesthetic psychology and ethnic emotions are exhibited and reinforced in black communities. Inevitably, the insightful Afro-American writers borrow in their literary creation the black sermonic tradition, which exerts a great influence on the Afro-American literary texts in both structure and theme. In this regard, Zora Neale Hurston and Alice Walker have set up an example to their kin writers.

As an anthropologist, Hurston accepts the black sermons as artistic treasures blending scriptures with artifice. Incorporating abundant sermons in her novels, she exhibits the great value the black sermons contribute to the black literature as well as the black aesthetics as a whole. *Jonah's Gourd Vine* gives an account of how the hero John grows from an ignorant rural juvenile to a prestigious folk priest. The multiple sermons delivered by John play a decisive role in the characterization and the plot development. They also add charm to the novel, sending out intense black folk customs. John has an inborn talent for languages. His verbal agility is first reflected when he prays in church after Lucy discovers his affair with Big 'Oman. The following is the final part of his prayer:

> You are de same God, Ah
> Dat heard de sinner man cry.
> Same God dat sent de zigzag lighting tuh
> Join de mutterin' thunder.
> Same God dat holds de elements
> In uh unbroken chain of controllment.
> Same God dat hung on Cavalry and died,
> Dat we might have a right tuh de tree of life—
> We thank thee that our sleeping couch
> Was not our cooling board,
> Our cover was not our winding sheet…
> Please tuh give us restin' place
> Where we can praise Thy name forever,
>
> Amen. (Hurston, 1995a: 75 - 76)

As it turns out, John is a good prayer. His outstanding performance surely could carry away anybody present. Deacon Moss sings high praise of him, saying that his praying is full of fire and he has a "strainin' voice." (76) Admittedly, in the praying a devout Christian stands out. The praying undoubtedly lays the groundwork for John's later success in preaching.

John's talent for preaching is first discovered by his fellow workers in the railway camp. One Sunday, John goes to church in town and hears the preacher's sermon. Back in the camp at night, he "preached the sermon himself for the entertainment of the men who had stayed in camp and he aped the gestures of the preacher so accurately that the crowd hung half-way between laughter and awe." (91) The fellow workers' approval, to a large extent, encourages John, who advisably builds the opportunity to bring his genius into full play in Florida. On a Sunday after he wanders to Eatonville, John makes a self-recommendation speech in Covenant Meeting:

> Brothers and Sisters, Ah rise befo' yuh tuhday tuh tell yuh, God done called me tuh preach. ... He called me long uhgo, but Ah wouldn't heed tuh de voice, but brothers ans sisters, God done whipped me tuh it, and like Peter and Paul Ah means tuh preach Christ and Him crucified. He tole me tuh go, and He'd go with me, so Ah ast yo' prayers, Church, dat Ah may hold up de blood-stained banner of Christ and prove strong dat Ah may hold out tuh de end. (95 – 96)

The speech itself has testified to his competence as a preacher. "The church boiled over with approval" the moment John finishes his speech. (96) Subsequently, he is agreed to deliver his trial sermon and logically ordained. Then he is taken to a larger church in Sanford and honorably settles down there. Fortunately enough, John wins the election while running for mayor later and becomes a prominent figure in the locality. It is his eloquent speechcraft that helps John and his family start a new life. In this sense, John is a winner.

As a matter of fact, John is remarkably successful in his preaching career. He is sure to preach at every crucial moment in his life to change his fate. In addition to the trial sermon, he delivers two other magnificent sermons that similarly help him turn the corner. When his career is in jeopardy due to his philandering with women, John listens to his wife Lucy's suggestion and preaches a long touching sermon to convince his congregation that he is the best preacher. Here is part of the sermon:

> My chillum, Papa Pearson don't feel lak preach' y'all tuh day. ... y'all been looking at me fuh eight years, but look lak some uh y'all been lookin' on me wid unseein' eye. When Ah speak fuh yuh from dis pulpit, dat ain't me talkin', dat's de voice uh God speakin' thru me. ...
>
> Course, mah childun in Christ, Ah been here wid y'all fuh eight years and mo'. Ah done set by yo' beside and buried de dead and joined tuhgether de hands uh de livin', but Ah ain't got no remembrance. Don't keer if Ah laugh, don't keer if Ah cry, when de sun, wid his blood red eye, go intuh his house at night, he takes all mah remembrace wid 'im, but some yuh y'all dat got remmebrace wid sich long tangues dat it kin talk tuh yuh at a distance, when y'all is settin' down and passin' nations thew yo' mouf, look close and see if in all mah doin's if dere wuz anything good mingled up uhmoungst de harm Ah done yuh. Ah ain't got no mind. Y'all is de one dat is so much-knowin' dat you kin set in judgment. (104 – 105)

By virtue of his God-given eloquence, John wins another good luck. Both the deacons and the congregation are deeply moved. When he is about to step down the pulpit, John is thrust back, and "[t]he church surged up, a weeping wave about him." (105) Naturally he holds down the pastorate.

John Pearson has been a pastor for seventeen years when he realizes that it is impossible for him to remain at his post. The moment he has to leave the church, he delivers his last sermon titled "the wounds of Jesus." (145) The several-page-long sermon hints at John's wounds as well. Or rather, John alludes to the biblical stories to express his own feelings so as to effectively exculpate himself from the awkward circumstance. After the needed warming-up, John begins:

> Jesus was not unthoughtful. He was not overbearing. He was never a bully. He was never sick. He was never a criminal before the law and yet. He was wounded. Now, a man usually gets wounded in the midst of his enemies, but this man was wounded, says the text, in the house of his friends. It is not your enemies that harm you all the time. Watch that close friend. Every believer in Christ considered His friend, and every sin we commit is a wound to Jesus. (145)

Evidently, the last sermon is as sensational as his any previous one. Apart from his moral quality, it cannot be denied that John is an exceptional preacher. To end up the sermon, John turns back to the topic of being wounded:

> He died for our sins.
> Wounded in the house of His friends.
> That's where I got off de damnation train
> And dat's where you must get off, ha!
> For in dat mor-ornin', ha!
> To dat Judgement Convention
> When de two trains of Time shall meet on de trestle
> And wreck de burning axles of de unformed ether
> And de mountains shall skiplike lambs
> When Jesus shall place one foot on de neck of de sea, ha!
> One foot on day land, ah
> When His chariot wheels shall be running hub-deep in fire
> He shall take his friends thru the open bosom of an unclouded sky
> And place in their hands de "hosanna" fan
> And they shall stand 'round and 'round his beatific throne
> And praise His name forever,
>
> Amen. (151)

Thus John ends his preaching career with his fascinating sermon as he begins it. Sermons are what really matters in John's life. For him, where there is preaching, there is life. Badly hurt by his congregation, he leaves the church as if he were the wounded Jesus. Hurston skillfully integrates the sermons with the plot of the novel, or, to be exact, with the hero's fate so that, without sermons, his life is gray and colorless: A pastor no more, John is nothing; he even does not make his own living and dies a dishonorable death. Almost all the sermons preached by John stem from the black folkloric materials Hurston recorded on the folklore-collecting expeditions. These authentic materials not only reveal John's potential personality defects (i. e., duplicity and betrayal of love) but also season the novel with life reality and cultural connotation. Every time he preaches in the church, John rolls his African drum up to the altar and calls his Congo gods by Christian names. Fusing the black cultural element with the white Christianity in his preaching, John, like the author, practically demonstrates the beauty of the black folk culture, reconstructs the black cultural identity, and appeals for the black-white equality as well.

In *Their Eyes Were Watching God*, Hurston depicts a funeral of the yellow mule, who dies of overwork, in a teasing tone. The townspeople gather together to hold the funeral. The whole course of the ceremony appears solemn and orderly. The Mayor Starks delivers the eulogy for the mule. And Sam preaches a sermon, imitating John Pearson, the local preacher:

> He spoke of the joys of mule-heaven to which the dear brother had departed this valley of sorrow; the mule-angels flying around; the miles of green corn and cool water, a pasture of pure bran with a river of molasses running through it; and most glorious of all, *No* Matt Bonner with plow lines and halters to come in and corrupt. Up there, mule-angles would have people to ride on and from his place beside the glittering throne, the dear departed brother would look down into hell and see the devil plowing Matt Bonner all day long in a hell-hot sun and laying the raw-hide to his back. (Hurston, 1995d: 223, italics original)

The sermon has an obvious allegorical presentation. The mule symbolizes the oppressed blacks while his former master Matt Bonner (or the people as a whole) the oppressing whites. The mule-heaven presents the ideal life black people aspire to live. Through the mouth of the mocker, Hurston accurately expresses black people's dream of a bright future.

After the funeral, when the crowd fades away and the soul of the mule is supposed to rest in peace, the buzzards, having already hovering over the corpse of the mule, immediately fly down and surround it in circles, and a grand banquet is about to be held. Ridiculously, all the buzzards have to wait till the appearance of the white-headed leader, who plays the role of Parson in its species. Then, under the leadership of "the Parson," the birds also hold a ceremony just before the feast. The sermon is preached in the call-and-response pattern of the black folk tradition:

> "What killed this man?"
>
> The chorus answered, "Bare, bare fat."
>
> "What killed this man?"
>
> "Bare, bare fat."
>
> "What killed this man?"
>
> "Bare, bare fat."
>
> "Who'll stand his funeral?"
>
> "We!!!!!"
>
> "Well, all right now." (224)

Even after death, the mule cannot escape the misfortune of being dismembered and devoured. This probably hints at the harsh reality that black people have to face. If the funeral held by the townspeople is a farce Starks performs to show his pretended benevolence and generosity in front of the townsfolk, the preaching of the buzzards before devouring the corpse of the mule incisively and vividly manifests the leader buzzard's strong desire for power. The two ceremonies are disparate yet imperceptibly coherent, and achieve complementarity. The leader buzzard in the birds' ceremony is the Mayor in the human ceremony, and vice versa. This unique two-in-one creative technique presents Starks' character traits of hypocrisy and greed to the full.

Moreover, the catchy sermon with clear-cut rhythm represents the preaching scene in the black church in a comic yet realistic way. It effectively combines solemnity with fun, and majesty with ridicule, and produces the effect of funny comics. It demonstrates the charming uniqueness of the black religion and conveys the strong ethnic content of the black customs as well. It thus adds the artistic appeal to the novel.

As a literary daughter, Alice Walker knows well about the negritude contained in the preaching and sermons of the black race. Nonetheless, as a fighter for black emancipation and women's rights, she endows black preachers with a different preaching style, expressing adequate concern for the human rights, the black rights to be exact, instead of the devout worship for God, which she knows has never existed at all. In other words, Walker's are more revision than repetition of Hurston's texts, as far as the sermons are concerned in her literary writing. In *Meridian*, there is a description of a memorial service in a black church for a young black victim, who has died for black civil rights. The author records the special preaching scene from the perspective of the civil rights activist Meridian. In his so-called preaching, the minister, in a voice so dramatically like Martin Luther King's, "launched into an attack on President Nixon," "forbade them (the young men) to participate in the Vietnam war," "told the young women to stop looking for husbands and try to get something useful in their heads," "told the elder congregants that they should be ashamed of the way they let their young children fight their battles for them," and "abused the black teachers present who did not... work hard enough to teach black youth because they obviously had no faith in them." (A. Walker, 1976: 195 – 196) The sermon has nothing to do with God or Christianity except the mention of "David and Goliath" at the beginning and the sound of "ah-mens." Essentially, the minister delivers a political speech rather than a religious sermon. What he does to Meridian and the other congregants is not religious indoctrination but political brainwashing. Walker's layout here, which seems counterintuitive, not just gives readers a refreshing stimulus but roots the novel deeply in the black culture as well. As a consequence, the black traditional religious practice is involved in the modern revolutionary atmosphere.

If *Meridian* witnesses the fighting course of Walker the fully-matured Afro-American warrior, *The Third Life of Grange Copeland* rests on the formative stage of the author's revolutionary thought. Instead of converting the traditional content of sermons directly as *Meridian* does, this novel indirectly presents the inanition and vapidity of the black sermon in the congregants' response, particularly little Grange's. In so doing, the work warns the black congregants about the dangerous effect of the black sermon that might imprison their souls, and appeals to them to reexamine its spiritual connotation so that it can both keep the black religious tradition and show concern for the life reality of black people. Recounting Ruth the story about how he comes to join the church, Grange depicts a funny preaching scene in the black church. In his childhood Grange hates the white and their religion and refuses to convert to Christianity. One day, his uncle, his mother's brother, forcibly takes Grange to church and threatens to give him "a horse-whipping" if Grange does not "get religion" this time. (A. Walker, 1970: 130) At the beginning of the service, a silence pervades the church. It seems as if all the congregants are concentrating on the preacher, so Grange has to pretend to be listening. But there comes whispering and snoring very soon. Looking about curiously, Grange notices women "gossiping like so many peacocks" and "spitting out of windows and into the stove," while the snores are from his uncle, who is now fast asleep. (131) All of a sudden, he finds that there is "a huge fat house-fly" playing around his uncle's "wide-open mouth." (132) This gives Grange the simple and absurd idea—"if the fly got inside Uncle Buster's mouth, *and if Uncle Buster swallowed it*, he would jump right up, claim he had found the Holy Ghost and join the church." (132, italics original) The moment Grange has made the decision, "the fly very cautiously sneaked into Uncle Buster's mouth, and Uncle Buster, waking to find everybody in the church gazing in his direction, or so it must have seemed to him, snapped together his ponderous whiskered jaws, and in a pious self-righteous gulp, downed the fly!" (132) As a matter of course, Grange becomes a Christian at the end of the sermon. Through the mouth of an honest and innocent child, the novel humorously details the ridiculous course of a new Christian's birth, which veritably reflects the belief crisis of the black religion and black people's resistance to the religious assimilation of white people. Thus the insignificant episode not simply plays a vital role in enriching and highlighting the character, but also mirrors the vulnerable foundation of black preaching and foreshadows the awakening of the black race.

7.2.2 The Black English Vernacular

Poetic and rhythmical, the black English vernacular is peculiar to the Afro-Americans and encompasses their wit, humor and emotion. It creates a new sphere for them to establish their cultural identity. Houston A. Baker, Jr. (1998: epigraph) points out, "unlike the white Americans who could assume literacy and familiarity with existing literary models as norms, the slaves found themselves without a system of written language… He (the black slave) first had to seize the word. His being had to erupt from nothingness. Only by grasping the word could he engage in the speech act that would ultimately define his selfhood." The black English vernacular is therefore acknowledged not simply as the Afro-Americans' means of survival, by which they adapt to the complicated living surroundings, evade the white oppression, and maintain their independence and freedom, but as their cultural strategy of constructing the ethnic identity and manifesting the ethnic individuality. However, due to its speakers' low position in the American society, the black English vernacular has been greatly devalued by American whites as vulgar and inferior. Even some Afro-American intellectuals have internalized the white notion and feel ashamed of their own language. With the enhancement of their sense of equality and justice, more and more Afro-Americans strive to live with dignity, which, for some of them, means the rejection of black folk traditions, including the black vernacular. As an anthropologist, Zora Neale Hurston knew very well the significance and value of the cultural history and its link to the ethnic and cultural identities. Therefore, as an Afro-American author, she took it as her duty to affirm the Afro-American history and propagate the black folk culture in her literary writing. Compared with the other folkloric materials, language is the most direct expression. The abundant use of black English vernacular is another salient feature of Hurston's black folk literary works.

There is a story about Hurston's attitude toward her mother tongue. To collect and record the folk tales of her natal community, Hurston returned to her hometown just before she completed her study at university. She turned up, speaking Standard English, before the natives and was decidedly refused. The "fabricated Zora," a black speaker of Standard English, was a stranger and outsider to the natives, who would provide strangers with no information about their history, culture and customs. When she switched to speaking black vernacular, she received a warm welcome and the native informants offered a great many valuable materials so that her research agenda was thoroughly executed. The black English vernacular is in practice the language of authenticating one's membership in a black community—those who speak it are insiders, and those who do not, outsiders. The natives' refusal of the Standard English speaking Hurston embodied their rejection of her academic pretentiousness. The rejection indicated the Afro-Americans' strong sense of identity and their collective resistance to the external agency, to any control and domination. If the course studying and academic training at university equipped Hurston with the theoretical knowledge of anthropology, the experience of being refused in her natal community taught her what an Afro-American anthropologist was supposed to do to carry forward the black folklore. From then on, Hurston was really attached to her mother tongue and was committed to heightening the communal pride of black folk by portraying a series of true-to-life characters, speaking black English vernacular, in her fiction.

By exploiting prodigious amounts of black vernacular, Hurston developed a distinguishable style of her own and managed to demonstrate the cultural politics of language through her black folk literary works. In this regard, *Jonah's Gourd Vine* is a good illustration. Its successful use of dialect has been the focus of academic circles at one time. Herschel Brickell (1934: 13) once asserts that the only reason "that will stop *Jonah's Gourd Vine* from being popular" is that "[m]any people do not read dialect." While Margaret Wallace (1934: 6) sings high praise of the magnificent phraseology of the southern black dialect, affirming that the essence of the novel lies "in the rhythm and balance of the sentences, in the warm artlessness of the phrasing," H. R. Brock (1935: 4), a white critic, concentrates on the authenticity and vividness of the hero's language, which the critic thinks is "rich with flavor and alive with characteristic turns of speech." Brock (4) declares that those "who have known the Southern Negro from our (their) youth find him here speaking the language of his tribe as familiarly as if it came straight out of his own mouth and had not been translated into type and transmitted through the eye to the ear, which is to say that a very tricky dialect has been rendered with rare simplicity and fidelity into symbols." Admittedly, both John Pearson and the other characters in the novel speak fluent southern black dialect, which is distinguished by lyrical pathos and ironic humor the outsiders hardly get at. The strong local accent permeating the novel creates a warm and cordial atmosphere of blackness, in which the characters speak their black dialect, follow their black conventions, and express their black (their own) thoughts and feelings. In a word, they try to enjoy freedom and relaxation, and maintain black dignity and selfhood. Evidently, here Hurston aims to strengthen the subject consciousness and the national pride and confidence of the Afro-Americans, and create a literary world for the Afro-American culture. Similarly, *Their Eyes Were Watching God* is dressed in the typical southern black dialect. The author mines its rich resources and continues to use her special literary language of distinct negritude in this work. On the one hand, she uses the idiomatic expressions in abundance from black English vernacular. Some of the typical examples are: "Ah ain't had a thing on mah stomach today exceptin' mah hand"; "Put me down easy Janie, Ah'm a cracked plate"; "love ain't somethin' lak uh grindstone dat's de same thing everywhere and do de same thing tuh everything it touch." (Hurston, 1995d: 178, 190, 332). On the other hand, she endows each character with a unique gift of language, which fits his/her position in society and reveals his/her peculiarities of character. By virtue of the black dialect, Hurston sets the characters in the southern black community and brings them to life so that each appears vivid, realistic and believable; by virtue of the language, the author manages to narrate Janie's stories with an infectious energy and enthusiasm which is hard to leave behind; by virtue of the language, the author succeeds in clothing the novel with local color and rural flavor; and by virtue of it, she reaches the goal of intensifying the Afro-Americans' cultural consciousness and manifesting their cultural identity in her literary works.

In a long time after the emergence of the black English vernacular, the white linguists ascribed its discrepancy from the Standard English to the inferiority of the black race. They refused to acknowledge the black vernacular as a variant of the English language and make a deep related study. With the enhancement of the Afro-Americans' social position in the American society, the American whites have abandoned their negative attitudes toward the black English vernacular; more and more linguists, black and white, begin examining its difference from the Standard English in a just, objective, and scientific way. As is known to all, mother tongues, along with linguistic diversity, matter for the identity of the speakers. So the application of the black vernacular is closely related to the Afro-Americans' cultural identity. As a pursuer of the womanist ideal, Alice Walker understands that "the master's tools cannot dismantle the master's house" (an expression from Carolann Louise Daniel's essay title "The Master's Tools Cannot Dismantle the Master's House"). To subvert the white thesis that the black English vernacular is inferior and vulgar, Walker, like Hurston, freely employs the southern black dialect to display its charm and vitality in her literary works. In *The Color Purple*, the black woman Celie makes a long journey of seeking independence and constructing her self-identity. Her struggle against sexism and racism is embodied in her preference for black vernacular and her persistence in speaking it all the time. Jacques Lacan once points out that "the subject was not an origin of discourse but a result of discourse construction and that the subject did not produce language but was constructed through language." (岳凤梅, 2005: 52 – 53) From the initial obedience through the gradual awakening to the complete independence, Celie always expresses herself and communicates with others in pure southern black rural dialect. It is the original narrative language that characterizes Celie as a self-reliant independent black woman of the new generation. In this sense, Alice Walker keeps up Zora Neale Hurston's narrative technique of hitting back at the hegemony of the white culture by sticking to the black vernacular. In the novel, the black rural dialect is not only a communicative tool, which has its own artistic beauty, but also presents the speaker's strong sense of self-identity and belonging in terms of culture.

All in all, thanks to the abundant use of the black English vernacular in their novels, Hurston and Walker have successfully formed a simple, lucid, natural yet fresh, peculiar, and fascinating language style. Their works abound with lively black men and women, whose daily life, permeated by the distinct local flavor, fully displays the black folk culture. In the meantime, they voice the Afro-Americans' protest against the white supremacy and social injustice, and thus underscore the "racial health; a sense of black people as complete, complex, *undiminished* human beings, a sense that is lacking in so much black writing and literature." (A. Walker 1983: 85, italics original)

7.3 The Religious Folkloric Materials in Hurston's and Walker's Fiction

Like other ethnic groups, the Afro-Americans have a long history of religion, which, originating in the African religious tradition, was affected by the white Christianity. The Afro-American religion lays emphasis on the harmony between humankind and nature, and has a firm belief in animism. Its core is blacks' reverence and worship for God, by which black people mean nature, and their ancestors. In other words, the Afro-American religion is strikingly characterized by ancestry adoration and nature worship. It is concretized in Voodoo, animism and some other superstitious manners and customs. All these religious folkloric materials abound in Hurston's and Walker's fiction, and thus strengthen the bond between the two generations of the literary figures in the Afro-American women's literature.

7.3.1 The Psychic of Voodoo Conjury

Voodoo, also known as Hoodoo, West African Vodun or Haitian Vodou, stems from the black religion in West Africa. It is a primitive religion of integrating ancestry worship with animism and psychic, and "a religion of creation and life," as Hurston (1995c: 376) describes it. It, combining its sympathetic magic with black people's life reality, has the peculiarity of black culture. An alien religion on the American Continent, Voodoo is to the American blacks what Christianity is to the American whites. However, slavery and racism contributed to its tough situation in the Christian world. It has long been suppressed and excluded as a heresy. It was not until the rise of cultural relativism in modern anthropology in the early twentieth century that Voodoo began arousing the attention from the mainstream culture and became thriving in the Afro-American community. Nowadays, it is no exaggeration to say that, where there are blacks, there are Voodoo practices. In New Orleans and some other southern American places, and the countries like Haiti and Jamaica, Voodoo has become a prosperous business, passed down by Voodoo conjurers/doctors/medicine men/herbalists. The blacks in these places are accustomed to turning to a Voodoo conjurer when they get ill or in trouble, notwithstanding white people often debase him/her into "a charlatan or a fraud." (Mbiti, 1990: 2) In its long history of confrontation with Christianity, Voodoo has not simply abided by the black religious beliefs but also borrowed some rituals from its opposite to innovate in its own religious practices so that it becomes more instrumental in comforting black souls.

On her folklore-collecting expeditions, Hurston once studied with the local celebrated Voodoo conjurers and acquired proficiency in the Voodoo rituals. In effect, she took great interest in Voodoo and its forms of expression, especially its beautiful sermons in prose poetry, which have been classified in the linguistic group, due to its obvious verbal expression, and have been discussed about in the previous section in spite of its religious nature. As an anthropologist, Hurston attached importance to the uniqueness of Voodoo as a religion. She accepted Voodoo as another distinct identity-mark of the Afro-Americans and depicted different Voodoo practices in her novels—*Jonah's Gourd Vine*, *Their Eyes Were Watching God* and *Moses, Man of the Mountain*—to add their negritude.

Narrated in a mixture of biblical rhetoric, black dialect, and colloquial English, *Moses, Man of the Mountain* traces Moses' life from the day he is launched into the Nile River in a reed basket through his development as a great magician to his transformation into the heroic rebel leader, the Great Emancipator. Moses is portrayed as a Voodoo saint, a fusion of Christian form and Voodoo spirit. As the embodiment of supernatural forces, he owns the deity power, even greater than God's, and excels in black idioms and magic. The Voodoo conjury is his source of power and helps him to attain his glorious achievements, namely, to accomplish the three missions—finding the Book of Thoth, leading the Hebrews to leave Egypt, and assisting them in building their own country. The story of Moses is based on the folktales Hurston collected on her research expeditions in Haiti, Jamaica, and the southern America. Moses is so popular among the African diaspora that, "[w]herever the Negro is found, there are traditional tales of Moses and his supernatural powers that are not in the Bible, nor can they be found in any written life of Moses." (Hurston, 1995c: 378) Transformed from the white original, Moses is created to satisfy the black tellers' own needs; he has been elevated to a status similar to that reserved for Jesus Christ and the Virgin Mary. There are so many parallels to the American slavery in the black version that tellings and retellings of the Exodus tale quickly become a staple of Afro-American sermons. Correspondently, Hurston portrays a black Moses, a Voodoo practitioner, whose most salient attribute is working wonders by his right hand, the symbol of his magic power. Her Moses straddles the line between a trickster magician and a powerful leader. To lead the Hebrew slaves out of bondage, Moses returns to Egypt and plays tricks on Pharaoh and his priests so that Pharaoh permits the

Hebrews to leave. In the whole course of his dramatic confrontations with Pharaoh, his right hand plays a decisive role; it enables him to defeat Pharaoh and his priests with tricks, ranging from the rampancy of different pests like frogs, lice, flies and locusts to the plague of cattle murrain and the like. The following is the description of the plague of frogs:

> Moses didn't lose any time. He walked to the made pond in the garden and lifted up his rod in his right hand and frogs swarmed out of the pond all over the garden. They filled the garden and the grounds and still they poured out of the fish pond. Hundreds and thousands and millions struggled over each other in the shallow water, clambered to the stone wall about the pond and leaped off in all directions. Moses still stood with his right hand lifted and the frogs kept on coming. Little frogs, big frogs, green frogs, toad frogs, rain frogs, bull frogs, every kind of frog that ever leaped or hopped. The foundation of the world seemed made of frogs and they came pouring out of that pond. The world croaked and leaped. The party fled inside but the palace was full of frogs. (Hurston, 1995b: 478)

As Pharaoh constantly breaks his promises, Moses has to play a series of tricks, all of which are vividly described in the novel, to force him to give the Hebrews permission to leave. Having won victory after victory, he eventually leads the people out of Egypt and marches them to the Promised Land flowing with milk and honey. In essence, the novel is a compelling allegory of power, redemption and faith, viz., an allegory for the Afro-Americans' struggle against slavery. Moses' magic power, brought into full play in Hurston's writing, is the key to the emancipation of the oppressed. It not simply decides the narrative clue of the story but also works as a cultural strategy in the author's attempt to subvert the white supremacy in religion. With the magic power, Moses is an invincible savior. His identity of a Voodoo man undoubtedly elevates his religion to the dominant position and thus threatens the established authority of Christianity.

Moses, Man of the Mountain is also a metaphor for a complex set of religious and social beliefs that are alien to those of a different social group and generation.

There is the sense that much lies under the surface, waiting to be discovered. Hurston recasts Moses' other events to fit in with the way the Afro-American communities, particularly those in the New Orleans area, interpret Moses and the Exodus. In this sense, the novel is a worthwhile read for those who want to see in novel form how such black religious practices as Voodoo differ from the white religion in the surrounding white communities.

Similarly, Hurston skillfully blends the Voodoo conjury into *Jonah's Gourd Vine* and makes the plot full of twists and turns. What is different is that Moses' magic power plays a positive role in changing the Hebrews' fate and life and brings the story to a happy ending while the Voodoo conjury in *Jonah's Gourd Vine* is a mysterious destructive force, which pushes John Pearson into an impasse. In order to get married to John, Hattie wants to kill his wife Lucy, so she turns to An' Dangie Dewoe, a Voodoo woman, who has the magic power to help her clients to fulfill their wishes. After Hattie tells her wish to her, An' Dangie fetches "a light handful of wish-beans" from "an old tin safe" with "the screw top of a fruit jar" and gives her the instructions about what to do to attain her goal: "Stan' over de gate whar he sleeps and eat dese beans and drop de hulls 'round yo' feet. Ah'll do the rest." (Hurston, 1995a: 106) Then, after Hattie leaves,

> An' Dangie crept to her altar in the back room and began to dress candles with war water. When the altar had been set, she dressed the coffin in red, lit the inverted candles on the altar, saying as she did so, "Now fight! Fight and fuss 'til you part." When all was done at the altar she rubbed her hands and forehead with war powder, put the catbone in her mouth, and laid herself down in the red coffin facing the altar and went into the spirit. (107)

As is expected, Lucy falls seriously ill and dies soon after. Nonetheless, the marriage to John does not bring Hattie happiness she longs for. Without Lucy's guidance, John does not know how to deal with all the troubles in life and work. Frustrated and depressed, he vents on Hattie. They often squabble and he even beats her. So Hattie turns to Voodoo again. Since An' Dangie has died, Hattie goes to another Voodoo doctor for the ways to ruin John's career as a pastor. Although she has kept "feeding" him for years, John comes to know the truth, finds all the "weird objects" she has hidden "in bottles, in red flannels and in toad-skin," and throws them away. In fact, it is a general formula for a Voodoo believer to put strange objects in bottles, or wrap them in red flannels or toad-skins to reach his/her goal of cursing one to bad luck or death. The similar formula is described in *Great American Folklore* by Kemp P. Battle (1986: 258): "Get bad vinegar, beef gall, filet gumbo with red pepper, and put names written across each other in bottles. Shake the bottle for nine mornings and talk and tell it what you want it to do. To kill the victim, turn it upside down and bury it breast deep, and he will die." The Voodoo practices have magical effects. Even if he quits Hattie's practice, John fails to escape from the doom: his divorce with Hattie stains his reputation in the community, which results in his failure in the election of the pastor. (Hurston, 1995a: 135) Leaving the church, John becomes down and out and gets away alone. He dies a tragic death in a car accident. Besides the detailed account of Voodoo practices, the novel gets to the sensitive issue of the white supremacy. It challenges the authority of Christianity not only in that John Pearson, a popular preacher in a Christian church, can do nothing with the magic power of Voodoo practices, but also in that Harris, a deacon in the church, believes that Moses is the "greatest hoodoo man dat God ever made." (124) When asked whether he believes in the mysterious power of the Voodoo conjury, Harris admits frankly:

> Yeah, Ah do, Mrs. Rev'und. Ah done seen things done. Why hit's in de Bible, sister! Look at Moses. He's de greatest hoodoo man dat God ever made. He went 'way from Pharaoh's palace and stayed in de desert nigh on to forty years and learnt how tuh call God by all his secret names and dat's how he got all dat power. He knowed he couldn't bring off all dem people lessen he had power unekal tuh man! How you reckon he brought on all dem plagues if he didn't had nothin' but human power? And then agin his wife wuz Ethiopian. Ah bet she learnt 'im whut he knowed. Ya, indeed, Sister Pearson. De Bible

is de best conjure book in de world. (124)

Comparatively, Voodoo is not so typical in *Their Eyes Were Watching God*. But it is not hard to find one or more examples here. When he suffers from kidney disease and is going to die, Joe Starks refuses to see any good medical doctor but the root-doctor, believing that he will "appear the old-time body" "as soon as the two-headed man found what had been buried against him." (Hurston, 1995d: 240, 242) This incident reflects both Joe's suspicion of Janie and his rooted belief in the miraculous effect of the Voodoo practices. Joe's persistence in relying on the root-doctor is an eloquent proof of the vital force of Voodoo as a living tradition in the Africo-Americans' daily life, notwithstanding its marginal status in the white-dominated American society.

If the Voodoo conjury plays a decisive role in changing the protagonists' fate in Hurston's works, what Alice Walker highlights in her writing is its punishing effect on sins, guilt and social injustice. The title character of her short story "The Revenge of Hannah Kemhuff" is a tough, strong-willed, and self-respecting black woman. Once during the Great Depression, she goes to accept the relief food donated by the US Government but is humiliated and denied any food by Sarah Holley, a white woman working in the town relief station, only because Hannah has not dressed herself up as a beggar. As a consequence, her four children are starved to death and Hannah herself embarks on the road of degeneration. To have Sarah Holley got her retribution and win justice for herself and her family as well, the exhausted Hannah first resorts to God and converts to Christianity so that He will do justice and punish the victimizer. But, much to her disappointment, the white God is completely indifferent to her suffering. She therefore turns to the Voodoo woman Tantie Rosie and is promised that "within a year's time the earth will be rid of the woman." (A. Walker, 1973: 70) Despite the detailed account of the Voodoo practice, such as how to chant the curse words, how to use the black candles, and the like, the story concentrates on how the cursed Sarah Holley, informed of the Voodoo woman's decision to help Hannah take revenge, becomes extremely terrified, goes through a nervous breakdown, and meets with her final tragic death. Tantie tells her assistant to ask Mrs. Holley for the weird objects—her fingernails, stray hairs from her comb, and urine and excrement in barrels and plastic bags in her closet—rather than collect them secretly. What's more, the assistant is allowed to tell the white woman the truth about Hannah's revenge. Of course, Mrs. Holley agrees to offer nothing the Voodoo woman needs. And she sticks in from then on, collecting each of her loose hair, devouring her own nails, allowing nobody to flush her urine and excrement, and storing all the leftovers. Her house begins smelling and even stenching. Subsequently, she goes to pieces, and pays the debt of nature soon after Hanna's death. Like Hurston, Walker believes in the magic power of the Voodoo conjury to help the blacks fulfill their wishes. But, unlike Hurston, who seems to exaggerate the mystery of the conjury more or less, Walker attaches much importance to its psychological effect on the cursed. Mrs. Holley is not cursed but frightened to death. She dies of her own great psychological pressure. If Hurston's writing highlights the popularity of Voodoo and of the black folklore as a whole, Walker's is alive with black people's wit and humor. Along with the protest against the racial discrimination and social injustice in the white society, Walker expresses her respect and admiration for the courage and intelligence of her people.

Just as is stated in the title of one of Walker's essays, "only justice can stop a curse." The Afro-Americans take Voodoo as a weapon to protect themselves, just because there exist so many injustices and inequalities in the American society as well as in the black community that they can do nothing but curse. As a dauntless womanist, Alice Walker never distracts her attention from gender issues within the black race. When Celie, the heroine in *The Color Purple*, eventually makes up her mind to leave Mr. —— and go to Memphis to earn her own living, her husband, flying into a fury, speaks malicious and insulting words to her and threatens to give her a good beating. In the face of his abuse and threat, she curses him, saying "[u]ntil you do right by me, everything you touch will crumble"; "everything you even dream about will fail." (A. Walker, 1982: 213)

These curse words are similar to the Voodoo believers' incantation recorded by Hurston in *Tell My Horse*. Here the punishing effect of Voodoo is underscored again. Evidently, Walker is willing to believe that evil is bound to be rewarded with evil. As an Afro-American woman, she echoes Hurston in the hope that Voodoo will mete out punishment to the villains like Mr. —— and Sarah Holley. In so doing, she expresses both her sympathy for the powerless and her burning desire to do away with the abusers, be it whites or black men.

7.3.2 The Harmony of Animism

Animism is the religious belief that souls or spirits pervade the universe, existing in all creatures—humans and non-humans like animals and plants—and in various objects like rocks and geographic features such as mountains and rivers, and even other entities of the natural environment, including thunder, wind, and shadows. It may further attribute souls to abstract concepts such as words, true names, or metaphors in mythology. Animism holds that there is no separation between the physical (or material) world and the spiritual. It is the oldest known type of belief system in the world. And it is still practiced in a variety of forms in many traditional societies. Animism is used in the anthropology of religion as a term for the belief system of many indigenous tribal peoples, including the African religious tradition. Although each culture has its own different mythologies and rituals, "animism" is said to describe the most common, foundational thread of indigenous peoples' "spiritual" or "supernatural" perspectives. The animistic perspective is so widely held and inherent to most animistic indigenous peoples that they often do not even have a word in their languages that corresponds to "animism" (or even "religion"); the term is an anthropological construct.

In the African tradition, animism is characteristic of nature worship. For Africans, everything in the world is divine, so they—trees, flowers, rivers, mountains, the sea, the sun, the moon, etc. —are all worth respecting and worshiping. Janie in *Their Eyes Were Watching God* has lived in such an animistic world since childhood. She grows up in conversations with grass, gets mature by watching the intimacy between bees and the pear blossom, and finds hopes and gains courage and confidence in the new sun every morning. As divine beings, grass, pear blossom, bees and the sun all carry God's gospel, and guide Janie to understand true love, shake off the chains of traditional marriage and enter the temple of free love. Her spiritual attachment to natural creatures shines with an animistic light. Animism permeates all of Hurston's account of Janie's growth. Janie's is a spiritual world bathed in the black religious tradition. Here human beings are Nature's children and Nature is the softhearted Mother, nurturing humankind. There is an unbreakable interdependent relationship between humankind and Nature. Janie is inspired by the natural phenomena, which witness her maturity, awakening and rebellion. Animism advocates humans' contact, dialogue and communication with Nature. In Janie's eyes, everything in the world has thoughts and feelings. Hurston writes her intuitive understanding of nature into her writing and develops a unique way of looking at life and the world, which brings readers back to the primitive harmony between humankind and nature. If the Voodoo practices unfold a life picture suffused with hatred, racial and sexual, but lacking love, the animistic philosophy creates a sweet, harmonious, and promising world in Hurston's works.

Animism in Hurston's writing is also echoed in the works of Alice Walker, who once claims,

> If there is one thing African-Americans and Native Americans have retained of their African and ancient American heritage, it is probably animism, a belief that makes it possible to view all creation as living, as being inhabited by spirit. This belief encourages knowledge perceived intuitively. It does not surprise me, personally, that scientists now are discovering that trees, plants, flowers, have feelings... emotions, that they shrink when yelled at; that they faint when an evil person is about who might hurt them. (A. Walker, 1983: 252)

Admittedly, Walker is a typical animist. She has internalized the basic idea of animism. On the part of Walker, there is no essential difference between human beings and non-human beings. This is evidenced in *The Color Purple*, which writes in its foreword to the second edition, "[p]erhaps like a pagan, I transform God from an extremely super man into a tree, stars, wind and all other things." (qtd. in Benevol, 1994: 178) Walker's animistic philosophy is based on a comparison with Christianity. She highlights the animistic traits of respecting humanity, worshiping nature and pursuing harmony and equality, while deconstructing the image of the Christian God with a sharp subversion, and unmasking and criticizing the Christian oppresson of humanity. Thanks to animism, Walker has successfully portrayed a series of new black women, who cast off the racial and patriarchal fetters and rebuild the fine spiritual homestead of humankind.

Racism and patriarchy resulted in God's image as a "white man" in the Western traditional culture. This God is not meant to free black women or black people as a whole out of their awful situations. Therefore, Walker's women characters are expected to care about their own feelings and believe in their own beliefs. Just as Celie says it in *The Color Purple*, "us have to find a road going off into the bushes to relieve ourselves." (A. Walker, 1982: 212) What has happened to Celie makes anyone with a conscience shocked and infurited. Even so, she dare not resist because God say that one (a woman) must honor her parents and obey her husband at all events. She has nobody to tell her grievance and misery but God, whom she has piously believed in since childhood. She keeps writing to Him in the hope that she might receive His protection and blessing; yet she receives no reply. Her "benevolent" God just listen to her complaints silently and watch her suffering serenely. He neither tell her how to protect herself nor punish the villains Himself. He "act just like all the other" white men Celie knows, who care about black women's suffering in no circumstances and will of course uphold their justice by no means. (199) What He give to Celie is just "a lynched daddy, a crazy mama, a lowdown dog of a step pa and a sister probably I (Celie) won't ever see again." (199) She is thus impelled to study her God again and is pained to discover that He turns out to be a "big and old and tall and graybearded and white" man. (201) Accordingly, Celie revises her own notion of God and accepts Shug's—"God ain't a he or a she, but a It"; "It ain't something you can look at apart from anything else, including yourself." (202) Celie's acceptance of the new notion of God is attributed to Shug's inspiration and guidance. As Mae Henderson (1989: 73) points it out, "[u]nlike Celie, who derives her sense of self from the dominant white and male theology, Shug is a self-invented character whose sense of self is not male-inscribed. Her theology allows a divine, self-authorized sense of self. Shug's conception of God is both imminent and transcendent." To put it simply, Shug is an animist instead of a Christian. Through the mouth of the animist Shug, the author expresses her own understanding of God, "God is inside you and inside everybody else. You come into the world with God. But only them that search for it inside find it. And sometimes it just manifest itself even if you not looking, or don't know what you looking for. ... God is everything, ... Everything that is or ever was or ever will be. And when you can feel that, and be happy to feel that, you've found it." (A. Walker, 1982: 202 – 203) God, for an animist, exists not simply in everything in the nature but also in every individual in the human world. God is everything, and every thing and every body has God inside. It just depends on the individual himself/herself whether or not there is God inside him/her. Everyone is everyone's God; everyone is a divine being. Obviously, in advocating animism, Walker virtually declares freedom, autonomy, self-reliance, and self-improvement. That is why the acceptance of Shug's notion of God becomes a turning point of Celie's life.

In the novel, Walker creates one other animist Nettie to convince Celie of the existence of an interior, self-invented genderless God and help her fulfil her conversion from Christianity to animism. In her letter to Celie, she affirms: "God is different to us now, after all these years in Africa. More spirit than ever before, and more internal." (264) As an American missionary in Africa, Nettie tells Celie her perception of God concluded from her nearly thirty-years' practice and eventually persuades Celie to try experiencing "that feeling of being part of everything, not separate at all." (203) And Celie succeeds: "I (Celie) knew that if I cut a tree, my arm would bleed. And I laughed and I cried and I run all around the house. I knew just what it was." (203) The moment Celie gets the "feeling of being part of everything," that is, she becomes an animist, marks the beginning of her rebellion and her new life. She determinedly leaves Mr. —— and goes to Memphis, where she not only lives a self-sufficient life but also owns her own business. An animist, confident, optimistic, and self-reliant, Celie is the master of her life at last. It is in the process of self-perception, self-perfection and self-development that Celie embraces the Afro-American God, the integration of nature with humanity.

Deconstructing the image of God is the core of Walker's animistic philosophy. The image of the Christian God is negated again in the Mundo traditional animism-based religion in *By the Light of My Father's Smile*. The Mundo God is the sun rather than the white moody Christian God. The Mundo take trees and wind as humans' familiars. As the Mundo young man Manuelito states it, the Mundo believe that "[t]he cathedral of the future will be nature" and that, "[i]n the end, people will be driven back to trees," to "streams," and to "rocks that do not have anything built on them." (A. Walker 1998: 193) That humans, like everything in the universe, are part of nature is emphasized once again here. For the Mundo, nature is what humans depend on for survival, so humans should pay tribute to nature. Different from the Western traditional concept that mankind is the supreme of all creation, the Mundo notion encompasses obvious ecological significance, which in turn affects their perception of gender roles. In the Mundo tradition, men and women are equal; women are the incarnation of nature and "the mother of corn"; they are great and divine and synonymous with good luck. As a matter of course, the Mundo accept it "the biggest lie" of white Christians that "woman could be considered evil" because of "her original sin of eating the forbidden fruit." (81) Evidently, Walker, reinterpreting God's image from the animistic perspective, attempts to overset the Christian view on gender and remove the mental blocks to women's emancipation. In the meantime, her animistic philosophy, respecting women and nature, questions the Christian practice of stressing rationality and suppressing emotion.

7.3.3 The Mystery of the Other Superstitious Beliefs

Religion is characteristic of superstition. The Afro-American religion is no exception. Both Voodoo and animism have supernatural powers as their cornerstones. Nonetheless, the word "superstition" is generally used to refer to the religion practiced by the minority of a given society. Hence the third group of the religious folkloric materials, namely, some other "superstitious" beliefs, along with Voodoo and animism. Superstition is the belief in supernatural causality—that one event causes another without any natural process linking the two events. To put it differently, superstition is a belief or notion, not based on reason or fact or knowledge but on association of ideas, as in magic. Superstitious beliefs and practices often thrive in rural or backward areas. They are quite influential and have long been an indispensable part of the local people's life. Usually set in the rural south of the United States, Hurston's and Walker's works cannot dispense with such superstitious beliefs and practices. Steeped in the typical Afro-American religion, the two black women authors are familiar with the superstitious practices of the local folks and skillful in handling the raw materials in their writing.

In this regard, *Jonah's Gourd Vine* is again a good illustration. Lucy Potts' dying request for her daughter Isis is taken from Hurston's personal experience, which stems from the superstitious version in Eatonville, the author's hometown. According to the local custom, the pillow under the head of a dying person must be taken away just before he/she breathes his/her last breath. Only by so doing can the dying die easy. Besides, to prevent the dying from leaving a bad luck to the family, the clock(s) and the mirror(s) within sight must be covered. Hurston's mother did not want to follow the custom while she was dying, so she told Hurston to stop it, believing her daughter would not make her disappointed. However, Hurston was just a nine-year-old girl. Nobody would listen to her, though she tried her best to do what her mother told her to. She failed in the end. Troubled by the lasting repentance, the author copies the scene into the novel:

"Irie, when Ahm dyin' don't you let 'em take de pillow from under mah head, and be covering up de clock and de lookin' glass and all sich ez dat. Ah don't want it done, heah? Ahm tellin' you in preference tuh de rest 'cause Ah know you'll see tuh it." (Hurston 1995a: 110) Similarly, things do not happen as Lucy liked. Although she does her best to follow her mother's dying words, Isis does not stop her father from taking the pillow under her mother's head away. She feels so sorry and so guilty that, "[a]s her father pulled her away from her place above Lucy's head, Isis thought her mother's eyes followed her and she strained her ears to catch her words." (113) This insertion at once expresses the author's own guilt and self-accusation of not fulfilling her mother's last wishes and faithfully represents the spiritual outlook of the local folks in the southern American communities so that the daughter's deep remorse is imbued with the strong local color.

Hurston's short story "Spunk," set in a place of Florida, which is similar to Hurston's hometown, is also rich in religious and superstitious color. The title character has an affair with a villager's wife. Humiliated and infuriated, the husband tries to assassinate him but is killed by Spunk instead. Soon after the husband's death, the killer moves to the wife. On their first night together, a big black cat appears around their house. Like the other villagers, Spunk believes that the dead husband has revived in the black cat to take revenge on him. In the days ahead, he becomes uneasy and restless and lives in panic. Consequently, he falls down on the sawteeth one day while at work and dies a dog's death. Before his death, he tells the villagers that the husband has pushed him from behind. Spunk's death is a corollary of his belief in "revival after death." It illustrates how black religion curses sin and punishes the wicked. The story is therefore a thriller shining with the light of justice.

In fact, superstitious beliefs and practices spread over Hurston's fiction, particularly *Their Eyes Were Watching God* and *Jonah's Gourd Vine*. Some other characteristic ones include the booger man (an evil spirit) invented by the black adults to scare children into obedience in the former, and the spider on the wall foretelling Lucy's death and Ole Pheemy's burying John's "nable string" under a "chanyberry tree" in the latter, to name just a few. (19) Each belief or practice is wrapped in mystery and closely related to the believers' life. For instance, by burying a newborn's nable string under a chosen tree, the parents hope to bring good luck to the baby. And ever since then, the child's life is inseparate from the tree's. He/She is obliged to protect the tree from being damaged or chopped down, or else, he/she will meet bad luck. All superstitious beliefs reflect the Afro-Americans' view of life as well as death. Perhaps that is why they have been transmitted from generation to generation and continue to thrive in the southern religious climate, despite their lack of reason.

As is expounded in the previous sections, Walker's texts revise and transcend Hurston's rather than repeat and imitate them only. While Hurston's interpretation and exploitation of the black superstitious customs still rest on the representation of the black folk culture, and her works are centered on the transformation of the individuals' fate and emotion, Walker appears to pay more attention to the social issues mirrored in black people's adherence to or rejection of the customs. Thus the junior offers readers the possibility to experience an amazing shock in heart and rethink the future of the black race. Her short story "Strong Horse Tea" recounts a tale about a black woman Rannie Toomer, who tries to save her son's life by every means. Although living in the southern black community of the United States, Rannie rejects blacks and does not want to make contact with any of them. She blindly believes white people, including each lie in their brochures. She believes that the white postman will send anything she wants free of charge once she asks him to. She lives a poor, benighted, and helpless life. Her son is all that she lives for. However, nothing is so certain as the unexpected. Her son has caught pneumonia and whooping cough, and is badly in need of medical treatment. Although the black woman Sarah has an effective folk remedy for her son's disease, Rannie refuses to try it. Instead, she resorts to the white postman in the hope that he will "deliver" a white doctor to her. After begging him time and time again, and receiving nothing but disappointment from him each time, Rannie seems to understand that it is impossible for the white postman to agree to help her. Just when her son is dying, she is impelled to have Aunt Sarah try the folk remedy. Unfortunately, when she goes out to look for the weird object needed—"strong horse tea" (i. e., the urine of a horse)—in the rain, when she finds it and scoops a shoeful of it and is about to go back home, her son breathes his last breath and leaves her forever. Rannie's is not just her personal tragedy but also that of the black race. Enslaved by the white ideology, she despises blacks and negates the black culture. She lacks her own thought and has no dignity. She is fully unaware of the postman's deception and contempt. Her tragedy not simply lies in her belief in white people but also in her rejection of black people, the black folk remedy and the black culture. Rannie is representative of those blacks who admire the white culture blindly. Her refusal and denial of the black folk remedy plunges her into the rootless state, a state of no ethnic identity. Rannie's story reveals the cultural crisis the Afro-Americans are confronted with. It warns the black race that abandoning traditional culture is tantamount to digging their own graves. The frustration of the black folk healer in "Strong Horse Tea" awakens the identity consciousness of the Afro-Americans on the one hand, and appeals for their united effort to carry forward the black folk culture on the other.

Argus-eyed, Hurston and Walker catch the truest part of black religion, be it Voodoo or animism or some other superstitious beliefs. They both think highly of the black traditional religious beliefs and devote themselves to the identity propagation through absorbing the traditional ritual elements into their fiction-writing and/or exploring the cultural issues hidden in the Afro-Americans' attitudes toward the religious tradition. In so doing, they not simply present the charm of black religion but also call on the Afro-Americans to stick to their ethnic religion and strengthen their ethnic identity.

7.4 The Artistic Folkloric Materials in Hurston's and Walker's Fiction

As a significant component of folk culture, the artistic folklore refers to the tradition or customs—existing in the art forms like music and dance—developed by an ethnic group to express thought and emotion. The black folkloric art forms mainly include black music, black dance and patchwork quilting. Closely bound up with black people's life and labor, these art forms are characteristically natural, lively and simple. They serve as a channel for the people to reflect thought and emotional attachment and get spiritual solace. Deprived of the educational opportunity, most blacks practically had no access to written language and had to rely on oral expression and body movement to communicate with each other or convey ideas and feelings, or to amuse themselves. Naturally, music, dance and quilting become popular in the southern Afro-American communities. Full of deep love for the black folk culture, Hurston and Walker take great interest in black art and seize every chance to display its charm. Consequently, black music and dance and quilting dot their novels and stories.

7.4.1 Black Music

Black music fused in Hurston's and Walker's fiction falls into two broad categories: the folk music represented by blues and the religious music represented by spirituals. Blues was born on the plantations in the Deep South of the United States around the end of the 19th century. It is rooted in African musical traditions, Afro-American work songs and Euro-American folk music. Having incorporated work songs, field hollers, shouts, chants, and rhymed simple narrative ballads, blues is characterized by the call-and-response pattern and sometimes cannot be separated from the religious music distinctly. The early traditional blues verse consisted of a single line repeated four times. It was only in the early twentieth century that the most common current structure became standard: the AAB pattern, consisting of a line sung over the four first bars, its repetition over the next four, and then a longer concluding line over the last bars. Blues belongs in the category of common people's music, as it used to relate the troubles experienced in the Afro-American society. It lays emphasis more on the expression of emotions than on the sound effect. The call-and-response format usually presents a harmonious picture of an individual's pouring out the bitterness and the crowd's offering comfort.

Hurston weaves the blues patterns seamlessly into the narration of *Their Eyes Were Watching God*. On the one side, the story is told in flashback: Janie relates her life story while her friend Pheoby listens to her and makes comments from time to time. Then, more importantly, she retells Janie's story to the villagers (the crowd) so that they could understand Janie and show compassion for her. Thus the novel follows the call-and-response pattern of blues. Here Pheoby is a bridge between Janie and the black community. As a listener, she approves of Janie's choice, including her shooting Tea Cake, and gives her moral support. As a spreader of Janie's story, she would retell it according to her own understanding in the hope that Janie will not be censured for what she has done (especially her marriage to Tea Cake and her final choice to kill him) by the villagers. Only then can their black sisters get inspiration from Janie's experience and intend to pursue their own dreams. On the other side, Janie's three marriages follow the AAB pattern of blues in the sense that her first two marriages are both characterized by the male oppression—the only difference is that the first oppression is physical while the second is spiritual—and the third is based on true love and equality: Janie is free and happy in the last marriage. The three husbands' social status, their attitudes toward the black culture and their relationships with Janie all, without exception, correspond to the AAB pattern of blues.

Similarly, Walker designs a three-stage life, in parallel with the blues AAB pattern, for Celie in *The Color Purple*. Before marriage, Celie, raped by her stepfather at the age of fourteen, is always on tenterhooks because of his threat and her mother's suspicion. With her son and daughter given away by their father (the raper), she tastes the pain of losing children to the full. Subsequently, she is sold to the widower Mr. —— as wife, and thus begins her life as a maidservant and sex object. During her married life, she is often abused and beaten by her husband. In the two stages of her life, Celie serves two different masters (first her stepfather then her husband) but leads a similar miserable life. The unutterable physical and mental torture surrenders her to the masters' despotic power. She has learned to be numb and obedient. The appearance of the blues singer Shug starts Celie's new life—the third stage of her life. Shug's enlightenment and friendship bring Celie courage and strength, and awaken her self-esteem and confidence. She comes to be no longer coward, voiceless, or long-suffering and uncomplaining. She not only gains independence in personality, and dares to love and hate, but also has her own successful business and becomes financially independent.

Blues is an oral and non-material cultural heritage and embodies the Afro-Americans' collective wisdom. Acknowledged as the quintessence of the ethnic culture, it is widely sung by the Afro-Americans. The two black blues singers—Shug Avery and Mary Agnes—in *The Color Purple* have a passion for singing blues. Their life is filled with blues. They cannot do without singing. Ms. Walker (1983: 234) once expresses the impossibility of their people's life without singing by questioning "what might have been the result if singing, too, had been forbidden by law." Indeed, singing blues is not simply a life habit of the black women like Shug and Mary, but also an effective approach to express their inner feelings and eliminate their physical fatigue. By singing blues, they "bring together the transformative powers of feminist polities and the African American blues matrix." (Winter, 1997: 53) Thus the blues singers actually launch a war against the objectification and oppression of women within the patriarchal order and attempt to create women's independent subject position in the man-woman relationship. For the Afro-Americans, the blues music is variously a refuge, a cry from the heart, a flag of defiance and a token of freedom. It provides the blacks with a special forum, where they resist oppression, pursue independence, and realize self-fulfillment, where they get indulged in reveries about their bright future. In this sense, *The Color Purple* is a full set of blues music. It presents black women's strong will and their unremitting efforts to achieve self-worth, and therefore crystallizes the author's compassion for her black sisters and deep feeling towards the black ethnic culture. By depicting the performance of the blues singers, Walker demonstrates the core-and-soul position of the blues music in the Afro-American culture.

As a product of the oppressed culture, blues is "a comprehensive reflection of language intersecting with economic system, political hierarchy, theology, sexuality as well as all the other aspects of the Afro-Ameircan life." (程锡麟, 1994: 171) It is a linguistic response of the Afro-Americans to the white cultural oppression. Whether through imitating the structural pattern of blues or through depicting the singing itself, Hurston and Walker reveal the fact that blues is a black cultural phenomenon rooting in the southern American soil and that it is not a dream but a living reality originating in the Afro-American communities. Giving full play to the negritude of blues, they increase the artistic appeal and mental penetrating power of their works and display the innate artistic talent and cultural awareness of the black folks. Ultimately, they gain their ends of disseminating the black traditional culture.

Spirituals (or Negro spirituals) are generally religious hymns or Christian songs that were adapted from black music by African slaves in the United States. They were originally an oral tradition that imparted Christian values while also describing the hardships of slavery. They are usually Afro-American interpretations of the Bible stories according to their own circumstances. Improvised, spirituals are short, full of melody and sense of beauty, and have a clear-cut rhythm. The common musical structure includes the repartee and the refrain. As carriers of blacks' inner feelings, spirituals integrate religion with secularity. They are characterized by the grand vigor of religious music and the worldly passion of folk music. In *Their Eyes Were Watching God*, when she notices her granddaughter Janie date an idle black youth, Nanny falls into despair and agony, worrying that Janie would follow in both her and her daughter's footsteps, and get impregnated before marriage and have a child, whose father might be an unreliable and irresponsible man. To stop the similar tragedy befalling Janie, the helpless grandmother begins to sing spirituals. She "half sung, half sobbed a running chant-prayer... Lawd have mercy! It was a long time on de way but Ah reckon it had to come. Oh Jesus! Ah done de best Ah could." (Hurston, 1995d: 186) Through singing, Nanny attempts to feel the power of the Lord and prays for His help and salvation. And, through singing, she could easily get herself to calm down. As a matter of fact, the old woman almost invariably sings spirituals when she is in trouble and needs help. Singing spirituals could at once aid Nanny in acquiring inner peace and bring her the hope to live on. Likewise, black Americans express delight and celebrate holidays or special events by singing spirituals. In the novel, when the first street lamp the Mayor buys with his own money appears before the townspeople, it is first put up "on a showcase for a week for everbody to see. Then he (Joe, the Mayor) set a time for the lighting and sent word all around Orange County for one and all to come to the lamp-lighting." (209) At the ceremony of the lamp-lighting, all the townspeople cannot help but sing a spiritual:

We'll walk in de light, de beautiful light
Come where the dew drops of mercy shine bright
Shine all around us by day and by night
Jesus, the light of the world. (211)

They sing it over and over. The joyful song carries the townspeople's desire for a bright future and their passion for the traditional ethnic music. It also adds a strong local flavor to the novel.

If Hurston's text is more or less confined to the religious content in choosing spirituals, Walker's boldly displays their secularity and realistic effects. In *Meridian*, at the open-air funeral for The Wild Child, whose casket is forbidden to be carried into the campus chapel, Meridian and her schoolmates in Saxon College sing their self-produced spiritual through tears:

We shall overcome...
We shall overcome...
We shall overcome, someday...

Deep in my heart, I do believe..

We shall overcome, someday... (A. Walker, 1976: 48)

Despite its exquisite refrains, the verse completely gives up the religious content in the traditional spirituals. It betrays neither the students' awe for the Lord nor their prayer for His help and salvation. All that it encompasses is their revolutionary enthusiasm and high morale, and their resolution to win a victory over the oppressor represented by the president. As the female intellectuals of modern times, the students in Saxon College know well that God is not meant to change the social injustice and that only through their own struggle can they gain justice and equality. The funeral for The Wild Child is practically their protest against the college authority and marks the beginning of their struggle for their own rights. Through singing the special spiritual, the students both defend the dignity of the dead and show concern for the future of the living. They sing their hearts out and the singing is their cry from the depths of their souls. Touching the hearts and souls of the audiences, the singing causes a strong psychological resonance of the Afro-Americans, and thus strengthens their resolve to fight for equal rights and their confidence to build a better future. By enlarging the secularity of the negro spirituals, Walker implants her womanism in the rich soil of the black folk culture and thus offers it an opportunity to take root and yield positive results.

7.4.2 Black Dance and Patchwork Quilting

The Afro-Americans are not just good at singing but also dancing. They have enjoyed the world reputation for their extraordinary gifts as both singers and dancers. Whether at weddings and funerals, or at festivals and holidays, or during breaks and after work, they cannot help dancing as long as the drum or music starts. They express their emotions and desires with the rhythms and movements of their bodies. The Afro-Americans have a long history of folk dances like the fire dance, the jump dance, to name just a few. It was in the company of dance as well as music that they went through the long, dull and harsh life as slaves on the strange continent. Dance constitutes an important part of the Afro-American popular art. It is another illustration of Hurston's love for the black folklore to absorb black dance into her literary creation, which is an important channel to display the beauty and charm of the black folk culture.

In *Jonah's Gourd Vine*, the author depicts a scene of the black workhands' carnival. On the Pearson plantation, where the hero John works, when the cotton is picked, the master Alf Pearson allows John and his workfellows to celebrate the harvest, giving them two hogs to barbecue. After the big barbecue with the negroes from three other plantations, they begin to sing and dance joyously. When the carnival begins, a man named Bully cries out, "Hey you, dere, us ain't no white folk! Put down dat fiddle! Us don't want no fiddles, neither no guitars, neither no banjoes. Less clap!" (Hurston, 1995a: 28 – 29) Subsequently, some beat the drums brought from Africa, and others sing and dance to their rhythm. Different types of drums, beaten in different ways, produce different rhythmical tones and sounds. "With their hands they played upon the little dance drums of Africa. The drums of kid-skin. With their feet they stomped it, and the voice of Kata-Kumba, the great drum, lifted itself within them and they heard it. The great drum that is made by priests and sits in majesty in the juju house. The drum with the man skin that is dressed with human blood, that is beaten with a human shin-bone and speaks to gods as a man and to men as a God. They beat upon the drum and danced." (29) The drum effectively controls the mood and movements of the dancers. Intoxicated with the transient pleasure and happiness, the workhands sing and dance until deep into the night, though they will continue their struggle for survival the next day. The cheerful scene, suffused with a rich artistic flavor, intensifies all the participants' sense of identity.

Echoing the carnival, the author gives a picture of John's funeral at the end of the novel. The drum here is also an important prop to express the mourners' sorrows. "They beat upon the O-go-doe, the ancient drum. O-go-doe, O-go-doe, O-go-doe! Their hearts turned to fire and their shin-bones leaped unknowing to the drum. Not Kata-Kumba, the drum of triumph, that speaks of great ancestors and glorious wars. Not the little drum of kid-skin, for that is to dance with joy and to call to mind birth and creation, but O-go-doe, the voice of Death—that promises nothing, that speaks with tears only, and of the past." (168) The funeral is ended "[w]ith the drumming of the feet, and the mournful dance of the heads, in rhythm." (168) Opposite as they are, the two scenes obviously share the author's writing intention of highlighting the richness of African drum culture and the popularity of black dance. The Afro-Americans use different types of drums to convey their moods and emotions on different occasions. Sold to the southern America as slaves, they made every effort to get their drum and dance culture preserved. The drum is the soul of blacks and black dance. Where there is the African drum, there is black dance. As a trope of the native African culture, the drum and black dance are practically respected as the Afro-Americans' spiritual habitat all the time.

Black dance is "not only a recreational activity of self-entertainment but also an integral part of the social activities." (艾周昌, 1999: 231) Characterized by "sociality and popularity," it embraces the connotation of the black folk carnival culture. (233) In the latter half of *Their Eyes Were Watching God*, Hurston gives a detailed account of Janie's happy life with her third husband Tea Cake, a guitar player and blues singer. As a black youth, Tea Cake epitomizes the desirable qualities like vigor, vitality, self-confidence, and rebellion. He operates outside the white standards of a "good" Negro, as he is neither hard-working nor obedient. He works just to earn enough money to last for a few days and then starts to enjoy himself. He is portrayed as a carefree and optimistic music lover, with "guitar hanging round his neck with a red silk cord and a grin hanging from his ears." (Hurston, 1995d: 273) After meeting and falling in love with Tea Cake, Janie resolutely leaves Eatonville, giving up the wealthy and comfortable town life, and follows him to the Everglades marshland. Though she undergoes the fatigue of laboring in the field, Janie lives a meaningful and pleasurable life. Different from the confined porch life, she can join the blacks in picking beans and enjoy the rich and happy night life with the local residents. After the hard work in the daytime, the blacks in the Everglades get together, entertaining themselves. "All night now the jooks clanged and clamored. Pianos living three lifetimes in one. Blues made and used right on the spot. Dancing, fighting, singing, crying, laughing, winning and losing love every hour." (282) The night life in the marshland brings Janie the unprecedented freedom and happiness, not just because she and her husband play a dominant role among the revelers, but also because she is free to choose to listen or to laugh or even to interrupt if she likes. "Work all day for money, fight all night for love"—this is a true portrayal of the life of Janie and the other people in the Everglades. (282) The freewheeling lifestyle and the friendly carnival scene present a utopia of liberty and equality, which reifies the Afro-Americans' dream of a healthy and harmonious society. Focusing on the carnival scene produced by black dance rather than on the dance movement and its artistic value, the novel reinforces the uniqueness and vitality of the black carnival culture in the marshland as well as the amusement of black dance in the daily life of the ethnic group.

In brief, as one of the prominent characteristics of Hurston's fiction, the insertion of black dance realistically reflects the Afro-Americans' life attitude and spiritual world. Through the vivid depiction of drumming, singing and dancing, Hurston not only expresses her approval of black art and her resistance to the white cultural assimilation of the black folk culture but also demonstrates the cohesive force of black art in building a close relationship within the black communities. By emphasizing the vivacity of the black folk life, the author eulogizes the tough spirit of the rural Afro-Americans to promote humanity as against white inhumanity.

While Hurston discovered the cultural root of the Afro-Americans in their music and dance, and caught the strong spirit conceived in black art, Walker reads the black sisterhood and black people's hope in the artistic form of patchwork quilting. The origins of quilting remain unknown but the sewing techniques of piecing, appliqué and quilting have been used for clothing and furnishings in diverse parts of the world for several millennia. Patchwork quilting in America dates to the 1770s, the decade the United States gained its independence from England. It became popular in the American colonies in the nineteenth century and gradually developed into a cultural custom. As a traditional skill, patchwork quilting is supposed to be acquired by the female adults. Each grown woman must make a patchwork quilt for herself, which will be used as her own dowry. Moreover, if a woman gets married, the women in the same community will hold a quilting bee to make a wedding quilt for her. Therefore, the multicolored patchwork quilt is not just a symbol of a girl's puberty and adulthood but also the crystallization of women's collective wisdom. It at once carries the kinsfolk's best wishes and great expectations, and embraces the deep sisterhood and the national emotions among the women in the community.

The Afro-American quilting has a long tradition, beginning with quilts made by slaves, both for themselves and for their owners. During the early period, the style of these quilts was determined largely by time period and region, rather than race, and the documented slave-made quilts generally resemble those made by white women in their region. After 1865 and the end of slavery in the United States, the Afro-Americans began to develop their own distinctive style of quilting. In their culture, patchwork quilting, like blues, is an important component of the black aesthetic tradition. Symbolizing friendship, solidarity and harmony, it is a common theme of the literary works by the Afro-American women writers of modern times. For instance, in the short story "Everyday Use for Your Grandmamma" by Alice Walker, the central image is the two patchwork quilts made by Grandma Dee and then Aunt Dee (Big Dee) and Mother (me). "One was in the Lone Star pattern. The other was Walk Around the Mountain. In both of them were scraps of dresses Grandma Dee had worn fifty and more years ago. Bits and pieces of Grandpa Jarrell's Paisley shirts. And one teeny faded blue piece, about the size of a penny matchbox, that was from Great Grandpa Ezra's uniform that he wore in the Civil War." (A. Walker, 1973: 56) A remembrance of the family ancestry, the quilts epitomize the hard work and painstaking effort of Grandma, Aunt and Mother, and embody their rich imagination and extraordinary artistic talent. In this sense, they symbolize the accumulation of the Afro-Americans' spiritual culture and witness their pursuit of liberty and beauty. In a word, they are both the transmitter of the family history and affection, and the witness of the (grand)mothers' wisdom and genius. Therefore preserving the quilts means not only protecting the family history and appreciating the (grand)mothers' artistic talent and aesthetic taste, but also recognizing the Afro-American identity and taking over the black folk culture. For Walker, true art not only represents its culture, but also is an inseparable part of that culture; only if it remains connected to its culture can art have meaning.

For the Afro-American women, patchwork quilting is a way of releasing their feelings, displaying their artistic creativity, and exploring their spiritual space. *The Color Purple* presents a couple of harmonious pictures of Celie making patchwork quilts with other characters like Shug and Sofia. The one in which Celie sits between Shug and Mr. —— is the most impressive. As Celie herself recalls it, "[f]or the first time in my life, I feel just right." (A. Walker, 1982: 60) Although Mr. —— does not change her attitude toward Celie, he is seated by her after all. This episode unwittingly prepares the way for Mr. ——'s later transformation. Patchwork quilting is a metaphor of sisterhood in the novel. The quilters, usually a group of black women (sometimes including black men like Mr. —— as well), sit together, designing, cutting, and quilting. Getting closer to each other, they begin opening their hearts and telling their stories. Quilting together offers a communicative platform for both Celie and Sofia and Shug. The more they know about each other, the more they are willing to share their joys and sorrows with each other, and to help each other, the more easily they develop a deep sisterhood between them. As is analyzed earlier in this book, sisterhood is the spiritual pillar of the women characters like Celie, Sofia, Mary Agnes as well as Shug. In brief, patchwork quilting makes it possible for the women characters to display their artistic talent on the one hand; on the other, it helps them retrieve the long-lost trust, intimacy and harmony; they begin feeling warm and secure, and ultimately have a happy and harmonious family reunion.

On the part of Walker, patchwork quilting is not simply an epitome of national emotion and cultural memory but also an embodiment of an aesthetic ideology and a narrative strategy, which can construct the cultural position and discourse space of the Afro-Americans. The fragmented plot of *Meridian* results from the patchwork-quilting narrative. Throughout the novel, in addition to the stories about Meridian, there are numerous embedded fragments, which are seemingly irrelevant to the plot development. They include the funeral for Martin Luther King, Jr., Meridian's great-grandmother's experience of ecstasy at the Sacred Serpent, the history of Meridian's family, some folktales, and the like. These fragments are collaged together deceptively at random so that they look like digressions, which lack coherence within the context. However, just as Barbara Christian (1993: 50) comments it, the author "takes seemingly ragged edges and arranges them into works of functional though terrifying beauty." Consequently, the novel, like a multicolored patchwork quilt of various-shaped pieces of cloth stitched together, not just keeps a record of every unforgettable history, but also provides a complete picture of the Civil Rights Movement. With the "bits and pieces" originating in the south, Alice Walker "concentrate[s] on the sensibility of the South as a way of perceiving the perennial conflict between the human spirit and societal patterns." (Christian, 1993: 50) She seems to suggest that the cause of civil rights Meridian is devoted to is beset with difficulties and the outlook for it is still clouded, as she "has long insisted that until the solids and prints of the South are sorted out and stitched into clarity, the relationship in this country between men and women, blacks and whites, will continue in disarray." (50)

The enslavement of the Afro-Americans has determined their longtime subordinate position and state of "aphasia." Hence, their awakening and awareness of identity are surely expressed in their approval and acceptance of the ethnic culture. The great Afro-American poet Langston Hughes once pointed out that, if it wanted to get out of its long-term marginalized state of "aphasia," the black culture had to boldly display its ethnic characteristics before the white. The absorption of a myriad of black folkloric elements into Hurston's and Walker's fiction not simply proves their strong sense of national pride and ethnic identity, but also indicates that the black literature is a major platform for the Afro-Americans to demonstrate and publicize their ethnic culture in the Euro-American cultural context.

Acclaiming Hurston as her "literary mother," Alice Walker has made great contributions to Hurston's revival. She not only rediscovered Hurston and her literary achievements but also models her literary writing on Hurston's. She adheres to Hurston's great concern for the black folk culture in particular. Their folk literary works do not aim to satisfy the curiosity of the white readers about the so-called "primitive" culture, but to deconstruct the white cultural hegemony, and to articulate Afro-Americans' desire to reconstruct their black cultural identity and build their national identity as Americans. Only with their cultural identity restored can the Afro-Americans construct their national identity or charm away their fractured identity (double consciousness in Du Bois' term). Neither do they desire to Africanize America nor do they want to "bleach" their souls and be assimilated into the white American culture. They just want to transmit their African folk cultural heritage or, to be exact, their Afro-American folklore. By celebrating the unique Afro-American folk culture, Hurston and Walker tend to enhance their national pride and reinforce their sense of community. In this sense, they have created a spiritual habitat for the hopeless and helpless Afro-Americans in the white hostile world. Meanwhile, their fiction might press for the Euro-Americans to reevaluate Afro-American culture and reflect on the cultural differences between the races and ultimately take more effective measures to solve the racial issues in the American society so that there will stand an ideal country, as is described in the US constitution: "That all men are created equal; that they are endowed by their Creator with certain unalienable rights; that among these are life, liberty, and the pursuit of happiness."

Bibliography

Abbandonato, Linda. "Rewriting the Heroine's Story in *The Color Purple*." *Alice Walker: Critical Perspectives Past and Present*. Ed. Henry Louis Gates, Jr. & K. A. Appiah. New York: Amistad Press, Inc., 1993. 296 – 308.

Andrews, William L., et al (Frances Smith Foster, Trudier Harris) ed. *The Concise Oxford Companion to African American Literature*. New York: Oxford University Press, 2001.

Awkward, Michael. *Negotiating Difference: Race, Gender, and the Politics of Positionality*. Chicago: University of Chicago Press, 1995.

Awkward, Michael. "A Black Man's Place in Black Feminist Criticism." *African American Literary Theory: A Reader*. Ed. Winston Napier. New York & London: New York University Press, 2000. 540 – 556.

Bambara, Toni Cade. Foreword. *This Bridge Called My Back: Writings by Radical Women of Color*. Ed. Cherrie Moraga & Glorie Anzalda. New York: KITCHEN TABLE: Women of Color Press, 1981. vi – viii.

Barker, Deborah E. "Visual Markers: Art and Mass Media in Alice Walker's *Meridian*." *African American Review* 31.3 (1997): 463 – 479.

Baker, Houston A. Jr. *The Journey Back*. Chicago: University of Chicago Press, 1998.

Bartelme, Elizabeth. "Victory over Bitterness." *Commonweal* CX. 3 (1983): 92 – 95.

Bartky, Sandra Lee. "Bosy Politics." *A Companion to Feminist Philosophy*. Ed. Alison M. Jaggar & Iris Marion Young. Malden, MA: Blackwell Publishing, 1998. 321 – 29.

Bates, Gerri. *Alice Walker: A Critical Companion*. London: Greenwood Press, 2005.

Battle, Kemp P. *Great American Folklore: Legends, Tales, Ballads, and Superstitions from All across America*. New York: Doubleday and Co., 1986.

Bell, Bernard W. *The Afro-American Novel and Its Tradition*. Amherst: The University of Massachusetts Press, 1987.

Benda, Julien. *Le rapport d'Uriel*. Arles: Actes Sud, 1992.

Benevol, Dina. *Excel Studies in Literature: Alice Walker's The Color Purple*. New South Wales: Pascal Press, 1994.

Berlant, Lauren. "Race, Gender, and Nation in *The Color Purple*." *Alice Walker: Critical Perspectives Past and Present*. Ed. Henry Louis Gates, Jr. & K. A. Appiah. New York: Amistad Press, Inc., 1993. 211 – 238.

Boggs, Ralph Steele. "Folklore: Materials, Science, Art." *Folklore Americas*. June 1943.

Bradley, David. "Telling the Black Woman's Story." *New York Times Magazine* 1 (1984): 29 – 37.

Brewer, Krister. "Writing to Survive: An Interview with Alice Walker." *Southern Exposure* 9 (1981): 12 – 15.

Brickell, Herschel. "Review of *Jonah's Gourd Vine*." *New York Post*, May 5, 1934.

Brock, H. R. "Review of *Jonah's Gourd Vine*." *New York Times Book Review*, November 10, 1935.

Bunch, Charlotte. *Passionate Politics, Essays 1968 – 1986*. New York: St. Martin's, 1987.

Butler, Robert James. "Making a Way Out of No Way: The Open Journey in Alice Walker's *The Third Life of Grange Copeland*." *Black American Literature Forum* 22.1 (1988): 65 – 79.

Butler, Robert James. "Alice Walker's Vision of the South in *The Third Life of Grange Copeland*." *African American Review* 27.2 (1993): 195 – 204.

Butler-Evans, Elliott. "History and Genealogy in Walker's *The Third Life of Grange Copeland* and *Meridian*." *Alice Walker: Critical Perspectives Past and Present*. Ed. Henry Louis Gates, Jr. & K. A. Appiah. New York: Amistad Press, Inc., 1993. 105 - 125.

Byerman, Keith. "Walker's Blues." *Alice Walker*. Ed. Harold Bloom. New York: Chelsea House, 1989. 59 - 66.

Byrd, Rudolph P. "Sound Advice from a Friend: Words and Thoughts from the Higher Ground of Alice Walker." *Callaloo* 6.2 (1983): 126.

Byrd, Rudolph P. "*By the Light of My Father's Smile*—Review." *African American Review* (Winter 1999), http://findarticles.com/.

Christian, Barbara. *Black Women Novelists: The Development of a Tradition*. Westport: Greenwood Press, 1980.

Christian, Barbara. *Black Feminist Criticism: Perspectives on Black Women Writers*. New York, Oxford, Toronto, Sydney, Paris & Frankfurt: Pergamon Press Inc., 1985.

Christian, Barbara. "Novels for Everyday Use." *Alice Walker: Critical Perspectives Past and Present*. Ed. Henry Louis Gates, Jr. & K. A. Appiah. New York: Amistad Press, Inc., 1993. 50 - 104.

Christian, Barbara. "We Are the Ones That We Have Been Waiting for: Political Content in Alice Walker's Novels." *Contemporary Literary Criticism*. Ed. Deborah A. Schmitt. Vol. 103. New York: Gale Research Company, 1998. 384 - 89.

Coetzee, J. M. "The Beginnings of (Wo)man in Africa." *New York Times Book Review*, April 30, 1989.

Collins, Gina Michelle. "*The Color Purple*: What Feminism Can Learn from a Southern Tradition." *Southern Literature and Literary Theory*. Ed. Jefferson Humphries. London: The University of Georgia Press, 1990. 75 - 87.

Cornwell, JoAnne. "Searching for Zora in Alice's Garden: Rites of Passage in Hurston's *Their Eyes Were Watching God* and Walker's *The Third Life of*

Grange Copeland." *Alice Walker and Zora Neale Hurston: The Common Bond*. Ed. Lillie P. Howard. London: Greenwood Press, 1993. 97 – 108.

Darwin, Charles Robert. *The Origin of Species*. Cambridge: Cambridge University Press, 1958.

Davis, Thadious M. "Alice Walker." *Dictionary of Literary Biography Vol. 6: American Novelists since World War II*. Ed. James E. Kibler, Jr. Ser. 2. Michigan: Gale Research Company, 1980. 350 – 58.

Davis, Thadious M. "Alice Walker's Celebration of Self in Southern Generations." *Women Writers of the Contemporary South*. Ed. Peggy Whitman Prenshaw. Jackson: University Press of Mississippi, 1984. 39 – 53.

Day, Frank, ed. *Alice Walker*. New York: Twayne Publishers, 1990.

Driscoll, Margarette. "The day feminist icon Alice Walker resigned as my mother." *The Sunday Times*, May 4, 2008. http://entertainment.timesonline.co.uk/tol/arts_and_entertainment/books/article3866798.ece.

Duggan, Lisa. "Lesbianism and American History: A Brief Source Review." *Frontiers: A Journal of Women Studies* 4.3 (1979): 80 – 83.

Dundes, Alan. "The Devolutionary Premise in Folklore Theory." *Journal of the Folklore Institute* 6. 1 (1969): 5 – 19.

Eagleton, Mary, ed. *Feminist Literary Theory, A Reader*. 2nd ed. Massachusetts: Blackwell Publishers, 1996.

Elliott, Emory, ed. *Columbia Literary History of the United States*. New York: Columbia University Press, 1988.

Ensslen, Klaus. "Collective Experience and Individual Responsibility: Alice Walker's *The Third Life of Grange Copeland*." *The Afro-American Novel since 1960*. Ed. Peter Bruck & Wolfgang Karrer. Amsterdam: B. R. Grüner Publishing Co., 1982. 189 – 216.

Fenton, Alexander. "The Scope of Regional Ethnology." *Folklore: Critical Concepts in Literary and Cultural Studies*. Ed. Alan Dundes. New York: Routledge, 2005.

Gates, Henry Louis, Jr. *The Signifying Monkey: A Theory of Afro-American Literary Criticism*. New York/Oxford: Oxford University Press, 1988.

Gates, Henry Louis, Jr. "Color Me Zora." *Alice Walker: Critical Perspectives Past and Present*. Ed. Henry Louis Gates, Jr. & K. A. Appiah. New York: Amistad Press, Inc., 1993a. 239 - 260.

Gates, Henry Louis, Jr. Preface. *Alice Walker: Critical Perspectives Past and Present*. Ed. Henry Louis Gates, Jr. & K. A. Appiah. New York: Amistad Press, Inc., 1993b. ix - xiii.

Gentry, Tony. *Alice Walker*. New York: Chelsea House Publishers, 1993.

George, Olakunle. "Alice Walker's Africa: Globalization and the province of fiction." *Comparative Literature* 53. 4 (2001): 354 - 372, http://findarticles. com/.

Gomez, Christine. "Alice Walker's *Meridian* as a Feminism *Bildungsroman*." *Feminism and Recent Fiction in English*. Ed. Sushila Singh. New Delhi: Prestige Books, 1991. 253 - 267.

Gray, Paul. "A Myth to Be Taken on Faith." *New York Times* 133. 18 (1989): 69.

Gruesser, John Cullen. *Black on Black, Twentieth-Century African American Writing about Africa*. Kentucky: The University Press of Kentucky, 2000.

Halio, Jay L. "Review of *The Third Life of Grange Copeland*." *The Southern Review* IX. 1 (1973): 465 - 66.

Harris, Trudier. "Folklore in the Fiction of Alice Walker: A Perpetuation of Historical and Literary Traditions." *Black American Literature Forum* 11. 1 (1977): 3 - 8.

Harris, Trudier. "On *The Color Purple*, Stereotypes, and Silence." *Black American Literature Forum* 18. 4 (1984): 155 - 161.

Harris, Trudier. "Violence in *The Third Life of Grange Copeland*." *Twentieth-Century American Literature*. Ed. Harold Bloom. Vol. 7. New York: Chelsea House Publishers, 1988. 4108 - 111.

Harris, Trudier. "Our People, Our People." *Alice Walker and Zora Neale Hurst-*

on: The Common Bond. Ed. Lillie P. Howard. London: Greenwood Press, 1993. 31 – 42.

Hellenbrand, Harold. "Speech, after Silence: Alice Walker's *The Third Life of Grange Copeland*." *Black American Literature Forum* 20.1 – 2 (1986): 113 – 128.

Henderson, Mae G. "*The Color Purple*: Revisions and Redefinitions." *Alice Walker*. Ed. Harold Bloom. New York: Chelsea House, 1989. 67 – 80.

Hendrickson, Roberta M. "Remembering the Dream: Alice Walker, *Meridian* and the Civil Rights Movement." *MELUS* 24.3 (1999): 111 – 128.

Hernton, Calvin. "The Sexual Mountain and Black Women Writers." *Black American Literature Forum* 18.4 (1984): 139 – 145.

Hoffman, Daniel. *Harvard Guide to Contemporary American Writing*. Cambridge, Massachusetts & London: The Belknap Press of Harvard University Press, 1979.

Hollenberg, Donna Krolik. "Teaching Alice Walker's Meridian: From Self-Defense to Mutual Discovery." *MELUS* 17.4 (1991): 81 – 89.

hooks, bell. "Sisterhood: Political Solidarity between Women." *Feminist Review* 23 (1986): 125 – 138.

hooks, bell. "Reading and Resistance: *The Color Purple*." *Alice Walker: Critical Perspectives Past and Present*. Ed. Henry Louis Gates, Jr. & K. A. Appiah. New York: Amistad Press, Inc., 1993. 284 – 295.

hooks, bell. "Black Women: Shaping Feminist Theory." *The Black Feminist Reader*. Ed. Joy James & T. Denean Sharpley-Whiting. Massachusetts: Blackwell Publishers Ltd., 2000a. 131 – 145.

hooks, bell. *Feminist Theory: From Margin to Center*. Cambridge, MA: South End Press, 2000b.

Huang, Xinhua, ed. *The Bible Story*. Guangzhou: Zhongshan University Press, 1998.

Hubbard, Dolan. *The Sermon and the African American Literary Imagination*. Columbia: University of Missouri Press, 1994.

Hudson-Weems, Clenora. *Africana Womanism: Reclaiming Ourselves*. Troy, Michigan: Bedford Publishers, 1993.

Hughes, Langston. *Simple Speaks His Mind*. New York: Simon and Schuster, 1950.

Humm, Maggie. *Feminist Criticism: Women as Contemporary Critics*. New York, London, Toronto, Sydney, Tokyo & Singapore: Harvester Wheatsheaf, 1986.

Humm, Maggie. *The Dictionary of Feminist Theory*. 2nd ed. New York, London, Toronto, Sydney, Tokyo & Singapore: Prentice Hall/Harvester Wheatsheaf, 1995.

Hurston, Zora Neale. *Jonah's Gourd Vine*. In *Zora Neale Hurston: Novels and Stories*. New York: The Library of America, 1995a.

Hurston, Zora Neale. *Moses, Man of the Mountain*. In *Zora Neale Hurston: Novels and Stories*. New York: The Library of America, 1995b.

Hurston, Zora Neale. *Tell My Horse*. In *Zora Neale Hurston: Novels and Stories*. New York: The Library of America, 1995c.

Hurston, Zora Neale. *Their Eyes Were Watching God*. In *Zora Neale Hurston: Novels and Stories*. New York: The Library of America, 1995d.

Joannou, Maroula. *Contemporary Women's Writing: From The Golden Notebook to The Color Purple*. Manchester and New York: Manchester University Press, 2000

Kaplan, Carla. *The Erotics of Talk: Women's Writing and Feminist Paradigms*. New York & Oxford: Oxford University Press, 1996.

Kerber, K. L. *Psycho-Feminism* (Vol. 1). Delhi: Global Vision Publishing House, 2002.

Lauret, Maria. *Feminist Fiction in America*. London & New York: Routledge, 1994.

Lerner, Gerda. *The Creation of Patriarchy*. New York: Oxford University, 1986.

Lewis, Rodis. *Decartes and Rationalism*. Paris: University of France, 1992.

Marvin, Thomas F. "'Preachin' the Blues': Bessie Smith's Secular Religion and Alice Walker's *The Color Purple*." *African American Review* 28.3 (1994): 411-421.

Mason, Theodore O., Jr. "The Dynamics of Enclosure." *Alice Walker: Critical Perspectives Past and Present*. Ed. Henry Louis Gates, Jr. & K. A. Appiah. New York: Amistad Press, Inc., 1993. 126-139.

Matuz, Goger, ed. *Contemporary Literary Criticism*. Vol. 58. Detroit, Washington, D. C. & London: Gale Research Inc., 1990.

Mbiti, John S. *African Religions and Philosophy*. Portsmouth, NH: Heinemann, 1990.

McDowell, Deborah E. "New Directions for Black Feminist Criticism." *Black American Literature Forum* 14.4 (1980): 153-59.

McDowell, Deborah E. "The Self in Bloom: Walker's *Meridian*." *Alice Walker: Critical Perspectives Past and Present*. Ed. Henry Louis Gates, Jr. & K. A. Appiah. New York: Amistad Press, Inc., 1993. 168-178.

Moi, Toril. "Feminist, Female, Feminine." *The Feminist Reader: Essays in Gender and the Politics of Literary Criticism*. Ed. Catherine Belsey & Jane Moore. London: Macmillan Press Ltd., 1997. 104-116.

Moore, Geneva Cobb. "Archetypal Symbolism in Alice Walker's *Possessing the Secret of Joy*." *Southern Literary Journal* 33.1 (2000): 111-121.

Moses, Nicole. "Heart Matters." http://januarymagazine.com/fiction/openyourheart.html 2009/11/23

Mohanty, Chandra Talpade et al, ed. *Third World Women and the Politics of Feminism*. Bloomington: Indiana University Press, 1991.

Munro, C. Lynn. "*In Search of Our Mothers' Gardens*: A Review." *Black American Literature Forum* 18.4 (1984): 161-62.

Mvuyekure, Pierre-Damien. "Alice Walker's Colonial Mind." December 6, 2009. http://www.ishmaelreedpub.com/articles/mvuyekure.html.

Nadel, Alan. "Reading the Body: *Meridian* and the Archeology of Self." *Alice Walker: Critical Perspectives Past and Present*. Ed. Henry Louis Gates, Jr. &

K. A. Appiah. New York: Amistad Press, Inc., 1993. 155 - 167.

Nowak, Hanna. "Poetry Celebrating Life." *Alice Walker: Critical Perspectives Past and Present*. Ed. Henry Louis Gates, Jr. & K. A. Appiah. New York: Amistad Press, Inc., 1993. 179 - 192.

Ntiri, Daphne W. "Reassessing Africana Womanism: Continuity and Change." *The Western Journal of Black Studies* 25.3 (2001): 163 - 67.

O'Brien, John. *Interviews with Black Writers*. New York: Liveright, 1973.

O'Brien, John. "Alice Walker: An Interview." *Alice Walker: Critical Perspectives Past and Present*. Ed. Henry Louis Gates, Jr. & K. A. Appiah. New York: Amistad Press, Inc., 1993. 326 - 346.

O'Brien, John. "Interview with Alice Walker." *Everyday Use*. Ed. Barbara T. Christian. New Brunswick: Rutgers University Press, 1994.

Ogunyemi, Chikwenye Okonjo. "Womanism: The Dynamics of the Contemporary Black Female Novel in English." *Revising the Word and the World: Essays in Feminist Literary Criticism*. Ed. VèVè A. Clark et al. Chicago & London: The University of Chicago Press, 1997. 231 - 248.

Omolade, Barbara. *The Rising Song of African American Women*. New York: Routledge, 1994.

Parker, Pat. "Revolution: It's Not Neat or Pretty or Quick." *This Bridge Called My Back: Writings by Radical Women of Color*. Ed. Cherrie Moraga & Glorie Anzalda. New York: KITCHEN TABLE: Women of Color Press, 1981. 238 - 242.

Piercy, Marge. "*Meridian* (1976)." *Alice Walker: Critical Perspectives Past and Present*. Ed. Henry Louis Gates, Jr. & K. A. Appiah. New York: Amistad Press, Inc., 1993. 9 - 11.

Pifer, Lynn. "Coming to Voice in Alice Walker's *Meridian*: Speaking Out for the Revolution." *African American Review* 26.1 (1992): 77 - 88.

Plato. *Protagoras and Memo*. Guthrie. W. K. C., trans. England: Penguin Books Ltd., 1956.

Pope, Alexander. "An Essay on Criticism." http://poetry.eserver.org/essay-on-criticism. html.

Prescott, Peter S. "A Long Road to Liberation." *Newsweek* XCIX. 25 (1982): 67 – 68.

Rapi, Nina. "Hide and Seek: the Search for a Lesbian Theater Aesthetic." *New Theater Quarterly* 34. 9 (1993), http://findarticles. com/.

Rich, Adrienne. "Compulsory Heterosexuality and Lesbian Existence." *Signs* 5. 4 (1980): 631 – 660.

Richards, Mary Margaret. "Alice Walker." *African American Writers* (Vol. 2, 2nd ed.). Ed. Valerie Smith. New York: Charles Scribner's Sons, 2001.

Robinson, Lillian S. *Modern Women Writers* (Vol. 4, Sabgal to Ziyadab). New York: The Continuum Publishing Company, 1996.

Royster, Philip M. "In Search of Our Fathers' Arms: Alice Walker's Persona of the Alienated Darling." *Black American Literature Forum* 20. 4 (1986): 347 – 370.

Schechner, Karen. "Sexual Healing: Alice Walker's *By the Light of My Father's Smile*." *Weekly Alibi* (November 11, 1998), http://www. luminarium. org/contemporary/alicew/fathereview. htm.

Selden, Raman, et al. *A Reader's Guide to Contemporary Literary Theory*. Beijing: Foreign Language and Teaching Research Press, 2004.

Selzer, Linda. "Race and Domesticity in *The Color Purple*." *African American Review* 29. 1 (1995): 67 – 82.

Sheldrake, Philip. *A Brief History of Spirituality*. New Jersey: Wiley-Blackwell, 2007.

Smith, Barbara. "Toward a Black Feminist Criticism." *The New Feminist Criticism: Essays on Women, Literature and Theory*. Ed. Elaine Showalter. New York: Pantheon Books, 1985.

Smith, Barbara. "Toward a Black Literary Criticism." *African American Literary Theory: A Reader*. Ed. Winston Napier. New York & London: New York University Press, 2000. 132 – 146.

Smith, Dinitia. "*The Color Purple* (1982)." *Alice Walker: Critical Perspectives*

Past and Present. Ed. Henry Louis Gates, Jr. & K. A. Appiah. New York: Amistad Press, Inc., 1993. 19 - 21.

Smith, Felipe. "Alice Walker's Redemptive Art." *African American Review* 26.3 (1992): 437 - 451.

Spiegel, Marjorie. *The Dreaded Comparison: Human and Animal Slavery*. New York: Mirror Books, 1996.

Spillers, Hortense. *Fabrics of History: Essays on the Black Sermon*. San Diego: Harcourt Brace, 1978.

Stanford, Ann Folwell. "Dynamics of Change: Men and Co-feeling in the Fiction of Zora Neale Hurston and Alice Walker." *Alice Walker and Zora Neale Hurston: The Common Bond*. Ed. Lillie P. Howard. London: Greenwood Press, 1993. 109 - 120.

Stein, Karen F. "*Meridian*: Alice Walker's Critique of Revolution." *Black American Literature Forum* 20.1 - 2 (1986): 129 - 141.

Stiff, Anne. *Words of Women*. New York: Bloomsbury Publishing Ltd., 1995.

Stine, Jean C., ed. *Contemporary Literary Criticism*. Vol. 27. Detroit: Gale Research Company, 1984.

Tate, Claudia. "Alice Walker." *Modern American Women Writers*. Ed. Lea Baechler & A. Walton Litz. New York: Charles Scribner's Sons, 1991. 511 - 520.

Tate, J. O. "*The Temple of My Familiar*—Book Reviews." *National Review*. http://findarticles.com/p/articles/mi_m1282/is_n12_v41/ai_7689753/, 2009 - 11 - 23.

Tucker, Lindsey. "Alice Walker's *The Color Purple*: Emergent Women, Emergent Text." *Black American Literature Forum* 22.1 (1988): 81 - 95.

Tucker, Lindsey. "Walking the Red Road: Mobility, Maternity and Native American Myth in Alice Walker's *Meridian*." *Women's Study* 19 (1991): 1 - 17.

Waaijman, Kees. *Spirituality: Forms, Foundations, Methods*. Leuven: Peeters Publishers, 2002.

Walker, Alice. *The Third Life of Grange Copeland*. San Diego, New York & London: Harcourt Brace Jovanovich, Publishers, 1970.

Walker, Alice. *In Love & Trouble: Stories of Black Women*. New York: Harcourt Brace Jovanovich, Publishers, 1973.

Walker, Alice. *Meridian*. New York: Washington Square Press, 1976.

Walker, Alice. *The Color Purple*. New York: Pocket Books, 1982.

Walker, Alice. *In Search of Our Mothers' Gardens: A Womanist Prose*. San Diego, New York, & London: Harcourt Brace Jovanovich, Publishers, 1983.

Walker, Alice. "Finding Celie's Voice." *Ms. Magazine* 12 (1985).

Walker, Alice. *Living by the Word: Selected Writings 1973 – 1987*. San Diego: Harcourt Brace Jovanovich, 1988.

Walker, Alice. *The Temple of My Familiar*. San Diego, New York & London: Harcourt Brace Jovanovich, Publishers, 1989.

Walker, Alice. *By the Light of My Father's Smile*. New York: Random House, inc., 1998.

Walker, Alice. "The Universe Responds—Or, How I Learned We Can Have Peace on Earth." *At Home on the Earth: Becoming Native to our Place—A Multicultural Anthology*. Ed. David Landis Barnhill. Berkeley: University of California Press, 1999.

Walker, Alice. *Now Is the Time to Open Your Heart*. New York: Random House, 2004.

Walker, Alice. "An Open Letter to Barack Obama." http://www.theroot.com/views/open-letter-barack-obama, 2009 – 7 – 27.

Walker, Melissa. *Down from the Mountaintop: Novels in the Wake of the Civil Rights Movement, 1966 – 1989*. New York: Yale University Press, 1991.

Wall, Wendy. "Lettered Bodies and Corporeal Texts." *Alice Walker: Critical Perspectives Past and Present*. Ed. Henry Louis Gates, Jr. & K. A. Appiah. New York: Amistad Press, Inc., 1993. 261 – 74.

Wallace, Margaret. "Real Negro People." *New York Times Book Review*. 1934 –

5 – 6.

Washington, J. Charles. "Positive Black Male Images in Alice Walker's Fiction." *Contemporary Literary Criticism*. Ed. Deborah A, Schmitt. Vol. 103. New York: Gale Research Company, 1998. 395 – 405.

Washington, Mary Helen. "Teaching Black-Eyed Susans: An Approach to the Study of Black Women Writers." *Black American Literature Forum* 11. 1 (1977): 20 – 24.

Washington, Mary Helen. "An Essay on Alice Walker." *Alice Walker: Critical Perspectives Past and Present*. Ed. Henry Louis Gates, Jr. & K. A. Appiah. New York: Amistad Press, Inc., 1993. 37 – 49.

Watkins, Mel. "*The Color Purple* (1982)." *Alice Walker: Critical Perspectives Past and Present*. Ed. Henry Louis Gates, Jr. & K. A. Appiah. New York: Amistad Press, Inc., 1993. 16 – 18.

Wehrs, Donald R. *African Feminist Fiction and Indigenous Values*. Gainesville: University of Florida Press, 2001.

White, Evelyn C. "Alice Walker: On Finding Your Bliss." *Ms* 9.2 (1998): 42 – 50.

White, Evelyn C. *Alice Walker: A Life*. New York: W. W. Norton & Company, Inc., 2004.

White, Lynn, "The Historical Roots of Our Ecological Crisis." *Science* 155. 6 (1967): 1203 – 07. http://findarticles.com/.

Williams, Sherley Anne. "Some Implications of Womanist Theory." *African American Literary Theory: A Reader*. Ed. Winston Napier. New York & London: New York University Press, 2000. 218 – 223.

Willis, Susan. Willis, Susan. "Walker's Women." *Alice Walker*. Ed. Harold Bloom. New York: Chelsea House, 1989. 81 – 96.

Willis, Susan. *Specifying: Black Women Writing the American Experience*. London: Routledge, 1990.

Wilson, Mary Ann. "'That Which the Soul Lives by': Spirituality in the Works of Zora Neale Hurston and Alice Walker." *Alice Walker and Zora Neale*

Hurston: The Common Bond. Ed. Lillie P. Howard. London: Greenwood Press, 1993. 57 – 68.

Wilson, Sharon. "A Conversation with Alice Walker." *Alice Walker: Critical Perspectives Past and Present*. Ed. Henry Louis Gates, Jr. & K. A. Appiah. New York: Amistad Press, Inc., 1993. 319 – 325.

Winchell, Donna Haisty. *Alice Walker*. New York: Twayne Publishers, 1992.

Winter, Kari J. "Blues." *Encyclopedia of Feminist Literary Theory*. Ed. Elizabeth Kowalewski-Wallace. New York: Garland Publishing, Inc., 1997.

Woloch, Nuncy. *Women and the American Experience*. New York: Alfred A. Knopf, 1984.

Zimmerman, Bonnie. "What Has Never Been: An Overview of Lesbian Feminist Literary Criticism." *Feminist Studies* 7.3 (1981): 451 – 475.

"An Interview with the Author: Alice Walker." http://www. penguinrandomhouse. com/books/184875/now-is-the-time-to-open-your-heart-by-alice-walker/9780812971392, 2016 – 10 – 3.

"Book Shows Lessons from Ancient People." http://www. femmenoir. net/Leaders—Lengends/Alice Walker. htm, 2009 – 1 – 12.

"Inner Light in a Time of Darkness: A Conversation with Author and Poet Alice Walker." http://www. democracynow. org/2006/11/17/inner_light_in_a_time_of, 2016 – 10 – 28.

"Sisterhood." *Longman Dictionary of Contemporary English*. http://www. ldoceonline. com/dictionary/sisterhood.

"Sisterhood." *Oxford Advanced Learner's Dictionary*. http://www. oxfordlearnersdictionaries. com/definition/english/sisterhood.

"Summaries and Analysis of *The Temple of My Familiar*." http://www. bookrags. com/shortguide-temple-of-my-familiar/, 2009 – 11 – 24.

http://www. amazon. com/Now-Time-Open-Your-Heart/dp/1400061733.

http://www. merriam-webster. com/dictionary/humanity.

http://www. newworldencyclopedia. org/.

http://www. readinggroupguides. com/reviews/by-the-light-of-my-fathers-smile.

艾周昌:《非洲黑人文明》,中国社会科学出版社 1999 年版。

程锡麟:《美国黑人美学述评》,《当代外国文学》1994 年第 15 卷第 1 期。

岳凤梅:《拉康的语言观》,《外国文学》2005 年第 3 期。

张玉红:《左拉·尼尔·赫斯顿小说中的民俗文化研究》,博士学位论文,上海外国语大学,2008 年。

Appendix I Alice Walker's Published Works

Novels

1. *The Third Life of Grange Copeland* (1970)
2. *Meridian* (1976)
3. *The Color Purple* (1982)
4. *The Temple of My Familiar* (1989)
5. *Possessing the Secret of Joy* (1992)
6. *By The Light of My Father's Smile* (1998)
7. *Now Is the Time to Open Your Heart* (2004)

Short story collections

1. *In Love and Trouble: Stories of Black Women* (1973)
2. *You Can't Keep a Good Woman Down: Stories* (1982)
3. *The Complete Stories* (1994)
4. *The Way Forward Is with a Broken Heart* (2000)

Children's books

1. *Langston Hughes* (1974)
2. *American Poet* (1974)
3. *The Life of Thomas Hodge* (1974)
4. *To Hell with Dying* (1988)
5. *Finding the Green Stone* (1991)

Poetic works

1. *Once* (1968)
2. *Revolutionary Petunias and Other Poems* (1973)

3. *Good Night, Willie Lee, I'll See You in the Morning* (1979)

4. *Horses Make a Landscape Look More Beautiful* (1984)

5. *Her Blue Body Everything We Know: Earthling Poems 1965 – 1990 Complete* (1991)

6. *Absolute Trust in the Goodness of the Earth: New Poems* (2003)

7. *A Poem Traveled Down My Arm: Poems and Drawings* (2003)

8. *Collected Poems* (2005)

9. *Hard Times Require Furious Dancing: New Poems*

10. *The World Will Follow Joy Turning Madness into Flowers (New Poems)* (2013)

Non-fiction books

1. *In Search of Our Mothers' Gardens: A Womanist Prose* (1983)

2. *Living by the Word* (1988)

3. *Warrior Marks* (1993)

4. *The Same River Twice: Honoring the Difficult* (1996)

5. *Anything We Love Can Be Saved: A Writer's Activism* (1997)

6. *Go Girl!: The Black Woman's Book of Travel and Adventure* (1997)

7. *Pema Chodron and Alice Walker in Conversation* (1999)

8. *Sent By Earth: A Message from the Grandmother Spirit after the Bombing of the World Trade Center and Pentagon* (2001)

9. *We Are the Ones We Have Been Waiting For* (2006)

10. *Devil's My Enemy* (2008)

11. *Overcoming Speechlessness* (2010)

12. *Chicken Chronicles, A Memoir* (2011)

13. *The Cushion in the Road: Meditation and Wandering as the Whole World Awakens to Be in Harm's Way* (2013)

Edited Work

I Love Myself When I Am Laughing …and Then Again When I Am Looking Mean and Impressive: A Zora Neale Hurston Reader (1979)

Appendix II Alice Walker's Selected Awards and Honors

1. Ingram Merrill Foundation Fellowship (1967)
2. MacDowell Colony Fellowships (1967 and 1974)
3. Radcliffe Institute Fellowship, Harvard University (1971 – 73)
4. Lillian Smith Award for *Revolutionary Petunias* from the National Endowment for the Arts (1973)
5. Rosenthal Award from the National Institute of Arts & Letters (1974)
6. Guggenheim Fellowship (1977)
7. Front Page Award for Best Magazine Criticism from the Newswoman's Club of New York
8. Pulitzer Prize for Fiction for *The Color Purple* (1983)
9. National Book Award for Fiction for *The Color Purple* (1983)
10. O. Henry Award for "Kindred Spirits" (1986)
11. Honorary degree from the California Institute of the Arts (1995)
12. "Humanist of the Year" named by American Humanist Association (1997)
13. Induction into the Georgia Writers Hall of Fame (2001)
14. Induction into the California Hall of Fame in The California Museum for History, Women, and the Arts (2006)
15. Domestic Human Rights Award from Global Exchange (2007)
16. The LennonOno Grant for Peace (2010)

Afterword

My interest in Alice Walker dates back to my study for a master's degree more than ten years ago. By some chance I was reading about the feminist movement when the word "womanism" leapt to my eyes. Frankly, it was completely fresh to me at that time, both as a word and as a term. I looked it up as a common new word but fortuitously caught its inventor and the philosophy. Then, out of curiosity I began accessing the relevant information about womanism and got to know more about the great Afro-American woman writer. As a consequence, the author's early novels, as the texts, came into my master's thesis, out of which grew the present book, *A Study of Alice Walker's Novels*.

It is my longtime dream to expand the thesis into a book, yet the work had been delayed until four years ago when my project on the tradition of the Afro-American women's literature was approved by Northwest Minzu University. In the following years, I managed to read a lot about the author and the relevant studies, which laid the groundwork for the writing of the book. I embarked on the manuscript about three years ago. Having survived a few abandonments, the book is now to be published. Nevertheless, I am feeling no sense of relief and overwhelmed with anxiety instead. For I know quite well that it abounds with flaws and errors due to my limited vocabulary and superficial understanding of Walker's writing and philosophy. Like a pupil who has just handed in her homework, I am looking forward to corrections and comments from whoever will have taken the trouble to read the book.

I am choosing to end my writing with sincere thanks to all those who have offered me inspiring advice, unwavering support, and constant encouragement. Without their trust and understanding the book would have remained just a wonderful dream.

December 28, 2016